THE FINAL THIRTY-FOUR

Stories in the Make 100 Challenge

DEAN WESLEY SMITH

wmg
PUBLISHING

The Final Thirty-Four: Stories in the Make 100 Challenge
Copyright © 2020 by Dean Wesley Smith
Published by WMG Publishing
Cover and layout copyright © 2020 by WMG Publishing Cover art copyright © by
SassinP/Depositphotos

ISBN:13 - 978-1-56146-246-9
ISBN:10 - 1-56146-246-2

CONTENTS

INTRODUCTION

There Are Even More Stories

As I put these thirty-four stories together for the last group of the Make 100 Paperback Challenge, I was struck by two facts. First, one hundred short stories is a lot of stories. Wow.

And second, I have hundreds and hundreds more. And I am still writing short stories every year, a lot of them, sometimes over fifty stories in a year on a normal year.

Can't tell I love short stories, can you?

How did this challenge of singling out one hundred of my short stories come about? As I said in the introduction in the last volume, from the start of the indie publishing movement, I have wanted to get my short stories into paper books of their own. Stand-alone books, short-story paperbacks in other words.

It has sort of been a passion, to be honest.

And for about eighty of my short stories in 2010, I did that as a challenge. But that was a decade ago now. Up until now I just never had the reason to spend the time and energy to do the covers and get the remaining two hundred to three hundred stories into paper form.

Or for that matter, redo the covers of the eighty I did ten years before, rebrand them. In fact, in this third volume, about twenty or so of the short stories already have paperbacks from ten years ago, but I will be redoing them completely so that all one hundred in this challenge are branded the same.

INTRODUCTION

This challenge started with the Kickstarter Make 100 Promotion. It dawned on me that with a lot of help, a bunch of learning curves for me, and some time, I could do one hundred paperbacks of my short stories.

The Kickstarter got more support than I had hoped it would, which was wonderful. But it turned out the learning curves I had to go through slowed down the process. I wanted to redesign a website to get the new branding on, and completely rebrand collections and redo covers from my *Smith's Monthly Magazine.*

And to do all that I not only had to learn better website design, but I had to completely relearn both InDesign and Photoshop. Not small tasks.

But now, after a year, I am working away at redoing *Smith's Monthly* covers, and are about halfway through the one hundred covers and gaining speed. As the first part of 2020 goes along, the paperbacks will be appearing and now I feel I can put together the three anthologies of the one hundred stories that I promised in the Kickstarter.

In this volume are the last thirty-four stories of the Make 100 Challenge. Just as the first two volumes, these stories cover many of my series and also many that stand alone.

The introductions ahead of each story will be basically the sales copy, with a few changes, on Amazon and other sales sites. So my name gets repeated a lot. But in these collections, I wanted you to see the sales copy.

I hope you enjoy these short stories. All three volumes, all one hundred of them. I can say that not only was it fun to write them over the years, but even more fun to get them up as stand-alone paperbacks and in these three volumes.

Dean Wesley Smith
Las Vegas, Nevada.
December, 2019

MISS SMALLWOOD'S GOODIES

A Pilgrim Hugh Incident

Sent to investigate the sudden appearance of the statue of a naked woman in a park, Pilgrim Hugh must first decide if placing a statue without permission constitutes a crime?

And why the statue of the naked woman lost all her personal parts? Are those missing personal parts the answer to the origin of the statue?

Another strange Pilgrim Hugh Incident.

One

PILGRIM HUGH STARED at the lifelike statue of the naked and blue woman.

Actually, she wasn't completely naked. She wore a large cowboy hat and carried a large revolver in her right hand pointed upward. Her finger was on the trigger like she was about to blow a hole in the rim of her hat.

The last days of summer were just starting to fade, but the temperature for the Portland, Oregon, area still seemed too high at eighty-five. The statue stood in a park in a suburban town of Portland called Hillsboro. The Chief of Police of Hillsboro had called Pilgrim to figure out where the statue had come from. The statue seemed to have just

1

appeared late last night and a couple mothers of small children had complained this morning.

Hillsboro, it seemed, wasn't used to getting statues donated to their parks in the middle of the night.

Over the last few years as a freelance private detective and lawyer, Pilgrim had gotten some strange calls, and this was another of the strange ones, of that there was no doubt.

After he'd gotten out of law school, he had tried to work in corporate law. He had managed two years, the exact same amount of time his first marriage lasted. Basically he had become bored with both.

Then his grandmother on his long-dead mother's side, a woman he barely knew, died and left him more money than even he could imagine or try to spend.

Two months after being divorced and out of work he had become free to do what he wanted.

His choice, as any young person might do, was a year of drinking and traveling around the world. Somewhere in the alcoholic haze, there was another even shorter marriage.

Eventually he went back to school to become a private detective, figuring that wouldn't be as boring as the law practice was.

Most of the training was not like the books about private detectives he loved to read. In fact most of what he had done was learn how to track someone by computer and look up financial records.

Finally, out of desperation to do something interesting, he set up his own combination law and private detective firm, hired a couple of talented associate lawyers to handle the really boring cases, and offered his services for free to the different city police departments around the Portland metropolitan area.

Hugh and Associates now occupied three floors in a downtown Portland high-rise. He had started out rich from his grandmother and managed to get even richer by hiring the right people and taking the right cases over the last few years.

Carrie, Pilgrim's assistant, limo driver, and best friend, stood beside him, staring at the blue statue. Today Carrie had on a green University of Oregon sweatshirt (that didn't hide her figure much at all) and a pair of white shorts that also hid little. Even in her late thirties, she could still have been modeling.

Pilgrim was over six feet tall and Carrie usually seemed to tower over him because of tall heels. But today they were the same height since she had on a rare pair of tennis shoes that matched her outfit perfectly.

Carrie was about to finish her last year of law school at the University of Oregon and join the legal side of Pilgrim's firm. But until that day, she paid for her apartment and food and school by being his assistant and driver when she wasn't in class.

He was going to miss her when her last year of law school started back up later in the month. They were such a good team.

The statue was anchored to what looked like a concrete slab and on the face of the slab was a name. "Miss Smallwood."

"Very lifelike," Carrie said, moving around the statue.

The blue statue did look very, very lifelike. No question there. Except the skin was perfectly smooth, the naked breasts had no nipples and were perfectly smooth, and the crotch of the statue looked like it came from a doll, also perfectly smooth with no attempt to make it lifelike in any way.

The eyes were open, yet showed no detail.

The entire thing felt creepy. Even in the bright sunlight and hot day.

Two

The park that now held the Miss Smallwood statue was only one block wide and a block long, surrounded by a sidewalk. A few other sidewalks wound into the trees and to a new playground in the far corner. A very nice neighborhood park, very well maintained.

The statue had been placed near the sidewalk facing an apartment complex across the street. In fact, it seemed to really be staring at that apartment building.

Pilgrim looked over at it, following the direction of the statue's look. The apartment looked to be a renovated old hotel of some sort. Stone and brick exterior, large windows. A nice place from the looks of it.

Pilgrim moved over and stared at the large revolver in the statue's hand. It looked real and from what he could tell the artist had depicted it with one shell missing.

"Know anything about guns?" Pilgrim asked Carrie.

"It's a revolver," Carrie said. "That's about it."

Pilgrim laughed. "I knew that much."

"Frank from the estate planning part of your office is a gun nut," Carrie said. "You want me to send him a picture?"

"Might as well," Pilgrim said. He doubted it would make any difference but it never hurt to get the details together.

Carrie started back toward the limo that served as an office for them. Pilgrim had every possible modern device he could think of in that car, from high-speed computer connections to sophisticated camera and listening equipment.

He moved closer and tapped the hard surface of the statue. It felt like a plastic resin of some sort.

He moved around the statue, studying every tiny detail. Clearly the statue had been made by a mold. And then polished and finished with a clear, thick blue resin compound. The resin looked to be almost a quarter inch thick in some places.

Fantastic work. Not a mark or seam anywhere.

The statue was clearly made from the mold of a real woman. Her legs were slightly too long for her final height, her hips just a touch too wide, and the right breast was slightly larger than the other.

A perfect statue, no marks at all, yet not a perfect woman as the subject.

Pilgrim stepped back and realized he was shivering slightly even with the heat of the day.

This statue just flat gave him the creeps.

He walked in a large circle around the statue, just trying to let his mind take in the details. It had been placed near the entrance to the park, between where a sidewalk split. But it hadn't been placed looking directly at the walkway, but instead at a slight angle staring off at the nearby apartment across the street.

With as perfect as this statue was done, why mess up the placement? Pilgrim would bet it wasn't messed up. It was intentional.

Carrie came back with the camera, snapped a couple of close-ups of the revolver in the statue's hand and then sent the images from the camera back to the office.

Then she put the camera down and picked up what looked like an iPad and aimed it at the statue.

"Shit!" she said, staring at the device in her hands.

"What?" Pilgrim asked, moving over toward her.

She had turned her back on the statue and was clearly trying to catch her breath.

4

"You all right?" he asked.

She shook her head yes, then showed him the image on the device.

"I wanted to see what the inside of the statue looked like," she said.

All Pilgrim could do was stare at the image on the device. No wonder the statue wasn't perfect. It was an actual woman inside that resin.

He could see every detail of her skeleton. Her insides had been cleaned out like they did with embalming. Metal bars ran up both legs. Another was up her spine and through her neck to hold her head.

Pilgrim turned to look at the woman frozen like a statue. "Whoever did this cut off the woman's nipples and smoothed over any sign."

"And covered or removed her crotch as well," Carrie said. "And covered or removed her eyes."

"Took and kept all the goodies," Carrie said.

"Better call Chief Benson," Pilgrim said, "tell him he has a crime scene here. The statue isn't a statue, it's a body."

"He's going to love this," Carrie said. "To find the killer he has to look for a woman's nipples and crotch."

"Might not want to tell him that on the phone," Pilgrim said.

"Not a chance," Carrie said, heading for the limo again, picking up the camera along the way.

Three

Pilgrim did another slow walk about the woman's body, looking at it with a new perspective. He was convinced that the placement in this park, in that exact position had something to do with all this.

He needed to find out what she was looking at with those blank eyes.

He headed back for the coolness of the limo and crawled into the back just as Carrie hung up. "Detectives and crime scene crew on the way. Benson said he would be here in fifteen minutes and we're not to move."

"Yeah, I bet," Pilgrim said.

"So," Carrie said, "any idea on The Case of Miss Smallwood's Goodies?"

Carrie loved to give each of the investigations they did a strange case name that almost always stuck.

"Some," Pilgrim said. "Search the area databases for a woman of that height and size and age being reported missing in the last month. Might want to go all the way down to San Francisco and up to Seattle as well in the search."

"Got it," Carrie said.

She was sitting with her back to the front compartment and a large computer complex of keyboards and screens opened out of the seat beside her, sliding out to almost surround where she was sitting with a keyboard on her lap and a large screen in front of her.

Pilgrim was on the seat near the wet bar. He turned and punched a hidden button on the bar, letting it turn into another computer center with a large screen and two small screens where the drinks had been.

He loved this limo. He felt like a superhero at times. The car was the most sophisticated computer center on wheels that he knew of. He loved it and never once questioned the costs to build it and keep it completely outfitted with any new device that would help him with a case.

In this car he could almost see through walls, hear something whispered two hundred yards away, and tap into any phone line he wanted to. This was a dream car for any private detective.

He immediately typed in the address of the apartment complex the woman statue was looking at.

Then on one screen he pulled up a floor plan of the building and on the other a list of tenants.

The landlord, a man by the name of Steven Frome, lived in a large apartment on the main floor with his wife, Sue. It was the only apartment on the first floor; the rest of the space was filled with a large lobby and entrance area. He had been right, the building had been an old hotel at one time in the past called The Wellington Inn. It had been converted to apartments in 1962 and Frome had bought it in 2001.

There was nothing in the full basement that showed on the floor plan and four apartments per floor from the second floor through the fifth, all fairly large.

Pilgrim couldn't see anything at all odd about any of the tenants or the building or the landlord.

"No missing person meets her look, size, or shape," Carrie said, "anywhere in the Pacific Northwest in the last six months."

"Yeah, that would have been too easy," Pilgrim said, shaking his head.

"So why would someone do this to a person and put them in this park?" Carrie asked as outside the first police car arrived on the scene.

"Figure that out and I bet we find Miss Smallwood's goodies," Pilgrim said. "I'll go talk to the police. Bring up pictures and background checks of anyone in that building there. I'll bet anything there is a reason she's looking in that direction."

Carrie nodded and went to work as Pilgrim crawled back out in to the heat.

"Where's the body?" the dark, heavy-set policeman asked. His name on his uniform was Wells.

Pilgrim pointed at the shiny, blue statue that seemed to be glistening in the sunlight as if she was sweating, even with the big cowboy hat and revolver.

"You're kidding?" Officer Wells asked. "That statue?"

"I wish I was," Pilgrim said.

Pilgrim went back to staring at the statue for a moment as Officer Wells started to tape off the area. More than likely the hat and gun the woman had were clues as well, but damn if Pilgrim could even figure out how to start on them.

At that moment Chief of Police Benson pulled up and got out into the heat.

"You're telling me that's a body?" he asked, as Pilgrim met him halfway across the lawn toward the statue.

"Sealed in resin and disguised, yes," Pilgrim said.

"You mean like that traveling science exhibit where bodies were frozen in movement in some sort of resin. The one that showed all the body's muscles and other parts most of us didn't want to see or even know about?"

"Might be like that," Pilgrim said, shaking his head. "I didn't know you were into science, Chief?"

"The kid loves the Omsi Center. That exhibit just grossed me out and I've seen a lot of bodies in my day." Chief Benson stopped a few feet from the statue. "What happened to her nipples and crotch?"

"The killer must have wanted to keep them. Or thought them too private to show," Pilgrim said.

Suddenly he realized what he had just said. The missing parts were the answer after all.

Four

"Hang on, Chief. I'm not so sure this is a crime after all. At least not a murder."

Pilgrim turned and headed back for the limo with Chief Benson right behind him.

Inside the cool interior, the Chief sighed as he closed the door. "I sure wish the city would spring for one of these for me."

"More than the city budget for a year," Carrie said, not looking up from the computer screen in front of her.

"Carrie," Pilgrim said, "can you do a search of death notices in the last year. Pictures of woman the age of the statue out there."

"Sure," Carrie said, frowning.

While she was doing that, Pilgrim looked up the occupations of all the tenants in the building, including the landlord.

He found exactly as he figured he would find. Steven Frome, the owner of the building, owned three of the area funeral homes.

"Look for a death notice for Sue Frome," Pilgrim said to Carrie.

"Already found her," Carrie said, swinging around he computer screen showing a picture of Sue Frome. "Maiden name Smallwood."

There was no doubt it was the woman in the statue.

"She died three months ago of terminal brain cancer," Carrie said. "She went very quickly. In fact, this park is named after her since her husband donated a ton of money in her memory to upgrade it and put in new kid's swings and such."

"He made her into a statue and stuck her here?" Benson asked. "Creepy."

"Death makes people do strange things at times," Pilgrim said.

"She liked to spend time in the park her last weeks," Carrie said. "And she was a top shot and loved to ride horses. All in the obituary."

"That explains the gun and the hat," Pilgrim said, nodding.

'Oh, shit, now what am I supposed to do?" Benson asked. "I'm fairly certain there's a rule against this somewhere."

"I'd go talk to Steven Frome, get him to remove her to a more appropriate place and then put a real statue in her place."

"Yeah, makes sense," Benson said. "Better than the press getting wind of this. Can you imagine the news?"

"Ask him what he did with her goodies," Carrie said as the Chief started to climb out.

"Her what?"

Pilgrim shook his head. "Never mind. Just Carrie's name for this case is all."

"You two are weird," Benson said, smiling. "But thanks."

After Benson got out and the computers were back into their hiding places, Carrie said, "Don't you want to know what happened to the woman's goodies?"

"Not even in the slightest," Pilgrim said, shaking his head. "Curiosity about another man's wife's private parts can only lead to problems."

"And you know this how?" Carrie asked, smiling.

Pilgrim dug out a Diet Coke for himself and handed Carrie a regular Coke. "How about we just let your imagination and memory work on that one while you drive us back to the office."

"You are no fun at all, boss," Carrie said, smiling as she took the offered can and started to climb out of the limo to move up to the front seat.

"That's not what she said," Pilgrim said, smiling.

All Carrie did was groan and then slam the door.

NOSTALGIA 101

One thousand years in the future, humans live very long lives in domes on the frozen surface. Boredom never poses a threat, but nostalgia does.

When it becomes deadly to focus on the past, teaching nostalgia solves the problem.

USA Today *bestselling writer Dean Wesley Smith takes a peak into the final exam of the class called Nostagia 101.*

"Nostalgia 101" was first published in 2001 in a slightly different form in Millennium 3001 *from DAW Books, edited by Marin H. Greenburg and Russell Davis.*

One

WE LEFT the domed city of Portland through the western gate, moving along the old Columbia River bed. Centuries ago, ice had jammed up the Columbia Gorge to the east of Portland, forming an ice field that stretched for a thousand kilometers. Nothing existed in, on, or under that ice field. It moved and shifted too much to be safe.

The wind bit at my shield-protected face, cutting through even my special thermal suit. An unprotected human body in this cold would die in less than a minute. A bad suit tear could kill if not fixed quickly enough.

The danger of being out of the dome always excited me, got my heart racing, made all the research and work leading up to this trip worth it. I loved going out of the domes, had since I was a kid a few hundred years before. Just as everyone did when leaving a dome directly into the snow, we got the standard lecture of too much time in the cold can kill, too much time free-breathing can kill, and on and on. Exciting stuff the first time, the two hundredth time, it was real boring.

"Rees, can you hear me, son?" the Professor asked through the com-link in my ear. "Stay to the right and in the river basin."

I was leading, Lara followed me, then Torman, then Jeanette, then the Professor. Five sleds, five self-contained living units if they had to be. We didn't plan on being out long enough to use those features.

"Will do, sir," I said.

I always addressed Professor Barren Stanton as sir. I never called him by name. I didn't feel I had the right to call a man almost a thousand years old by his name. Besides, he insisted he be called Professor or sir and who was I to argue?

As I accelerated away from the base of the dome, the wind force field on the front of the hoversled rose into place, blocking any blowing snow and ice from hitting my environmental suit. I eased the sled up to one hundred and twenty and settled there, the agreed-upon speed.

The snow-covered terrain sped past in a blur. There was really nothing to see, since the ice and snow had killed everything hundreds of years ago. I clicked on the hoversled autopilot controls and sat back, adjusting the controls only when I thought the computer needed the help to make a bend in the riverbed.

Thankfully, mankind had discovered the cooling of the sun hundreds of years before it happened and had prepared, after a period of panic and religious insanity. As the sun's cooling phase started, some people had left the planet, moving into self-sustaining stations closer to the sun. Some day I hoped to visit one of those stations on vacation from my job managing a restaurant. I just hadn't had the chance yet.

Other groups had built large spaceships, Generation Ships as they were called, and simply headed off slowly toward other stars in search of a new home, one that wasn't about to be covered in ice. Nothing had been heard from those ships in hundreds of years. Nothing was expected for hundreds more.

Most of the population of Earth had decided to stay and wait the sun's cooling phase out. With the help of nanites back in the early twenty-first century, humans now lived thousands of years, maybe longer. No one was sure, since only a thousand years had passed. With nanites, humans had time to wait for the melt. Scientists predicted the sun would start into a heat-up cycle in less than five hundred years. I wouldn't even be as old as the professor by then.

Two

It took just over an hour for us to reach the frozen Pacific. Millions and millions of humans lived under the frozen oceans of the planet, in the depths near thermal trenches, in domes that hugged the ocean floors like ancient coral. I had been into an ocean dome twice and both times didn't like the damp feel and the darkness that seemed to creep in from all sides.

I liked surface domes, with the intense white of the snow and the constant of the deep blue sky in the day and star fields at night. Surface domes were kept clear, ocean domes opaque. I loved the openness, the whiteness of everything. I had been born in the Reno dome three years short of two hundred years ago. I sure didn't feel that old, especially around the Professor. Nevertheless, on my two hundredth birthday, I planned on closing the restaurant and throwing a private birthday party for myself. I always figured that starting a person's third century of living should be celebrated and I planned on doing just that.

How could anyone get anything done in a short seventy to one hundred years of living? I worked full time, sure, had had a couple of marriage contracts with women, but basically, I was still in school, and would be off and on for another thirty years. Only after finishing all my classes would I feel really ready to contribute to society.

This class had become a prerequisite to any professional jobs above waiting tables. Nostalgia 101. The problem with living a long time had not been boredom, as many had predicted, but nostalgia.

Dreams and thoughts of a time that seemed better, seemed more comfortable, seemed easier, often pulled a normally productive human down to a complete standstill. Or worse, it made them collectors of things from the long dead past. Collectors wasted dome space, inflated prices of worthless things, and basically contributed nothing to the forward progress of society.

Five hundred years ago, nostalgia had become such a debilitating factor in society that suicide became the main cause of death above accidents. Classes were mandated to cure the problem. Hospitals were set up to treat the worst inflicted. Living basically forever was a wonderful thing, as long as you remained looking into the promise of the future.

For me, the dreaded nostalgia so far hadn't become a factor. I liked new everything, didn't collect anything, and didn't even much like old movies. I was happy with my life now, but even still, I had to take the class, prepare myself for the time when nostalgia might take me over.

I turned south along the old Pacific shoreline and kicked the speed up to two hundred kilometers per hour, skimming over the frozen ocean surface. The others followed at safe distances.

I couldn't imagine being born into a pre-dome life, back before nanites. But as the professor said, this expedition was going to help me with that lack of understanding. We were in search of a home he had known existed when he was born. A cave home that had survived the big Pacific fault quake of 2067. He claimed that after the quake, the house had been closed down and sealed by its owners. It might be possible that artifacts from over a thousand years ago were still in that home.

The problem was, of course, finding it under the hundreds of feet of snow and ice, using only records from three coastline shifts before the freeze. The five of us had signed up for this class with the professor four years ago. We had traveled the world searching through ancient stored information and books, arguing, learning, pinpointing what we thought might be the exact location of the home.

One of the main things I had learned in the process was that looking into the past was a very time-consuming and expensive thing to do. Why anyone would do it as a hobby was beyond me. It had to be a sickness, of that I was sure.

Now, we were approaching the agreed-upon site, the one place all our research led us to believe we might find the old building and thus discover something about ourselves, human history, and more importantly, nostalgia.

Three

My screens showed I had almost reached our destination.

I slowed and turned the sled toward the slopes and ice cliffs that indicated the old coastline. Hundreds of thousands of people had lived along this ocean's shores before the freeze. I had seen images of these places, old movies of walking on sandy beaches. I just couldn't imagine it. My entire life had been in the comforts of the domes and the white nothingness of the snow.

I eased my sled up onto a slight incline and then stopped when my computer told me I had arrived at the right coordinates. I did a quick sounding of the slopes and cliffs above me, checking for any chances of ice slides, then signaled the all clear.

"Well done, son," Professor Stanton said to me as he pulled up his sled beside the rest of ours. I nodded and stayed on my sled. I could monitor all the progress of the search from there on the sled's screens.

Torman and Lara already had out their equipment and were scanning the ice field below us. They looked almost identical in their environmental suits and masks. We all looked the same, even the Professor.

"There's something down there," Lara said, her voice level.

I could feel the excitement of a possible find surge through me. Could we get lucky enough to actually find the old cave house so quickly?

I watched the information come over my screens. The details were correct, the shape of the opening that we had trained to look for, the age of the blockage in the cave mouth. All fit. Thirty-six meters down.

But something about the ice and snow around it didn't seem right. I couldn't put my finger on exactly what it was.

"We have found it," Professor Stanton said, his voice flat as always. "Jeanette, are you ready?"

"I am, Professor," she said.

I could hear the excitement in her voice. She was the youngest of the four of us at just under one hundred and fifty. Like me, her job in the Portland dome was to manage a restaurant. I would have been interested in a contracted relationship with her if she hadn't already been in contract with another woman. And she seemed neutral to me, so I never pushed anything.

"Then, open us a path to the cave home."

Jeanette moved her sled back away from the hill, then watching her screens instead of the white in front of her, she turned on her heat drill attached to the front of her sled.

I watched as the drill melted the ice, fusing it into a ten meter in diameter tunnel down toward the cliff house.

The tunnel formed very quickly, almost too quickly.

I ran a few non-connected scans of the snow and area we were in. I could see traces of the remains of other closed-up tunnels.

Many others.

Maybe thousands.

Jeanette drilled down right along the path of a former tunnel, which caused her much easier digging.

I said nothing about my findings, but I instantly lost the excitement I had been feeling about the find.

Excitement that Professor Stanton had warned me to contain.

He had said, "From this excitement comes nostalgia, and from nostalgia comes death. As a society, we must never look back. We must always look to the future. It is in the future that the true excitement lays."

Realizing that this wasn't an original find, that we were only going over the same stuff a hundred or thousand classes before us had gone over, made the professor's point very clearly.

Finally, Jeanette reached the mouth of the cave and shut off the tunneling device.

Professor Stanton climbed off his sled for the first time and using hover pads on his feet, moved to the mouth of the tunnel. "Shall we take a look at the past?" he said.

I wondered if he said the exact same thing to every class he taught. More than likely, he did. I didn't know if I should be angry at the years we had spent researching to find this place. I wasn't sure of the point of that part of the lesson.

I sat there as the others went to join the Professor.

"Are you coming, son?" he asked after a moment.

"Wouldn't it just be easier to look at the images recorded by earlier classes?"

The others spun to look at me through their environmental visors, but the Professor just nodded. "Yes, it would be, Rees. But that's not the point of this class, is it?"

"I'd be very interested in what *exactly* the point might be," I said.

"To give each and every one of you an understanding of nostalgia. That was in the course description. I'm sure you read it."

"By going to an old site where hundreds, maybe thousands have been before?"

"Of course," the Professor said. "History is where people have been before. Did you expect anything different?"

I started to say something, then realized he was right.

He went on. "Nostalgia is the disease that makes us continually want to be where others have been before, where we have been before."

"And what's the point of wanting that?" Jeanette asked.

"There is no point," the Professor said. "True excitement is always the unknown ahead. Torman, Lara, you saw in your scans that there had been many tunnels here before us."

"We did," Lara said.

Torman nodded.

"How did you feel?" the Professor asked.

"Disappointed," Lara said.

"Tricked," Torman said.

"And you, Jeanette, you saw it as well. How did you feel?"

"The same," she said, nodding.

"Yet, for the last few years, our mission in this class was to find this cave house in which people had lived, where people had been before. What is the difference that others had visited this site in the last hundred years, or a thousand years ago when it was built?"

I was starting to see his point. "The search for anything in the past is always the search for where someone else has been."

"Exactly, son," Professor Stanton said.

"But no one has been to tomorrow yet," Jeanette.

Professor Stanton nodded. "Now are you starting to understand why nostalgia is so dangerous? You just spent almost four years of your time to discover a place that others had been to, that others had lived in. Couldn't your time and money have been spent so much more constructively?"

I nodded, as did the others. Point made.

"So," Professor Stanton said, indicating the tunnel "anyone want to take a look at the past?"

"Why bother those who are dead and buried?" Jeanette said.

We all agreed with her and she closed up the shaft so that the next class might have its object lesson.

"Come in for one final discussion next week," Professor Stanton said. "I can safely say, you all passed with top marks."

After a few minutes, I turned my sled back north up the coastline, setting the speed at two hundred kilometers per hour. I had to admit, I was glad we hadn't wasted any more time going down that hole. It would be nice to get back in the dome, maybe check in with the restaurant and see how the dinner rush was doing.

And it felt very good passing this class. Now, I could sign up for my next class. "The Proper Use of Nanites in a Sexual Act."

That promised to be very informative.

SHE ARRIVED WITHOUT A SONG

A Jukebox Story

Stout, the owner of the Garden Lounge, always thought he could control the time machine disguised as a jukebox by keeping it unplugged.

Then one day the jukebox started up without power and a visitor from the future asked a very important favor. A favor that would not only save lives, but maybe everyone.

One

"STOUT!"

The shout wasn't really something I paid much attention to. I was standing with my back to the bar working on my bar order that needed to be done by three in the afternoon or the four regulars behind me weren't going to be drinking this weekend.

"Stout! You had better turn around real quick!"

That was Big Carl's voice and in all the years he had been coming into the Garden Lounge, I had never heard him raise his voice until now.

I spun around to find all four regulars turned and staring to my left. And they all looked shocked.

Big Carl, the farthest down the bar to the right looked almost panicked.

Fred and Billy, both retired older men in for an afternoon "bracer" as Fred liked to call his drink, looked like they had seen a ghost.

Richard, my friend who sometimes helped me out behind the bar when I needed a break was on the right and leaning back as if he was trying to move away from something that might bite him.

It took me a moment to see what they were staring at. Then it hit me like a hammer and I had to catch myself against the back bar.

The jukebox was on!

That jukebox was never to be plugged in or turned on unless I did it. And everyone knew that. At least everyone sitting at the bar at the moment and there was no one else in the bar on this sunny July afternoon. Even in the faint light of some of the booths, I knew no one else was in here. In the summer, when someone came in or left, the bright sunshine from outside lit up the normally fairly dark Garden Lounge like the insides of a spotlight.

And every time a person came in they had to stop, let the door close, and then let their eyes adjust before moving.

The jukebox was on.

Not possible.

For a second I thought it was one of my regulars playing a joke on me, but they all looked as shocked as I felt and they knew I wouldn't consider anyone messing with the jukebox any kind of joke at all.

So I clicked off the stereo behind the bar and eased toward where the old Wurlitzer jukebox sat tucked behind a planter off the open end of the bar.

It was out of sight from most of the tables in the bar and on busy nights I just covered it with an old gray cloth to keep anyone from deciding to plug it in and play a song when I wasn't looking.

That old jukebox was very special. It could take a person back to the actual memory of the song being played. And the person, while there, while the song was playing, could change the memory, their own history if they wanted.

And that made the jukebox frighteningly dangerous. It only got turned on for the seven friends that knew about it on Christmas Eve every year, friends who understood the danger of tinkering with their own past in the slightest.

But there the jukebox sat on this hot July afternoon, lights bright, the hum of whatever secret time travel device was inside it filling the now deadly silent bar.

I eased around and looked behind the jukebox.

"It's not plugged in," I said out loud, more to myself than the other four in the bar as I backed away.

"Not possible," Richard said softly. "That power is coming from somewhere."

At that moment the motor started to whir that brought up a record.

I wanted to just run for the street and the heat outside, but instead stumbled back behind the bar, too shocked to even think.

Somehow that jukebox, without power, was about to play a song. Not possible. It could take all of us out and back in time to memories we didn't want to go to.

Suddenly, I realized what I had to do and my mind broke free of the shock for the moment. In two steps I reached the drawer under the cash register and yanked it open. In the back was the box of high-grade earplugs clipped together in pairs. I yanked out a handful and scattered them in front of everyone along the bar, then grabbed two for myself.

"Quickly, get these in and think about a pleasant memory."

All of them moved as one, grabbing earplugs and stuffing them into place.

I did the same, moving back around the end of the bar to the jukebox to see which record the thing was going to play.

It picked the slot A-1, where I used to have the record that took me back to Jenny. I hadn't had that record in the jukebox for years, so the pick-up arm of the jukebox picked up nothing and moved toward the platter as I watched.

"It doesn't have a record!" I shouted so everyone could hear me over the earplugs.

But the machine kept pretending it did have a record, dropping the imaginary record on the turntable. A moment later it spun up and the playing arm moved into place, resting over the empty, spinning turntable like a record was actually there.

I had to be dreaming.

That was the answer. This had to be an ugly nightmare. I had come to respect the jukebox and whoever had built it. Time travel in any fashion was dangerous and I had had many nightmares about that machine as well.

But never one where the jukebox played without being plugged in.

That was always the control I had over the thing. No power, it didn't work.

Up until now.

Two

Then, as some imaginary song on an imaginary record started to play, there was a shimmering in front of the jukebox, or actually more accurately right over the jukebox, and the image of flowers and colors and bubbles appeared surrounding a beautiful woman.

She looked almost see-through and she was wearing what looked like sound-dampening headphones.

She smiled and started to speak, but I couldn't hear her because of the earplugs. She indicated I should take them out.

Trying to think of the best memory I could, I eased the plug out of my right ear.

There was no song. No music at all, just this image of a woman shimmering over the jukebox, sort of fading in and out.

"It's clear!" I shouted to the others and everyone pulled out their earplugs. They were all looking as stunned as I was feeling.

All of us had seen people disappear and then reappear as the jukebox took them back to a memory and then brought them back when the song ended. But only once before had a song brought a person to us.

And never had someone come to the jukebox without it being plugged in and with no actual song playing.

The woman floating over the jukebox smiled and the area around her sort of radiated the joy of her smile, the colors becoming brighter and the swirling lines moving faster.

She did not take off her headphones.

"Hi, Stout," she said, nodding to me.

I had never met her before that I could remember, and she was attractive enough I'm sure I would have remembered.

Then she turned to Richard and the look in her eyes changed slightly in a way I couldn't tell. "Thank you for giving me this chance. It looks like it worked, at least the first part of this."

I glanced around at my friend.

Richard just sat there, looking shocked, his mouth slightly open as he stared at the beautiful woman floating above the jukebox.

I finally managed to swallow, then through a very dry mouth asked the obvious first questions.

"Who are you and where are you coming from?"

I wanted to ask how, but figured I needed the first two questions answered first.

"My name is Donna Neff. I'm thirty-seven and you don't know me yet. I am coming back from a future I hope to change."

I nodded, tried to swallow again without much success. She was a young-looking thirty-seven.

She smiled and answered my next question. "I don't know how this is being done either. In the future Richard figures some of this sort of stuff out about this fantastic jukebox."

Again I glanced at my friend, but he wasn't moving. His gaze was just locked on the woman.

"The song is half over," she said, glancing down at the jukebox and where the arm was in its position on the imaginary record.

"What can we do to help you?" I asked. "And why should we?"

"The why is the easy part, sort of," she said. "To save the world, to put it bluntly."

I didn't like the sound of that, but I just let her go on. I didn't much like any of this at this point.

"Please don't ask me how I know, I just do, just as I know about this wonderful jukebox. Time travel is very possible, as you all know. My son Danny will invent a device when he is in college that will eventually solve a lot of the energy problems of the world. That's all I can say because it's pretty much all I know."

I nodded and glanced at the jukebox. Whatever song that had sent her was getting close to being over.

"Go on," I said.

"I am told that in about ten minutes a girlfriend and I will come through the front door of the Garden looking for a cool drink and you all will treat us wonderfully, since you are all great people. And we will become regulars, using the Garden as a sanctuary away from our children and divorces and crummy ex-husbands."

"And you changed your past, right?" I asked. I knew the answer because she said that she had been told. She had gone through the jukebox at some point in the future and changed her past.

She nodded. "One Christmas, because I was slightly drunk and not really thinking, I went back through the jukebox and said something to my future and ex-husband on our first date."

"And you never got married and Danny was never born to save the world."

She nods. "That's what I am told by others from yet another future."

"You and Richard found me again, because I had never come into the Garden in my new life, and invited me back to the Garden and I met my old friend and she told me everything, since she was touching the Jukebox when I left."

I still didn't understand the part about her son inventing something in a future that no longer existed. How could anyone come back from that future, that timeline to tell her anything?

She smiled at Richard. "A while after you found me again, Richard, you got a visit from a son you had in my first world, our son, actually, a son that somehow crossed over timelines to warn us."

She smiled. "In the timeline I changed, you and I were talking about getting married and we had had a child. But you didn't remember it either because you hadn't been touching the jukebox when I screwed up."

As she started to fade, she glanced at me and then looked directly at Richard. "Please don't let that happen to my first son, and to our son. Don't ever let me go through the jukebox. Ever."

And then she was gone.

Three

A moment later the jukebox ran through the return routine, put the invisible record back in the A-1 slot and then went dark.

The quiet in the bar was so intense, it felt like my ears were ringing.

I forced myself to take a deep breath and move back behind the bar, staying a good distance away from the now clearly unplugged and powerless jukebox.

I was almost afraid to even look at Richard, but I did.

He sat there, mouth open, staring at the now dead jukebox.

"I've got to admit," Fred said as I clicked on the stereo to break the silence. "You sure know how to put on an afternoon's entertainment."

Everyone but Richard drank to that.

I stared at my old friend. He was in his early forties, had never been married, and didn't drink, although he used to. He was a plant manager by day and spent his evenings here in the Garden with friends sipping on orange juice and grenadine and helping me when I needed help. Sometimes, on long lunch breaks, like today, he came in to cool down. In the Garden we didn't call his drink a Shirley Temple, as they did in every other bar. We called them "A Richard," and Richard was proud of that fact.

I took my glass of fresh-brewed iced tea and leaned against the backbar, trying to put aside the shock and deal with what had just happened.

I was used to thinking about time travel over the last years of owning the Garden and that jukebox. And if we didn't welcome the women who were about to come in the door, we would feel a faint shimmering and we would never remember she had come to visit us.

I knew that for a fact. If we chased the two women away, we would have changed the future, the future where she and Richard meet and have a child. She would save her first son, but not Richard's son. If we chased the two women away we would kill the child who would grow up to understand time travel well enough to cross timelines.

Somehow we had to save both sons.

And I knew exactly what I had to do. What we all had to do. We had no choice.

And we had to do it quickly, before that door opened and let in the outside sun and heat and two women looking for a cool drink.

"Listen up!" I said, not shouting, but getting everyone to look up at me instantly, including Richard.

"That never happened," I said, pointing at the jukebox. "We never saw her, never heard what she had to say."

"But Stout," Fred said, "that would mean she would lose her son."

"No, it won't," I said. Then I turned to Richard. "You and I will never, ever allow her to go back through that jukebox. Ever. Once she learns about what the jukebox can do, we will just never let her travel in time."

Richard nodded. "At some point we'll have to tell her why."

"I'll leave that up to you," I said, smiling. "When the time is right."

He just shook his head, staring down at his drink.

I grabbed a pair of earplugs from the bar in front of Richard, quickly hooked them back together, then took a bar napkin and wrote in large black ink, "Donna."

Then with a tack I put the earplugs up on a post above and to the right of the cash register. "For the future," I said.

I turned back around to my four friends. "We can't tell a word of this to anyone. Not even the other regulars. This is a very, very important secret. Lives are at risk, maybe in the future of our world. Are we in agreement?"

All four of the regulars facing me across the Garden Lounge bar nodded, their expressions very serious and intent.

"Then pick up your glasses for a toast," I said as I grabbed my iced tea.

All four regulars did and I raised my glass upward. "To the different possible futures."

"To the futures," they all said and we all drank.

A moment later the front door opened, flooding into the Garden Lounge bright sunlight and warmth. And through the door walked two attractive women. One was a slightly-younger Donna Neff.

Again, my stomach sort of flipped over.

It hadn't been a dream and the secret we had all just agreed to keep really did have lives and worlds at stake.

"Not a word," I whispered just loud enough for the four at the bar to hear me.

They all nodded as they all turned toward the front door, clearly staring at the two women.

Both women stopped just inside the door as it closed, trying to look around as their eyes adjusted to the dim light.

"Put on your most charming smiles, gentlemen," I whispered again.

Then I motioned for Richard to scoot down two stools closer to the jukebox to allow room at the bar for the two women to sit.

Then I went around the bar with a wide smile to greet a woman I had just met a few minutes before.

"Welcome to the Garden Lounge. Your eyes will adjust in a moment."

Somehow I kept myself from saying, "Welcome back to the Garden Lounge."

But I did.

And that boded well for the future. Maybe a number of futures.

A LIFE IN WHOOPEES

Great moments exist for all of us at different times in our lives. From a simple taste of a cookie to meeting the love of our life.

Bill Wallace lived through five of those special moments. Bill considers himself lucky to experience five. Many people never get any.

USA Today bestselling writer Dean Wesley Smith peeks inside Bill Wallace's life and his special moments.

My name is Bill Wallace, I'm seventy-two years old, and I feel like one of the lucky people in life. I had a good marriage, great children and grandchildren, a good career. And I had five whoopee moments.

I hear some people never even have one.

My First Whoop

I was ten. It was the last day of school before Christmas, and it was snowing lightly outside our family house in Madison, Wisconsin. As I came through the door, the warmth of the house hit me in the face, combined with the fantastic smell of Mom baking Christmas cookies.

"Yes!" I shouted. I dropped my backpack on the hall table and headed toward the kitchen.

"Billy!" my mom shouted from the kitchen. "Take off your boots at the door."

I stopped, yanked off my boots and went sliding in my stocking feet on the hardwood floors to get a cookie.

That Christmas turned out to be the best Christmas ever, since Grandma and Grandpa were there, Dad was still living at home, and Mom seemed happy. None of that would ever happen again, so I still look back at that Christmas as the best ever.

My Second Whoop

Debbie pushed me away and slid back across the front seat of the car. She was clearly breathing hard and as excited as I was.

We had parked on a canal road a good four miles outside of town. The only thing close was a farmer's house a half mile away. I still had the car radio on, and the light from it and the moon through the steamed-up windows was enough for me to see Debbie's face.

Her short brown hair was messed up slightly, and her cheeks were red.

Debbie and I were both sophomores in high school and had been sort of hanging out for a month or so together. It was common knowledge that we were together, and we went out on sort-of dates a lot, but that was about as far as it had gotten.

Twice after I had gotten my driver's license, we had parked out here on the canal bank, and both times all we had done was kissed. I was hoping tonight might be a little different, but so far it was turning out to be the same.

The seat between us was one of those bench seats that only Dodges and pick-up trucks had during the seventies. Luckily my mom had bought a Dodge.

"Billy, you promise you won't tell anyone we're parking?"

"Who am I going to tell?" I asked. "Of course I promise. What happens here, what we talk about here, is just between you and me."

She looked at me for a long time, but of course, in that situation, any amount of time seemed long. Then, in a quick motion, she slipped her sweater over her head and tossed it into the back seat.

Her white bra was like a beacon in the night. All I could say was "Wow!"

Five years later, during our second years in college, we were married. I have to admit that even after we were married the sight of her in a bra still took my breath away.

My Third Whoop

The letter came from the State Bar association. Four years of college and three years of law school and it all came down to one stupid envelope in my hand.

I just stood there in the doorway of our apartment, staring at the envelope. I couldn't stop my hand from shaking.

Debbie, who had spent seven years putting me through college, looked at what I was holding, then gently took it out of my hand.

I was already an associate at *David, David, and Jennings*, one of the best law firms in town. But I still had to pass the bar, and the results of that bar exam were inside the envelope. Three weeks ago I had walked out of the exam convinced I had passed, but with every day since I became less and less sure, to the point where I could hardly sleep I was worrying about it so much.

I couldn't watch as Debbie quickly opened the letter.

Then, in the loudest release of breath I had ever heard, she handed me the letter and then hugged me, smiling and crying at the same time.

I glanced at the letter. I had passed.

"Oh, thank God!" I said.

"You did it," Debbie said.

I looked her right in the eye and shook my head. "We did it."

All both of us could do after that was just smile.

My Fourth Whoop

My secretary knew what I liked. We'd been having an affair for almost a year, and she said that she had something very special for me for Christmas this year.

Debbie and I had had two kids, a boy named Ben and a daughter named Karen. With Debbie focusing on the kids and me focusing on building my law practice, we sort of drifted apart. At some point a few years back we just sort of stopped making love, one or the other of us seeming to always be too busy. We talked about it once in a while, but never really acted on the talk.

We also fought a lot, especially right after the kids were born. It seemed I never knew when I went home if Debbie was going to be angry or not.

I don't think Debbie knew I was having an affair with my secretary, Heather, and I never wanted her to find out. She had developed a real temper over the years, and I sure didn't want her letting that temper loose on me for something as major as an affair. It was bad enough on the small stuff with the kids and the house and money.

Heather knew I was never going to leave Debbie, and she didn't much care. She was open sexually and had no thoughts at all of wanting me as a husband.

"So what's this surprise you've been talking about?" I asked Heather as I came back into my office after my last meeting. It was a little after six in the evening three days before Christmas, and Debbie didn't expect me home for at least another few hours.

Heather beamed at me, her twenty-something smile lighting up the room. She had long blonde hair, even longer legs, and a body that looked far too good in a lace bra and underwear.

"This way," she said, motioning me with a finger.

She had that sexy look on her face and I knew I was in for something fun.

She led me into my darkened office, and then before I could turn on the light, she put her hand on mine and said, "Not yet. I'll tell you when."

She closed the door and turned the lock, sending the room into almost complete blackness, since the blinds were down on the window and it was a dark night outside.

I could hear a faint rustling in the dark. Then Heather said, "Go ahead."

I snapped on the light. The sight that greeted me was something I could have only dreamed about. Heather and another young woman were both sitting on the edge of my desk. Both were wearing only lace underwear. The sight took my breath away, so it was a moment before I finally said, "Wow!"

Heather smiled at me. "This is Heidi, a friend of mine. She's going to help me give you a very special Christmas present."

Two and a half hours later I finally managed to stagger to my car. Never, in all my life, had a Christmas been like this one.

My Fifth and Final Whoop

I was just over an hour late getting home after my special present from Heidi and her friend. I expected to find Debbie sitting in her favorite chair, watching television, wrapped in her blue bathrobe, more than likely angry at me. But instead, when I opened the door, I was greeted with the wonderful smell of baking cookies.

I took off my coat and dropped my briefcase on the hall table, then headed for the kitchen. I had skipped dinner because of Heather's little surprise, so the smell of the cookies was almost more than my rumbling stomach could handle.

When I went through the kitchen door, I got a sight that not in a million years would I have expected to see. Debbie was leaning over the stove in her white lace bra and underwear, taking out a fresh batch of cookies.

Until that moment I hadn't realized just how attractive she still was. Even after having two children, she had kept herself fit.

"Wow!" I said, for the second time in the same night.

She looked up at me and smiled. "Welcome home. I thought I'd give you a little surprise."

I glanced around, then back at her. "Where are the kids?"

"At my mother's for the night," Debbie said, smiling her old sexy smile. "So we're all alone."

She put the hot batch of cookies on the stovetop, closed the oven, and moved over to a plate of cookies already frosted. "I bet you're hungry," she said, offering the plate to me.

"I am," I said, taking two cookies. "And these smell wonderful. And you look wonderful."

I almost swallowed the first cookie whole, it tasted so good.

"I do, don't I?" she asked, turning around so that I could see her from all sides.

"You do," I agreed between bites of the second cookie. "Really good."

"As good as Heather and her friend Heidi?"

I froze in mid-bite, staring at her smile.

She laughed, twirling around to give me another look. "I'm surprised you would even be interested after what those two young things put you through in your office."

I had no idea what was happening, how she knew about Heather and what had happened in my office, or how she was even going to react. So being a good attorney and a fearful husband, I ventured nothing, and said nothing.

She leaned against the counter across the kitchen from me, that damned white lace bra of hers making her look very sexy. "Surprised, huh?"

I nodded slightly and she laughed.

It was getting damned hot in that kitchen at that moment. Too hot.

"Didn't you know I would find out what you were doing? Hell, I went to take you to dinner to talk about things and even got a little show tonight."

Damn, she had a key to my office. I had made her one years ago.

"So I thought I'd just come home and give you a little show of my own."

I could feel my heart racing, my blood pounding through my head. I couldn't seem to think straight.

I tried to say something, but the words didn't want to come out.

"Oh, good," Debbie said, laughing and coming toward me, "the poison is working."

I wanted to say, "Cookies?" but again nothing came out.

The next instant, instead of staring at Debbie's white bra, I was watching the tile Debbie and I had picked out specially for the kitchen come rushing up at my face.

I woke up six hours later in the hospital. A woman who looked like a doctor was standing over me, frowning.

"Poison," I managed to croak out.

"We know," she said, nodding and staring at some instrument beside me. Then she patted my arm. "Just rest."

I must have rested, because the next thing I remembered was waking up to the blinding light from the window, my head pounding so hard I thought it might explode.

Debbie was already in jail. She served a total of six years in prison for trying to kill me.

I lost my position in the firm and had to hang out my own shingle because it came out in court what Heather and I were doing that caused Debbie to snap.

The kids lived with me, with my parents helping out, and visited their mother every other Sunday while she was in jail, and every other week after she got out and got a job. I never did make as much money as I had been making at the firm, but I did all right for myself over the years. And never once hired a secretary.

I never remarried either. Couldn't see much point in it.

I was thirty-two when Debbie poisoned me with that cookie. Now I'm seventy-two, no longer practice law, and have three wonderful grandkids. But in all those years, I never had another whoopee moment.

I guess I should be happy to have a five-whoopee life.

From what I understand, some people never even have one.

I feel sad for them.

BETWEEN SHOWERS

All he wanted to do was wash his green Rambler Classic, but the volcano blew and started dumping ash everywhere.

And just wouldn't stop.

An end-of-the-world story for one man who just really wanted it to rain.

And yes, I lived downwind from Mount St. Helens in 1980, and that is where this story came from.

One

IT RAINED YESTERDAY, which was the day before the volcano blew.

I was annoyed at the rain, because it caught me by surprise. Actually, I was napping at the time, but I was still surprised when I woke up. Not a fun-surprise sort-of-thing, either.

The rain, in its untimely arrival, had given me no time to get my freshly-washed-and-waxed green Rambler Classic under the shelter of the overhang on the back of my house. I usually wash my car three times a week, and when I saw, to my surprise, that it had rained, I figured I was going to have to wash it again today. In fact, I prepared myself last evening for a morning of car washing.

But that was before the volcano blew.

Everything changes when volcanoes blow.

Now, as ash drifts down outside my living room like a lazy snow, covering everything in a gray blanket, growing deeper by the hour, I hope for rain.

Rain, I believe, would clean out the air, turn the ash into mud, and make it safe.

One day I am mad at the rain, the next I hope for it. I am clearly divided in my rain loyalties.

I am also a divided surprise junkie, it seems. Yesterday, I was angry at the surprise of the rain, now I want to be surprised again by it. I have even thought of napping to see if the rain would come. But after tossing and turning on the couch for a half hour I came to the conclusion that sleeping just after a volcano blows is not possible for me. It might be for some people, but not for me.

So maybe my inability to sleep will hold off the rain.

I feel powerless without the ability to nap. I can only now hope for rain, wish for rain, think about rain.

I thought for a short time about praying for rain, but on that strategy I have a problem. I am not a religious man. Religion hasn't come to me in a flash of lightning, or even an itch like a bad fungus between my toes. I haven't caught it like a cold, or ran into it like a car wreck. It just hasn't happened to me, so I can't pray for rain. No god to pray to.

Just hoping and wishing and thinking are my choices, and I alternate between those choices as the ash builds up outside.

Two

Looking through my front window feels like viewing the world through an old black-and-white television.

I had bought an old black-and-white television a number of years back from a thrift shop. It had a big wood cabinet with carved legs and round marks on the top where people had left glasses and scarred the wood. It only worked for a day and then smoke came out of the back. I now use it for a stand to hold up the smaller color television with no circle stain marks that I bought six months later from the same thrift shop.

Right now that color television is working just fine, only there is no picture. Just gray fuzz like the ash outside.

I walk back and forth in my living room, first staring out the window, then going back to stare at the empty television. The gray in the television and the gray in the windows is turning my entire life gray, sucking the colors from my green living room carpet, my old maroon reading chair, even the covers of my books stacked in the corners.

Everything is becoming the color of a road surface, bland and without contrast.

I love contrast in things. A day without contrast just isn't a good day for me. Today is not a good day. It needs to rain to change that. The wet of the rain needs to contrast with the dry of the ash. That would make it a good day.

I stare at the television again. The man who did the nightly news had looked alarmed when he had come on and said to stay tuned for further emergency messages, but that had been a half hour ago.

I figure it was lucky, at least so far, that the power hadn't gone out. If it does, I am prepared, with candles and matches and everything, even though it is still sort of light outside.

Actually, it is just a little after two in the afternoon, but the cloud of ash falling from the sky has turned the day into dusk.

I stop and put my face against the window like a kid staring into a candy store. Outside the ash is halfway up the post on my slightly-tipped mail box that sits just off the edge of my driveway.

I have been meaning to straighten the post because I hate to leave a message to the world that I thought the mail was a crooked thing. Actually, I have no opinion of the mail system in this country. I have just never got around to fixing the mailbox post.

Getting around to things often is my worst problem, or at least that was what my mother used to say.

The one girlfriend I had had since I got out of school had said the same thing. It seemed I didn't get around to her often enough either. I would have, if she hadn't slammed the door in my face and left.

I stare out the window again as I pace. The ash looks light and fluffy and fun to walk through. It might be. At one point I thought about going outside to test the theory, but then the emergency folks warned over the television that everyone should stay inside because the ash might be poisonous.

That warning had made me look at the gray stuff completely

differently, shifting my perspective from fun and light to gray and dangerous. Amazing how a simple warning can change perspectives of a person like that.

Poison gray snow is falling from the sky. That is worse than yellow snow I figure. Yellow or gray, either way I am going to do what the man on the news channel had said to do, and stay inside.

The power flickers.

I hold my breath as if holding my breath will help the power stay on.

Maybe it did, because the power stabilizes again, leaving the television still showing gray, and the window still showing gray.

I go back to hoping and wishing and thinking about rain, which is better than thinking about the power going out.

Before my phone had stopped working, I had talked to my old buddy Mike about the ash coming our way. That had been just after the volcano blew this morning, and the first warnings about a heavy ash fall to the west of the volcano were being sent out.

That was also before the big gray cloud rolled in from the east. It had been a sunny day. Perfect car-washing weather. And the man on the radio had said as I was waking up that there was no chance of rain for the next few days.

Mike had said that rain would eventually wet down the ash and turn it into mud, and that we were all going to be stuck in our houses until the next rain.

After seeing the ash reach halfway up the mail box post, I am starting to believe him, even though I hadn't when he said it.

Now I hope for rain, and wait for the man on the television to come back on to tell me what to do.

And I pace.

Pacing is something to do. I take turns staring at the gray television and the gray world outside the window, and pacing between the two.

But pacing doesn't seem like enough. There has to be something I can do.

Then the thought comes to me: Maybe I can bring rain.

I dig through a pile of books behind my reading chair and find an old Native American rituals book. Actually, the title is *Indian Rituals and their Practice*. The book had been published at least fifty years before the turn of the last century. I still make myself think of the book as the Native American rituals book, and never look at the real title.

In chapter six the author talks about the different types of rain dances. I stare at the old black and white pictures. I could look the part of a Native American. I could get a few feathers left over from an old Halloween turkey decoration I had in the attic, then stick the feathers in the headband I use for jogging.

I think about the idea for a moment. I could also use some lipstick left behind by my old girlfriend as ceremonial paint on my forehead. She had used it for ceremonial occasions on her lips, so I figure it would work fine.

I could be a real rain dancer.

Then I realize I don't know the steps. I had never been a good dancer, and more often than not girls in school had laughed at my attempts. It is bad enough having high school girls laugh at you. Having the rain laugh would be another matter. Much worse I am sure.

And there is no Rain Dancing school that I can attend to learn in enough time to make a difference.

I put the book behind my reading chair and go back to pacing and watching the different versions of the same show. Gray world through the window, gray television on the air.

On the television nothing happens, outside the window the ash has now reached the top of the mailbox.

Suddenly the television blares out an alarm, reminding me that I had kept the sound up earlier when I had gone into the bathroom, just in case it had come back. If I had been in the bathroom and that alarm sounded, I would have heard it just fine. Standing beside the television, it gives me a very sharp surprise.

And not a rain surprise.

I turn the sound down to normal levels just as a man's face replaces the sign that reads "Emergency Broadcast System."

I pay the man close attention because he does not look happy. In fact he looks very upset, and in all my years of watching men with perfect suits and hair repeat news stories to me, I have never seen one look upset. Even his tie is crooked and looked upset.

"The National Guard, State, and Federal agencies have advised that everyone remain inside. The ash cloud is still growing, and there is no sure idea when it will pass."

I do not like the sounds of those words, but I keep listening and he keeps talking.

"Testing on the ash has been inconclusive as to its dangers. Medical agencies at this time do not know the extent of the content of the ash and warn that you do not breathe in any of the ash, or let it touch your skin."

I turn the sound down some as he starts into how far the road closures were extending, how far the ash cloud might drift, and so on. It seems clear to me that all my hoping and wishing and thoughts of doing a rain dance have done no good. The ash is continuing to fall, and no one really knows anything more.

The television goes back to the sign and then back to gray after a few minutes. I pull my maroon reading chair around so that it faces the window so I can watch the gray, lack of contrast show going on outside.

The falling flakes of ash seem hypnotic.

Three

At some point, those flakes must have put me to sleep, because when I wake up I have another surprise waiting for me. My window is completely covered in ash. And little bits of it are seeping in around the edges of the single pane window where normally only a draft and a few drops of water appear.

That surprises me.

That is the second time in two days I have woken up from a nap and been surprised.

Plus the fact that the power is still on surprises me.

Sort of a bonus surprise.

I have no upstairs in my small, one-bedroom house with a lean-to on the side for a garage. So I can not run up and see how deep the ash has gotten while I napped. But the clock on the wall says I have been asleep for two hours. Clearly ash falling is a very peaceful thing.

Around me the house creaks slightly, as if a wind is blowing outside. After two house creaks the alarm sounds softly on the television, startling me just like it had done before my nap when it was turned up loud.

After a few moments the man with the crooked tie comes back on. Only this time the tie is gone and his eyes look red. Clearly he needs a nap like I had just gotten.

He goes through the same speech he gave the last time I had

listened. The ash continues, and is spreading. And from all aerial shots that they could get, which look very beautiful on television, the volcano continues to spew out ash at an ever increasing rate.

I stare at the beautiful blue sky around the volcano above the ash. It is a very sharp contrast to the gray outside my window.

I pay even more attention as the tie-less man gets to reports of the depth of the ash in certain places around the metropolitan area. With some of these numbers he cannot look at the camera, but instead just reads calmly.

He is like a doctor telling a patient he is about to die. When he gets to my area of town, and says that the depth of the ash has reached forty feet and is continuing to build up, I know I am the patient.

I have been buried alive while I napped.

And my little house is my coffin.

Now that is a surprise I had never dreamed I would wake up to find.

Again the house creaks and adds in a groan. The man without a tie on the television says he will return in fifteen minutes. Before the alarm signaling the end of his little talk can end, the power goes off.

It seems that for the near future I will not be able to check on the progress of the man and his tie.

I sit in the dark for a moment, letting my eyes adjust to the lack of light, then move slowly to find the candles on my small kitchen table. The first match seems extra bright, and after a moment and three matches I have five candles burning, giving the house a warm feel, and a sulfur smell.

I look around deciding that I have to think about my house differently than a coffin. I have to think of it as a safe, warm cave.

Only my cave has a limited supply of oxygen and might collapse under the weight of the ash.

I stop the thought and make myself think of the house, lit by the orange glow of the flickering candles, as my cave.

I get settled on one of my two kitchen chairs, repeating the word "cave" over and over. I am in the fifth or sixth repetition when there is a huge crash and the area around me fills with swirling ash.

Thinking quickly, I lean forward over the table and shelter one candle and a box of matches as best I can.

Somehow I manage to keep the candle burning as the ash swirls like a gray river filling up a space.

The heat from the candle burns my neck a little, but I ignore that. And I try to ignore the bone-dry feel of the ash and the smell of rotting eggs that fills every sense I have.

I take slow, shallow breaths through my nose, trying not to let too much of the stuff into my lungs.

Slowly, so slowly, the stuff settles and I grow used to the smell.

I look up, using the one candle to see how the ash now coats everything I own with a layer of gray that makes all my things look faded.

The other candles have gone out, but moving slowly, so as to not swirl up too much more ash, I get two of them lit, giving me enough light to see the living room.

My big front window is smashed inward from the pressure of all that ash against it. My living room is full of ash, and the televisions are buried.

Around me the house creaks again, but nothing else happens. Maybe the window breaking open has relieved some pressure, but I didn't know how that might work. It is just the best positive thought I can come up with at the moment.

Four

I look around, staring at all the odd differences a thin layer of ash can make with things. My mirror still reflects, but it also scatters the light. The table is covered, but not much of the area under the table, leaving the faded green tile as a contrast.

Every corner in the place seems rounded by the ash, every edge dulled.

I slowly open my fridge, get out a red apple and a bottle of water, then take my three candles and crawl under my kitchen table. Now the next time something breaks and lets in more ash, I will be protected. The table is like a second home, giving me another roof over my head.

Suddenly, as if someone had stuck a feather down my throat, I cough. I manage to cough into the kitchen and away from the candles.

They stay lit.

Dust swirls with the cough.

The house creaks.

I lay down on the floor, on my back, trying not to cough again while staring at the underside of the kitchen table. It is a sight I had never expected to see. I would think that no one would ever expect to see the unfinished underside of a table by candle light. But still it has a beauty all its own as the flames give the surface odd shadows.

I focus on the shadows for a moment trying not to cough.

Then, while staring at the underside of the kitchen table, I think about washing my Rambler.

I can remember the feel of how much I had wanted rain today, how much I was angry at the rain the day before.

Now I have changed again. I don't want it to rain. Rain now will make the ash even heavier, and more than likely crush my poor little house.

For the third time in just two days, my feelings about rain have changed. Part of me is glad that I had never tripped on religion and prayed for rain, because I might have been successful.

And it was lucky I can't dance.

I laugh at the idea that my not being able to dance might save my life.

I yawn, while at the same time trying to not breathe in any of the dry ash still floating in the air.

I have no idea why I am so sleepy. Maybe there is a sleep drug in the ash. Maybe, after all this was over, they would shovel up the ash and put it in bottles and sell it to the rest of the world for a sleep-aid.

It would work well. I am getting very tired.

I yawn again, and then close my eyes.

Maybe, just maybe, a little nap might help.

Maybe the ash is doing me a favor, allowing me to sleep so that when I wake up there will be yet another surprise.

Maybe by then the power will be back on, and a wind will have come up and blown all the ash away, and then I can again hope for rain to help clean up the yard.

Surprises after naps are always interesting. I just have to think they are going to be good.

As I drift off into my nap, I yawn again and think about how much fun it will be to again wash my Rambler.

SQUATTER'S RIGHTS ON THE STREET OF BROKEN MEN

Conrad found Tani, the woman of his dreams. Beautiful, sexy, and soft fine hair all over her body that drove him wild.

And Tani found Conrad, exciting, fun, and primitive, something she loved and needed to escape her boring job.

A perfect match? It might have been, except for one minor problem. Tani wasn't from Earth.

Originally written and published under the pen name Dee. W. Schofield.

One

"FUR," Conrad Weir said, trying to keep his voice low enough that not every one of the twelve people in the Golden Dragon Bar would hear him in his excitement. "I'm not kidding. She was covered in a fine blonde fur, all over her body. Hottest thing I have ever seen. Or hell, felt."

"Yeah, right," his companion and best friend, John "The Clump" Benson said, staring at his glass of beer on the bar in front of him. "You were so drunk, you just ended up in the zoo screwing one of the bears. Lucky you didn't get your balls chewed off."

A woman in the booth under the fake plants looked over at them and gave them a disgusted look. John's voice could sure carry. But hell, what did she expect being in a local bar like this one? The Dragon, as everyone called this bar, was a place for locals in the afternoons and early evenings, and college kids at night. Conrad was usually gone long before the kids arrived, moving up the street to the Elks Club bar to listen to whatever local band was playing for the week.

The Dragon consisted of five booths against a back wall, a half dozen small tables, and a long bar across the back with ten stools, usually filled with regulars. Dave was the normal afternoon bartender, a quiet kid who had come to town to go to college and had just never left. He could pour a mean drink and listen to just about anything with a straight face. Conrad had no idea what he did outside of the Dragon.

Conrad ignored John's zoo comment and went on, telling him about last night, remembering every detail of the wonderful night with Tani. She had been real, very real, that much he was sure of. He had met her at the Elks when she came in with a group of about six people, one of who must have been a member. He had asked her to dance. At first she had resisted, so he bought her a drink, then another, and after a little talking, he finally got her out onto the dance floor.

That was when he discovered the fine layer of fur all over her skin and he was hooked.

"I couldn't keep my hands off her," he said, letting the memory just flow. "I drove her nuts."

"You drive me nuts," John said, finishing his beer and signaling Dave for another.

"Yeah, but with her, I did it by stroking her arms and legs and stomach and breasts. I couldn't get enough of the fur. Softest, finest hair I have ever felt."

John looked at him like he had lost a bolt and his head was about to fall off. "She had *hair* on her stomach and boobs? Not for me."

Again the woman in the booth snorted and stared into her drink, trying to ignore John's comments as much as she was ignoring the poor guy sitting beside her.

"Fur," Conrad said, making sure his voice didn't carry. "Soft, golden fur, softer than anything you've ever touched. From more than a foot away you can't see it. She has normal skin, wonderful skin, just coated with this fine fur. I loved it. Hell, I think I might be falling in love with her."

"You fall in love with light poles when you're drunk enough," John

43

said. "I've seen it. Remember? I don't think that pole down off of Third Street is ever going to get over you."

Conrad ignored him, even though John was right. Drinking did tend to lower Conrad's restrictions and his judgment. But at the moment, he was cold sober and still felt that way about her. All he could see was her green eyes and wonderful smile. She had a bright wit, a contagious laugh, and oh, *that fur*. A perfect package. What more could any thirty-year-old man want?

"This one might be real," Conrad said, motioning for Dave to bring him something besides the sparkling soda he had first ordered. "Honest."

"Her last name, Einstein?" John asked, looking over at Conrad. "Or maybe a phone number?"

Conrad had to admit he didn't know her last name. Just her first name. Tani. And she had been gone from his apartment like a dream when he woke up this morning. She hadn't even left a note. But that didn't matter. He had met her once, he could find her again. This town wasn't that big.

"That's what I thought," John said when Conrad didn't answer him, again shaking his head and turning back to his beer. He did a lot of that head shaking every time Conrad met a new woman, or had a new idea to make them both rich. But this time, Conrad was determined to prove him wrong.

"So, you going to help me find her?" Conrad asked his friend as Dave slid his scotch and water, light on the water, onto a napkin and put it in front of Conrad.

"And why would I do that?" John asked. "I helped you find Debbie, remember, and look where that got you."

Debbie had been Conrad's wife, now his ex-wife. John had introduced them at a party up on campus. She had left Conrad for a lawyer and then got remarried and left the state. Good riddance as far as Conrad was concerned. That had been four years ago.

"Friendship," Conrad said, sipping the sharp taste of his drink. He didn't know why he drank scotch, other than to avoid hangovers. The stuff tasted like it could chew the enamel off his teeth. But after a few drinks, he didn't much notice the taste. But he did notice the lack of headaches and driving the porcelain steering wheel in the morning. Made the taste worthwhile as long as he was going to drink.

John snorted and said nothing about the "friendship" comment.

John and Conrad had been best friends since high school, had gone to college together here. When John had started a construction firm, he had wanted Conrad to join him, but Conrad had instead just worked for him part time. Conrad had ended up going on to more school, getting a graduate degree in math, and then getting hired to teach at the university.

Both of them had been married once and divorced once. They now had a habit of meeting every late afternoon, with a bunch of other locals, in the Dragon for a drink or two. At thirty, Conrad had never expected to end up divorced, hunting for women in bars, and unhappy in his job after only a few years. But he was.

Tani might change that if he could find her.

John had sworn off women after his divorce, taken up drinking beer and building homes for other people, and was slowly but surely getting a beer gut and very rich.

He had also been a process server while in college and had developed a knack for finding people who didn't want to be found. If anyone could find this Tani, John could.

"So, what do you say?" Conrad asked. He took another sip of the biting taste of scotch, then turned to his best friend.

"You're serious, aren't you?" John asked.

"Very," Conrad said. Again, the image of Tani's green eyes and wonderful smile filled his mind. He wouldn't mind looking into those eyes for a very long time.

John just shook his head, but Conrad knew he had him.

"Tell you what," John finally said after taking another long drink. "You don't find her in the next week, and you still want to find her, I'll help you. But you're on your own for a week."

"Perfect," John said. "For all I know, she might come walking back into the Elks tonight looking for me, or maybe leave a note at my apartment."

"Sure," John said. He finished off his second beer and signaled for another. "But I'd check the zoo. See if one of the sheep is missing from the kids petting area."

Conrad tried to give his friend a serious look. "Not nice. That's the second Mrs. Conrad Weir you're talking about there."

"Baaaaaaa," John said, loud enough to echo clear out into the restaurant.

Conrad laughed, the woman in the booth snorted again, and the night went on.

Two

Tani-Areas-Fol-Dan-Peet floated into the Doorways Bar and Fine Dining and let her robot lifts carry her around the tables and to her two friends sitting near a Punk-Tac game. From the looks of it, they had both just arrived a moment or two before her. Neither had a B of C in front of her, and since they had been here every cycle for the past thirty, the robots knew their orders perfectly.

She drifted into her seat and a moment later, all three of their drinks appeared in front of them, freshly made with the exact liquors from any one of a thousand planets. For Tani, her B of C was the Earth drink called a "Screwdriver" made up of a fruit grown on the planet and a real distilled alcohol called "vodka" packed over frozen water cubes. Very strange but very tasty.

Kreble, who loved her drinks sweet, had a B of C from a planet called Diken, where they drank a form of pure sugar, fermented to a degree Tani had not thought possible, then flavored with different types of plant roots.

Too-Tight-Tootie-Two loved her drinks sour, in the same degree that Kreble loved them sweet. Too's B of C had some mixture minerals from a planet with a name no one could pronounce, blended firmly with roots from two of the planet's trees, then mixed with a type of acid.

If Too had too many, her lips turned an ugly black and Tani and Kreble had to lift her back to her place for the night. Tani hated that and she didn't want that to happen tonight. They only had two more days of their vacation on Doorway, before they had to return to their home world, Lind, and return to work.

All three of them worked in an anti-gravity chip plant there, waiting for the right moment to take a mate, have children, and then return to work. Last year Tani had done that twice, spawning her 42nd and 43rd child. She was scheduled for two more matings the coming cycle and two more children.

Boring didn't begin to describe how she felt about that. Especially after last night on Earth with the man who called himself Con-Rad.

She was required by custom to produce child 44 and 45 in the coming cycle, but she could pick with whom and Con-Rad might just be a likely mate. It would add to her diversity quota since seldom did anyone mate with creatures from Earth. They were considered far too primitive.

Actually, she wasn't even sure if it was possible, but she would be willing to find out.

But right at this point in her life, Tani needed an adventure, and going into a backwards planet like Earth to mate might be the adventure she needed.

Unlike her two friends, Tani had saved her money and was rich enough to not work. She only did so because she had nothing else to do, and her friends were there. But she had been unhappy with her job for a long, long time. It was time for a change.

And it was this bar that was going to help her make that change, on this vacation.

She looked at her two friends as they took first sips of their drinks, then blurted out, "I'm going back."

"Why would you go back to work two days early?" Too asked, stunned into not drinking for a moment.

"Not back to work," Tani said. "Back to Earth."

"Did you leave something there?" Kreble asked.

"It's that Earther you were doing rubbing with," Tani said.

Tani gave them both her most seductive smile.

"Did you show him your true form?" Kreble said.

"No," Tani said. "I maintained human form. But Earth excites me. Earthers excite me."

"So you're going to use another day of your vacation there?" Too asked. "After we planned on hitting Solo-Prime for their chalk baths and system-clearing tongue-licking?"

"Sounds heavenly," Tani said, not mentioning to her friends they had done the same thing for the last five cycles and once you've had one Solo-Prime insect-tongue clear your system, you've done it more than enough.

"Actually," Tani said. "I'm going to spend the next cycle on Earth exploring the wilderness. I'm going to take a leave from work."

Both her friends just sat staring at her.

Then Too looked like she might get sick. "Seriously, you are considering mating with an Earth creature?"

Tani nodded, sipping the wonderful-tasting screwdriver. "Two of them, actually."

"Is that even possible?" Kreble asked.

Tani just smiled. "I'm sure going to find out."

Three

After a couple more drinks and then an hour searching through the phone book for any first name that even resembled the name Tani, Conrad gave up and told John that he would buy him dinner if he joined him again at the Elks.

"The Golden Dragon here isn't good enough for you?" John asked.

"Tani can't find me here," John said.

"How can you be so sure?" a woman's voice asked from behind Conrad.

Both men spun on their bar stools, Conrad a little faster than John. He knew that voice anywhere. Even being drunk last night, that voice could soothe even the wildest beast. And excite the hell out of him.

"Tani!" Conrad said, standing and giving her a long hug, which she returned in a wonderful fashion. "I've been looking for you, hoping to see you again."

"You mentioned you liked this place," Tani said, smiling. "So I took a chance."

Conrad almost fainted with that smile. Wow, she was far, far more beautiful than he remembered. And she had done something different with her hair tonight. It was a light brown and looked longer. Clearly the booze last night had done him no good. But right now he was only two scotches into the evening and he planned on doing no more.

Tonight she had on a thin sweater that showed most of her assets and tight slacks that looked more painted on that anything.

"I'm John," he said, extending his hand.

Conrad could tell John was stunned at Tani's beauty as well.

Tani smiled and Conrad thought John's knees might just melt out from under him as he shook her hand.

"Conrad mentioned you," Tani said. "So I brought two friends tonight that you just might find interesting."

Tani turned as two women just as stunning as Tani walked in, looking around at the small bar. Both also had on pants that left nothing to the imagination and tight blouses.

"This is Too," Tani said, introducing the woman with long red hair. "And Kreble."

The woman with short blonde hair shook Conrad's hand, then smiled at John with a smile as powerful as Tani's.

Then Tani looked directly at John and smiled. "Think you can handle my two friends?"

John's mouth opened, then closed, then he just nodded as he swallowed.

Both women giggled as each took one of John's arms and headed for the door.

Tani took Conrad's arm as he stood there, mouth still open, just staring in shock at his best friend. "Let's go with them, find a more private place."

"We can go back to my apartment again," Conrad managed to croak out.

"Perfect," Tani said, stroking his arm as they headed for the door. "My friends want to know if we are compatible. After last night, I'm fairly certain we are. You willing to try that again?"

Flashes of the wonderful night in bed with Tani appeared in Conrad's mind like a movie and he just nodded.

Actually, he just kept nodding all the way to his apartment.

Four

Somewhere around six in the morning the squeals and moans from John and the other two women in Conrad's second bedroom stopped.

Conrad was just trying to catch a third or fourth wind. It might be more but the sex and the night had become a long, wonderful blur. Tani didn't seem to be slowing down at all.

"Tani," the woman named Kreble said from Conrad's bedroom door. Conrad was so tired, he didn't even try to cover up the fact that he was nude and sprawled on his back on the bed.

"Yes," Tani said, smiling up at her friend.

"It seems you were right," Kreble said as the other woman appeared beside her. "This species seems to be suitable for mating. And they are fun."

"That they are," Tani said, giving Conrad junior a tug right there in front of her friends.

Conrad just didn't care. Far, far too tired. He hadn't had a night like this ever, let alone at his age.

"Have fun," Kreble said. "We'll see you next cycle."

"If not before," Tani said, smiling.

Then it was if the two other women just vanished. Conrad blinked then started to say something as Tani went back to the job of trying to revive him for another round.

They couldn't have just vanished. He must have dozed off for a micro second.

He reached for Tani to indicate she might want to give him a little more rest, but then his hand found the fine hair on her back and he started stroking it and even to his own surprise, he was soon ready to go again.

John left a few hours later with a smile on his face and an "I owe you, buddy."

Tani didn't leave.

She also didn't know how to cook or even use some basic house-hold appliances like a faucet on the sink or an electric toothbrush. She kept saying that where she was from they didn't have those sorts of things.

But she wouldn't tell Conrad where she was from, other than a name that didn't sound very real. When asked she said her last name was Peet.

But Conrad didn't much care if she was backward and had a weird last name. Tani tended to spend most of her days in the nude and as time went along Conrad stopped drinking, lost weight, and gained stamina that he hadn't even dreamed of as a teenager.

Tani just never quit smiling.

Then one day about a month after Tani moved in she said, "Mating cycle has started. Are you ready?"

She stroked his arm and he touched her fur-covered naked back and he was as ready as he always was.

That was the last night of sex.

On the second day he asked her what happened and she said, "It is forbidden to have sex until the child is born."

She would explain no more, so he left the apartment without her and went back to the Golden Dragon.

"Wow, are you looking good, friend," John said. "Tani getting you in shape, huh?"

Conrad decided to not talk about what had happened with the sudden lack of sex and talk of a kid. So he had two drinks and went home.

Tani was nude, and now clearly pregnant.

He stood staring at her, his mouth open, then just pointed at her stomach. "What is that?"

"Our child," she said, nibbling on a box of chocolates while watching *The Price is Right* rerun.

"When did that happen?" he asked.

She looked at him, puzzled. "Two nights ago, of course. He will be born in two days. My 44th child, but my first with an Earthman. You should be honored."

Conrad just opened his mouth and not a damn word came out. He just couldn't think of anything to say.

He turned around, went back out the door and back to the Golden Dragon. John managed to get him home at closing, but he was so drunk he just stumbled into bed.

The next morning a very, very pregnant Tani awoke him, still nude.

He took a shower, looked at her one more time, then said, "Let me know when this nightmare is over."

He again drank himself into a stupor, took a cab home, and woke up the next morning to the sound of a crying child.

And Tani was back looking like her normal self.

"Would you like to see your son?" she asked, carrying him to the side of the bed for Conrad to see.

The kid looked cute, as most babies do. He had Conrad's slightly thin nose, but like Tani was covered in a fine layer of hair.

How the hell did he have a kid? He had never wanted a kid, and he had only been playing around with Tani for less than a few weeks. Maybe a month at most.

A moment later two strange-looking women with flat faces and black dresses who smelled of mothballs appeared in the bedroom right out of thin air.

"I've got to stop drinking again," Conrad said.

"Say goodbye to your child," Tani said to Conrad.

"What?"

Tani stood and took the child to the two faceless women.

51

The both held their palms over the child, then nodded. "You risked a great deal, Tani," one of the women said without any sign of a mouth moving anywhere that Conrad could see "to mate with such a primitive creature. But the baby is fine."

Tani nodded and handed them the baby.

A moment later the two faceless women in black and the baby vanished.

Tani turned to Conrad, completely nude. "Now that's finished, let's have some fun."

She jumped on the bed, yanked the covers off him, and sat on his crotch.

"Hold on, hold on," he said, taking her by both arms and keeping her from moving on him. "What just happened?"

"Our duty, of course," Tani said, smiling. "Wonderful isn't it, helping our different races survive and mingle."

She started to move again and his crotch started to respond again, being a traitor, but he needed more information.

"Different races? What do you mean?"

Tani smiled. "I told you, I'm from Lind."

"I have no idea where that's at," he said.

"About a hundred thousand light years from here," she said, still moving on him even though he was holding her two wonderful-feeling arms.

"You're kidding, right?"

"I am not joking," Tani said, smiling at him. "I am very different from you. I am from another planet."

"John put you up to this, didn't he?" Conrad asked.

Tani again smiled. "Would you like to see my actual form?"

"I would love to," he said. "I have no idea what just happened with that baby thing and I need some answers."

She sort of shrugged. "I was warned that you might not be able to understand my original form, which is why I have maintained this body."

"I like this body," he said, stroking the fur on her arms. "But it's always better to know the real person."

Again she shrugged.

And a moment later a huge, fur-covered spider with eight legs, two eyes on stalks, and large green lips with rows of teeth behind them was straddling his naked body.

The last thing he remembered before waking up screaming in the hospital was Tani saying, "Can't say I didn't warn you."

He couldn't stop screaming for a very, very long time.

Two months after being committed to the State Mental Hospital, a small spider crawling down the wall near his bed caused him to have a heart attack and he died at the age of thirty.

Five

Tani-Areas-Fol-Dan-Peet floated into the Doorways Bar and saw her two friends just getting their drinks on this first day of their vacation. It felt wonderful to see them again. She had so much to tell them about her adventure of the cycle.

"How did the mating go with the primitives?" Kreble asked after the ritual greetings were finished.

Tani smiled, her eye-stalks swirling. "They are wonderful playthings and produce adequate children."

"But..." Too said, leaning in and matching one eyestalk with Tani's. "I hear a reservation."

"They ask too many questions," Tani said. "I showed Con-Rad my original form and he ran from me so I had to find another mate for the second child of the cycle."

"Are you going back?" Too asked.

"No," Tani said. "I had wonderful adventures I can share, but I want to keep exploring."

Both of her friends looked and acted relieved. "So where are we going first this vacation?"

"I hear there is a little planet of ocean-swimmers that might be fun."

Both Too and Kreble pretended to be shocked by swirling their eyestalks and twisting their front legs together.

Tani smiled. She knew they were as excited about the idea as she was. Sex with creatures with four sex organs and ten arms under a mile of ocean could promise many, many good times.

She sipped her last Screwdriver from the planet Earth and nodded to her friends. It was good to be home.

THE EMPTY MUMMY MURDERS

A Poker Boy Story

For the second time in his life, Poker Boy finds himself trying to help a woman stalked by the alien-looking Silicon Suckers.

He failed the first time and they killed an old girlfriend of his.

This time the Silicon Suckers have killed three other women. Can he save the woman asking for help and more importantly help her save herself?

One

IT WAS a good ten minutes into the conversation over vanilla milkshakes and a side of fries with Scary Mary, as her friends called her and she called herself, before she got to the point.

Scary Mary deserved the name. She had bright red hair tied up so tight on the top of her head that it pulled the skin of her face and scalp upward. She wore more makeup than a bad rodeo clown, and had breasts that must have arrived at the restaurant a good minute ahead of her.

Her tight red dress, if you could call the small piece of cloth covering her largest assets a dress, I'm sure didn't cover her butt when she slid into the leather booth at The Diner. But I didn't look. In Vegas you saw all types, and a long time ago I had learned to not judge a person by their look or a woman by the expanded size of her chest.

Some friend-of-a-friend had given Scary Mary one of my real-world names and told her I might be able to help with her problems.

As Poker Boy, I find people to help in all sorts of ways. Sometimes I find them, sometimes they come to me, sometimes my boss, Stan the God of Poker, assigns me the task of helping someone. It never seems to make any sense how I find the people who need saving, but I do. Just as I find the people at poker tables who need me to take their money. It seems to be a natural way of the world.

I had told Scary Mary to meet me at The Diner in downtown Las Vegas. The Diner serves the best milkshakes on the planet, and the waitress who is always there is Madge, a superhero in the food service business. The Diner is decorated like a fake 1960s diner. I am convinced there were no places in the 1960s that looked anything like The Diner, with records stapled on the walls and photos of Elvis, Marilyn, and James Dean on most walls.

But the booths were comfortable and the milkshakes huge and made like old milkshakes from the 1930s. And it was where my team met when we had a job to plan.

It was two in the afternoon. No one but Madge was with us in The Diner, and she was working up behind the counter. Scary Mary and I were in a booth near the front door. It was a perfect time to get to the bottom of her problem.

Scary Mary kept looking at me in a worried fashion, so I sort of turned on my Trust-Me power and let it wash over her. I had on my black leather jacket and black fedora-like hat that was my superhero uniform, and I could feel the power they gave me drawing from the nearby casinos. It should be more than enough to get Scary Mary to talk.

After a moment she blushed, which looked washed-out next to her blazing-red hair and beside her thick, blue eyeliner and red lipstick.

"You're not going to believe me and I just don't know what you can do to help," she said, her voice deep and throaty.

"Try me," I said, turning up my Trust-Me" power a little and adding a little Empathy power to it as well. "You would be surprised at what I might be able to do."

"That's what my friend in the poker room at the MGM told me. But you just won't believe me."

"Let me decide that," I said.

She signed, looked both directions. "I'm being harassed by aliens."

"Oh, no," I said, sighing and stirring up my milkshake. This felt like a problem I had had three years before with an old girlfriend. She hadn't let me help her and she had ended up dead.

"I told you that you wouldn't believe me," Scary Mary said, clearly disgusted.

"Oh, I believe you," I said. "The aliens you are seeing have large heads, big eyes, and are gray. Right?"

"Yes, yes," she said, jumping a little in the booth in excitement and almost knocking over her milkshake with the large extensions on her chest.

I sighed again. "Those aren't aliens. Those are creatures called Silicon Suckers. And my bet is they are after your breasts."

Both her hands went to cover a few inches of the mass on her chest, her eyes wide, her mouth open.

Silicon Suckers are the reason the UFO nuts think there are aliens visiting earth. They have big oblong heads with long thin excuses for chins. Their bodies are thin, humanoid, but all gray in color. Their feet are huge and they walk like they are floating through the air without a sound. And they have lived in their caves in the deserts for far longer than there have been humans around.

What drives me nuts about them are their huge eyes. They don't seem to blink, and that can just unnerve a guy, even me, a superhero.

They have no smell, but can suck moisture out of an area faster than a hundred dehumidifiers on full blast. And for some stupid reason, of all the people and superheroes and gods that exist, I am the one who has become the go-to-guy for dealing with the Silicon Suckers.

I keep wanting to tell people I play poker for a living, I work for Stan, the God of Poker, and I do my best work in casinos helping people who come into poker rooms solve their problems. As far as I know, Silicon Suckers don't even know what poker is.

Now here I was again, talking to a woman who needed help with the Silicon Suckers. If this trend didn't stop, I might start being called Silicon Sucker Boy. And I would hate that.

"So what have they been doing?" I asked, dreading the answer.

She still had her hands firmly planted over small areas of her massive breasts.

"What do you mean they might be after my breasts?"

"First tell me what they are doing," I said, sending as much Calming Power as I could generate her way. I wasn't in that good of control of that superpower yet, but by simply trying to calm a person, I sometimes could.

She took a deep breath and then nodded. "I first saw them in the parking garage off my apartment, out near the airport. They just stood there, staring at me."

"Two of them?"

"Yeah," she said. "At first I figured them for nutcases from a convention, but they are very skinny and I couldn't see costumes."

"You've seen them more times?"

She nodded. "A couple of dozen times and twice they got into my apartment. Made the place so dry I was afraid it was going to burst into flames."

"Silicon Suckers live under the desert and take moisture out of the air," I said, nodding. "Have they tried to touch you?"

"No," she said, shaking her head and shivering.

I stared into her worried eyes and knew I was way out of my depth. Any question I might have next about changes to her chest would sound bad coming from me. I needed some help.

"Hold on just a minute, would you?" I asked. "I want to call a friend to make sure there haven't been any other sightings lately."

She nodded and I motioned for Madge to come over as I stood.

"You interested in a hamburger?" I asked Scary Mary. "On me."

She nodded and I turned to Madge who had heard me. "My normal burger, one for Mary, and a shake and burger for Patty as well. I'll be right back."

Madge nodded. She would entertain Scary Mary until I got back with Patty. With luck, it would only be a minute.

Two

I stepped outside the door into the warm fall day, then jumped to a spot in front of the MGM Grand main hotel lobby check-in desk. Then, before a camera could pick up my sudden appearance, I pulled myself and Patty out of the flow of time.

I loved being able to teleport, and even more being able to stop time. Actually, I couldn't stop time but it looked like I could. I actually just could step between moments in time. And I could take others with me into that moment, which made everyone else look frozen around me.

My girlfriend, Patty Ledgerwood, aka Front Desk Girl, had just finishing checking in a woman with two kids. The woman and the two kids were frozen in place moving away from the counter and Patty was smiling at me.

"Thank you," she said. "I needed a break."

"My pleasure," I said, smiling back. Just seeing Patty always made me smile. She had long brown hair that she had tied back while working. Her wonderful brown eyes were deep enough for me to get lost in and I had many, many times. Today she had on a white blouse and black slacks and a light tan MGM jacket that was the uniform of the day. She looked good in anything, but I was in love with her, so my opinion was clearly not one anyone could trust.

"So what's happening?"

"I need some help with a woman who's being visited by Silicon Suckers," I said.

"Oh, oh," Patty said. "Does she…?"

"Bigger than I thought possible," I said, indicating how large Scary Mary's breasts were.

"And you want me to help you question her about them?"

"I screwed this up once," I said. "I'd kind of like to get it right if her breasts are the problem."

Patty knew about my old girlfriend and how she had refused to give back her breast implants made out of silicon from a sacred Silicon Sucker's burial ground. The Silicon Suckers had eventually removed the breasts through her ass, for some reason the only way they know of to get inside a human body, and it had killed her.

Failing to save her always felt like one of my biggest mistakes.

Patty nodded. "Meet me in the hallway down near my car. I'll be right there."

I nodded and jumped to that spot while also stepping back into the flow of time. In Vegas a person couldn't just jump around through space without also being careful to not be picked up on cameras. Patty and I had a regular camera dead spot.

It took Patty exactly four minutes to get off work and meet me. Her boss at the MGM Grand knew what she did and that sometimes she just needed some time away. In fact, her boss was another superhero working the same area.

I jumped us out of there the moment Patty hit the camera safe area and back to a spot just in front of The Diner.

I led the way inside, telling Patty what I had ordered her. Madge was just heading back to the kitchen and Scary Mary was sitting nervously in the booth twisting the straw in her milkshake. Clearly Madge had stood and talked with her for a few minutes while I was gone.

I introduced Patty to Scary Mary and then said, "Patty knows all about the Silicon Suckers."

Patty nodded as Scary Mary sort of beamed behind all the makeup.

"I've seen them a number of times," Patty said. "And even been down in one of the caves they call sand castles."

"Wow," Scary Mary said. "I thought for sure I was going insane."

"Far from it," Patty said. "But these creatures are very dangerous, and we need to try to figure out what changed for you that started them visiting you."

"That way we have a chance of stopping them," I said.

Scary Mary nodded and I hit her again with another wave of my Relax and Trust-Me super power. She seemed to calm a little more.

Patty, who was sitting beside me in the booth, patted my leg and then leaned toward Scary Mary. "So what day exactly did you first see the Silicon Suckers?"

Scary Mary twisted her face and layered makeup around, clearly trying to think, then said, "May sixteenth."

"So, anything major happen the week before that?" Patty asked. "Anything change?"

"I got a new job," Scary Mary said without hesitation. "Five days before. I remember because it was May Eleventh, one year from the day exactly that I had my sex change operation, and I figured that was a good sign."

So Scary Mary used to be Scary Martin, but I doubted that was going to have anything to do with this case. Patty clearly didn't either because she said nothing. Again, this was Vegas. We had seen most everything.

"What was your new job?" Patty asked.

"Dispatcher," she said. "Desert High Sand and Gravel. I used to drive a truck, but after my operation Ben, the owner, said that once I got recovered, he'd find a place for me. And he did."

"What happened to the previous dispatcher?" I asked, afraid of the answer.

"Sharon? She vanished one day," Scary Mary said. "No sign of her but her ex-husband was knocking her around at one point so they're looking at him."

Patty sighed and looked down.

I would bet anything that the previous dispatcher had been killed by the Silicon Suckers. But it would never be proved. Somewhere, at some point, the trucks that Scary Mary was sending out were doing something to anger the Silicon Suckers. And since she sent them out, they were blaming her. And clearly they'd blamed the woman who had her job ahead of her.

Then Patty asked a question I hadn't thought to ask.

"Did any other dispatchers disappear besides Sharon?"

"Joyce," Scary Mary said. "And there might have been another, but I'm not sure."

Then, suddenly she realized where we were going. "You don't think that these aliens caused them to vanish?"

Both Patty and I nodded and Scary Mary turned white under all the makeup.

Three

Madge brought the food at that point, and it gave me a chance to think. My entire premise that the Silicon Suckers were after Scary Mary's breasts had gone out the window. Most of the time I dealt with the Silicon Suckers because of land problems. They were very, very protective of their land, and had negotiated with the gods, including Lady Luck herself, a compromise that allowed humans to build Las Vegas. But with the recent expansion, there had been many dust-ups lately over land.

This was looking like another one of those. And clearly the Silicon Suckers were warning each dispatcher in their own way, giving them time to stop, then killing them when they didn't and starting over with a new dispatcher.

Scary Mary had had no idea her job was so deadly when she took it.

After Madge put down the wonderful-smelling hamburgers and fries and left, I started to quiz Scary Mary about the business as we ate.

Turns out the company only had one large sand quarry in the desert outside of town. And the first mile of road from the pit was gravel across desert as well.

Scary Mary's job was to dispatch the trucks full of gravel or sand from the quarry to different jobs around the city or concrete mixing plants. She had to keep track of forty trucks, but in the boom times the dispatcher had managed over a hundred and had them on the go constantly for two shifts a day. She said she used to drive one of those trucks.

"I need maps of the quarry and the road in and out of it," I said. "And then I'll compare them to Silicon Sucker lands."

I took a big bite of my hamburger, then stood. "It won't take long," I said.

I headed out the door, and the moment I was on the sidewalk and the young couple walking toward Freemont Street had their back turned, I shouted to the air, "Stan. Need help in your office."

Since I didn't have an office and I didn't want Scary Mary to know what I could really do, I figured Stan's office would be as good as any.

A moment later I found myself in a standard business office and Stan in his normal black slacks and tan shirt stood facing me beside an oak desk with a computer and chair. A couple plants filled the corners and the windows looked out over Vegas from high in the air. Far higher than any office building.

"I got to teach you how to build yourself an office when you need it," he said, shaking his head.

"I can do this?" I asked, stunned, looking around at the furniture and the fantastic view of the invisible floating office. I had always figured that only the gods could build offices.

Stan just shook his head in slight disgust and then said, "What do you need?"

I told him which maps I needed and a moment later they appeared in the air, the map of the Silicon Sucker lands floating on one side, the map of the quarry and road on the other.

"You going to tell me why you need these two maps?" he asked.

"Just put them at the same scale and overlay them," I said. "We just might see why."

He did, the two maps floating until they merged. The quarry was a long ways from the Silicon Sucker land, but the road was another matter.

"There," I said, pointing to one area where the road seemed to touch the Silicon Sucker's land. "Can you make that larger?"

The road clearly had been laid out to go around a corner of the Silicon Sucker's land, making a ninety-degree corner.

I was betting that corner had been cut off. And people had been dying because of it.

I glanced around. "Can you put us and this office right over that corner?"

An instant later we were over the corner of the dirt road, floating in the air still inside the office, only now part of the office floor under our feet was invisible.

That felt kind of creepy and cool at the same time. I really needed to learn how to do all this.

Below, I could still see the old road, but clearly a new one had been constructed a few years back that cut directly across Silicon Sucker land. More than likely the owner just figured it was desert land and no one would care. As we watched, floating invisible in an air-conditioned office above, a truck full of gravel powered through the corner leaving a trail of dust.

"Oh, shit," Stan said.

"The Suckers have been warning and then killing the truck dispatchers," I said. "Blaming them for sending the trucks across their lands. The newest one came to me because she thought she was seeing aliens."

"It was worse," Stan said.

Then something on the old road caught my eye and I could feel my stomach drop. I wished I hadn't had that bite of hamburger.

"Hang on," I said and teleported to the old section of road.

The heat of the desert hit me hard and it was a moderately cool day in the fall. I couldn't imagine how hot it was out here in the summer.

Right square in the middle of the road was a long mound of sand built crosswise to the road. Beside that were two others.

"Oh, don't tell me," Stan said, appearing beside me.

I eased over and carefully moved a little sand on one pile with my shoe, just enough to uncover the mummified remains of a human hand, drained of all moisture.

"Shit!" Stan said.

All I wanted to do was be sick. I stepped back and tried to take a deep breath of the hot air, but that didn't help much.

Four

"Where is the woman you are helping now?" Stan asked, also still staring at the three mounds clearly covering three bodies. He was the God of Poker and been around for thousands of years. And I was a superhero. That didn't mean that we had gotten used to things like this. You could never get used to this kind of thing. Ever.

"She's with Patty and Madge at The Diner," I said.

"Let's go there and figure this out," Stan said.

"Scary Mary doesn't know who we are or what we can do," I said.

Stan shook his head. "She's going to know now."

We jumped back to the booth and Scary Mary jumped so hard against the back of the booth, her large breasts just about hit her in the forehead.

Patty looked shocked as I slid in beside her and took a long drink from a glass of water. Stan pulled up a chair and took another glass of water and drank it.

Then he reached across the table and extended his hand. "I'm Stan."

"Mary," she said, taking his hand carefully. "People call me Scary Mary. And how did you do that?"

"There's a reason you came to us for help," Stan said. "Just trust us."

She nodded and said nothing, but I could tell she wanted to bolt for the door. Seeing aliens was one thing, seeing two men appear out of thin air was another.

"This has to be bad," Patty said, "or you wouldn't have come in like that."

"Very bad," I said. Then with Madge listening, I explained about the corner and what we had found on the old unused part of the road.

Mary now looked like she would be sick. "I drove for two of them," she said. "How is this possible?"

"Silicon Suckers are very, very protective of their land," I said. "They consider what they have been doing with you a warning to stop sending trucks over their land. They must have done the same thing with the other three."

"But you said they might be after my breasts," Scary Mary said.

"My first assumption; I was wrong," I said. "I had an old friend who ended up with silicon breast enhancements that were made from a sacred Silicon Sucker burial ground. She wouldn't give them back, so the Silicon Suckers took them."

"But the issue this time is the road and that shortcut," Stan said. "You said you used to drive for this company?"

"Before my operation," Scary Mary said. "A bunch of drivers built the shortcut across that corner back in the boom times, when we were all in such a hurry to do as many loads as possible. God, such a stupid thing to kill three women over."

"Not to the Silicon Suckers," Patty said. "All their land is very sacred."

"Poker Boy," Stan said, "you deal with the Silicon Suckers more than anyone. Any idea what we need to do now?"

I honestly had no idea. There were three bodies on the old road that the police were going to need to do something with. And more than likely that would be a crime scene for some time. If the trucks kept using that shortcut, Scary Mary wouldn't live very long.

I turned to Scary Mary who was looking shocked and puzzled, or at least that's how I thought she was looking under the layers of makeup. Clearly sex-change operations didn't come with lessons in makeup.

"Is there another way in and out of that quarry?"

"South toward the freeway and then into town past the airport," she said.

"That's directly away from Silicon Sucker land," Stan said, nodding. "I'll get the police on the bodies and work with Laverne to talk with the Gods of Land Use to get permission to use the road past the Silicon Sucker lands revoked."

I nodded. Stan would take care of the surface problems. My problem still sat across from me.

"Good luck," he said. Then with a nod to Scary Mary, he vanished.

"How…how…how…?"

Scary Mary just kept staring at where he had been.

I tried one of my French Fries, but it just no longer tasted good. Somehow I still had to figure out a way to save Scary Mary's life. We would get the trucks stopped, but I had a hunch Scary Mary had insulted the Silicon Suckers for just too long a time. She would need to apologize or end up dead.

Finally Scary Mary moved her attention from the vanishing Stan to the quiet that rested over the table. She looked at Patty, then at me. "I'm still in danger, aren't I?"

Patty nodded. "I'm afraid so. But give us a little time. We'll protect you until we can get something figured out."

"Think fast," Madge said as two Silicon Suckers appeared near the door and the air in the restaurant got suddenly very, very dry.

Five

I didn't know they could teleport. That explained a great deal.

I stood and stepped toward the two alien-looking creatures. Then in their language of clicks and snaps and grunts, I said, "It is an honor to be in the presence of such great beings."

"Thank you, Poker Boy," the one on the right said in clear English without seeming to move his lips. "The honor is ours. Today you visited the great scar in our lands."

"Yes, I did not know about it until today," I said, having no idea what to say but the truth. "I have become very upset at such an insult to my wonderful friends, the Silicon Suckers. The human vehicles that crossed across your sacred lands and damaged them are being stopped and will not come near your lands again. The humans must retrieve the dead that caused such damage, but then that path near your sacred lands will be closed completely."

The restaurant was becoming tinder dry and Patty and Scary Mary sat perfectly still in the booth. Madge stood near her counter, also not moving.

"When will this ceremony take place?" the Silicon Sucker asked.

I had no idea what he meant by ceremony, but with that corner being a crime scene, we wouldn't be able to do anything there anytime soon. I bowed slightly. "May we beg for one half of a moon cycle to prepare and for the humans to finish removing their dead?"

The Silicon Sucker bowed slightly, then said, "Yes, that will be acceptable."

I had just bought us and Scary Mary two weeks. I hoped that would be enough time.

Then the Silicon Sucker turned and looked at Scary Mary for a moment, then back at me. If they stepped toward her, there would be nothing I could do to stop them that wouldn't insult them deeply and maybe cause a war between the gods and Silicon Suckers. So far, in my understanding, there had only been two such wars throughout all time. Both fought over land.

Scary Mary had damaged their land in their minds. No god or superhero could or would stop them if they wanted to take her.

"Will the human that sent such machines over our land be at the ceremony?"

"She did not understand what she was doing until she received your warnings and came to me. She is disgusted at her carelessness, and is the reason it is stopping now. She will bow in great respect and offer herself and her gifts in hopes the great Silicon Suckers will allow her to live."

He bowed slightly again and then said, "We will be watching."

"It was an honor as always," I said, bowing to them.

Both bowed in return and then vanished.

"Open the door and let some moisture in here," Madge said after a moment.

I did as I was told and then went back to the booth and drank three glasses of the water that Madge brought.

We had two weeks to save Scary Mary's life.

Six

We failed.

That afternoon at The Diner we tried our best to convince Scary Mary to keep her mouth shut about the murders and what she knew. And never say anything about the Silicon Suckers, but it ended up under questioning she didn't remain quiet.

Or couldn't. I never knew.

The murders hit the headlines, of course. When it became known that the corpses had been hollowed out, with most of the insides pulled out of the victims' asses, it got even more sensational. The press called them the "Empty Mummy Murders."

I didn't want to mention to the press that most mummies were empty.

After the police were done, Stan got the Gods of Land Use to go in and close off and destroy any sign of any road across the Silicon Suckers land, and even had them replant new desert grass and weeds.

Two major rocks were placed at both ends of the old shortcut to make sure no one went out there over the Silicon Sucker land.

And, of course, the road to the crime scene was closed off completely from the quarry to the location of the bodies and also from the highway to the location at the corner.

But Scary Mary just couldn't keep her mouth shut. She started insisting that it was aliens who had killed the women. And that there were people in The Diner who could appear and disappear.

That sounded totally insane, so the police started investigating her past and her sanity and came up will all sorts of things that didn't look good besides her makeup.

Scary Mary was tossed into custody not only as a suspect in the murders, but also for other events that happened in her past, including the accidental drowning in a pool of Scary Mary's first wife when Scary Mary was a he.

Her picture in all its strange made-up glory hit the front page of the newspaper as a primary suspect in the Empty Mummy Murders.

So on the day of the ceremony, Scary Mary could not attend.

I wanted to jump into jail and spring her for the ceremony, but Stan wouldn't let me. He said we didn't do things that way.

I did the best I could in the ceremony, leaving offerings of five thermoses of hot chocolate at each end of the now repaired scar in the land. Silicon Suckers treasured hot chocolate as a sacred drug that allowed them to produce more Silicon Suckers. I figured five at each end would show them how serious I thought the scar was.

Denton, the God of Land Use Planning, who was the God who had originally negotiated the settlement of lands around Las Vegas, appeared and begged for the forgiveness of the great beings.

There just wasn't much else we could do.

No Silicon Suckers showed up, so we left the thermoses sitting in the sand in the desert.

Four days later Scary Mary vanished from her holding cell. Her body was found where the others had been found two days earlier. All her organs had all been cleaned out through her ass and her skin was mummified.

Scary Mary became the fourth known victim of the Empty Mummy Murderer. Of course, the case was never solved.

I was batting zero-for-two. Two women had come to me for help with the Silicon Suckers and both had been killed. I moped around for a few days until finally Patty got fed up with me and went with me to talk with Stan.

We ended up in another floating office far over the city. The view was stunning, but I noticed Stan had his windows turned so that he couldn't see in the direction of the quarry.

He was sitting behind a big oak desk with nothing on it. Patty and I dropped down onto the leather couch.

With Patty pushing me on, I mentioned what was bothering me to Stan.

He just shrugged. "Nothing you could do when a person won't help themselves and just keep their mouth shut."

"I mentioned that a few times as well," Patty said, shaking her head. "But he's determined to feel bad."

"It feels like crap," I said. "Even though I couldn't do anything."

"Yeah, it does," Stan said. "But do you win every hand you play at a poker table?"

"Of course not," I said, almost angry that he had suggested that. "But when I lose a hand there I don't have someone die."

"True," Stan said, "but you win a hell of a lot more than you lose in the saving-people game. And that's the key to remember."

"Yeah," Laverne said, suddenly appearing standing beside Stan behind his desk, "remember the ones you saved."

Patty and I both jumped to our feet, because when Lady Luck appears, you don't sit there slouching on the couch.

Lady Luck went on. "Remember you and your team saved me once. And the entire human race another time. And you've even saved a few people from the Silicon Suckers over the last few years, which is more than most have done."

All I could do was nod. She was right.

"So get over it and get back to work," she said, smiling at me.

When Lady Luck smiles at you, trust me, you can feel it. And I did. I felt a ton better, and was suddenly back thinking again instead of just feeling sorry for myself for losing Scary Mary.

"Stan," Lady Luck said, "teach Poker Boy how to build himself an office, would you? It's about time he and his team have one of their own, don't you think?"

Then she vanished.

Stan laughed and stood from behind his desk. "That's the first time I have ever heard her give a pep talk."

"You're kidding?" I asked, feeling stunned.

"Three thousand years, never seen it happen."

Suddenly even more of the weight seemed to lift from my shoulders.

Patty gave me a hug and then a big, long kiss.

"Hey, not in my office," Stan said.

I broke away from Patty just long enough to say, "Then teach me how to build one of my own." Then I went back to kissing Patty.

"Nag, nag, nag," Stan said.

AFTER THE DANCE

Billy meets Laura at the dance. She loves to dance. But she has a problem. She died on the night of her first dance.

But when the dance falls on her 16th birthday, she gets to go to the dance again. And this year she meets Billy, a wonderful, gentle boy.

She hopes he will understand.

A dead teenager story about what happens when the song ends.

FROM THE MOON-CAST shadows of the night I watch Billy pick up his gray wool sweater from the newly mowed grass of my grave.

He holds the sweater away from him, as if he has never seen it before, let alone worn it to the dance last night.

Those gentle hands of his shake, and even across the darkness of the cemetery, I can see the fear clouding his green eyes. His brown hair is mussed by the night breeze and I can tell he is about to panic and run.

I want to step out of the shadows, to let him kiss me again as he did at my parents' front door, to feel his strength against me, but I know that would send him fleeing, now that my father has told him the truth. I can't have him leave. There are only a few hours before the sun

70

breaks over the tops of the hills and I will be forced to return to my grave. I must act before then.

But at this moment the time is not right.

I stand in the night shadows and watch him hold his sweater. He stares at it and then at my headstone.

I know the words he reads.

LAURA JANE ROBERTS
Born September 22, 1946
Died September 22, 1962

Nothing more. A simple statement of facts.

Even frightened, Billy seems unable to tear himself away from those words that are carved in the cold, smooth stone. He must love me as much as I came to love him in the few short hours of the dance.

I almost laugh out loud, but then stop. That would scare him too, so I hold my hand over my mouth and let the laugh die with the wind in the trees.

Billy sits down beside my grave, his sweater beside him on the grass.

Good. He is not going to leave yet. I can wait a little longer, until the night air chills him and forces him into my arms.

I move to a group of shadows closer to him and stand thinking about my first fall dance twenty-eight years ago tonight.

That night had started out so special.

I went to the dance with my best friend, Donna. I remember my stomach twisting with excitement. The first dance of my sophomore year. And my birthday would start at midnight.

Donna and I had planned to stay out late, until one in the morning, dancing with every boy we saw and celebrating the arrival of my birthday.

Only Donna started drinking. Rum and Coke that some stupid kid from another school gave her.

Before midnight, before my birthday had even started, she was sick. She had ruined everything.

I remember telling her I hated her, yelling at her, calling her names as she threw up time after time.

I stormed out of the bathroom and into the parking lot and the cold night air.

That's where I met Craig.

He was sitting in his blue Chevy, with the radio blaring and the windows wide open. He said he was from downtown.

Looking back now, from the cemetery, the dark shadows, and all the years, I should have known better. But I was so mad at Donna and the cloth seats of his car felt so soft and he liked the same music that I did. After all, at midnight it was going to be my birthday. I had a right to have a good time.

At eleven he suggested we go driving around.

I knew better, but I didn't want to go back into the dance and face Donna, so I said yes.

At first we only went downtown and cruised. But by quarter to twelve, he had driven out to the edge of town and pulled off onto a dirt road next to an empty field.

He stopped, shut off the car, the radio, and the lights.

The darkness seemed to scream in my ears and I was so frightened, my hands were shaking. He tried to kiss me and I wouldn't let him. I told him I wanted to go back to the dance, but he just laughed.

I started to get out of the car like my mom had told me to do, but he grabbed my arm, yanked me back, and hit me.

From that point everything was sort of fuzzy. I think he hurt me real bad with that first hit.

I remember crying and him laughing at me. A high, nervous sort of laughter that I knew didn't sound right.

He kept trying to kiss me and touch me.

Every time I tried to make him quit he hit me.

I screamed once and he hit me so hard I could taste the blood.

Looking back now I mostly remember him laughing. That and thinking about my birthday and how it was ruined.

I guess he finally hit me too hard, because everything went completely black.

The next thing I knew it was years later, the dance was again being held the night before my birthday, I was standing on my grave, looking at my own headstone, and thinking how odd it was to be dead because I didn't feel dead.

In fact, I didn't feel a thing.

Nothing.

I didn't even care what had happened to Craig. I just wanted to meet someone and dance.

Now, four dances later, Billy, my date and dance partner for the evening, is sitting next to my grave. I think he is shivering.

Maybe it is time for me to talk to him.

Maybe now he will listen if I go slow.

Very, very slow.

"Hi, Billy," I say as I move forward, my voice as friendly and as sweet as I can make it in the night air.

He jumps and scrambles to his feet, clutching his sweater to his chest. His eyes are wild and his face is twisted in fear.

I know he is about to run.

"I'm sorry about lying to you about where I lived," I say.

I stop far enough away that he does not feel threatened.

He looks around as if searching for an escape route, then back at me.

I just stand there in the seemingly bright spotlight of the moon, looking as timid as I can, waiting, hoping he will stay without me forcing him to.

After a moment he chokes out a question. "Are you really dead?"

I nod, making my best sad expression, even though I feel no sadness. I know that's what he expects.

"But how..."

He leaves his question open. "I don't know," I say. "I really don't. I just knew I had to go to the dance, maybe to meet you. I don't know."

I give him my best lost-girl shrug. I am surprised at how calculating I can be. I could have never done this while I was alive.

He turns and points at my headstone. "Is that really you? I don't believe this."

"That's really me," I say.

He shakes his head. "No way. Someone is playing a joke on me. That's it, isn't it? This is just a big joke and you set that old man up in the house to tell me you had died. Right?"

I shake my head slowly, thinking back over the night. After Billy and I danced for hours, dream hours, he took me home. On the way to his car I asked to borrow his sweater. I told him I was cold. He took it off and gave it to me to wear. Then he kissed me, softly, and left me at my parents' house.

Down the street he remembered his sweater and went back to get it. I watched from the shadows as my father answered the door. Even after having this happen four times on the anniversary of the night I died, my father does not believe I return.

He refuses to believe.

So four times he has yelled at a boy.

He told Billy, in no uncertain terms, that I was dead and that Billy was rude for doing such a nasty thing to him. Then he slammed the door in Billy's face.

I feel so sorry for my father, but he is part of the pattern and I cannot break it.

Billy, very confused, found his way to the cemetery and to my head-stone. I knew he would.

They all did.

"This has to be a joke," he says.

He glances around the night shadows and up and down the rows of headstones.

"All right!" he yells. "The joke's over."

But his call is swallowed up by the darkness and the cold light of the moon. Nothing moves.

No one comes forward.

After a moment he is forced to turn back and face me.

"I don't believe you," he says.

Again I shrug. "There is nothing I can do to prove it to you. I only have a short time. I must leave at sunrise."

"Why?" he asks.

"I really don't know. Anymore than I know how I got here. I just know. Would you stay a little while and talk?"

He glances quickly around. Then it is his turn to shrug. "Why not?"

I smile and move closer to him, to my grave.

He backs away until he sees that all I am going to do is sit down on the grass near where he was sitting. Then, slowly, he comes back and joins me, keeping his distance.

I smile at him and after a moment of studying me, he shakes his head. "You don't look dead."

I laugh softly. "I don't feel dead. I enjoyed the dance. The decora-tions were wonderful. Especially how they made the gym look like the insides of a space ship."

He nods. "I had a good time," he says. "But this is a strange way of ending it."

I sigh and shake my head. "I had it worse."

His face becomes serious, as if he suddenly believes that I am dead. "What happened?"

I shake my head. "It was too ugly and it no longer matters."

Of course, that's a lie. But I cannot tell him so. And I could never tell him what happened. He would never understand.

"How often do you come back?" he asks. "Every year?"

He is unlike the others. They refused to believe right up to the last moment. He is asking questions as if he truly believes that I am dead. Maybe the world is changing.

"I only go to the dance when it falls on the night before my birthday."

That is the truth. I find it funny how I can mix the truth with lies and make them both sound so convincing.

Billy nods. "That makes sense."

Now it is my turn to be amazed. He is the first one who has been so understanding. I hope he has not guessed what I have planned for him. I might not be able to hold him if he knew.

I do not let my worry show.

Instead, I turn the conversation to questions about him, about his life, about the world he lives in. The same world that was taken from me and that now I only get a few hours every few years to see.

As the others did, Billy follows my lead and gladly talks about himself.

After an hour he has relaxed.

Behind him the eastern sky starts to fill with light. My time is very short.

He notices me looking at the sky and he stops.

Then he asks the question the three before him asked in one form or another. "What happens next?"

I smile at him. "I have to go back."

I point at my headstone.

"But why did you come out in the first place?" he asks. "I don't understand."

"Because I'm lonely," I tell him. That is partly the truth.

The sun is about to top the horizon. I glance up at it and he sees me look. I think he sees the fear and the sadness in my eyes.

"My night is almost over," I say as I stand and he stands with me. "Thank you for being so kind."

He shakes his head and takes a step toward me.

They all did.

They all wanted to hold me, to not let me go.

"I have no choice," I say. I make my voice sound helpless, sad.

The sun is at the edge of the horizon.

I can feel the pull of my grave.

Now is the time.

I step toward him, gently, eyes down.

"Thank you," I again say. "You are very kind."

He steps close to me and I turn my head up as I did on my parents' front step for him to kiss me good night.

His lips touch mine.

It is a wonderful kiss and I wrap my arms around him just as the sun casts its first rays among the stones and the trees. The pull is hard, but it only lasts a moment.

Then I am back on the soft padding inside my coffin, still kissing Billy. Still holding him with my dead arms.

Still pressing against him.

I try to make the moment last.

It takes Billy a few seconds to realize what has happened.

Then he starts struggling and screaming.

His kicking messes up the crowded insides of the coffin.

He is choking because there is no air. It had all been used up years ago by Henry and Don and Brian. There is none left for Billy and I feel sad because I wish Billy would last a little longer, as Henry did.

But there is no hope of that.

My coffin is a very small bed.

So Billy realizes where he is, feels the bodies of my lovers, feels my body wrapped in his embrace, feels the thickness of the smell press over his face, feels his lungs gasp for air.

He screams and struggles.

But soon he too is dead.

I adjust his body so I can hold him and still touch the bones and dried flesh of my other lovers.

My soft coffin is now very crowded, but I don't mind. I'm sure that by the time I awake again the worms will have guaranteed that there will be room for one more.

Good night, my loves.

Sleep tight.

FOR THE BALANCE OF A HEART

A Poker Boy Story

As a superhero in the gambling universe, Poker Boy works directly for Stan, the God of Poker.

Poker Boy's job? To save those who need saving and take money at the poker tables from those who need it taken.

But when Lady Luck herself comes calling and asks for a personal favor, Poker Boy and his team must travel far beyond the edges of Las Vegas to find the Queen of Hearts.

One

I ALWAYS FIGURED that when Lady Luck needed a favor from me, things had to be really, really bad.

Laverne, aka Lady Luck, appeared a little after noon on a Friday. My entire team was in my new office eating take-out Chinese and talking about our plans for the weekend. I had a poker tournament I hoped to play in later in the evening at the Bellagio and Patty Ledegerwood, aka Front Desk Girl, my sidekick and girlfriend, had to work swing at the MGM Grand Hotel front desk.

In other words, a pretty standard weekend night for us.

Then Lady Luck appeared.

When that happens, normal becomes a laughing matter.

Laverne had on her standard business casual gray pantsuit. Her dark hair was pulled so tight into a bun on the top of her head that it had to hurt. Her eyes looked neutral as they always did. Lady Luck seldom showed anyone any emotion and it was always impossible to get a read on what she was thinking.

She looked around my new office and smiled and then nodded. "Original."

I thought that meant she liked my new office layout. At least I hoped that was what she meant.

She glanced at Stan, the God of Poker, who was trying to choke down the remains of a spring roll. "Good job."

Stan, who had on his standard gray cardigan sweater and gray slacks, only nodded. Compliments from Lady Luck herself were rare and Stan knew that. The expression on his face and in his dark eyes never changed.

At times I couldn't believe my new office, or the fact that a super-hero poker player like me even had an office. But I did, and it was invis-ible and floated above the city of Las Vegas, about a thousand feet above the MGM Grand Casino and Hotel.

I doubted I would ever get used to how amazing that was.

Since Patty worked at the MGM Grand, I figured directly above the MGM Grand just seemed like a great place to anchor the office. Besides, since I got a lot of my superhero power from casinos funneled through my black leather coat and Fedora-like hat, being parked over a major casino never hurt.

And I seldom took off my coat and hat. Even now over a Chinese lunch that was about to get very cold.

The office in this spot also allowed for a great view of all of Las Vegas and the surrounding mountains and desert since all four walls were glass and perfectly clear. At first that had scared me so much I stayed to the center of the room. Finally, after a day of almost crawling around the room on my hands and knees for fear of falling off the edge of my office tile floor, I had decided to put in a wooden rail about a foot wide and waist-high across the glass. On all four walls. That helped. I now could actually go to the edges of my own office and look down.

Compared to normal offices, mine really wasn't much of an office. No desk, no couches, no pictures or awards hanging on the glass walls.

The entire center of the square office was filled with a large, oblong wooden booth. It was an exact replica of the booth in the Diner Restaurant from downtown Las Vegas where we had all met for the last couple of years.

Plastic-covered booth seats and a scarred tabletop made it feel real. Bottles of ketchup and mustard sat next to the salt and pepper and a pile of white paper napkins in the center.

Every detail was the same as in the Diner.

In other words, my nifty new office was nothing more than a hunk of tile floor and a diner booth floating in the air over a major casino. I liked it.

So did the rest of the team, or so they had said.

The booth was large enough to handle the six members of my team. There were two or three extra chairs in the room that visitors could pull up to the end of the booth and a couple of lawn chairs in one corner where Patty and I could just sit and stare out at the city and the mountains.

I'd only had this office for a week and I was starting to love sitting in those lawn chairs in the evenings before sunset.

Lady Luck turned around, grabbed a chair and pulled it toward the end of the booth where we were all sitting. It had been Lady Luck herself who had suggested that Stan, my boss and the God of Poker, teach me how to build and secure a floating office for me and my team.

Over the last few years my team had saved the world more times than I wanted to count, so it seemed like a great idea to me and it was turning out to be just that. But while I was building it, I hadn't been so sure.

It had taken two very long days and just about every ounce of energy I had, even with Stan helping, to put it all together and get it secured somehow in its floating and invisible location. But now it took no energy at all for me to keep it there.

Stan tried to explain to me how that worked, but I flat didn't understand a word he said. I figured there had to be some things only the gods could or should know. Since I was only a lowly superhero in the gambling universe, I wasn't meant to know what we had just done or how it even worked. Honestly, I was fine with that, as long as the office stayed in the air and we could go and come from it.

Lady Luck pulled the chair to the table and sat down. Then she sampled a bite of an extra spring roll and nodded. The food was from a restaurant called Larry's Chinese Place just off The Strip. The locals knew it was the best in town.

My entire team was there, plus Stan. I could tell they were all as shocked by Lady Luck's action as I felt. One of the most powerful gods in the universe just didn't join a bunch of superheroes and a poker god for lunch.

The Smoke and Screamer both eased away from her on the left side of the booth. The Smoke was basically a werewolf who could walk through walls. He stood about my height at six foot, but had shoulders so large it made him seem shorter. His most striking feature was his deep blue eyes.

Screamer was shorter than me and usually just wore Las Vegas tourist clothes like bright shirts and ugly shorts. He worked for the law enforcement side of the gods and seemed far, far harder than he actually was.

Madge, the food-service-superhero waitress who always wore a too-tight pink diner uniform and owned and ran the Diner, had been sitting on the end on the right side. She now stood and moved to a position behind the booth facing Lady Luck and behind Stan, who sat in the middle.

Patty and I moved closer to Lady Luck on the right side, taking up some of the room left by Madge.

No one said a word and the smell from the Chinese food filling the middle of the table wasn't helping my stomach any. Since my team covered five different branches of the gods, we were unusual, but I just never expected Lady Luck to join us for anything.

"Poker Boy," Laverne said, looking at me. Then she looked at Stan. "Everyone, I need a personal favor."

Now I really, really, really wished I hadn't just eaten that last piece of sweet-and-sour chicken. Lady Luck never asked for personal favors. She had been alive for longer than any written history. Civilizations over the centuries had come and gone, but Lady Luck had lived through them all. So her asking us for a personal favor had to mean things were really, really bad.

"Anything," I managed to say. Stan only nodded and even though he was the God of Poker with the best poker face I had ever seen, I could tell he was too surprised to even speak.

Everyone else nodded slightly, clearly too stunned to dare move much.

"Thank you," she said. Then she took a deep breath. "I need you to find Helen, my daughter."

I was fairly certain at that moment I had stopped breathing.

Lady Luck had just told me she had a daughter. I had thought I was starting to get a grip on all the different gods and superheroes and who worked for whom and who hated whom. But now it was clear there was still a great deal I didn't know about all the whos and whoms of the world of gods.

"Do you know where she was last seen?" Stan asked.

Thank heavens Stan knew about Lady Luck having a daughter and was managing to keep his wits about him. That was the difference between a god and a bunch of superheroes. He'd been alive a lot longer and could roll better with very, very strange requests.

And even better, he could explain it all to us after she left.

"Helen is somewhere here in Las Vegas," Lady Luck said. "And I have no idea what she is doing or why she has vanished. I can't even sense her."

"How long has she been gone?" I managed to ask, at least trying to sound logical and in control and leader-like. Thankfully, my voice didn't squeak.

"About twelve minutes now," Laverne said, clearly serious. "I am very worried."

She started to take another bite from the spring roll, then changed her mind and pushed it away.

"We'll do our best," Stan said.

"Thank you," Lady Luck said, nodding. "I know you will."

With that she vanished, leaving the chair empty at the end of the booth.

I stared at the empty chair for what seemed like hours, but it must have only been a few seconds. Then I turned back to the stunned faces of my team.

"Wow," Madge said from behind Stan. "The Queen of Hearts has gone missing. Imagine that."

Now all I could do was stare at Madge.

She just shrugged. "I'll get some milkshakes for everyone if someone gets rid of all that dead food. Looks like we got some planning to do."

With that she turned and vanished. I had put in an invisible door right behind the booth—with Stan's help—that allowed Madge and most of the team to move back and forth between the real diner in downtown Las Vegas and my office.

I also put a door from my office to Patty's apartment so Patty could be in the office as much as she liked as well, even when I wasn't here. I was the only member of the team besides Stan who knew how to teleport.

Across from me in the booth, The Smoke, a part-human, part-wolf superhero in the world of animals, looked completely shocked, his blue eyes wider than normal by a ways. That was going some.

Beside him, Screamer just looked down at the pile of uneaten Chinese food and shook his head. Screamer worked under the gods of law enforcement and his superpower was the ability to take thoughts from one person and put them in another person's head. He had seen more than I ever wanted to imagine and yet he seemed bothered by this.

I honestly couldn't believe what had just happened either.

Lady Luck had a daughter, who was missing, and Lady Luck had come to us to find her.

That did not bode well for anyone involved.

I looked out over the city of Las Vegas. Helen, the Queen of Hearts, was out there somewhere. And up until a moment ago, I didn't even know she existed beyond the faces of the cards I played poker with.

Had she been the one to pose for those early cards? Or was that just her nickname? So many questions.

In the distance, a Southwest airliner turned for final approach to McCarran Airport. Sometimes a plane landing at the airport got a little too close to this invisible office for comfort, but Stan assured me that a plane could hit the office and it would go right through and no one would notice. Something about the office and everyone in it being a half-turn out of normal time and space.

Again I didn't understand what he meant, but I was fairly certain I didn't want to be in the office the day a plane passed through it.

I was drifting. I had to get focused.

I turned to Stan who was just sitting staring out over the country-side as well, his eyes blank.

Beside me, Patty took my hand and squeezed it, sending waves of comfort and calm through me. She worked under the Gods of Hospitality. Calming people was one of her many superpowers. I loved it.

"Stan, can you tell us about Helen? And why Madge called her the Queen of Hearts?"

"Because for centuries, even before I was born, which was before Atlantis, she has been called that," Stan said. "Her beauty is legendary. Red hair, very tall, and a temper when unleashed that could level a city."

"And she's been gone now for thirteen or so minutes?" I asked. "How does Laverne know that?"

Stan shrugged. "Some sort of connection, a family bond, at a level I am not familiar with."

"And that clearly was broken," I said.

Stan nodded. "I can't sense her either."

I sat back and looked out at the view. I had no idea where to even start on this problem. And that scared me a lot.

"We're missing a lot of information here," Screamer said. "First off, who would have the power to cut the link between Lady Luck and her daughter?"

"Good question," I said. "Can't be many people I would imagine."

"Unless Helen did it herself," The Smoke said in his level, deep voice.

I glanced at Stan who sat calmly, not saying anything.

"Stan?" I asked. "You know who could do this, don't you?"

Stan nodded, but said nothing. Instead he made all the food on the table just vanish with a simple wave of his hand, leaving the scarred wood top as clean as if Madge had spent an hour wiping it down. I had no idea where he sent it all.

"Stan?" I pushed.

He looked up and seemed almost afraid to say what he was about to say. And when a god was afraid to say something, it couldn't be good.

Finally he put both hands on the table and looked first at Patty, then at me. "There is only one person who could break the link between Laverne and Helen purposefully."

"That's going to make the search a lot easier," Screamer said. "Who is it?"

"Laverne's husband," Stan said softly, again looking down at the table.

At that moment you could have heard a pin drop in my new

floating office over Las Vegas. Nothing is ever supposed to be that quiet in or above Las Vegas.

Two

I finally managed to choke out the most logical question we all had to be thinking, since we were all staring at Stan in shock. "Lady Luck is married?"

"Separated, actually," Stan said. "Centuries before I was born."

"His name?"

Stan shrugged. "He's gone by a lot of names over the centuries, just as Laverne has. Last I heard he liked Benny. Before that I think he went by Jonah. In Atlantis it was Belial."

"Evil one?" The Smoke asked, his voice almost a growl.

"Not really," Stan said. "Are you all familiar with the concept of Yin-Yang?"

I was slightly, only because that circle with the two black-and-white shapes inside it was sold as trinkets all over Vegas in just about every form.

Everyone else nodded and Stan went on.

Stan looked at me. "Ever wonder why you have as much bad luck as you have good over time?"

I honestly hadn't wondered that, or at least given it any meaning. I just knew it always balanced out in poker and skill always won out in the long run.

"Benny is the God of Bad Luck?" Screamer asked.

"Not really," Stan said, shaking his head. "Any more than Laverne is only good luck. But Benny and Laverne must both exist for the other to exist. Yin-Yang. Dark and Light. Masculine and Feminine. Only down through time the two sides of that have been confused when it comes to sex."

I was confused as well, but managed to ask "How?"

"Today the sunny, light side is called Yang," Stan said, "and is also associated with masculine. That got flipped. Actually, when all this started, Yin was masculine and in the shadow while Yang was sunny and feminine. The key is that everything stays on the Golden Mean."

"The middle between two extremes," Patty said.

"That's right," Stan said.

I looked at my girlfriend in awe, then back at Stan. I had no doubt I could keep asking him questions and he could keep me confused for hours, And Patty could keep impressing me with her knowledge, but it seemed we had a task to do, so I needed to get that task in motion somehow.

"So, why would Benny cut off connections between Laverne and Helen?"

Stan shook his head. "I can't think of one reason. They both love Helen."

"So if she went to visit her father," Screamer asked, "where would she go?"

"He lives right here," Stan said. "You don't see him out much. He has a walled compound over near the university. He mostly stays to the dark side."

"And we live on the sunny side?" I asked.

Stan pointed at the clear blue sky around the booth.

"Yin-Yang," The Smoke said, his voice very soft as if he understood.

I honestly didn't, and I had no doubt Patty was going to have to help me understand later. But right at this moment, with Helen the Queen of Hearts missing, my understanding of ancient philosophy and aspects of how the gods work didn't much matter. I hoped there would be time to learn it all. For some reason, this problem felt world-ending serious and I had no idea why.

"Would crossing into the shadow side cause the connection to break?" I asked Stan.

"And if we crossed over there, what would happen?" Patty asked.

"And how could we cross over?" Screamer added.

Before Stan could answer, Madge appeared carrying milkshakes, the drink of choice for all of us when working on a case.

"You guys talking about going over into the shadow world?" Madge asked as she put the milkshakes in front of us.

Mine was vanilla with whipped cream stacked high. I really wasn't in the mood for a milkshake, but I forced myself to take a taste anyway. It was as wonderful as usual. I had no doubt that if this meeting kept going for another ten minutes, I would down the entire thing.

Patty nodded thanks to Madge for the milkshake, then answered her question. "We're just discussing if Helen crossing over would cause the connection between her and her mother to be broken."

"In some extreme areas of the shadow world, I suppose it might," Madge said. "But I honestly doubt it."

"I agree," Stan said.

Madge went on as she moved around the table delivering our shakes. "I've worked both sides of the line over the years. Not much purposely crosses the line because that line is always moving for everyone."

"She's right," Stan said. "Every action, every reaction by everyone moves the line for that person."

I was so confused I just wanted to slump down into the booth and cover my head. So I focused on the first question that came to mind.

"Madge, what's it like living on the other side of the line?"

"Exactly the same as here," she said, finishing putting out the milk-shakes, napkins, straws and spoons for everyone. "You can't tell the difference, actually. It's the same world."

Banging my head on the table would probably do no good, but I sure felt like doing that. And clearly Stan read me like a book.

"You ever sat at a poker table with a cheater?" Stan asked me.

"Sure," I said.

"How about a guy who couldn't buy a good card if his life depended on it, or played just a little too long and lost all his money."

"Sure," I said. "A normal table."

"They are living on the other side of the line," Stan said. "At least for their time at the table."

"So the shadow side isn't an actual place?" Screamer asked just slightly before I could.

"Yin-Yang," Madge said. "They both exist together and one could not exist without the other. Although I have to admit there is very little Yin in this room. All Yang."

"We all have our dark sides," The Smoke said.

Screamer nodded.

"Of course you do," Madge said. "There are no exceptions. But this group tends to not use the dark side without reason. And that's why I like to hang around with you all. I've spent far too much time solidly over on the other side of that line."

I looked at Madge with a brand new level of respect. Some day I was going to have to ask her a ton of questions about her past.

Patty just shook her head. "So if crossing the line would not normally block any connection between Helen and Laverne, and visiting her father here in Las Vegas would not do that either, what would?"

I had the same question, but decided to ask it from another angle. I looked directly at Stan. "What exactly do you think Laverne is actually asking us to do?"

"Go into the tunnels," Stan said without looking at me.

"Not me," Madge said, turning and vanishing through the invisible door back to the Diner.

"I cannot go down there," The Smoke said, his eyes almost flashing anger.

"I understand," Stan said.

"Well, I don't understand much of anything we've been talking about," I said. "Laverne having a daughter, Laverne being married, Yin-Yang, and now tunnels. My head is starting to hurt. So would someone who understands these tunnels please explain them to me? Slowly."

Before anyone could say a word, Laverne appeared back in the chair at the end of the booth. She looked at Stan, her eyes intense. "You believe Helen might have actually gone down into the tunnels?"

"It would seem to be the only logical conclusion I'm afraid," Stan said.

"I came to the same conclusion," Lady Luck said and sat back, clearly shaken.

These tunnels, whatever they are, must be something very nasty to have Lady Luck act like that.

"I was so hoping it wasn't going to be that," she said. Then she took a deep breath and looked at Stan. "Explain to Poker Boy and his team everything you can about the tunnels and I'll go talk with Helen's father. I'll see if he has any suggestions or has heard from Helen. I would imagine he's getting as worried as I am."

With that she vanished again.

The Smoke pushed to the end of the booth and stood. "I am sorry, I cannot help with the tunnels."

"I understand," Stan said.

I stared at The Smoke as he moved around the booth and vanished into the doorway to the Diner. I considered The Smoke one of the bravest I had ever met. And now he didn't seem to be afraid either. There was something else.

"You want to explain what just happened?" Screamer asked Stan before I could. There were only four of us left now to try to save Lady Luck's daughter.

"In a very ancient agreement between gods to end a war, The Smoke's people were banned from certain ancient cities back when the cities were inhabited. The agreement still holds even after hundreds of thousands of years."

"The tunnels are a part of an old city?" I asked.

"An ancient one," Stan said, nodding. "From the time of the Titans."

"I didn't know they were real," Patty said, saving me from asking yet another stupid question such as who were the Titans?

"Very real," Stan said. "Far before my time. They ruled this planet for almost two hundred thousand years, then one day they all suddenly vanished."

"Anyone know why?" I asked. "And I thought there were only a few of them. Why did they need cities?"

Stan shook his head. "The myths of their leaders is all that has survived. There were millions of Titans at one point in time. They are said to have ascended to a higher plain, or gone into space, or got locked up by a powerful curse in a hidden prison."

"And the tunnels under Las Vegas is the remains of one of their cities?" Screamer asked.

"Actually," Stan said, "It is their main ancient city, their capital city. It is supposed to be completely preserved. It was buried by the gods who followed them into the position of ruling the planet. No one knows why. This area holds a great deal of unseen power, which is why so many of the gods live here, and why the city of Las Vegas even exists in this dry desert."

"And The Smoke can't go down there because his people got in a fight with the Titans?" Screamer asked.

Stan shook his head. "His area of the gods and a few others fought the Giants. In one battle they destroyed part of a Titan city and were forever banned from any Titan area ever since."

I took a deep breath and forced myself to focus through the thousand questions to stay squarely on the task Lady Luck had given us. "So Helen might have gone down there into an ancient protected city? Would that break the connection with her and her mother?"

"I'm assuming it would," Stan said. "The field surrounding that huge city is very powerful."

"How did she find her way in there?" Patty asked.

"Everyone knows how to get in," Stan said. "But no one has ever figured out how to get out."

"Wonderful," was all I could say.

Three

After a few more minutes of confusing me with more mythic history than I could begin to learn in a very long semester of college, I finally held up my hand.

"There is only one question we don't have an answer to," I said. "We don't know why Helen would go down there without a way back. What was she after?"

At that moment Lady Luck appeared. "She went after this."

In front of her and floating over the booth was an image of a golden key, turning slightly in the air. "Her father said she had been spending the last hundred years researching it and he says Helen thinks it is hidden in the old city."

As the key turned in the air over the table, it slowly transformed into a sneering, ugly man's face and then back into a golden key.

"That was one of the faces of Janus," Lady Luck said. "The key is one of his four faces. Some believe when combined with the other three keys, it will release the Titans to return to this time and space."

I had scooted away from the image of the floating key and finally Lady Luck snapped it out of existence.

"Why would she want to release the Titans?" Stan asked, his voice hushed.

I glanced at him. Clearly there was still a lot of very real history I had to learn.

Lady Luck sighed and dropped into the chair in front of the booth. "From what I understand, Helen has researched the Titans for centuries. Her father tells me she believes them to be an honorable race that has been unfairly imprisoned over time."

"And what do you believe?" I asked.

Lady Luck shook her head. "My beliefs are of little value now. We need to go into the old city and find Helen."

"No!" a deep voice said from just behind Lady Luck. "You cannot go into that city and you know it."

A small man, not more than five feet tall and as round as a basket-ball stepped up and looked into Lady Luck's eyes. If she hadn't been sitting down, she would have towered over him.

Now it was Stan's turn to push back as far as he could into the back of the booth.

Lady Luck said nothing.

After I stopped holding my breath for anyone talking to one of the most powerful gods in the world like a child, it dawned on me who the man was.

"Benny, I presume?" I asked.

He glanced at me. "Got it in one, Poker Boy."

Then he looked back at Laverne. "She's my daughter as well. But you and I both know you can't go in there after her. If you did not return, the world as we know it would collapse. We have both worked far too hard for that to happen. We must stay balanced. And to do that, you must stay here."

The silence in my little office felt like a heavy weight. Finally Benny looked away from his wife again and back at me, and then Stan.

"Find our daughter," he said softly. "We'll give you all the help we can from out here."

With that he and Laverne vanished.

I looked at the white faces of Screamer and Stan, then took Patty's hand in my own and squeezed it.

But all I could think about was that we were so screwed.

Four

For the next hour Stan explained to me and Patty and Screamer what "the tunnels" were. And how big they were supposed to be.

"But no one really knows what they can see from the doorways, since no one has ever returned after going in there."

Finally, I had to ask.

"So where is this entrance?"

Stan shook his head. "There is an old metal door right on the edge of Binion's Horseshoe Casino, about a hundred paces from Freemont Street down a side street."

"You're kidding," Screamer said.

"I'm not," Stan said. "No one notices it and you have to have some powers to open it. But all of you could do it."

"And no exit?" I asked.

"No one that I have heard of has gone in and come out again."

"Ever?" Patty asked.

Stan just shrugged, about as clear an answer as there was.

My stomach was so twisted into a knot around what was left of my Chinese food lunch, I couldn't even think of a response or another question.

"Well," Screamer said, finally, breaking into the silence, "let's hope we can find a way out once we are in there."

My mind was twisting again, struggling on what Screamer had just said. But I couldn't get it.

I turned to Screamer. "What you just said bothers me, but I can't put my finger on why."

"Bothers me as well," Screamer said, shaking his head. "For obvious reasons."

"Link us, would you?" I said, taking Patty's hand and then reaching my other hand across the booth between the empty milkshake glasses. "There's something I'm not seeing and I feel it might be the answer."

Screamer shrugged and glanced at Stan.

"I think I would only confuse the issue," Stan said. "Sometimes too much history and knowledge can hurt more than it can help."

I knew Stan was right, so Screamer reached over and touched my arm and suddenly he and Patty were both in my mind. We had done this sort of thing so many times over the years, it didn't even feel strange anymore.

It just felt familiar.

After only a few seconds, Screamer pulled his hand away from my arm and I was back alone in my own head.

Patty gave my hand a squeeze, but didn't let go, for which I was glad. Her touch kept me calm and thinking clearly, at least most of the time.

"See anything?" I asked Stan, then Patty.

"Something about the exit," Patty said.

"You were thinking we should find it first, before we go in."

Suddenly I knew the answer.

"That's exactly right," I said. "And I have an idea. I'll be right back."

I instantly teleported to the Diner.

Madge was scrubbing a counter far harder than it needed to be scrubbed. Clearly she was upset at herself for not wanting or being able to help.

"I need a thermos of hot chocolate," I said.

She looked at me and frowned. "Official or otherwise?"

"Official," I said. "How long?"

"Two minutes," she said, turning for the kitchen. "I'll bring it to you."

"Thanks." A moment later I was sitting next to Patty in the booth in my office.

And I was smiling. I knew how to find the exit, at least from this side.

"What was that all about?" Stan asked, looking as puzzled as the rest of my team.

"Call Laverne and Benny and I'll explain," I said.

"No need," Laverne said as she appeared again in the chair facing the booth. Benny was standing beside her and she still seemed taller than he was. "You think the exit is controlled by the Silicon Suckers?"

"I do," I said. "In fact, I'm convinced of it."

The Silicon Suckers were an ancient race of beings that lived in huge tunnels and caverns under desert regions of the planet. The gods, a long time ago, had negotiated a truce with them to keep humans and Silicon Suckers from fighting.

"How can you be so sure?" Benny asked, his voice deep and low and almost rumbling with power.

"There was a point when I was trying to save a superhero from the Keno side from her time with the Suckers. I had to watch her negotiate with the leader of the Silicon Suckers for an exchange of land for a number of thermoses every month of hot chocolate."

"Strangest thing I had ever heard about," Benny said, shaking his head.

"During the negotiation, the leader of the Silicon Suckers floated a map in the air of the land around Las Vegas, showing what humans controlled and what they controlled. There was a giant round area under the city of Las Vegas that had neither human nor Silicon Sucker color on it. At the time, I assumed it was that way because it was under the city and no one cared."

"The ancient city," Laverne said, nodding. "From what I understand, the original protective screen over it was a dome, so it would be round."

"I'm willing to bet," I said, "that the Silicon Suckers know of the exit and have just kept it locked or blocked."

"Worth finding out before going in there," Laverne said, nodding her head. "We'll be watching if you need help."

With that she and Benny both vanished again before I had a chance to ask them why they didn't just go and talk to the Silicon Suckers instead of me. More than likely there was some reason I didn't know about. Just another question I would have to ask later.

Before anyone could say anything, Madge appeared out of the invisible door carrying the thermos of hot chocolate, the most sacred and valuable of drugs to the Silicon Suckers.

I was going to need to negotiate for Laverne's daughter's life with hot chocolate. I just hoped I could offer them enough.

Five

Five minutes later, after making sure my plan was solid with Stan and Screamer and Patty, I found myself standing alone on the edge of Highway 95 leading north out of Las Vegas.

The Silicon Suckers' main entrance was under a billboard, hidden from view for anyone not welcome in their castles, as they called their caverns and tunnels.

The hot wind was whipping my coat around me and I had to hold my hat on my head with one hand to keep from having to chase it up the highway.

I waited until there were no cars coming in either direction, then slipped off my shoes and left them in the sand next to a sagebrush. I stepped into the wide tunnel and took ten steps into the sand tunnel, as showed respect, then stopped.

Silicon Suckers were big into respect. And rules. They had a million rules.

A few seconds later two Silicon Suckers appeared. They were, as normal, completely naked, but I had no idea what sex they were, or if Silicon Suckers even had a sex. Their bodies were very, very skinny and a pasty gray, but their heads were huge, with wide, unblinking eyes.

Over the centuries, humans who had seen them called them aliens and lately they had become known as the Grays. But as far as I knew, they had lived on Earth longer than humans, and that was going some I was starting to discover.

Both of the Silicon Suckers bowed slightly to me and I returned the bow, then followed them down through what seemed like miles of sandstone tunnels, illuminated by something I had never been able to figure out. The light just seemed to come from everywhere in the tunnel.

When we broke out into the open into the huge cavern that was the main area of this city, I was stunned. Never had I seen so many Silicon Suckers in this area, and they all seemed to be moving at a normal pace, clearly all busy.

From what I understood, hot chocolate not only was a wonderful drug to the Silicon Suckers, but it was a critical element in their health and ability to reproduce. And clearly they had been doing a great deal of reproducing in the year we had been giving them a number of thermoses of hot chocolate every month in payment.

After almost thirty minutes of walking behind my guides, I was shown into a large room I knew to be the Great One's throne room. Only it was as empty as every other room and tunnel I had seen in this place.

I was told to wait and my guides left me standing alone.

Then from one side of the room, a tall and clearly elderly Silicon Sucker appeared and walked slowly toward me. I knew, without a doubt, even though most of the Silicon Suckers looked identical to me, that I was facing their great leader.

I bowed very deeply.

"It is a great honor that you have blessed us once again with your presence, my friend," the Great One said.

"The honor is mine," I said, carefully respecting their tradition. "May I offer the people of this fantastic castle a gift?"

The Great One nodded slightly and I pulled the thermos of hot chocolate from my coat and sat it on the ground in front of me.

Two others came from a side tunnel and carefully picked up the thermos and carried it away.

After they had left, the great one indicated that I should sit and he did the same, facing me.

Then he nodded, a sign I had permission to speak.

"Great One," I said, bowing slightly as was the custom when

someone spoke in front of the Great One, "I am honored by your gracious gift of time to listen to me. I have a very serious problem that only you and your wisdom can help me solve."

The Great One just nodded, signaling I could continue.

"Helen, the daughter of Laverne and Benny, two of our greatest leaders, has vanished."

The Great One leaned forward, clearly reacting in some way to my news.

"Helen is such a wonderful child," the Great One said. "Full of spirit, yet very respectful, as are her parents."

I actually was so stunned he knew Helen, I got off my planned script and for a moment sat there not moving.

"Has she gone into the ancient city?" the Great One asked.

"We think she has, oh Great One," I said, bowing again. "And I am afraid we do not know where the exit is."

The Great One said nothing, so I continued on.

"We would be willing to offer four more containers of the sacred liquid per moon cycle for ten sun cycles if you knew where the exit is from the ancient city and would allow my team to enter the city from our entrance, find her, and bring her back to her parents."

"As I would expect of you, your willingness to risk yourself is admirable."

I bowed slightly in acknowledgement of the compliment. However, a sentence like that usually was followed by the word, "But…"

"We will create a special and separate tunnel from the exit of the ancient city to the surface and allow you to use it for ten sun cycles. But for such work and use, we will require six containers per moon cycle."

I sat dead still for a few seconds. I was expected to negotiate. It was a custom.

"Great One," I finally said, "your kind offer is very generous. If I am allowed to make a counter proposal?"

He nodded, so I went on.

"We can only bring five more than we are doing now per moon cycle for the first year. But then, after that, we can add one more per sun cycle for the ten years of the use of the tunnel you are so graciously willing to build."

I was making sure that he understood that we valued our thermoses of hot chocolate as much as he did, even though we did not. And yet I was giving him a chance to continue to let his people grow and multiply.

He nodded slightly. "Your proposal is very fair. We have an agreement. You can enter the ancient city from above at any time. It will take us only a very short amount of time to open the new tunnel from the ancient city exit to the surface."

"The first payment will be at your entrance tomorrow at sunrise and then with the other regular payment every moon cycle."

"It is always an honor," the Great One said to me, bowing slightly.

"The honor is always mine," I said, bowing as deeply as I could while sitting down.

He stood and without another word left the room.

I waited until he was gone before standing. My legs screamed at me for sitting cross-legged on the dirt floor, but I had had no option.

Two guides appeared a moment later and after thirty minutes of sweating in my black leather coat, we had climbed back to the surface.

I grabbed my shoes and an instant later was in the cool air of my new office floating over Las Vegas.

"Well done," Laverne said, looking like she wanted to hug me.

Benny just smiled and nodded.

"We're not done yet," I said as Patty handed me a large glass of water and I took off my black coat. "We still have to find Helen and get her out of that city."

"At least there's a way out now," Laverne said. "Thanks to you and your fantastic thinking. Not sure why someone hadn't thought of that before now."

With that she and Benny vanished and I slumped into the booth to tell the rest of my team what had just happened.

After I was done, Patty gave me a little kiss on the cheek and then squeezed my hand.

"So we're going in," Screamer said, nodding.

I nodded and turned to Stan. "Is there a map of the ancient city?"

"I'll find out," he said, and vanished.

"I thought you had the exit cleared with the Silicon Suckers," Screamer said.

"I do," I said, "But that ancient city is as large as the entire city of Las Vegas. We first have to find Helen. After that, I honestly have no idea where exactly that one door out is."

"Oh," Screamer said, looking shocked again.

I felt the same way.

Six

Laverne found a very old map of a city that seemed to be not only the size of Las Vegas, but a hundred times larger. In fact, from what I could tell from the old map, at one time the ancient city filled the entire valley.

Stan held that map and the rest of us carried supplies. In packs we had enough food and water to last us a month if we rationed.

We were standing on a side street off of Freemont looking like we were heading into the wilderness for two weeks instead of through a simple door I had never noticed before.

We waited until there was no one on the sidewalk around us, then Stan pulled the door open and held it for us to step through.

I glanced around once more at the city I loved, hoping I would see it again, then holding Patty's hand, I stepped through and into what looked like a long, simple hallway.

Screamer followed, then Stan who pulled the door closed, plunging us into complete blackness.

Patty was the only one who was thinking and had a flashlight in her hand. She snapped it on and pointed it ahead down the hallway that now looked a great deal like a tunnel.

Now I knew where the ancient city got its nickname of "tunnels."

My stomach was in a tight knot and I could barely breathe the stale, dust-smelling air. Only Patty's superpower ability to keep me calm allowed me to move forward. Otherwise I was sure I would have turned and fled for the door and the street beyond.

"Feel that?" Screamer asked.

"Sense of dread spell," Stan said, nodding.

A moment later it was gone as was my need to panic and run. Now all I felt was just plain old fear.

"Thank you," I said.

"Yes," Patty said. "I was barely holding on against it."

"You were doing fine," I said, squeezing her hand as I led us down the hallway and around a corner.

There the beam of her flashlight found another door made of old wood. It had a metal pull handle with strange inscriptions on the metal and the plate under the handle.

"Here we go," Stan said.

I nodded and pulled the door open, sending waves of dust swirling around us in the hallway.

It was now or never.

I stepped through the doorway and into the ancient city.

And stopped cold at what I saw spread out in front of me.

"How can that be?" Patty asked breathlessly beside me.

"Oh, oh," Stan said.

"You have got to be kidding?" Screamer said.

And then, behind us, I heard the door close with a loud thump that sent a chill down my spine.

We were standing on a high balcony with an iron railing protecting us from a very, very long fall. From the looks of it more than thirty or forty stories.

The ancient city was spread out below us. But it wasn't ancient and it certainly wasn't underground and it certainly wasn't empty.

In fact, snow was falling gently on the massive city and I could feel the faint wind and the not-so-faint sounds of a busy city very much alive below us.

We were no longer under Las Vegas.

Or if we were, this was the strangest illusion I had ever seen or felt.

Because we had stepped from a warm afternoon in Las Vegas to a cold, snowy night in a very strange city.

Seven

As I stared out over the fantastic city, suddenly I wished I had listened a little more carefully when Stan explained to me how my new office was out of time and space a half turn. Because I had a hunch this city was the same.

And if we went down into those streets, I was pretty certain we would meet some real Titans. Or at least the descendants of the real Titans from legend.

I really wished I had studied history and legends more back when I was in school. I just never expected to need it like this.

The city stretching into the light snow looked like a fantastic alien science fiction city you might see in the movies with towering beautiful buildings and walkways crisscrossing from building to building mixed up with an ancient Eastern city with arches and columns and narrow, stone roads.

A huge boulevard wider than The Strip in Vegas wound its way through the city and as far as I could see, lined by sleek glowing buildings that seemed to vanish up into the snow. Futuristic cars that looked like they were polished metal without windows seamlessly flowed up and down the boulevard only on the wrong side of the road as far as I was concerned, like they did in England.

There were a few pedestrians out along the roads, but we were so high in the air I couldn't get any idea of what they looked like.

The snow was thin and the lights from the bustling city made it all seem sort of like I was staring over a fairy tale city inside a snow globe.

For all I knew, I was. I was starting to learn that anything was possible when it came to my world. So maybe we were in a huge snow globe that was the prison to the Titans.

I tried to clear that thought out of my head without much success.

I turned and looked at the door we had come in.

It had vanished. Just a blank, gray cement wall filled the area behind us. No going back that way.

I knew that would be the case, but now being faced with it scared me more than I wanted to admit.

And I had a hunch that finding the exit from this huge city wasn't going to be easy.

We had all stood there on that high balcony in silence for a good minute before I squeezed Patty's hand and turned to Stan. "Got any idea how we might find Helen in this place?"

"I know exactly where she's at," he said, shaking his head and coming back to our situation.

"That's good," Screamer said. "But anyone besides Poker Boy here think to bring a coat?"

For the first time I noticed just how cold it was. Even my black leather coat didn't cut the chill.

An instant later all of us were wearing heavy parkas of varying colors. Patty's was a stylish pink, mine was plain and black like my leather jacket under it, so it matched my fedora-like black hat. Screamer's coat was green with deep pockets that he instantly stuck his hands into. Stan had put himself in a blue parka with a hood and gloves.

I was glad he hadn't given me and Patty gloves. I got a lot of strength from her touch.

"That help?" Stan asked, smiling.

"Thanks," Patty said.

"So how do you know where Helen is at here?" I asked Stan.

"We have a connection when we are close in distance," Stan said. "I've kind of ignored it for years, but it's still there."

"A connection?" Patty asked.

Stan nodded, turning to stare out over the beautiful and very alien city around us. "We were married once."

I just stared at my boss like he had become an alien.

Stan had been married to Lady Luck's daughter. That must have been some divorce.

"Can you jump us to her?" Patty asked, since I hadn't said anything.

He nodded and a moment later we were standing in the snow in what looked like a garden surrounded by stone walls. A brown stone patio filled the center of the garden and in the background was a single-story home with warm orange lights coming from the windows.

The most stunning, redheaded woman I had ever seen was smiling at us.

She wore a white dress that looked more like a thin nightgown. It sort of drifted around her frame and blew in the wind. She had to be cold since I was pretty certain I was seeing through most of that dress or nightgown or whatever it was.

She moved barefooted in the snow across the stone of the patio toward us, her bright red hair blowing in the wind.

All of us stood frozen as she approached and kissed Stan in such a way that most of the snow in the garden area must have melted.

Then she broke the kiss and said, "Wonderful to see you again, my husband."

"Ex-husband," Stan said.

She ignored him and extended her hand to me. "I'm Helen. You must be Poker Boy."

I'm not sure if it was the thin blowing white dress around the naked body in the snow, or her radiant smile, but something caused me to pause before extending my hand as well. "Nice to meet you."

Then Helen turned to Patty. "The famous Patty Ledgerwood, I presume."

"An honor," Patty said, shaking Helen's hand.

Then Helen turned to Screamer and nodded and said nothing.

"Nice seeing you again as well, Sheila," Screamer said, smiling.

I managed to take my eyes off of Helen long enough to look at Screamer with a puzzled look. Clearly he had met her before, only she had called herself Sheila to him.

Wow, did I have a lot of questions when we got out of here.

The woman in the thin, white blowing dress seemed like no Sheila I had ever met.

Screamer just kept his eyes on Helen, and she shrugged and smiled at him.

The next moment we all were inside in a warm living room with a crackling fire in a huge stone fireplace. Helen now had on regular jeans and a flannel shirt and her hair was pulled back. It didn't decrease her beauty in any respect. But it sure made her seem far more human.

Outside in the snow, she had been a goddess. Now she seemed almost normal, if that was possible.

I pretty much doubted it.

The room around us reminded me of a mountain lodge, with warm-brown logs as walls and high ceilings with log rafters. Tan over-stuffed couches and chairs surrounded the fireplace and a couple of scarred coffee tables filled the center area.

The air had a faint smoke smell from the burning logs and every so often the fire would pop or crackle.

Thick, dark-brown carpet covered all of the floor except a stone area in front of the fireplace. The carpet added to the feeling of warmth in the room.

I could spend a lot of time in a place like this, especially if it was snowing outside.

"Nice entrance," Stan said to her as he pulled off his parka and dropped down onto a couch.

"You know I always play the part, dear husband," Helen said, laughing. "Thought I was going to freeze off a part or two for a moment there."

"Ex-husband," Stan said more to himself.

"It was a show all right," Screamer said, taking off his parka as well.

"I thought it impressive," Patty said as we both took off our coats and sat on a couch facing Stan.

"Thank you," Helen said, nodding to Patty.

Screamer moved to a chair near the fireplace and Helen sat alone in a large, overstuffed chair facing all of us.

"So did you find what you came for?" Stan asked Helen, his voice clearly telling me he wasn't into any idle chatting, even though I had about a thousand questions I would have loved to have answered at that moment.

Helen smiled and her eyes lit up like a child's eyes with a new toy. "And what do you think I came for?"

"One of the keys of Janus," Stan said.

She laughed, a perfect laugh that might draw someone from across a room. "I did. I had researched it well and knew exactly where it was hidden. I found it within twenty minutes of arriving here."

"And how did you plan on getting back with it?" Screamer asked, also clearly not interested in just having a social visit.

She turned to me, then glanced at Stan. "I knew Mother and Dad would send a rescue party. And I knew it would be you and Poker Boy and his team. And I knew Poker Boy knew the Silicon Suckers and would bargain with them to open the exit, since I am pretty sure the exit has to go into their territory."

She turned to me. "You did that, didn't you?"

"I did," I said, stunned that she had played us like I played a sucker at a poker table.

"Great," she said, clapping her hands together. "Then let's get out of here before the Titans discover some of the gods are among them. I have a hunch they won't like that much."

"Do you know where the exit is at?" I asked.

Helen looked at me like I now had two heads. "No. Don't you?"

I shook my head. "The Silicon Suckers just promised me it would be open with a tunnel to the surface. They never showed me where it was."

She turned to Stan.

"Sorry," he said.

She looked at Screamer.

"We didn't even know this city was here," he said. "We thought we were going into ancient ruins to look for you."

"Oh, no," Helen said, slumping in her chair and covering her face with her hands.

I glanced at Patty, then back at Helen, the Queen of Hearts.

Looks like there was one little detail the Queen of Hearts hadn't figured out in her little scheme.

A very important one.

Eight

Actually, what she hadn't been thinking about, I had, from the very first moment I learned that Laverne wanted us to go down into the "tunnels" as this city was called by those who had never been here.

I wondered what people who lived in this beautiful place actually called it. And exactly where it was in reality. It certainly wasn't under Las Vegas.

"Okay, a couple of questions," I said to the group sitting silently around the fire. "Where exactly is this city in time and space? And what the heck is it called?"

Stan shrugged and looked at Helen.

"The city's name is Elysium," she said without looking up. "It exists in a time in the distant future from what I understand."

Patty coughed, glanced at me, then asked, "Elysium, like in Elysium Fields, like in a form of heaven?"

Helen shrugged. "All myth and rumors of this place. But it is actually a pretty nice city from what I have seen of it."

"Great, just great," Screamer said. "We haven't died and we're stuck in heaven."

I didn't know what to think about her answer. Something was nagging at me, but darned if I could figure it out. Something about this city being in the far future, yet we had come into it in our time, and it seemed to have a protected area in our time as well, under Las Vegas.

Maybe it really was a city inside a giant snow globe buried under Las Vegas.

Again I tried to clear my mind of that stupid thought.

I needed to ask another hundred or more questions, but like everything with this rescue mission so far, most of the questions were going to have to wait until after we got out of here.

If we got out of here.

So I picked the one question that bothered me the most.

"So when we came through the door, we stepped into the future?"

"I believe we did," Helen said, then sighed and slumped in the chair like a kid not getting her way.

The future. That was the key. I had an idea. It wasn't much of one, but it was all I had at the moment.

I stood and started to put my parka back on over my black leather coat. "Stan, could you jump us back to the balcony we came in on?"

He looked at me with that studying look that only the God of Poker could give a person, then nodded and stood and put on his coat as well.

Screamer shrugged and did the same and so did Patty.

"I'll be right here when you get back," Helen said. "I'm still chilled from my last little adventure out there."

Stan just shook his head and a moment later we were standing on the balcony looking through the snow and out over the beautiful city below.

The cold air hit my face with a bite, but actually it felt good and cleared my thoughts even more. The wind swirled the light snow through the buildings and now there seemed to be very few people on the streets below. Whatever the local time was, it must be getting late.

Back in Vegas it wasn't even dinnertime yet.

Patty took my hand and I could feel her calming influence push through me.

I looked at the blank wall behind me where the door from Las Vegas into this city had been.

"So what are you thinking, Poker Boy?" Screamer asked.

I pointed at where the door had been. "We came in level to Freemont Street in downtown Vegas. Right?"

Everyone nodded, so I turned and pointed down. "We have to be a good thirty stories above the street level here. And we know the exit is underground and against the Silicon Sucker's territory."

"So more than likely it's down on the main city level somewhere," Screamer said. "That's a lot of area to look for a door that is more than likely very hidden."

"I agree," I said.

I turned to my boss. "Stan, is it possible in our vision or in our minds, whatever, to overlay a view of Las Vegas from our time over this city? Same scale and everything?"

He looked at me and actually frowned. "We would need to be connected."

"Screamer?"

He nodded and I indicated everyone should step to the metal railing of the balcony and face out over the city. Screamer stood between me and Stan and Patty had my hand on the other side.

Screamer's main power was the ability to hook up thoughts, to see what others were seeing with a touch.

He touched my hand and suddenly he and I and Patty were all together again in my head. We had done this so many times over the last few years, I sometimes wondered if them being in my mind wasn't more comfortable than when they weren't there.

I like it too, Patty thought at me.

Me, not so much, Screamer thought back.

Then Screamer touched Stan and brought the God of Poker into the mix. And instantly a map of Las Vegas formed in my vision. Actually, more than a map, an image of the city as if we were in the air over the downtown area where we had gone through the door.

Rotate it so that the Strip is running along that big boulevard below, I thought to Stan.

He did, and suddenly the two main roads overlaid almost perfectly, only the one in this city kept going out into the distance, right through where the airport had been in our time.

This is a future Las Vegas, Screamer thought, clearly stunned.

"Stan, take us north, keeping the cities lined up, along our Highway 95 where the Silicon Suckers home castle is."

Suddenly we were no longer on the balcony, but instead flying through the snow with an image of Vegas below us overlapping the streets and boulevards of Elysium.

It was even colder up in the air like this. My face and hands were going to take some warming time when this was over. I just hoped my nose didn't freeze off.

I'd still love you anyway, Patty thought.

Knock it off you two, Screamer thought.

Stan took us north slowly until finally I indicated he should stop.

We were right over the edge of the Silicon Sucker's boundary. And clearly they still lived there, since there was nothing but huge mounds of sand and empty spaces over their Territory. The mounds of sand towered into the air over the edge of the new city.

The Silicon Suckers still exist, Patty thought, feeling as stunned as I felt.

I pointed to a wooden shack that had been built against the huge mound of sand. It looked very, very old and weathered. And sand covered the back half of the building. And on the front, facing the city, was a closed wooden door.

Is that the door home? Screamer asked in a thought that felt excited.

I could sense Patty was excited as well.

It might be, I thought back. *It would have been a long ways underground in our time. Stan, take us along the edge of the Silicon Sucker's territory to the west and then back to the east.*

We spent the next five cold minutes drifting through the air, the map of our time imposed over the city below. Then we ended up back over the old shack half buried in the sand.

We had found nothing else touching the Silicon Sucker's territory.

Looks like we might have found our door out, I thought to the others.

Part of me wanted to shout for joy.

And part of me was scared to death that we were wrong.

Nine

An instant later we were back in the warm room with Helen and the wonderful crackling fire.

Screamer dropped his grip on my arm and I was again alone inside my head.

"Any luck?" Helen asked.

"Maybe," Stan said to her. "Get on a coat and gather your things."

She jumped to her feet like an excited child and vanished.

Patty and I moved over in front of the crackling fire, holding our hands closer to the flames in a sad attempt to warm them.

In less than fifteen seconds Helen was back, bundled in a heavy coat with a bag over her shoulder. With a wave of her hand, the fire went out, the lights in the place dimmed, and white sheets covered the furniture.

"Planning on returning?" Screamer asked.

"You never know," Helen said.

An instant later Stan had us standing in the desert in front of the old shack. The wind was blowing harder here and the snow felt like small grains of sand against my cheeks.

Up close the door looked very similar to the one we had come through on the way in. Same rough metal handle with strange inscriptions, same old wood. That made me feel a little more hopeful.

I turned to face everyone and held up my hand for attention. Then shouting over the wind I said, "If this is our door out and we end up in the Silicon Suckers' tunnels on the other side, it is critical we say nothing and calmly walk to the surface."

I looked directly at Helen and she looked back, very puzzled.

She then started to say something and Stan held up his hand. "If you can't agree to Poker Boy's instructions, you stay here."

"And how can you make me do that?" Helen demanded, her eyes blazing as she turned to face her ex-husband.

She was so angry, I had no doubt that the snow wasn't getting near her. I know I wanted to step back, but I didn't.

Stan just kept his poker face and said calmly, "We will go through first and make sure the Silicon Suckers never open the exit again."

"You would do that to me?"

"I would," Stan said. "And I am sure your parents, once they know you are alive and living just fine, would agree with me."

She started to say something and then closed her mouth. She turned her back on Stan, staring at the wooden door in front of her. Her face was bright red, almost matching her hair blowing in the wind.

"It is critical we say nothing and walk to the surface," I said again, looking directly at her and keeping my voice as even as I can. "Please? The Silicon Suckers have opened this tunnel for us. The least we can do is honor their customs in their land."

Finally, she took a deep breath and nodded.

I glanced past her at Stan and he nodded. I had a hunch he was going to make sure she followed the instructions. I didn't want to think of dealing with the Silicon Suckers again if he couldn't keep her under control.

I took a couple steps through the sand and pulled on the door. It didn't move.

Stan stepped up and made a motion and then pulled the door open, scraping back sand as he did.

A dark concrete tunnel led into the mound of sand inside the small shack and again Patty snapped on her flashlight and I led the way, holding her hand.

Screamer followed us, then Helen, and Stan came in last, pulling the outside door closed behind us.

We walked silently for about thirty paces and then around a corner to face another door.

I indicated everyone keep quiet with a finger against my lips, then I pushed the door open.

Beyond the door was a sand tunnel that I knew was dug by the Silicon Suckers. It had the same light that seemed to come from everywhere and the same scraping marks on the walls.

But the question was had we gone back in time or were we just walking inside a Silicon Suckers' tunnel in the future without invite?

Patty instantly snapped off her flashlight and put it away.

I led the way up the steep slope of the tunnel, only glancing back to make sure Helen was still with us and that Stan had closed the door.

There were no side tunnels at all.

The climb had to be the longest in my life. But actually it took us less than ten minutes until the tunnel leveled and I walked out into the evening light and warmth of the desert outside of Las Vegas.

A bright red Ford pickup truck sped past on Highway 95.

As Patty stepped into the evening sun, Laverne and Benny appeared, both looking happy and angry at the same time. I didn't want to think about what this family meeting was going to be like.

As Helen stepped into the light, a bright smile crossed her face as she saw her parents. Then she turned to Stan.

"You can take off the shield now holding me here," she said.

"Not me," Stan said, smiling.

Helen turned to stare at her parents. "Mom?"

"We'll talk," she said.

And with that Helen vanished, and not to a place she wanted to go I would wager.

"Thank you again," Lady Luck said and behind her Benny nodded.

It never got old having Lady Luck thank you.

Lady Luck went on. "After we get family business taken care of, I would love to hear about your adventure on the other side. I'll come join you all for lunch one of these days."

Then she and Benny vanished as the four of us stood there with our mouths open.

An instant later Stan had us back in my office and we were all missing our parkas.

And I had about six thousand questions built up to ask.

Screamer shook his head and looked out at Las Vegas below my office. "Well, that was an interesting afternoon trip. I think there's a steak with my name on it at the MGM Grand."

"Mind if I join you?" Stan asked. "I would love to know how you knew Helen or Sheila, as you called her."

"You drive," Screamer said, smiling, and an instant later they were both gone.

Without answering a single question I had.

"So that leaves just the two of us," Patty said, looking at me with those big brown eyes of hers. "Any ideas?"

"Maybe trying to find out what just happened? And what those keys were all about. And why exactly that city is there. And who did it."

"More than enough time for that," Patty said, smiling. "I'm going to call in and cancel work tonight. I think they can get by without me, don't you?"

I took a deep breath and looked out over the city I loved. I was finally starting to catch her drift. It was time to celebrate being back and being alive.

"I do," I said, nodding seriously.

"Then after I call work I want to take a long hot shower," she said, smiling at me and giving me a quick kiss. "I'm still chilled. Then maybe some dinner."

"Mind if I join you?" I asked, holding her close. "I'm sure they can get along without me at the poker tournament tonight as well."

"For dinner?" she asked.

"I was thinking of the shower to be honest," I said.

"You drive," she said, smiling.

"With pleasure," I said.

And it turned out that with pleasure was a very good description of the rest of the evening.

I KILLED THE CLOCKWORK KEY

A Bryant Street Story

We are all born and raised with an image of a perfect life, an American Dream illustrated by a simple subdivision street called Bryant Street.

But in chasing and holding the American Dream, we often forget why we are in the race.

For those of us living on Bryant Street, I thought I just might get you wondering why.

THE EARLY MORNING on Bryant Street seemed like any other early spring-morning day in a subdivision that looked like most other middle-class subdivisions in America. Young trees, well-kept green lawns watered by automatic sprinkler systems, clean sidewalks, and a dozen for-sale signs every two blocks.

Half the houses along Bryant Street were bank-owned, and most of the other half had huge mortgages that would never be paid off and would soon also become bank owned.

Barb's and my place was no exception. The Bryant Street subdivision was a small, but beautiful subdivision that might as well be a ghost town.

And I was one of the only remaining ghosts. A ghost of past times on Bryant Street just as any ghost was from a past where life had once existed, but had been killed in a brutal and ugly fashion.

Tuesday had arrived. Monday was finished. The week stretched ahead of me like a dull highway across a flat desert. Or at least I thought it did, until I killed the Clockwork Key, the thing inside of me that wound me up and kept me moving along the same path, in the same circle day after day after day.

We all have Clockwork Keys, but most of us never notice we have them or seem to care.

When I killed my Clockwork Key, I was halfway to my sixty-three-payments-left black Lexus. All normal, until Barb came out of the front door.

"Ram!" she shouted.

She called me Ram because of my days playing football in college where we met. It had been my nickname and she still called me that, even though my real name and the one I liked was Raymond. To her calling me Ram reminded her of better times, better nights of sex and lots of drinking and laughing and throwing parties where kids threw up in garbage cans and behind hedges and called it the "good old days."

I turned, not really caring what she had to say. We had gone through the morning routine. I had kissed her at the door, she had said she thought she was going to have better luck today finding a job. I had told her I thought she would as well.

All simple morning lies to keep us walking along in our circles and not thinking about anything in our life or how we would eventually have to leave Bryant Street and her dream house that we had paid far, far too much to build back when "times were better" as people said.

I'm not sure I remember those times, but people do tell me they existed.

"You forgot your briefcase!" Barb shouted, as if I couldn't hear her in the complete silence of the early morning in a mostly-empty subdivision. I was usually the first out of the subdivision these days of the few people that actually left, since I was one of the few on the street who actually pretended to still have a job.

She held up the black briefcase and instead of coming down the sidewalk to bring it to me, she just stood there, waiting for me to come back to her to get it.

And I just stood there waiting for her to bring it to me.

We had a marriage standoff.

Barb and I had had many such standoffs over the years.

But back in the "good old days" or when "times were better," I usually was the one to break the marriage standoff. Now I couldn't care.

I had walked down the sidewalk, I had done my bit to keep the morning moving, to stay in my routine, to continue to pay for the house and the cars and the food for as long as I could, even though we were within six months of being out of money.

She had done her bit to cook the breakfast and to make small talk and to pretend she was preparing to go looking for a job even though we both knew there were no jobs to be had and she would never leave the house or get out of her bathrobe.

We had both played our parts perfectly, just as we did every morning.

Now, standing there on that wide sidewalk with the carefully manicured edges so that the grass wouldn't touch the pavement, neither Barb nor I knew what to do.

We did not know, in our perfectly ordered world, who had the responsibility for the briefcase.

A marriage standoff.

Sure, the black briefcase was supposed to have my job paperwork in it, paperwork I brought home to work on every night, but never did, because I hadn't had a job for over a year.

And in a year of looking, I had found nothing.

And had never told Barb I had lost my job. It just hadn't been worth the problems telling her would have caused me every day. We had long before stopped acting as partners.

And the last thing I had wanted to do was stay in the house with her all day long. I felt bad enough about losing my job and not finding a new one. I didn't need that kind of punishment as well.

My former job was nothing more than crunching numbers to determine who would be laid off next. I assigned numbers, calculations, statistics to people, real people, and then gave those special living numbers to my boss who pretended to check them and then give them to his boss and so on up the corporate ladder until someone decided to act.

Because of my numbers, a certain person or numbers of people each week had been laid off to keep the company profitable (on paper) for the shareholders who continued to send the stock higher and higher making everyone happy who owned the stock.

At first I had felt remorse for the people that my calculations had caused to lose their job. But then, after a few years of doing the same thing every day, every week, I no longer cared about the faces and the lives destroyed behind those simple numbers.

And then one day I had become a number as well. Someone above me had figured the numbers for me and I had been laid off.

Now in our marriage standoff, Barb, once a good-looking woman with brown hair and good teeth, stood there in her blue bathrobe and blue matching slippers on the brown welcome mat in front of our brown and tan home, smiling and holding the worthless lie of a briefcase that contained nothing of value in it.

My life had become nothing of value, either.

It seemed logical I should carry a briefcase that carried nothing.

I stared at her and she smiled at me, holding the briefcase.

And I smiled back and made no movement toward her.

The morning sun felt warm against my back, and I realized that in all the years of mornings I had walked from the house to the car I had never noticed any feeling about anything.

Now I felt warmth.

And the smell of the freshly-mowed grass suddenly caught my attention.

And the sounds of birds chirping in the young trees almost distracted me from staring at Barb.

Slowly, her smile faded.

"Ram, don't you need your briefcase?"

I turned my back to her and looked around at the neighborhood.

It was a perfect neighborhood, a perfect, Hollywood-version of a neighborhood, as if some screenwriter had written in a few words at the beginning of a script, "Standard Subdivision: Well-kept and manicured."

I had not really, really stopped and looked at Bryant Street and the homes along the street for a long time. And now that I had stopped, thanks to the marriage standoff, I could actually see what I had missed.

The paint on a few of the empty homes was starting to show weathering. The shrubs on a few homes hadn't been trimmed in years and had grown too large for the yards.

Windows on two of the closest bank-owned homes were dirty, and the drapes in one window were torn and looked faded.

And as I watched, a woman's face appeared beside the torn curtain, staring at me with sunken eyes and hair that looked like it hadn't been combed in weeks.

A ghost of a former resident, maybe.

I recognized her after a moment. DeAnna Sterling. Or what was left of DeAnna Sterling. She used to be a large, almost obese woman. Now she looked more like a model for a bad fashion designer.

Her husband, Dan had been laid off two years ago and the bank had foreclosed on their home over a year ago.

That home had been DeAnna's dream home, and she and Barb used to be best friends.

I had a vague memory of Barb telling me DeAnna had had a breakdown and had refused to leave her home.

Now I understood why our grocery bill had grown higher. Barb did the shopping, telling me about the inflation. The inflation was that we were feeding DeAnna.

I looked down the street. I wondered how many other ghosts were in these empty buildings and what they did when I was working.

DeAnna ducked back into the darkness of her home.

I turned back to face Barb who had that "worried look" I knew so well on her face. She had not expected a marriage standoff either this fine morning. More than likely she was missing her morning program and her second cup of coffee, and that was not right.

Or more likely she was worried that I had seen DeAnna.

I stared at my home. I had somehow managed to continue making payments on this "perfect" home. I had started to do the yard work myself when I could no longer afford a gardener, and I drained most of the remains of my estate from my parents to keep walking this routine.

To keep pretending that I was living a life I wanted to live.

I was nothing more than calculations and statistics and numbers as well. My entire life consisted of walking the same routine, doing the same thing, trying to find a job that didn't exist to pay bills I didn't want to pay so that I could keep doing the same thing again and again and again.

And now, because of a briefcase and a marriage standoff, I could see clearly for the first time what I had been doing.

I had broken the cycle.

I had broken my Clockwork Key.

I reached up and undid my tie because I was getting warm standing there on the sidewalk in my black suit.

Barb's "worry look" switched to her "puzzlement look" mixed with her "slight-panic look." I knew all her expressions. I knew how she thought at every moment of every day.

I dropped my tie on the grass I had mowed yesterday after I had gotten home from my pretend job.

"You keep the briefcase," I said to Barb.

"Ram!" she shouted, her voice rising to the level I hated, the level that made her sound like a record had spun up just a little too fast while she spoke. "What are you doing?"

"You keep it all," I said, waving at the home I had come to hate and the neighborhood I had never really looked at in years.

"Ram? What's wrong?"

She had still not moved off the porch, and was now clutching my briefcase against her chest as a symbol of the life she didn't want to lose. An empty briefcase that meant far more to her than I ever did.

"Nothing's wrong," I said, smiling at her. "I've got to go. You keep it. You keep it all. You win."

With that I turned and walked the short distance to my car and got in.

She still stood there in front of the worthless home, in her blue bathrobe with perfectly matching blue slippers, my empty briefcase clutched against her chest.

I still had enough savings left to get a divorce, give her the house in the settlement, pay off my car, get a nice, cheap apartment in some other town where there were still a few jobs to be had, and maybe eat for a year or more.

After all, I was a numbers man and I knew the numbers. I had lived those numbers for years now, walking in clock-like service to a life I did not want with a woman I had grown to hate.

I pulled out of the driveway and stopped in the middle of Bryant Street, giving it one more look.

Barb clutched my briefcase, staring at me.

I smiled at her, a real smile for the first time in years. Not a pretend smile, but a smile I actually felt.

I waved at her. Then, with my hand solidly planted on the horn, I drove down Bryant Street for one last time, letting the loud sound of my leaving echo off the ghost-like remains of my former life.

MATED FROM THE MORGUE

(Published under the name Dee W. Schofield)

Not really dead, not really alive. Debbie finds herself one fine day in a hospital morgue and the man of her dreams walks in to start her autopsy.

In just moments her wonderful body will be cut open.

And she can't move to stop him.

One

I'M on one damn cold metal table, bright lights shining on my naked body, my brand new, enhanced breasts aiming at the ceiling tile of this stupid hospital morgue like they were supposed to. And what do I feel? Annoyed. Just annoyed. Not cold, not embarrassed, just annoyed.

And just a little scared.

Panic?

Sure. That was in the mix as well.

I'm about to be very, very dead if someone doesn't catch a clue real quick that I am still inside this stupid body of mine and very much alive, even though it doesn't look like I am.

Some pimply-faced kid set up a tray of sharp knives and bone spreaders beside my table, looked at my breasts, then my crotch, and left.

This felt like sitting in a dentist's chair getting ready for the dentist to use all his nasty-looking instruments. Only, that tray of stuff was sitting there just waiting for some lowlife mortician to come in and cut me open like a stupid trout.

While I'm still alive and can feel it! Okay, maybe panic was a little closer to the surface than I thought.

Can't any of the idiots out there see that I'm still alive, that some blood was pumping? Otherwise, how could I be lying here on this damn cold metal table thinking that if I ever did get out of this, I was going to kill someone.

Anyone.

From across the embalming room I heard a door open. I sure as hell wanted to turn my head and smile at the person just to give them a shock. I tried.

Nothing.

Not even a muscle twitch.

Suddenly, a hunk of a good-looking guy in a rubber apron and a hairnet appeared over me like an angel. He had flashing dark eyes, longish, dark brown hair under the net, and a smile that just wouldn't stop.

And he was looking right in to my eyes.

"You are far too good-looking to be here on this table," he said.

I tried to shout, *No Shit, Sherlock!*

My mouth wouldn't move. Not even a grunt came out.

He walked slowly down along the table, clearly taking in all my naked assets.

Now I was starting to feel embarrassed. This was not really the way I wanted a hunk of a guy to see me. He looked at the toe tag on my foot, then came back up and checked off something on a clipboard.

"Debbie," he said, smiling at me again. "My name is Mathew. I'm here to try to find out why you just keeled over dead in your tuna salad."

I'm not dead! I tried to scream.

Nothing.

I was facing a young hunk of a doctor who talked to the bodies. Even with that bad habit, I still wanted to jump his bones.

I wanted to jump anything, actually. Getting cut open on a morgue table was not my idea of a good way to leave the planet.

How the hell did I end up here?

And what the hell was a guy like him doing here? He could be modeling for a men's magazine in sweaters with golf clubs in his hands. Instead he was cutting open dead people.

And more than likely a not-so-dead one in just a moment.

I had two degrees in business and ran my own company. He clearly had a medical license of some sort to call himself a doctor. He couldn't be dumb. Maybe, just maybe, he might figure this all out. The idiots in the ambulance and the bitch doctor in the emergency room sure hadn't.

Having yourself declared dead while you are listening is just not a good time. If I got out of here, I was going to need counseling for years.

The door to the room opened again, and Doctor Mathew turned those wonderful, dark eyes away from me.

"I won't need you anymore today, Jim," he said.

His voice sort of echoed, so the room had to be fairly large. More than likely he was talking to the kid with the face-full of pimples, but I couldn't see the kid.

Doctor Mathew disappeared from my limited sight, and I heard the kid mumble something, then the door closed.

And then there was the sound of a lock turning.

Oh, shit!

This might turn even uglier than it was. I just went from a horror sit-com to a full-out horror movie.

Two

Now the panic was starting to swell up. I had seen far too many movies where the good-looking doctor was some sort of perv.

My brain told me I wanted to swallow and then scream for help, but none of that was happening.

In horror movies, they always made the poor victim unable to move as well.

The hunk of a man appeared above me again, smiling. At least he was a good-looking monster.

"We're all alone now, Debbie. Just you and me. Maybe we could call this a date. You would be the first date I've had in a year. Since my wife died."

Oh, shit! Oh, shit! I was doomed. I just hoped I didn't remind the guy of his dead wife.

"You remind me a little of Marcie," he said, smiling and checking out my scalp with very tender fingers and a light touch.

Oh, shit! Oh, shit! Oh, shit!

"But she was shorter and had green eyes," he said, "instead of pretty blue ones like yours. She also wanted to have breast enhancements like yours, but was killed in a car crash before she got the chance. Life is so short. Clearly it was for you as well."

He kept working over my scalp, very carefully, like a lost hairdresser trying to pad her bill and find her way to the door by Braille.

"I'm afraid I won't be a very good date," he said, smiling at me and looking right into my eyes. "I just don't think it's been long enough for me since my Marcie left."

He laughed in a strained way and shook his head.

Wasn't it bad enough that I was on a morgue table, thought to be dead, and now some guy was going to get his jollies on my naked body?

"But don't worry," he said as he smiled down at me. "I have always been a complete gentleman on a first date."

I'd believe that if I wasn't as naked as the day I came into this stupid world. Except for the toe tag.

He started to check out my neck with those wonderful hands of his, then he stepped back, a frown on his face. "Your skin is still warm to the touch."

Could he be figuring this out?

He stepped away and I could no longer see him. From what I could tell he was flipping through some sort of paperwork.

"It's been three hours since you collapsed," he said, clearly still talking to me. "Two hours since you were declared dead. And you've been down here on this table for over an hour now. That's just weird."

I should be as cold as a rock. Right? Come on, Doc! Figure it out.

Next I could hear him rummaging through a drawer, and a moment later he was back, a stethoscope around his neck and a small device in one hand.

He held the device in my ear for a moment, then looked at it.

"Weird," he said. "Just weird." He looked into my eyes again. "You are as strange as you are beautiful."

If I could have even blushed I would have right at that moment. Maybe I did, just a little. I couldn't tell.

He put one hand on my chest, right on my brand new, specially-enhanced left breast, and leaned forward, not noticing at all what he was touching. I was still just dead meat to him, like I had been to my first husband for two years of that disaster laughingly called a marriage.

With his other hand he held the cold stethoscope to my chest.

For a moment he listened, then he moved the stethoscope to a location just under my enhancement and held it there. His eyes were distant, intense, as he tried to listen.

I'm in here, Doc! I wanted to shout.

After a moment he pushed down fairly hard on my chest with one hand while listening.

And then he pushed again, right on my breast.

Gentleman, hell!

But I knew he had no real idea what part of my body he was touching and pushing on. And that was damn fine with me. I wanted out of this nightmare—then he could push on my new breasts as much as he wanted. In a nice soft bed at his place or mine.

Suddenly he jumped back as if I had shocked him.

My new breasts were good, but not that good.

Three

"Not possible!" he said.

Then he was back at my chest, leaning over, breathing gently into my chin as he leaned way down and almost put his ear against my chest with the stethoscope pressed in hard.

He listened and listened and then suddenly jumped back again, knocking over the tray of instruments.

"Oh, hell, Debbie, are you still in there?"

If I could have moved I would have jumped up and kissed him.

Suddenly, he vanished out of my vision and I could hear him grab a phone. He called in some sort of code and unlocked the door. Then he was back at my side, staring into my eyes.

"Hang on, Debbie. Help is on the way."

He took my hand and squeezed it gently.

I just stared into those wonderful dark eyes of his and said nothing. Not like me, but I had no choice.

It was still a very, very nice moment.

What seemed like only a few seconds later the door exploded open and help arrived.

Six of them, including Doctor Mathew, moved me onto a stretcher, put an oxygen mask over my nose and mouth, covered me with a sheet, and banged me out of the room so fast I thought I was on a ride in an amusement park.

Doctor Mathew never left my side as he and two other doctors talked all the way down the hall and up an elevator, clearly headed into more tests than I wanted to think about. I had no idea what they were talking about, but to be honest, it all sounded wonderful. A ton better than having someone declare you dead when you were really just fine.

For the moment my nightmare in the morgue was over. Now if I died, it wouldn't be because I was sliced and diced. It would be with real doctors trying to save me.

They arrived in a place with dozens of people swarming around all seeming to talk at the same time. They hooked me up to a dozen monitors and confirmed I still had a very, very slowly beating heart.

And that my brain was still working.

I knew that, but it sure felt better to have some doctor say that.

"Oh, wow," I heard Doctor Mathew say as someone else announced the test results. "I could have killed her on that table."

Some other male doctor said, "But you didn't. Nice work, doctor."

So after what seemed like only a moment since they shoved me out of the morgue, Doctor Mathew leaned in over me again and smiled.

His smile got more wonderful every time I saw it. And those dark eyes of his could melt an iceberg.

I was almost dead and still in lust. How sad was that? It had clearly been too long since I had been laid.

"Hang in there, Debbie. We're going to put you under while we do more tests and figure out just what is happening to you. But don't worry, I'll be right here when you wake up."

Then he gently reached forward and closed my eyelids.

"Sleep well."

He could do that to me for years if he wanted to.

And that was the last thing I remembered as that little cloud of blackness sort of came in from all sides.

Four

And then the blackness pushed back.

Weird. It seemed I didn't want to be knocked out.

Or all of that had been some horrible nightmare.

Around me, I could hear the beeping of machines; and in the background, the sounds of a people talking.

And a television was on, softly going over some sort of news.

I blinked and opened my eyes to the lights of the room.

I was in a very different room than the one the tests had been in. And CNN was on the television. I had a light oxygen mask on my nose.

And holy crap, I had moved my eyelids!

I tried a finger and could feel it move as well.

And then an arm.

And then a leg.

Everything moved!

And I could feel I had a tube stuck in my arm.

And my chest hurt something awful.

And I was beyond thirsty.

"Water?" I tried to say, and I actually think what I managed to croak out sounded like a word.

Instantly Doctor Mathew was standing over me, smiling. He had been sitting beside my bed watching television.

"Glad to have you back, Debbie," he said, again giving me that wonderful smile of his.

He eased a tiny ice cube toward my lips and managed to help me get it in my mouth.

"Just let that melt for a moment."

In all my life, an ice cube had never tasted or felt as good.

Doctor Mathew smiled as I worked the tiny ice chip over like it was a seven-course meal.

"My name is Doctor Mathew Stevens," he said. "I have no idea how much you remember, but you were declared dead."

I nodded slightly, and indicated he should come closer. He leaned in and I somehow managed to whisper. "A weird first date, Mathew. Thank you for saving me."

He leaned back, smiling and blushing, realizing I had heard every word he had said in the morgue. Somehow, with that handsome face of his bright red, he managed to recover a little and go on.

"We had to remove your breast implants," he said. "You had an allergy to them that just shut you down. It would have killed you completely in another few hours. Don't worry, you can get the implants replaced with a different type later."

At that moment I didn't care. Who knew having large breasts could kill a woman? My original, factory-issued breasts weren't that bad in the first place. Dumb idea by me to think they might help me with men.

I just nodded to Mathew, so he went on.

"You've been out for about five days," he said, "in a drug-induced coma so the toxins could clear your system completely. You should be up and around in a few days and feeling back to normal in a week."

He leaned in and gave me another piece of ice, which again felt wonderful.

I sure liked having him close.

"Thank you for saving me," I said again, my voice gaining strength.

"That's what we try to do," he said, nodding and blushing a little again. "You are welcome."

A bashful doctor. Who knew there was such a thing?

I smiled at him.

"You have a beautiful smile," he said. "Glad I could see it."

"So am I," I said.

Then I smiled again. "I understand about your wife, at least what little you told me. But if you are willing to give it a try and are ready, I would be up for a second date. The first one turned out so well."

He stood there just staring at me, then, after a long few seconds, he finally laughed.

"Honestly," I said, "I don't expect you to save my life every date."

"That's good," he said, shaking his head and laughing. "I would love to try a second date. Especially since that was a first date I could never imagine happening. I normally don't date patients."

"Why?" I asked, smiling so hard I was going to knock the small oxygen mask off my nose.

"Because I'm a forensic pathologist," he said. "I only deal with the dead."

"Thanks to you," I said, "I am far from dead."

"Good. Because I only really date the living."

I just sat there smiling, trying not to laugh because my chest hurt too much. It seemed that those larger breasts really had helped me get a man.

ME AND BEANS AND GREAT BIG MELONS

When Innis went shopping to get ready for the Packers-Rams game, he never expected to meet one of them aliens.

But he also never expected to meet a woman who ate beans either.

A strange supermarket romance. Are there any others?

I HAVE NEVER THOUGHT, wondered, or even pondered the idea of having a supermarket love affair. If I had, I certainly wouldn't have thought it would start and end in front of the green beans. I'm the kind of guy who really doesn't eat green beans, red beans, black beans, or any other color bean. I'm not prejudiced in my bean selection. I pretty much just hate them all equally.

And I flat don't understand how anyone could even eat the things.

I met my supermarket lover as I tried to figure out which Hamburger Helper would work for the night. I was an expert in Hamburger Helpers and all the different incarnations of the stuff. I could almost make it without looking at the box. Almost.

"Excuse me," a soft, husky voice said.

I jerked around, realizing that my cart and my body had made an effective roadblock in the aisle. And I hadn't even set up any detour signs.

A woman stood there with one of those yellow baskets for small amounts of stuff. Just like me, she was wearing jeans and a blue tee-shirt, but unlike me she also had a brown purse over her shoulder.

The purse, oddly enough, accented the wonderful color of her hair. I wondered if she had bought the purse because of that, or changed the color of her hair to match the purse. It was a question I would never think to ask any woman, even a woman I didn't know.

But yet, for some reason, she had made me think of it. I made a note to myself mentally to write down the weird supermarket moment. I hoped to be a writer in the future, when I could find the time, and often made notes about things that might come in handy in a story some day.

I found myself attracted to this woman wanting to get past me, and I did an instant inventory of her appearance.

Before I was laid off down at Sears, I had done lots of inventories of the warehouse, and had become known as "Innis, the Inventory King." I had decided one day to practice the same craft on women I met, and grocery stores were great places, full of inventory.

Using my skills, I instantly looked her over while moving my cart out of her way. She wore a loose blue tee-shirt with nothing written on it, tight jeans, and expensive tennis shoes. Total inventory cost of two hundred bucks. She had on no jewelry at all, not even an earring. She was an easy inventory subject.

Miss Brown-Hair-Yellow-Basket: Two hundred bucks.

"Sorry," I said, as I finished my inventory and cart moving at the same time, leaving the cart in front of the green beans, never thinking that she might actually be trying to get to that area. If I didn't eat green beans, no one else did I was sure.

My first wife had called that self-centered-universe attitude my defining characteristic. I had considered that a compliment and still do.

"No problem," the brown-haired, two-hundred-dollar-woman said, giving me a wonderful, bright smile as she moved past me. The aroma of fresh soap caught me and I stared at her from behind for a moment, first watching her long hair move against her matching purse, then her ass under her tight jeans.

I had always been an ass man, staring at woman's asses before any other body part if the chance arose. This woman had a stareable ass, of that there was no doubt. Really tight.

A stareable tight ass wasn't worth anything on my inventory list, but it should be.

She walked a few steps and stopped, looking at the canned vegetables.

I went back to trying to decide which Hamburger Helper to pick to eat while the football game was on tonight. Packers against the Rams. Could be a real shouter.

"Sorry to bother you again," she said from behind me.

I turned around to look into the deepest green eyes I had seen in a long time. If all women had eyes like her, I would shift to being an eye-man instead of an ass-man.

She pointed at the bean section that my cart was blocking.

"Oh, sorry," I said, moving to pull the cart out of her way for the second time. "I didn't think anyone ate that stuff."

She laughed. "Usually I like my beans fresh. But when I can't get them fresh, I make do with canned."

Usually I'm not real honest with the women I meet, but this woman ate beans and had annoyed me by making me move my cart twice in the middle of my Hamburger Helper shopping. So I said the first thing that came to mind.

"I'm that way with women," I said. "When I can't find the fresh stuff, I resort to the canned as well."

She stared at me for a moment.

I returned her stare.

The faint store music went away; the sounds of the other shoppers went away. It was a movie moment.

Of course, I had no doubt this movie moment was going to end with the woman walking off in a huff. At least then I could watch her ass and get back to my shopping.

But she surprised me.

Suddenly her smile returned, followed by the richest, deepest laugh I had heard in a long time. It echoed off the cans of corn and surrounded me, pushing me back against the shelf of Hamburger Helper.

"Now that's an opening line I've never heard before," she said after she caught a breath from the laughter.

"Opening for what?" I asked.

She smiled. "My legs."

I looked her right in the eye. "Now tell me why I would want to get between the legs of a woman who eats beans?"

Again I was serious, and again she stared at me, stunned into a second movie moment right there on aisle four.

Then she damned near lost a lung laughing that wonderful laugh of hers. I guess to her I was a real laugh-a-minute kind of guy.

She finally caught her breath and stared at me, her bright smile lighting up everything.

"Well?" I asked. "I'm waiting for my reason."

"Because," she said, "beans go well with franks at a picnic."

She stepped forward and grabbed my crotch, never letting her green-eyed gaze drop from mine.

She rubbed me through my jeans a few times as again we were having a movie moment, only this time it was a sex scene right there in front of the Hamburger Helper. I doubted I was ever going to be able to eat Hamburger Helper without a hard-on again.

"I assume little Frank here wouldn't mind a picnic in the park."

"His name is Ben," I said as she kept rubbing. "Big Ben. And he likes melons on his picnics."

"I think that could be arranged," she said, rubbing one small, tight breast against my arm. Whatever she had thought, that wasn't a melon. More like an apple.

"Any other menu items?" she asked.

Any man with a woman rubbing his crotch on aisle four of a grocery store might have trouble answering a question like that. I didn't. "A television to watch the game while I eat."

Her hand came away from my crotch like Big Ben had lit a match and burnt her. She stared at me, then said, "My ex-husband would have rather watched television than make love to me."

"Did he like Hamburger Helper?" I asked, adjusting Ben a little to ease the tension of tight underwear.

"Yeah," she said, clearly upset at my request for a television at her picnic.

"Figures," I said.

Now she was starting to get angry. A moment ago she was offering me a picnic, basket, apples, and all. Now she was mad. I had never had a woman mad at me on aisle four in a grocery store before. Two things new in one day, both on the same aisle. I would really have to write this down for the story I would do some day.

"And why does it *figure*?" she demanded, as if I owed her an answer just because she had given Big Ben a quick rubbing.

I shrugged. "You eat beans."

She made a choking sound, grabbed two cans of green beans, held them up for me to see like she was giving me the finger, put them in her little yellow basket, and walked off.

I watched her ass until she turned the corner and disappeared toward aisle five. Because her ass was so nice and tight, and her hand had felt so good on Big Ben, I thought for a moment about following her. But I knew there was nothing I could say to her to calm her down.

Besides, she ate beans. I hated beans, and no amount of Big Ben rubbing was going to erase that difference.

Also, if I spent time dealing with her over on aisle five, it might carry on to aisle six, and then even into the frozen food section on aisle eight, and if that happened I might miss the opening kick-off.

No bean-eating woman with a nice ass was worth missing the kick-off to a Packers-Rams game. Even if she had offered Ben an offer he had trouble refusing.

It seemed that my supermarket love affair had started and ended on aisle four.

I went back to trying to figure out which Hamburger Helper to get, finally picked up just the standard, and headed for aisle two where the Pabst Blue-Ribbon Beer lived and breathed and waited for me. No Hamburger Helper football game dinner was complete without Pabst.

I turned the corner onto the aisle. There was a short woman with a nice ass and short red hair parked right in front of the Pabst. She was studying the beer on the other side of the aisle as if reading labels would make the stuff any better.

I knew right off she was an alien, off one of them big ships from some other planet that had landed a year or so ago. All the alien women that I had seen on Fox News had short, bright-red hair and great bodies.

There had been hundreds of thousands of them, and all the countries of the world welcomed them to live. After awhile, they weren't even headlines anymore unless one of them got drunk and punched a cop or something.

The aliens had said they had come in friendship and just wanted to learn about us, but I had read stuff, and I knew better. More than likely they were going to kidnap us all and take us away and make dinner out of us.

But still, alien or not, she was standing in front of the Pabst and I had a game to watch.

"Excuse me," I said.

She turned to look at me, a puzzled look on her very human but very alien face.

Her dark eyes were like magnets, swirling pink and orange and brown. They held me with some unseen force. She was dressed in jeans and a blue tee-shirt, just like I was. Just like Miss Brown Hair had been. Only instead of apples in the tee-shirt orchard, she sprouted the biggest melons I had ever seen, especially for an alien as short as she was.

I did a quick inventory. Same as Miss-Brown-Purse. Two hundred bucks. It seemed it was two-hundred-dollar-woman-day in the supermarket.

"Yes?" she asked. "Can I help you?"

Very formal, like the secretary at my doc's office. But oh, Miss-Alien-With-Melons' voice could melt grease in a cold frying pan.

I pointed to the beer. "Hamburger Helper and a hand job are never complete without Pabst."

For some reason it was my day to be honest with women. And aliens it seemed. Maybe someone had put something in the grocery store air to make me do it. Or maybe it was the excitement of a good football game that was causing it. I would have to think about it later, after the game, if I could stay awake long enough to do so.

She kept staring at me, then slowly smiled as she moved aside. "Aren't you forgetting one thing?" she asked.

"What's that?" I asked, figuring an insult to be next out of her mouth. Something about the rudeness of humans in social situations and that we all needed alien training or something. I grabbed my half case of beer and placed it next to the Hamburger Helper.

"A good Packers-Rams game."

Now it was my turn to stare at her like she was a winning lotto ticket. I didn't know alien women watched American football. Fox News had never mentioned anything like that. Maybe there was hope for all of us after all.

So, with that encouragement, I went ahead and asked the all-important question.

"Do you eat beans?"

She made a face. "Are you kidding? No human or alien should eat those things."

"Good," I said. "How's your ass?"

She turned around to show me, then said, "Engineered to be as tight as they make them. How's your big fella?"

"Big," I said.

She smiled and I smiled back.

I loved those alien eyes.

Then after my third or fourth movie moment of the shopping trip, this time right there in front of the beer, I stuck out my hand. "I'm Innis. I count things and hope to write stories."

She took my hand, her smooth skin sending wonderful warm sensations through my body right there in the cold beer section.

"Here on your planet, in your language, I'm called Melody," she said. "I'm not from around here. I rub things and hope to paint things. And if we don't hurry we're going to miss the kick-off. How big is your screen?"

Her eyes seemed to swirl and she smiled with that question.

"Sixty inches," I said, proud of the moment I could say that to an alien woman.

She smiled even wider and then reached down and touched Big Ben through my jeans. "Sixty inches, huh? Mind if I join you? I'll buy the hamburger."

"Deal," I said, enjoying the fact that Ben was getting a work-out right there in the supermarket.

She put a second half-case of Pabst in my cart, left her empty cart in front of the other beer, and helped me push mine to the meat section, letting one of her wonderful large melons rub firmly against my hand.

It pleased me that she hadn't intended on sharing my Pabst. I really had to know a woman, or an alien for that matter, before I let that happen. Even if she was sharing her melons.

On the way past aisle six, we passed Miss Brown-Hair-And-Matching-Purse, who gave me a very, very long and angry look.

"Wow, what is her problem?" Melody asked, turning with me to watch the angry woman walk away. "Besides the fact that she has a tight ass."

"Very tight," I said, agreeing. "But she hates football and eats beans."

"Oh, that explains it," Melody said, shaking her head. "One of my people's biggest puzzles about your planet is how anyone could eat beans. They are poison to us. It may be a mystery we will never solve."

I was starting to really like these aliens.

"Let me know if you do," I said.

"The moment we figure it out," she said, laughing a high laugh that sounded very off-worldish. With that, me and my first alien super-market lover headed for the check-out counter and a Hamburger Helper football game.

DON'T RUST ON ME NOW

Can romance be real between two androids on a poison planet with beach sand in all the wrong places?

Dr. Susan Taft discovers the answer to that question when her ship crashes in the middle of a lake in a very hostile place.

The only thing not hostile: Another android with her.

An Android with a great body and an even better mind.

THE ALARM BELLS were going off as I came up out of transwarp sleep, trying to remember where I was. Who I was, actually.

Oh, yeah, Susan Taft. Dr. Susan Taft, actually; originally from Canada on Earth, recently from the Mars city of Bensen.

I remembered now. Waking up from transwarp sleep was supposed to be calm and comfortable, like waking up from a long nap. Yeah, alarms blaring can really help a person be calm.

Damn I hated alarms.

The one echoing around me had a distinctive *whoop-whoop* screaming sound that I was sure could hurt a person's ears given time. What was going on?

And why didn't someone shut off the stupid alarm? And let me out of this sleep chamber. I didn't want to open my eyes because I knew there was nothing but padding about five inches above my face.

Everyone says that the human brain doesn't dream in transwarp sleep, but I'd had this uncomfortable dream about losing my body in an industrial accident, and having my mind temporarily put into an android body so I could make the journey to New Wells a couple of hundred light years away for a new and younger and healthier body.

On New Wells they grew the human replacement bodies tall, strong, and pretty in the organ beds in the light gravity. Anything would be better than the old, scarred-up and dying original body from my dream. I remember dreaming that I had ordered larger breasts as well, just to spend one life rotation seeing if the things might change my life in any way.

Then the dream firmed up and became a nasty memory, and I remembered.

No dream. I really was scarred up by an accident and I had really ordered new and larger breasts on my body replacement. Yeah, that was dumb.

And I really was in an android body right now.

Damn. I didn't want to open my eyes.

But I sure did want to shout for someone to turn off the stupid alarm. It seemed to be vibrating my sleep coffin. Even if I were dead, that sound would wake me up.

I sure hoped I wasn't dead.

I had come too close to that totally dead state in the accident back on Mars. I had plans to stay around for another ten body rotations—a good four hundred Earth years—if I stayed away from having a machine explode ten feet from me again.

The android body I was in had all the normal human shapes and bumps and curves and even the larger breasts I had ordered. It was a replica in every detail of the new body I had ordered that was waiting for me on New Wells.

The android body even functioned in all ways like a normal human body, right down to eating and drinking and other body functions. It even had soft, smooth skin over the metal alloy frame.

Only that soft-looking skin was a patchwork quilt of browns and whites, making me look more like an old movie monster that had been stitched together by an insane quilter.

Stupid Earth law. Any android with a human brain had to remain naked at all times and wear a patchwork-colored skin until the brain was transferred into a new human body.

Fear-based law. Politicians never seemed to understand anything about how androids worked. Androids were actually easier to disable than human bodies if you knew what you were doing, and they didn't last long at all because of the complexity of the systems inside.

A dumb law. I sure didn't much care to walk around naked. But with my new breasts I had gotten some nice stares while boarding from the Mars station crew.

I moved my hands and felt my android skin along the sides of my legs.

Seemed like everything was working.

Have I ever mentioned how much I hated alarms?

No one seemed to be turning off the alarm. This sure wasn't a peaceful wake-up from a long transwarp nap.

I had been told to just lay very still when coming out of transwarp sleep, but if someone didn't shut that alarm off I was going to be anything but still in a few seconds.

Back when I was a student working on my first doctorate in physics, I had used an alarm that sounded like a cross between a fire engine and a ride at Mars Disney just to make sure I got out of bed on time every day.

I kept smashing the alarms and replacing them. Cost me a very satisfactory three hundred extra credits during the term. Worth every damn credit.

If that alarm didn't get shut off, some part of this ship was going to be smashed in very short order.

Suddenly I could hear the lid of my chamber start to move. I opened my eyes.

Above me stood a very, very handsome, well-built, and very naked male android. I thought I was the only android transport on this ship. Clearly I hadn't been.

As he pushed the lid back and clicked it into place, his very personal, very male parts dangled just inches from my face. Now that also wasn't a restful way to wake up.

Nice, but clearly not restful.

"Dr. Taft?" he asked, staring down at me. His gaze first looked relieved as I nodded, but then he looked down the rest of my naked body and the part closest to my face twitched.

"That's me," I said, pushing myself up slowly as he stepped back. "What's going on? Where is the crew?"

He reached down and somehow managed to get his hands under my arms without touching my breasts and help me out of my sleep coffin.

"I don't know," he said finally, as I stood, leaning against the smooth metal of my coffin until my balance returned and the room slowly stopped spinning. "I haven't left the room yet."

There was another sleep coffin across from mine. It hadn't been there when they had put me to sleep.

"And you are?" I asked.

"Hugh Bensen," he said, smiling a smile that could knock down a dead woman, let alone an android with a human brain. I stared so long at his wonderful smile and his deep eyes that it took a moment for the name to register.

"Bensen of the Mars, Bensen City family?" I asked.

"Yup," he said, "Only son of the current mayor."

"So why the android?" I asked. "I seem to remember you were only into your second human cycle.

He laughed, and the laugh made me want to just hug him like a big patchwork teddy bear. "Fell off a cliff while doing some climbing up north of the city. Broke my back in three places. Lower gravity can hurt just as much as Earth gravity."

His voice also seemed perfect to my ears, even with the alarm blaring in the background.

"Great to meet you," I said.

"The honor is mine," he said. "I've been a big fan of your work since your first paper on the reality of dark space around dark matter."

Now I really stopped and actually looked at him. A rich guy with a brain *and* a nice voice *and* a fantastic body. Was that possible?

"Thank you," I said, smiling and staring into his eyes just a fraction of a second too long. God, I hoped android skin didn't blush. More than likely it did.

"Let's find out what's going on," he said, turning from me and heading for the door.

Damn, he had a nice butt as well. There had to be something wrong with this guy besides the patchwork android skin which would soon be changed for a human body when we got to New Wells.

I followed him as he opened the metal door and stepped into the hallway. He took two steps and glanced down; as did I.

We were standing in about an inch of water.

"This can't be good," he said, a hint of slight panic in his voice.

I didn't say anything, because the panic would no doubt be very real and clear in my words.

Water didn't belong on spaceships past a toilet or a shower or a glass of the stuff in the dining hall. I sure hoped this was just a sink overflowing somewhere.

His pace down the hall got faster and faster as we headed forward. The small transwarp ship was a private craft that the University had chartered to get me to New Wells. It only had a crew of four. Small ships and short, twenty-day jumps didn't need any more than that.

So where was the crew?

As we headed toward the bridge, the water got deeper, until, in front of the bridge door, it was knee-deep. And the damn alarm got louder and louder.

I hated alarms, sure, but not as much as a flooded spaceship.

The water smelled a lot like a lake I had grown up near in Canada. Not sour, just fresh and clear and wild. Not the slightly sterile, recycled smell of water on Mars.

Hugh pushed open the bridge door slowly, sending a wave of water across the control room.

"Oh, no," he said softly.

"Damn," I said, not really believing what I was seeing.

All four crew members were in their chairs and clearly dead. The front of the ship was mostly missing and the ship was nose-down and stuck in a shallow lake.

The light outside was soft, shining through high, white clouds. The air smelled slightly of almonds. I could see some sharp mountains in the distance.

The ship didn't seem to be sinking at all, so clearly the lake wasn't very deep, at least where the ship had crashed.

Hugh paused for a moment beside me, then went to the closest crew member and looked at him.

"Can you tell what killed them?" I asked, moving to stand over the captain I had met right before being put in my sleep coffin. Besides a nasty bump on the head and some saliva running out of his mouth and down his chin, he looked all right. But I had no training at all on the medical side of things.

"The air is poison," Hugh said, heading for a control panel that looked to be functioning. "We survived the impact and can breath the air because of our sleep coffins and these bodies."

I nodded. That made sense. Android bodies could actually survive in deep space for a short time without suits. Breathing was only an artificial function built in to keep the human mind inside from panic. Actually, everything about an android body was designed to react and let the brain inside feel it was actually still in a human body. I had learned that much a long time ago, long before my accident.

I moved to a blinking light and slammed my hand on the alarm controls to turn them off.

Silence, almost louder than the alarm itself, filled the bridge.

I could feel myself relax just slightly.

"Thank you," Hugh said, still bent over the communications panel. "Now I can hear myself think."

I sloshed through the water and checked the other crew members, just to be sure, then went back over to the captain's panel and clicked on the flight record.

I had been trained a number of years back in small craft flight, and this ship wasn't much larger than the ones I had flown in short, five-light-year jumps.

I fast-forwarded to the moment of the alarms.

"Looks like the transwarp drive caught something and had a catastrophic failure," I said out loud to Hugh. "It was ejected instantly, so the failsafe worked."

"Luckily," he said, "or we would have never even realized why we never woke up."

"The ejection dropped the ship and crew into regular space, and they spent two months real-time limping their way at sub-light to this system and this planet."

"Means a bunch of people are looking for us already," Hugh said. "How fast were they traveling?"

"One-tenth light," I said, finding the reference in the record.

Hugh nodded. "Good, then it has been less than six months, real-time."

I glanced over at him again. He had his back to me, still focused very intently on the communications board. How could someone with that nice a butt have such a powerful brain? He had figured out the real-time speed time deletion factors almost faster than I had.

138

I shook my head and went back to following the record. "There was engine damage from the transwarp drive ejection, so they ended up crash-landing here. When the front of the ship sheared-off, they died almost instantly."

"They are heroes," Hugh said, turning to look at me with a very serious expression. "They saved our lives."

"How's that?"

"They got sub-light distress signals out on the way here, and again before they crashed. Help is on the way."

He moved over through the water and clicked the alarms back on, killing the peaceful quiet.

"Why did you do that?" I asked. The sound just grated on me.

"Distress beacon," he said. "That's the signal that will lead the rescue ships to us."

I nodded. Made sense, but why the hell did it have to be so loud inside the ship. "Any idea how long?"

"Maybe up to two days," he said, smiling, as if enjoying a private joke on me.

I shook my head. "I don't think I can stand that noise for two days. Any way to cut the audio portion of the signal?"

Now his face was suddenly serious. "I don't want to risk our lives and even touch that thing."

Damn if he wasn't right. I didn't either, but that didn't help me with that alarm sound.

Hugh turned and took the captain by the shoulders. "Let's get the crew back into a dry room and closed off. Never know what's in this water."

That seemed like a logical plan. He seemed to be much better at emergency situations than I was.

I took the captain's feet and we headed back down the hall to the sleep coffin room.

When we had all four bodies there, we covered them with blankets from one of the crew quarters.

"When we get back," Hugh said, "Dad will make sure all their families are well cared for."

"And the university will help as well," I said. "They were very brave."

Hugh nodded. "They just didn't expect the lake to be so shallow or the nose of the ship to crack open to outside air."

In silence we went to the galley and found something to eat. Even though our android bodies didn't actually need the food, our minds believed they did, so we both felt hunger.

Sometimes the android bodies were just a little too efficient.

I just kept finding myself staring at Hugh, even though I tried not to. I hadn't had a real date for almost six months before the accident. Holo-dates, sure. Everyone did those. But no real dates, and I had been missing that.

The designers of these android shells could have easily unhooked the sex-drive part of the androids, but they hadn't. Everything was hooked-up and working from my brain.

And my brain kept my eyes staring at the naked hunk of a man I was with.

And I noticed he was staring at me as well, when he didn't think I was looking.

In the galley the alarms were muted, but even there it just pounded at my head and got in the way of my thinking. Of course, I wasn't real sure how well I was thinking considering everything that had happened.

After eating, he broke the silence and asked, "How about we take a walk outside? Get some distance from the alarm."

"I would so love that," I said. More than I wanted to admit to him, actually.

We went back to the bridge and Hugh checked the communications panel.

After a moment of my staring at his butt again, he turned to me, smiling that killer smile of his. "A ship called the *Tennison* will be here in less than twelve hours."

"Can you contact them?" I asked, feeling a huge sense of relief.

"Nope," he said. "We just have to wait and hold on."

I didn't say what I wanted to hold on to as he turned for the opening in the hull.

Carefully we worked our way outside and into the shallow water. Then holding hands like two kids at a swimming pool, we started for the nearest shoreline, a good two-hundred-paces away.

The lake looked like it could be a mountain lake back on Earth, with some sort of pine-like trees surrounding the shoreline and sharp, rocky mountains in the distance. It was stunningly beautiful.

But we were going to have to be very careful of any wildlife.

Android bodies possessed almost super-human strength and the metal under the skin was tough to hurt, but a head injury would be a disaster, especially this far away from good medical help.

The water never got deeper, only more and more shallow as we slowly worked our way along the sandy lake bottom and finally up onto the beach. It was a fine, white sand, and very soft.

And on the beach the alarm from the ship was only a very distant sound, not annoying at all.

Even with the yellow sun and the high clouds, I could feel the warmth of the air and the light bouncing off of the water.

"Do androids get sunburns?" I asked, not really having a clue to the answer.

He laughed. "I honestly don't know. I don't remember reading anything about that. Guess we'll find out."

He dropped down on the beach and put his back against a tree stump so that he could stare out over the water and back at the ship.

I sat beside him, wondering how hard it was going to be to get the fine, white sand out of the intimate parts of an android body.

"So this air is poison to humans," I said, taking a deep breath of what seemed like crisp, clean mountain air.

"Very," he said. "More than likely why this planet hasn't been settled."

I laughed. "When has that ever stopped humans?"

We sat for a moment in silence just staring at the ship.

"More than likely," Hugh said, "the crew thought the lake was deep and tried a water landing. I have a hunch they would have made it if the water had been even five feet deeper."

"Those ships float?" I asked, glancing at him.

"Like a top," he said.

"And how do you know that?"

And that question got the conversation rolling.

For the next five or six hours we talked about our pasts and discovered we had almost crossed paths a few times over the years. I was shocked to discover how really solid he was, considering his family past. And he seemed shocked to discover I was a real human with real emotions, considering my reputation and discoveries.

And he made me laugh a lot, something I would have never considered possible in this situation.

Actually, I wasn't the type to laugh much in any situation. But sitting on this lakefront with the beautiful alien sky and mountains, I seemed to laugh more than I had in years.

And I had never opened up to anyone like I opened up to him. I told him things about myself I had never told anyone.

As each hour went by I became more and more attracted to the man inside that android shell. To the brain, the personality.

Before I had wanted to jump him for sex. Now I wanted to spend time with him. A lot more time. Especially once we were both back in real human bodies.

I had no doubt I had fallen in love with Hugh. Never, in all my life, had I fallen for someone this fast and this hard.

Maybe it was the trauma of surviving a spacecraft wreck.

Or maybe it was Hugh.

I was betting it was Hugh, not the android-body-Hugh, but the mind and sense of humor and personality inside the body.

After six hours, the sun had only barely moved in the sky, clearly indicating this planet had a very slow rotation period.

"I have a hunch we need to be heading back," Hugh said, standing and brushing off sand and once again putting that magnificent body part of his directly in front of my face. "Besides, I'm getting hungry again."

Did he have any idea at all what that was doing to me?

He offered a hand and helped me to my feet.

I brushed off the sand, then laughed. "I think I need water to really get the sand out of some parts."

I headed back out into the water and when it got deep enough, I started brushing water up into my crotch, working the sand loose and enjoying the feel of the cool water.

"Need some help?" he asked, moving up beside me and splashing water in the direction of my crotch.

I sure didn't have any plans on objecting, and the two of us made sure not one grain of sand was left where it didn't belong.

Then I turned to him. "I can see you need help as well."

I splashed water at the part that was now clearly larger than it had been when he pulled me out of the sleep coffin.

"I might," he said, smiling and pulling me into his arms.

His kiss sent electrical sparks through my system like I had never felt before.

I pushed against him and he pushed back, his wonderful patched,

142

android skin feeling like satin against me.

After what seemed like forever, yet was far, far too short, he broke the kiss and looked me in the eyes. "Wow."

"Yeah," I said. "I'm tingling all over."

"So am I," he said, smiling, the look of lust very, very clear on his face.

"Are you sure these things don't rust?" I asked after another long kiss.

"That much I'm sure of," he said, starting to kiss me again.

Then suddenly my mind clicked back in over the lust and the desire.

I pushed him away and grabbed his hand and started toward the ship as fast as I could go. My legs were actually tingling and it had nothing to do with the kiss or what body part of his that had been brushing against them.

"These don't rust *in natural conditions*," I said, the fear clouding my mind more than it had at any moment before. This was alien water and alien air and this water could be very, very corrosive to android skin and parts. We had no way of knowing.

"Oh, shit," he said, clearly understanding what I was thinking. Then, as easily as picking up a bag of snacks, he had me out of the water and into his arms and was almost running in the shallow water toward the ship.

"I can run on my own," I said, the panic filling my voice even though I tried to act strong.

"No chance," he said. "I don't want those parts of yours rusting. I have plans."

I actually laughed. How could he make me do that?

In what seemed like only a moment, he was helping me through the damaged front of the ship and we were rushing back through the ship toward the crew quarters and the fresh-water showers that were still well above the lake water.

After a short time it became clear that we had gotten out in time.

We were fine. No real damage to our android bodies.

But we decided to make sure, and that second inspection took lots of soap and very, very close personal inspection of each other.

Very close.

Careful, careful inspection, right up to the moment the rescue ship arrived.

LONG DEAD NEW LOVE

A Buckey the Space Pirate Story

Sometimes you must go back to find the future.

Buckey the Space Pirate travels back in time with his friend Fred, the talking oak tree, to learn why Fred refuses to recite his new limerick, the last limerick in Fred's first poetry book.

Over a hundred years in the past, in a forest of oak trees, Buckey finds more than just the reason for the rhyme.

One

WHEN MY BEST friend is a talking oak tree named Fred who likes limericks, I suppose I shouldn't be surprised at anything that happens. I just never expected to meet the woman of my dreams, the woman I hope to marry, through Fred.

But there was only one major problem with this woman of my dreams: She has been dead for over a hundred years.

It made a relationship and a marriage just a little difficult.

Not impossible, just difficult.

It started because I needed help on a history paper due in three days and was stuck cold on what to write about. Fred could remember every detail from all his oak-tree ancestors over centuries and centuries.

And oak trees could and did grow just about everywhere on the planet, so it sort of made sense to ask him for help with history.

But it still felt like a last resort as I headed for my mother's house where Fred was planted in a nice suburb of Portland, Oregon. I should have been able to come up with something myself and research it like a normal student instead of having to ask a talking oak tree. But I just couldn't think of anything to write about.

I grabbed a cookie from my mother's kitchen counter. Peanut butter, my favorite. She was upstairs watching her afternoon soaps and wouldn't see me go out back to talk to Fred.

Luckily, the afternoon May rains had stopped. It was going to be a sticky afternoon by the time the day was done, but at least in Portland, the summer heat hadn't kicked in yet.

Actually, asking Fred for help should have been my first resort, but over the last year Fred had become even more focused on limericks of all sorts and kept asking me to write them down and at some point publish them for him.

He said he wanted to be the first oak tree in history to ever write a book.

Since he was the first talking oak tree in history, being the first one to write a book wouldn't be much of a stretch. But getting his help with my history paper was going to mean some trade-offs, of that I was sure.

I slid open the patio door and stepped through, letting the damp air smother me. I had on a Star Trek tee-shirt, Levis, and my old tennis shoes that would be soaked by the grass in the back yard before I even got out to the twenty-foot-tall oak tree.

I had only planted Fred in my mother's back yard four years ago, as a seed. He should never have been this tall, but he told me because of special skills and the great soil, he could grow far faster than he normally would have. I was kind of glad he got so big so fast. It saved me looking like a fool sitting in a lawn chair trying to get shade from a sapling.

And besides, Fred hated to be called a sapling. He hated it so much he didn't even make up limericks using the word. For Fred, that was some hate.

"Well, if it isn't Buckey the Space Pirate," Fred said as I headed out toward him, as normal his deep voice sort of coming from everywhere in the air around me.

The first time we had met, I had had on my Buckey the Space

Pirate costume, plumed wide hat, dark tights, black cape, and long sword. I wore the costume regularly still to science fiction conventions and Halloween parties.

Fred never called me anything else and I honestly didn't mind. He had been a huge old oak tree down in the park, about to be cut down. He made up a rude limerick about my girlfriend's private parts as I tried to get lucky, which had the result of me getting far from anything lucky or her body parts. In fact, after that night she wouldn't talk to me again since she thought I was the one who had made the crude joke about her private areas.

It hadn't been me. It had been Fred, the oak tree we were under at the time.

I didn't believe it either at first. In fact, I thought it was a joke. But he convinced me to doctor one of his acorns and plant it and I did and the next day he had been cut down to make way for a new road.

I planted the acorn in my mother's backyard and it sprouted and by the middle of the next summer, Fred was back and talking and spouting limericks once again.

It was kind of sad that a talking oak tree was my best friend. Third year of college, no girlfriends, no real close other friends. I was a typical nerd, only I talked to a tree.

Luckily the tree talked back, or I would have been in big trouble.

"Hey, Fred," I said, pulling up the lawn chair and knocking the last drops of rain off it before sitting down just under his newly sprouted leaves. I had my chair turned so that if Mom looked out, she wouldn't see me talking. She didn't know about Fred. She just thought I used her backyard to study.

I had always been a weird kid, so this behavior didn't seem odd to her at all. Luckily Dad wasn't alive. He would have been asking a lot of questions.

"So what do I owe this unexpected surprise?" Fred asked, not starting into a limerick as I had expected him to do.

"History paper," I said. "I don't even have a topic yet."

"The learning of history is a noble enterprise for any human," Fred said, his voice booming like he was a college professor trying to wake up a sleeping student in the back row of a large classroom theater.

"You feeling all right today?" I asked, glancing up at the fresh green of the leaves over me. Everything looked healthy enough.

"I am in the top of spirits," Fred said. "Spring rain, fresh sunshine, a wonderful summer of growth ahead of me. Add in your fine company, what is not to enjoy?"

Suddenly it dawned on me why he was so happy. "You finished the last limerick, didn't you?"

"I most certainly did," he said, his voice sounding so full of pride, it was lucky his bark didn't burst from his trunk from the pressure.

"Are you going to share it with me?" I said, dreading the coming recital.

"No," he said.

I damn near fell off my lawn chair. The day Fred didn't force limericks on me was a day I really should be worried about his health.

"No?"

"No," he repeated. "Not until you see the moment in history and the person from which I took inspiration for the final limerick. Only then will you understand."

"Can I write about that period of history?"

"You most certainly may," Fred said. "It is only just over one hundred years in the past, a short hop."

I stood and moved over to touch the rough bark of the oak tree.

Fred had the ability to take me back to any point in time along what he called "his family tree." His family tree, as far as I could tell, included every oak tree on the planet.

At first I wasn't sure if he actually physically took me or not, but once he had been worried about my safety while we were in another time, so that led me to believe I actually vanished from the present and traveled somehow to the past.

He eventually told me I did.

I glanced around at Mom's house. No sign of her watching.

"Ready," I said, holding onto the trunk of the oak tree tightly. Sometimes on the other end I found myself high in the air.

A moment later I was leaning in darkness in a light rain against the trunk of a huge oak tree. Going from the bright light of a May afternoon to darkness was going to take some time for my eyes to adjust.

Plus it was cold here and the light rain felt like it might turn to snow at any moment. My Star Trek tee-shirt just wasn't suited for this kind of weather.

"Fred?"

"I am here," he said.

I glanced around. It was clear I was near a log cabin that sat nestled in a grove of oak trees. I could hear what sounded like a small river nearby and nothing else. Flickering yellow light came from the open window and a wonderful smell of bread baking.

"What time is it?" I asked. "And where are we?"

"It's only a little after five in the morning on October 21st," Fred said. "We are on the edge of the town called Boise in the new state of Idaho. The year is 1871. Take a look in the window."

"How can I do that?" I asked, staring at the open window with the light beyond. I honestly wasn't sure I wanted to go peeking in windows on someone dead more than a hundred years. There seemed to be something doubly perverted about doing that.

"You can go anywhere under the leaves of this tree or over the roots of the tree or any oak tree in this grove," Fred said. "And the roots of this tree alone extend a long distance under the house to the latrine on the other side. A wonderful source of nourishment."

"Too much information," I said, shaking my head at the idea that Fred ate from latrines. Of course he did. He was an oak tree. I just didn't have to think about it.

"Go take a look," Fred said. "See the reason, the very inspiration for the last limerick in my first book."

"First book?" I asked.

"Of course," he said.

All I could do was moan.

I glanced at the window in the side of the cabin. The drapes on the inside were pulled aside and the rough windowpane of glass was pushed open. Every so often I could see a shadow of someone moving inside.

And the wonderful smell of baking bread just kept getting stronger and stronger. I really should have grabbed more to eat before seeing Fred than just a cookie. The smell was making me hungry.

"What happens if I happen to get beyond the branches or roots of the tree?" I asked.

"You will simply return to the backyard in your current time," Fred said, clearly starting to get annoyed.

An annoyed oak tree was not something I wanted to experience, so I stepped away from the trunk of the large tree and hesitantly moved toward the window.

It was darned cold out and I was already starting to shiver as I crouched near the window.

"You know this is illegal in all fifty states," I said. "And more than likely in most countries as well. I would hate to be arrested in 1871 for being a pervert."

"You will not startle her and there is no need to hide," Fred said. "I told her you were coming."

I stopped, stood up straight, and looked back at the large old oak tree sitting beside the log cabin. "You talked to her? I thought you couldn't talk until you were born in Portland."

"Have you noticed when and where you are at and that you are talking to me right now?" Fred asked, going into the mode where he treated me like I was as dumb as a first grader. I hated that mode.

He went on. "When I gained the ability to speak to humans, I also gained the ability to speak to humans at any point in time along my roots. I have struck up a number of friendships over the centuries."

"Oh," was all I could say. I actually felt a little disappointed because for some reason I thought I was the only one who talked with Fred.

I turned and moved toward the open window on the cabin. The wonderful fresh bread smell just kept getting stronger and stronger. And I could sense a little bit of frying bacon smell as well.

I moved up to the window sill that hit me just above my belt as Fred said, "Mary, we are here."

"Wonderful," a woman said. She turned from the stove to face me across the kitchen area of the cabin.

I suddenly just couldn't breathe and I am sure my mouth was doing the old guppy move of opening and closing.

The woman in the cabin was the most beautiful woman I had ever seen. She had bright red hair pulled back into a long ponytail, a bright smile that seemed to fill her face, and huge brown eyes. She wiped her hands off on a white towel over her shoulder as she started toward me.

She had on a thin plaid cotton dress in a white and red pattern that framed a thin, but wonderful body. The dress was protected by a long, white apron like you might see in a cooking magazine.

She seemed to be my age of around twenty-three, but that was a guess. She might be younger.

"Mary Elizabeth Smith," Fred said, his booming voice filling the area around the cabin. "I would like you to meet Buckey the Space Pirate."

She reached out her hand and I took it through the window, never letting my gaze drop from those deep brown eyes.

"Wonderful to meet any friend of Fred's," she said, her voice pulling me in even more.

"The pleasure is all mine," I somehow managed to say, even though my entire focus was on the wonderful feel of her hand and those huge brown eyes.

"Can you come in and share breakfast with me?" she asked, still not letting go of my hand.

I never wanted her to let go, to be honest.

Finally I said to the air, "Fred, is that possible?"

"Of course it is," he said. "But you will need to climb in the window or go in the back door. There are no roots under, or branches over, the cabin front door."

I smiled at her and indicated I would just climb in the window. "Do you mind?"

She laughed and let go of my hand and stepped back. "You may crawl in my window any time you would like."

At that moment I thought my heart would beat out of my chest. Somehow, with Fred giving advice, I managed to climb in the window without falling on my face. Pure luck since I could barely keep my eyes off her and didn't really pay a lot of attention to what I was doing.

Two

Over the next two hours we had a wonderful breakfast of fresh-baked bread, bacon and eggs, and tea. I helped her with the dishes and we laughed a lot.

The conversation with her and Fred was just wonderful, even with Fred sometimes becoming like a college professor and going into a lecture on some topic or another.

During that breakfast and conversation I completely fell in love, especially when I learned she had moved from Kansas to Boise with her brother who had gotten married a year ago and she had lived alone ever since.

"What do you do for money?" I asked and she told me about how her parents, when they died, had left her and her brother a sizable inheritance.

Finally, I realized that hours had passed in the wonderful conversation.

"Fred, is there a problem with me being gone? Is the same amount of time passing in 2011?"

I did have an assignment to get finished and classes to attend. I didn't want to, but I needed to.

"Time is always passing," he said. "But I can return you within a few seconds of when we left if that is what concerns you," he said.

"That would be helpful," I said.

"Wonderful," Mary said, clapping her hands together. "Then you can spend as much time as you would like with me here."

Then she realized what she had said and blushed. "If you want, of course."

"I can think of nothing I would want more," I said. "Fred, is that possible?"

"I see nothing at all impossible about it," he said. "I will leave you two alone. Please call me when you are ready to return."

"Thank you, Fred," I said.

There was no response. He was gone.

"He is a wonderful friend, isn't he?" I asked and reached across the wood table and gently squeezed Mary's hand.

"He is at that," she said as she put her other hand on mine and looked into my eyes.

I knew right at that moment that I had found a woman of my dreams, even though she had been dead for a long time before I was born.

After a long moment of silence, with only the sounds of the river running from the window, we went back to talking and laughing and later I helped her cook us both a wonderful dinner of venison and potatoes.

She let me wear a sweater she had knitted for her brother and promised to knit me one just like it. It had to be the softest thing I had ever put on.

And she forced me at one point to try to explain Star Trek, which got many laughs from her.

That night I slept on the couch, but for a time she sat with me in front of the crackling fire and we kissed and I never wanted to stop.

Finally she pushed me gently away and said, "We have all the time in the world."

"Thanks to our friend Fred," I said.

Three

The next morning she cooked us both a wonderful breakfast and then I suggested that I needed to go home to get some clothes and run a few errands.

She made me promise to come back quickly and I did.

We also have one thing we need to do for our friend," I said as we finished up drying the morning dishes.

She smiled. "Hear his limerick?"

"You got it in one," I said, surprised Fred had recited limericks to a woman of her caliber in 1871.

"Fred, please come back."

A moment later he said, "I am here."

I didn't want to ask how he did that. I had a hunch that Fred and I would be having a lot of conversations about time travel in the near future.

"I need to return to my time for some errands and such. But before I go, we were both hoping that you'd give us a recital of the last limerick in your first book. The limerick that brought us together."

"It would be an honor," Fred said.

I could tell he was clearly touched that we had remembered and he didn't have to force his limerick on us.

"You are going to produce Fred's book for him?" Mary asked, smiling.

"I am," I said. "But I am surprised you have heard some of his limericks?"

"I have been appropriate," Fred said, "in my telling and choice of subject matter."

"I find them wonderful and funny and unique," she said.

"They are unique," I said. "Now Fred, would you please honor us?"

"I would be glad to," Fred said.

Then there was a pause and if an oak tree could clear his throat, or even had a throat, I was sure Fred would have cleared it.

"There was a woman named Mary
Who found my voice to be scary.
But I told her of Buckey
And how she'd be lucky
To find a pirate to marry."

For a moment the silence in the room seemed to grow and then Mary smiled at me and raised her right eyebrow and I smiled back and then we both started applauding and cheering while smiling at each other.

Yesterday the idea of marrying anyone would have scared me to death. Now, even though Mary died many years before I was born, the idea of marrying her just made me smile.

It would take some figuring on how to be together, but I was sure we could do it with Fred's help.

"Thank you. Thank you," Fred said.

If an oak tree could bow, Fred would be bowing.

"I would be honored to put your book together," I said.

"Wonderful," Fred said.

"I might be able to actually give you a short introduction as well," I said.

"It would have to be in limerick form," Fred said.

I smiled at Mary. "Oh, it would be."

Then I said, "How about this?"

> "There was a pirate named Buckey
> Who one day was very lucky
> To travel in time
> To listen to a rhyme
> From Fred, a friend, an oak tree."

Mary smiled, stood and came over and gave me a long kiss that I did not want to break.

"That was wonderful," she said, finally, pulling away, but still holding me.

"It will do," Fred said.

"That's the nicest thing you have ever said about my writing," I said to Fred, winking at Mary.

"Don't push it," Fred said.

But I could tell the oak tree was as happy as I was.

SHOPPING CART LOVER

They met on a Tuesday, a hot Tuesday in Southern California, and filled up an entire shopping cart with groceries and conversation and dreams.

Sometimes not getting a shopping cart can lead to a lot more than just carrying your food to the checkout counter under your arm.

A grocery store love story.

I CALLED her my "Shopping Cart Lover."

It was Tuesday.

A hot Tuesday.

Middle of June.

The parking lot to my local Safeway Grocery Store was full and I should have realized there would be a problem right there and just went back to my small apartment overlooking Interstate Five, one of the best apartments in all of Southern California. It's a nice place, one bedroom, and the rumble of trucks and cars going by reminds me of the ocean.

I love the ocean, how the waves crash on the beach, the wind always blows, the smell of brine and fish fills the thick air. I didn't often make it to the ocean due to my living circumstances and no job and not having a car, but living near the freeway reminded me of the ocean all the time and I liked that.

My ex-wife used to say I could make a silk shirt out of an old cotton rag and a vivid imagination.

I would always say, "At least I have a silk shirt."

If she hadn't left me for that manager of the hardware store last year, I wouldn't have had a chance to meet my Shopping Cart Lover.

Lucky for me my wife left.

I only go to my local Safeway grocery store once a month, when my card is refilled from the State of California. I do maintenance around the apartment complex to pay my rent and I save most of unemployment except for a few dollars to buy my Pabst Blue Ribbon beer.

Today California refilled my food allowance on my card, so I could stock up on food that would last for the month. And maybe by next month the application I had put in three months ago at the local bike shop would work out and I would get hired. The store owner liked me and said I did good work, but with the economy he just couldn't hire me yet.

I had told him I would wait.

I had always wanted to work on bikes, the peddle kind, not the motor kind, ever since I was a kid, maybe even open my own bike shop. But out of high school I had ended up working construction instead and then had gotten married and the bike shop idea sort of went the way of those old cotton rags my ex-wife used to always talk about.

So when she left me and I found my nifty apartment overlooking Interstate Five, I decided that I would work for a bike shop now and just wait until an opening came around or I had my own shop.

I saved as much as I could so that if I got the chance I would start my own bike shop. But until then I fixed a few of the neighbor's bikes for their kids and tried to watch the dumpsters for old bikes and bike parts. My apartment was pretty full of bike parts now, so I had lots to work on and fix up for the time I had enough for my own shop. It kept me busy at night, listening to the ocean of Interstate Five and fixing bikes.

Life was pretty good.

The bike I rode to my local Safeway grocery store I had put together with parts of about seven others. I had built a sidecar on it made out of parts and baskets from kid's bikes to carry my groceries and more bike parts when I found them.

It really was amazing what a guy could find in dumpsters.

I locked up my bike in the bike rack near the front door of the Safeway grocery store and went inside.

It was much cooler inside, which instantly felt good and put me in a good mood for my afternoon of shopping. It was always better to be in a good mood when shopping. I knew it never did much good to buy food angry. The food just never tasted the same.

My ex-wife thought that attitude was weird, but I tended to always get good food when I shopped happy.

Inside, by the produce section, was a big empty room where hundreds of grocery carts were normally stored in rows jammed into each other. The shopping carts were always hard to get apart like they resented being wheeled once more around the store they knew so well.

There were no grocery carts in that large area.

None.

It was cool in that grocery cart room, much cooler than the hot afternoon outside, but still there were no grocery carts.

It seemed that when California filled everyone's cards with money for food, the store got real busy.

I went back out into the parking lot and the heat to find a used cart there, but two kids with Safeway uniforms were already doing that and by the time I watched them push the rows of carts into the store, the hordes of shoppers waiting for a cart had grabbed them all.

I was left standing next to the produce section near the main door without a cart, waiting.

It was cool there, so I didn't mind. A cart would come to me soon enough.

A woman with brown hair, glasses, and a long nose stood beside me, also waiting.

She didn't look annoyed at all, which my ex-wife would have been. This woman had this calmness around her that attracted me to her and I looked at her even harder without actually looking at her and being rude and pervert-like.

She wore an old, blue-cotton tee-shirt with a light-blue cloth jacket covering it, not because it was cold, but because the tee-shirt was torn slightly from what I could tell. The jacket and shirt together still looked nice.

She had on faded jeans and well-worn leather sandals that showed toes with blue-painted toenails. She clearly was no better off than I was, except more than likely I had a nicer apartment with my ocean sounds of Interstate Five.

Her brown hair was long and pulled back and tied. Her skin looked well-washed.

A kid with greasy hair and a nose ring who worked for the store came in with one cart and pushed it toward us.

I laughed and turned to her. "Want to share?"

"That's all right," she said, her voice soft and wonderful. "You go ahead. I'm in no hurry."

"Neither am I," I said, smiling at her.

People used to say back ten years ago in high school that I had a good smile, a smile that made people feel good, so I gave her my good smile.

For the first time she actually looked at me over the shopping cart waiting to be claimed by one of us.

I wasn't a handsome man, but I had showered. I also had my long brown hair combed back and tied out of my face. And I was thin. Besides that, running around looking in dumpsters for bike parts kept me tanned.

My ex-wife said that my staying thin as I got near thirty was one of the best things I had done for myself. I don't think I gave it much thought. I just didn't eat much and now couldn't afford to drink more than two Pabst Blue Ribbons a night if I wanted the Pabst to last the month and still save money for my bike shop.

Besides, more than two and I screwed up the bike part I was working on every time. Two was my limit.

I guess that kept me thin.

"You go ahead and take it," she said, smiling. "But thanks."

I smiled back and nodded, but didn't touch the cart.

"To be honest," I said, "I thought it would be fun to share a shopping cart again. I haven't done that since my wife left last year."

"It's been two years for me," she said, smiling. "Although for the last year he didn't shop with me much."

"Come to think of it, I did all of the shopping the last year of my marriage," I said. "So I guess it's been longer than two years for me as well."

"Who knew a person could miss joint shopping," she said, smiling, a sort of wistful look in her eyes.

I really liked her smile even though she had one chipped tooth on the right side. It gave her character and made her even more unique.

"You sure you don't want to give it a try again?"

She hesitated, looking at the door to see if another cart would roll to her rescue, but there wasn't one in sight that wasn't firmly attached to another shopper's hand.

"You have a lot of things to buy?" she asked.

"Just basics," I said. "They don't give me a lot of money on my card every month."

At that she smiled even wider. "I don't get much either," she said. "It would feel nice to actually have a full shopping cart for a change."

"If we combine forces, we might just do that," I said, again giving her my best smile.

"You are very nice," she said, nodding. "Let's do it."

"We'll trade off pushing," I said. "You first."

I bowed like I had seen some movie star do in a movie once and she laughed and took the position behind the cart.

At that point I suppose I should have asked her name, but I just liked the idea of not knowing her name and she clearly didn't want to know mine either.

It was a great adventure.

An adventure in the aisles of the Safeway grocery store.

Who knew going to the Safeway grocery store on a hot Tuesday would be an adventure.

It is a wonderful world.

She picked up a bag of oranges.

I picked up a bag of potatoes.

Then she picked up some lettuce and bagged it and weighed it.

"How do you keep that fresh for a month?" I asked.

"I don't," she said. "I come back and buy more oranges and lettuce in two weeks. I use part of my unemployment for that."

"Where did you work?" I asked.

"Construction firm office," she said. "Bookkeeping."

"Construction as well," I said. "The driving nails department."

Suddenly, besides a shopping cart, we had something else in common. That felt good.

She kept track of what she was spending on a small calculator. I had one of those tiny spiral notebooks and an old pencil and I marked down each dollar.

"I hate to get to the register and not have enough on my card," I said, indicating the notebook in my hand.

"Yeah, I did that once," she said. "Had to leave stuff I really wanted."

Now we had three things in common. I had more in common with my shopping cart lover than I did with my ex-wife.

We kept going, me talking about how I loved to work on bikes, the peddle kind, not the motor kind, and she talking about how she was slowly trying to set up her own accounting firm.

"When I get my bike shop open, I'll hire your company to do my books," I said.

She beamed at that. "Thanks."

Finally we both had run out of money on our cards and our shopping cart was almost full.

Wonderfully full.

I had been pushing it the last few aisles, so I said, "You want to push it the last distance to the check-out line?"

"I would love to," she said. "Thanks."

She pushed it like it was the most important job on the planet and I followed along proud of the moment.

In line she sorted out her groceries first, then put that rubber thing between our stuff, which felt odd to be honest. We had shared so much in the last hour.

Now we were divided.

A simple strip of hard rubber indicated the wonderful adventure was almost over.

The clerk checked her out and she stayed under her card limit by two dollars.

A bagger with good hair and no nose ring at the end of the counter had found another cart and was putting her groceries in that.

Now we were very separated, in two carts.

And we had stopped talking.

When she was all done and had her receipt in her pocket, she turned to me. "Thank you for an enjoyable day."

I could tell she was nervous and didn't know what to say. We had shared a great deal in the last hour.

"It was my pleasure," I said. "How about next month on payment day we meet right here again at two o'clock and share a cart again."

Her smile returned, chipped tooth and all. "I would love that."

"So would I," I said, giving her my best smile again as the clerk worked at checking out my groceries.

"Until next month then," she said.

"Until then," I said.

She turned with a smile and pushed her own cart out of the door of the Safeway grocery store.

I watched her walk away like watching the end of a good movie. It felt good to have happened, but sad that it was over.

Usually I didn't feel conflicted, but for the moment I did.

I smiled at the clerk who just shook her head and finished my groceries and the bagger put them in the now only half-full cart.

My groceries looked small and sort of sad sitting in that cart all alone. It seems my food had shared the same experience I had. My food would taste great.

"Next month," I said to my groceries as the clerk handed me my receipt and I headed out of the store toward my bike.

I had a date with a wonderful woman in one month.

A date with my shopping cart lover.

I smiled and almost started to whistle.

Between my shopping cart lover, fixing bikes, and listening to the ocean sounds of Interstate Five, life just couldn't get much better.

THE ATLANTIS FIFTY

A Poker Boy Story

The desire to party often causes all sorts of problems. But Poker Boy never expected one of those problems to be getting frozen in time.

But being frozen inside a time bubble seems to be the least of the problems. They don't play poker in Atlantis.

First published in Fiction River: Universe Between.

One

I GOT STUCK in an instant of time on Saturday afternoon at 12:37 and seven seconds, exactly.

Actually, I woke up stuck.

I knew something was very wrong the instant I woke up. Not only was my warning voice telling me something was wrong, but the sounds were gone from the Las Vegas Strip that normally filled the background of Patty's apartment like a faint sound of the ocean when you stay near the beach.

I could hear nothing.

Either I had gone deaf while sleeping, or something else was going on.

I tapped the bed stand with my alarm clock and heard the sound of my knuckle on the fine oak just fine.

Nope. Not deaf.

Patty wasn't in bed beside me, but I figured she hadn't been up long. We had both been up until after four in the morning last night, her working until three at the MGM Grand and me playing in a tournament in the poker room there.

And then we had enjoyed a wonderful half hour before sleeping.

That memory made me smile.

I strained to hear anything, at that point not thinking I was between moments in time. That usually takes me some focus to do and focus while I am sleeping is not one of my superpowers.

No sound.

My warning sense that something was very wrong was dinging in the back of my head like an annoying microwave timer that wouldn't shut off.

I rolled out of the big bed, shoving the thick tan comforter aside, and padded to the window across the soft brown carpet in my boxer shorts.

I pulled the blinds aside slightly and the night shade and after my eyes adjusted to the bright light, I knew instantly what the problem was.

There over Las Vegas, at about two thousand feet, was an airliner turning to make a final approach into the airport. Only it wasn't moving. It was just stuck there, as if someone had glued a decal to a phony blue-sky ceiling in a bedroom.

Now, don't get me wrong. I love my ability to step into a moment of time, out of the normal time flow. It's my second favorite superpower right behind being able to teleport. But unless I do the stepping between moments purposefully, or have another superhero or god put me in a time bubble, I didn't much like being out of whack with the real ticking of time.

I took a deep breath and imagined myself back in the normal flow of time. That's what I always did to drop a time bubble that I made.

Nothing.

Intense silence.

Not even the deep breath helped.

No wonder my alarm dinger was going off in the back of my head. Something was very wrong.

I headed for the bathroom. Patty Ledgerwood, aka Front Desk girl and my girlfriend, was in the shower, her head thrown back as water ran down her long brown hair.

Only the water wasn't actually running, more like glistening in sparkling droplets all over her as if someone had taken a still picture of her.

I can say without any chance of argument that she had a perfect body. And every detail, from her smooth skin to her deep brown eyes fit together.

Now I was no different than any other young man growing up. What stood frozen in front of me was any teenage boy's fantasy. A beautiful woman with a perfect body, naked in a shower, caught in a moment of sheer beauty, every perfect detail magnified by the wetness.

Even as a superhero, I wasn't immune to that, so for an instant after I opened the shower door, I stopped and stared.

Sometimes even emergencies can take a back seat to an opportunity of a lifetime.

So I stood there for a moment, just a moment, staring. Honest, it was only a moment.

And all I could do was ask myself how I had gotten so lucky as to have that woman in my life?

Finally I eased forward, feeling almost guilty, and touched her shoulder, bringing her into the time bubble with me.

The water around her ran off, but no more water came out of the faucet.

"Up for a rematch from last night?" she asked, turning to face me and giving me that smile that often made me forget everything around me.

And her being nude and wet like that was just damn near impossible for me to resist.

"In a little bit," I said, leaning forward and kissing her. "We have a problem I can't seem to get a handle on."

Her expression turned serious, and she turned to shut off the water. Then she realized it was no longer running, even though the faucet was turned on.

"Are we between moments in time?" she asked, looking at me.

Wow, another reason I loved this woman so much. She was scary smart. I nodded.

"How come?" she asked, quickly stepping past me and wrapping a blue bath towel around that fantastic body, making me slightly sad I had said anything.

"I woke up out of time," I said.

Back before I was a superhero, those were words I never would have imagined saying unless I was late for an appointment, or the start of a poker tournament.

"Can you clear us?"

I shook my head. "I don't think I did this one."

"Let's get some clothes on and call Stan," she said. "See if he has any idea what's happened."

"That's why I came to get you out of the shower," I said.

She laughed as she worked to dry off. "Sure it wasn't just to stare?"

"Well," I said as I headed back into the bedroom, "I did a little of that as well."

"Pervert," she shouted after me.

"Guilty and loving it," I shouted back.

I could hear her laugh as I worked to get dressed.

Two

Patty put on her comfortable clothes, which were jeans and a white blouse. She pulled her hair back and didn't bother with any make-up. She looked fantastic and I told her so.

I also had on jeans, but wore a tee-shirt under my black leather jacket and fedora-like hat that served as my Poker Boy uniform. The hat and coat somehow helped me focus energy. I didn't need them inside the apartment, but in emergency situations like this, I felt better having them on.

When we were both completely dressed and had breakfast bars half eaten, we moved into the center of Patty's living room. I had tried a couple of times to drop back into the normal flow, without success.

And I had Patty stand across the room from me and I made myself concentrate on releasing her.

Nothing.

Around us the tan furniture and tan rug seemed completely normal. Everything seemed normal except the clock on the wall near the kitchen door was stopped.

So I was stuck between instants of time, and from what I could tell,

I had brought Patty into the mess as well. But if I hadn't, she would have been really, really mad at me. I just never considered not including her these days in anything I did. We were so much stronger together than we were on our own.

"Stan, a little help?" I said at the ceiling. For some reason, every time I called out to my boss, the God of Poker, I shouted upwards. I was fairly certain he could hear me if I just said his name softly, but the old habit died hard.

Patty and I both stood there in her living room, waiting. Usually he appeared almost instantly, but after about five seconds I looked at Patty and shook my head.

"Laverne?" I shouted at the ceiling, hoping that Lady Luck herself would hear me.

Nothing.

We had no access to my team this time around.

"Let me see if I can jump us to my office and get out of this," I said.

Instantly I had alarm bells go off in the back of my head and Patty touched my arm and shook her head. "That feels wrong."

"I agree," I said, pushing back the alarm bells.

My little voice was telling me the problem was here and we needed to stay here and solve this. But it was really, really odd that my calling Stan or Laverne couldn't get out of this. They never had had troubles with coming into time bubbles before.

I went over to the window in the living room and looked at the frozen city below. The cars on The Strip were frozen in place, a couple of birds were stopped in midair a few floors below, and flags on the top of a building across the street hung at odd angles, clearly blown by a wind, but yet not moving.

I looked back at Patty who stood there staring at me.

"Do you have any idea how many gods or superheroes have the power to take a person between moments of time?" I asked, moving back over toward her.

She shook her head slowly as she thought, her long brown hair flopping around on her back as she did. "It's not many, I know that. And you are the only superhero that I know that has that power."

I wasn't sure what to think of that, but at the moment I didn't let myself dwell on it.

"Seems we have some spare time on our hands," I said, smiling at the worried look on her face and in her wonderful dark-brown eyes. "We might as well enjoy it."

The worried look turned to puzzlement.

I shrugged.

"We're trapped in a moment in time," I said. "Someone did this. It's either a wide-spread thing or a focused event and I'm betting on focused around the person who did it, since it takes some real power to hold a time bubble for very long that's very large. And to include us, it has to be pretty large, so I don't expect this to last that long."

She nodded. "Good point. Any way to know how far this bubble extends?"

I stopped and thought about that for a moment. In the past, when I held a time bubble, as I called them, keeping myself and others out of the flow of regular time, there was a limit. I once had a dog inside a time bubble and it couldn't get out, the edge of the bubble held it until I released the bubble.

I remember thinking that it would be a good and easy trap for anything wild, except that so far I hadn't learned how to project a bubble I wasn't inside of. And being trapped inside a time bubble with something wild hadn't really appealed to me, so I had tossed that idea out.

"I have a question," I said. "Was I supposed to be part of this bubble or just an accident?"

"If you are included only by accident, by bringing me in as well must be draining more energy," Patty said.

"Of whoever is doing this," I said.

"Let's go exploring and see if we can find the edge," I said, heading for the front door to her apartment.

Patty's apartment was on the seventeenth floor. Outside the corridor looked like a plush hotel hallway, with lamps scattered along the hallway and each door recessed into its own entryway.

The carpet was light blue and the walls painted off-white with hotel-like art that depicted nothing hung on the walls. Four elevators were near the center of the building.

No one was in the hall.

"What's going to happen when we find the edge of the bubble?" Patty asked.

"My gut sense is that it will be like walking into a wall," I said. "So walk slow and protect your face."

"Good to know," she said, laughing and shaking her head.

We slowly walked the entire length of the hallway with arms extended in front of us. We must have looked pretty silly, almost walking like movie zombies.

No edge to be found.

"That's an impressive-sized bubble," I said when we reached the other end of the hallway and stopped.

There were two floors above hers and we headed for the stairs to the left and slowly worked our way upward.

We made it all the way to the top floor without finding the edge to the time bubble.

"This is someone very powerful," I said to Patty as we stood outside the stairway door in the upper hallway, the blue carpet making me feel more like standing on water than a floor. Here there were only four doors to the four expensive penthouses that filled this floor. I had no idea who lived on this floor, but my gut sense it was someone powerful and very rich in the local area.

The fear I was starting to feel suddenly twisted my stomach around the breakfast bar. I pushed it down and took a slow breath, getting my nerves under control.

"This might be generated mechanically," Patty said.

I looked around at the building and walls and windows and the lights on the walls. Damn she was smart and had the ability to see things I just flat missed.

"I think you might be right," I said. "This kind of field could be generated or amplified through the electrical system. So it would cover the entire building like a skin. A mechanical field might block calling out to Stan or Laverne because natural fields have never blocked me calling them before."

"Good thing we didn't try jumping out of here," she said.

"We'd have smashed right into the bubble wall," I said, glad our warning senses had stopped us. "That might have been painful or worse."

She nodded. "We still don't know why anyone would do this."

"I'm getting the sense that whoever did this is not after us," I said. "My warning bells are not going off, except when I suggested we jump to the office."

"Neither are mine," Patty said. "I bet that whoever did this didn't realize you were here and that the time field wouldn't get to you."

"I wonder why it didn't," I said.

"We'll ask Stan about that later," Patty said, smiling at what must have been my puzzled look. "Now we need to figure out who is doing this and why."

However, I had no idea how to find out that simple thing.

At that moment, the stairwell door at the other end of the hall rattled and stated to open.

"Freeze," I whispered to Patty and we both struck a pose we could hold that made us look like we were just two people frozen in time standing in the hallway.

It looked like we were going to find out who was doing this sooner, rather than later.

Three

"There you are," Stan, the God of Poker, said as he came through the stairwell door and into the hall.

I released the breath I think I had been holding and relaxed.

Stan had on his normal button-down sweater and tan slacks. He could blend in anywhere and right now he seemed to almost blend in with the hallway as well, even though his colors seemed to clash with the blue carpet. It wouldn't surprise me if I looked away and looked back, he would be wearing blue slacks.

Right behind him was Screamer, dressed in jeans and a dress shirt with the sleeves rolled up. Screamer was a superhero who worked for the police. He got his name because he could put images in criminal's minds that made them scream in terror.

He was my height at about six foot and had intense dark eyes that seemed to see through things.

Through the door behind Screamer came Ben, a god in the library area and the oldest of our team. He was panting from climbing the stairs.

I had no idea how old Ben really was, but his old-fashioned suits and wrinkled face and hands made him look like a grandfather from a classic movie.

I was very, very glad to see them.

"Did you hear my call?" I asked as Patty and I stepped toward them.

"I did," Stan said. "But I couldn't jump into the building, so I stopped time for me and Ben and Screamer and we managed to merge fields with this time field down in the lobby."

"Twenty floors. Long climb," Ben said, still panting.

"So ever seen anything like this before?" I asked Stan. "Ever have anyone do a time bubble this large?"

He shook his head. "And neither has Laverne. It basically covers this entire building like a skin."

"More than likely run through the electrical system," I said.

Stan looked at me for a moment, clearly thinking, then nodded. "Possible."

"But why?" Patty said.

"I've been wondering the same thing," Screamer said.

"As have I," Ben said, still panting slightly.

"Anyone in a personal time bubble," Patty said, "can walk around just fine without generating something this large to take an entire building out of time. You would get the same effect with just a personal bubble."

That very problem had been bothering me as well. Clearly, if Stan and the rest entered down on the main floor and came up, the bubble holding this building was in the walls and covered the entire building. Patty was right, there was no reason to do that.

None.

Unless…

"Maybe doing something like this," I said, sort of sweeping my arms around me in a grand fashion, "in the walls or electrical wiring of a building, is the only way for whoever did this to generate a time bubble field."

"Mechanical only," Ben said, nodding. "Not a god power. Possible."

"Seen anything like this before?" Patty asked just a fraction of a second before I could.

"Crystals," Ben said, nodding. "In the old Atlantis days."

It always freaked me out a little when someone I knew as a regular person here in Las Vegas started talking about Atlantis. Not the casino, the actual continent and civilization that had actually existed and then had been destroyed. And more often than not, that person had actually been alive during the time of Atlantis.

Stan nodded. "I sort of remember hearing something like that from Laverne once."

"Do you remember who was doing it back then?" I asked Ben, then realized how stupid my question was. His memory was amazing and he could remember every detail and information in every book he had ever read.

"The God of Electricity," Ben said. "Actually, the real experiments in time and electrical powers were done by her assistant."

"Oh, no," Stan said, shaking his head.

Screamer and Patty and I just stared at my boss until Screamer finally said, "You want to fill us in on the problem?"

Ben nodded and took over from Stan, who for the God of Poker, looked suddenly very upset.

"Far before Atlantis, a giant by the name of Arges was the God of Lightning. He was a fan of Zeus and gave him the power to fire electrical bolts, which is why Zeus became known after centuries as being able to use lightning as a weapon."

I so wanted to ask about so much of this, because as I had discovered in my short years of being a superhero, the gods of mythology had often existed, and some of them still did. I had never heard if Zeus was still around, and had never had the courage to ask, to be honest.

Ben went on, with me saying nothing.

"When the gods and the giants managed to banish the Titans to the city that lies under Las Vegas, Arges was injured in the battle and he stepped down and gave his duties over to his daughter, who was a god. He died from his injuries before Atlantis came into being."

"Who was his daughter?" I asked.

Ben looked at me very puzzled, then said, "I need to spend some time with you getting you up to speed on the history of the gods, don't I?"

"I've been saying that," I said. "At least to myself."

"When this is over," Ben said, giving me that grandfather look he sometimes gave me, "we'll make the time."

"Laverne is Arges's daughter," Stan said. "Back in Atlantis, as Laverne was taking over more and more duties, she gave the duty of electricity to the Goddess Horae, a good friend of hers who also had control over planting and seasons and things like that."

"And a young man, a superhero of sorts," Ben said, "began work for Horae as Atlantis boomed. Over the centuries there, he got himself in and out of many troubles with his experiments with electricity and using it in different forms of travel and controlling time."

"What's his name?" Patty asked, again right before I could.

Ben shrugged. "Nothing worth pronouncing right now. Last I heard, in Atlantis, he went by Nicky."

"Still a superhero?" Screamer asked.

Ben nodded. "Last time I heard, still officially working for Horae, when or if she can ever track him down. He used to throw some wild parties, which is what caused part of his problems."

"And he could do things like this time bubble over the building?" I asked Ben.

"More than likely he could."

I didn't like the sounds of that. "When was the last time anyone saw him?"

Ben glanced at Stan, who only shrugged. "Atlantis," Ben said, "about sixty years before it was destroyed."

Okay, that silenced our little group standing in the blue and white plush hallway inside a giant time bubble.

For some reason my friends thought a guy who hadn't been seen in more thousands of years than I wanted to think about had done this to a modern apartment building here in Las Vegas.

I managed to not laugh. "I think we need another suspect."

And that also sent the entire group back into silence.

Four

"There are no other suspects," Screamer said after a moment of silence in the hallway.

I just didn't think a guy who hadn't been seen since Atlantis was the logical choice, so I changed the point of focus.

"How about we do a search of the entire building," I said. "See if we can find anyone moving."

Stan and Ben both nodded, so I sent Ben and Screamer to one apartment, Stan to another, and Patty and I would handle a third on this floor. Then we would check the last one and work our way down.

However, the search ended just about as quickly as it started.

As we neared the four doors to the four penthouses near the elevators, modern jazz dance music blared out over the hallway, almost vibrating one of the doors. The music seemed to be right out of the 1940s big band era.

Patty looked at me with a puzzled look and all I could do was shrug.

"That form of music was very popular in Atlantis," Ben said softly.

I just shook my head for a moment. Great, just great. Maybe this Nicky guy was inside.

I had no idea what I was walking into, but with Stan at my side and Patty and Ben and Screamer close behind, I used one of my superpowers to unlock the door and slowly eased it open, letting the intense loud music smack me in the face. It sounded like an entire band was just around the corner in the main area of the penthouse apartment.

And then, over the intense music, I caught the sound of laughing and talking.

Lots of laughing and lots of talking. Actually more like shouting, since that was all anyone could do over that amount of noise.

I eased around a corner of the entryway so I could see the huge main room of the penthouse and then just stood there, my mouth open, staring at about fifty people dancing, all dressed in brightly-colored robes and togas and all barefoot on the plush white carpet. The expensive white furniture had been pushed back to the sides to form the large dance floor.

The main room of the big apartment was completely full of people.

Everyone was young and all clearly having a great time.

I felt like I had walked into a college frat party. I hated drunken kids' parties when in college, thought them stupid beyond words and never went to a one, mostly because I never joined a fraternity or any other group for that matter.

I didn't much care for the party I was staring at either.

There were so many colors jumping up and down and swirling around, I almost got dizzy trying to watch it.

Suddenly, one of the dancers on the edge of the mob spotted us and smiled and broke away from his partner, a blonde with far too much long hair that seemed to function as a second robe and only allowed glimpses of her smiling face.

The guy coming toward us had long brown hair that looked like it was cut by putting a bowl over his head. He had on a brown robe that seemed a cross between a bathrobe and a toga.

He was smiling a huge smile that lit up his face and the smile reached his eyes. Beads of sweat had formed on his forehead from the dancing and I noticed the apartment had started to heat up.

None of my alarms were going off about him, so he wasn't a threat. At least I didn't think my alarms had sounded. Even inside my own head, I wasn't certain I would have heard them in this noise.

The music still pounded at me like a hammer and I could tell it was everything Patty could do to not cover her ears.

As the kid got closer, he went straight at Ben and gave him a hug.

"Uncle Ben," the kid shouted over the noise. "What are you doing here?"

Finally Stan couldn't take it any longer. He took us out of time, instantly silencing the music. I almost staggered at the relief.

"Thank you," Patty sighed softly.

Screamer just shook his head as if trying to clear it.

I didn't know it was possible to have a time bubble inside another time bubble, but it seemed it was. Thankfully.

My ears were ringing and even with that I could tell this guy wasn't a threat.

All the dancers were now frozen in wild positions of movements, bright-colored robes and hair flung all over the place. From a few of the loose robes, I could tell that underwear wasn't a fashion these kids believed in.

"Sorry," the kid who had hugged Ben said, still smiling. "A little loud I suppose, but figured we weren't bothering anyone."

Ben just shook his head and turned to face Stan and the rest of us. "This is my nephew, Nicky."

"From Atlantis?" I blurted out, not even wanting to know how he was Ben's nephew.

"Where else?" Nicky asked, still smiling.

Oh, wow. And I thought I had a lot to learn about history.

Five

Ben introduced us all.

Nicky gave Patty a very broad smile and a slight kiss on the back of her hand. He was a real charmer, this guy.

After the introductions, Ben said, "Your mother and Horae have both been very worried about you."

I didn't want to even ask who his mother was.

Nicky actually looked puzzled at that and my alarm bells suddenly went off at full force. This kid had no idea where or when he was.

Not a clue.

"Nicky," I said, indicating the kid should come with me, "I want to show you something."

Ben nodded and I led the young superhero across the room toward the big windows. The others followed me through the frozen crowd until we all stood beside one of the huge floor-to-ceiling windows.

I pointed at The Strip below and then at the desert around the city. "You know where you are?"

He shrugged, looking out over the city. "Never seen the place before," he said. "North quadrant, maybe."

"North quadrant of what?" I asked as Ben shook his head and looked down at the soft white carpet.

"Of Atlantis," Nicky said. "Where else."

I turned to Ben. "What was this area called in the time of Atlantis?"

"This was mostly all ocean and swamp," Ben said softly. "This land mass was much lower at the time, so we really had no name for this area."

Nicky looked at me, then at his uncle, a look of panic starting to cross his face.

"What exactly did you do to make this building be in a time bubble?" I asked.

"Any building," Nicky said. "We all jam into a mountain cabin that I put the bubble around. I can jump the field out of time and have it go around a larger building. That gives us all a place to party and not even be gone more than an hour or so."

"How do you pick the building?" I asked.

He shrugged, looking out over the city below. "I don't. My machine does. Chronos is going to be angry at me for jumping in time, isn't he?"

I ignored that question. "How do all these people get here?"

"Portal near the device down on the ground floor," Nicky said. "Everyone was already in the cabin before I locked up the building. So a portal down on the main floor is the only way in and out. When exactly is this?"

Silence. I couldn't answer him because I honestly didn't know the answer.

Finally Ben said softly, "This time is about eleven thousand years after Atlantis was destroyed."

"Destroyed?" Nicky asked, looking like he might faint at any moment.

"You haven't been seen since about sixty years ahead of the destruction, Ben said."

Now the kid simply dropped to the floor, his eyes blank, his smile long gone.

So we had a young inventor superhero that had brought about fifty people with him through time to the present. We couldn't let him or any of them just go back, because in this history, our history, my history, he didn't go back.

This was going to take a time travel expert far, far smarter than I was to unravel the mess that Nicky had just caused.

I looked around at all the dancers frozen in a moment of pure enjoyment, then down at the young man sitting on the floor staring down at the depths of the plush carpet.

My warning voice was tingling.

Something was still very, very wrong. And I needed to figure out what.

But for the life of me, at the moment I just couldn't ask poor Nicky another question.

Not after the reality he just faced.

Six

We all stood there in silence until finally what had been worrying me crawled its ugly way to the surface of my mind. And when it poked out, I shuddered.

I turned to my team, letting Nicky sit on the floor and stew in his own thoughts.

"If this time bubble gets shut off, the bubble is going to haul us back to the past as well with it."

"But it doesn't go back to the past," Stan said, staring at the dancers. "We know that because Nicky disappears."

"In this timeline," I said.

Stan started to open his mouth and shut it, suddenly lost in his thoughts.

"Have I ever said that time travel gives me a headache?" I asked.

Patty smiled at me as I turned and kneeled down beside Nicky.

"How is this time bubble around the building set to recall?"

"One day exactly from the moment it left," he said. "Automatically. It will return within thirty minutes of leaving."

"And it takes everyone who is inside it at that moment with it?"

"I don't know," he said, shrugging. "I would assume so. This is the first time I've ever tried it. I figured if the bubble took along anyone who didn't belong, I would just send the hitchhikers back where they belonged before they noticed."

Now my stomach was really twisting. We had an untested machine that could take us all at any moment.

I stood and looked at Patty. "Any idea how many people live in this building?"

"Oh, my," she said, her face white. "Maybe around 500 people at any given time."

It was the middle of the afternoon on a Saturday, so not all of them would be in the building, but a large number of them would be.

Stan and Ben and Screamer had been listening and all three of them were just shaking their heads slowly, Stan staring at the dancers.

All my team looked like I was feeling.

Shocked.

Around us, all of Nicky's friends from Atlantis remained frozen in different positions of dance, their brightly-colored robes spread out or twisted around them, smiles covering their faces.

If we were inside this building when it shifted back, we would end up in a timeline where Nicky returned to Atlantis with his friends. And everyone from Las Vegas time in this building would go with him and suddenly find themselves thousands of years in the past. And all of them would be lost to this world and all their families.

That would be a missing person's case for the ages.

And if we stopped this, Nicky and his friends would be stuck here, lost to all their families.

And since it was a new invention, who knew if the timer was right or would even work.

Or if it went off, where or when it would send any of us.

Wonderful. Just wonderful.

We were so screwed.

I had to admit, Nicky here had really invented something to cause problems.

"I'm open to ideas," I said, glancing around at my team.

I didn't even have one of my normally stupid ideas or random thoughts.

Patty, Screamer, Ben, and Stan all just stood there looking blankly. We all seemed to understand this was a disaster where no matter what we did, no one won.

"So what's going on?" Laverne demanded as she walked into the room. Lady Luck had on her normal power suit and her hair was pulled back. She also had on tennis shoes instead of her normal dress shoes. More than likely she knew she was going to have to climb twenty flights of stairs when she came into the time bubble.

She looked at the crowd of frozen dancers with a puzzled frown, then looked at Ben. "Why are those kids dressed like they are from an Atlantis college party?"

"Because they are," Ben said.

That made the frown on Lady Luck's face just get deeper.

Behind me, Nicky was climbing to his feet. "Hi, Aunt Laverne," he said, stepping up beside me, his voice soft and his eyes not meeting hers, but instead staying focused firmly on the carpet in front of him.

"Oh, shit," Lady Luck said, seeing him. She clearly understood the situation, or at least part of it, instantly.

She stepped forward and seemed to tower over the cowering Nicky.

"So you are responsible for the greatest mystery in all of Atlantis, the Lost Fifty," she said.

She glanced at Stan, then focused back on Nicky.

Ben was nodding slowly, his gaze also aimed directly at the carpet.

Nicky wisely said nothing.

Lady Luck shook her head, clearly disgusted and saying nothing. Having Lady Luck disgusted at me was my worst nightmare. And I had some horrid nightmares at times, but having her disgusted at me was the worst one.

Finally, Lady Luck turned to look at the frozen dancers, then at Stan, touching his arm slightly for a moment, and then finally she looked at me. "We can't let these kids go back. They did not return in this timeline. They were lost to their families a very long time ago."

I nodded.

"We know that," I said. "But we have another problem as well.

Nicky thinks his machine will just take everyone in the building when it automatically jumps."

Beside me Nicky nodded.

"Even the people from this time period who are in time stasis in the building?" Laverne asked, her voice as cold and as angry as I could ever imagine it getting. The windows seemed to vibrate from the tension in her words.

I know I did.

"I think so," Nicky said. "I don't know for sure. It might. I don't know."

I thought the poor kid was going to break into tears, but somehow he just kept staring at the carpet and managed to hold it together.

"Can you just shut it off?" I asked Nicky. I hoped my voice was a little less angry and powerful as Laverne's, but I was so mad at this point, I wasn't sure.

Nicky did exactly as I feared he would do. He shook his head.

"It will return the moment I shut it off," he said.

"Perfect, just perfect," I said to myself. "Where is it exactly?"

"Ground floor, very center of the building," Nicky said.

"Does it have a visible timer on it?"

Again he shook his head.

"Any other way outside this field but through the door on the ground floor?" Stan asked.

Again Nicky just shook his head.

I was stunned. Not only had this kid just destroyed the lives of fifty of his closest friends and their families, if we didn't figure something out quickly, he was going to take all of us as well and who knew how many hundreds with him in this building.

"How long do we have before the time field returns to Atlantis?" Laverne asked directly at Nicky.

"At most ten hours," he said. Then softly he said, "It might be a lot less. I'm sorry."

"Not as sorry as you're going to be when your mother hears about this," Laverne said.

Then Lady Luck turned to me and said simply.

"I'll talk with Chronos and the Fates and see if I can come up with a solution. In the meantime, get everyone out of this building. I'll have the portal downstairs hooked into real time to move with your time here in the building."

I had no idea how she was going to do that, but decided this was not the time to ask.

Then with Nicky by the arm, she turned and yanked the poor kid by the arm toward the apartment door like a mother with a misbehaving three-year-old.

Seven

We all watched them go. I looked at the fifty dancers and took a deep breath. "We're going to need help and a really amazing cover story for the residents."

"And we're going to need counselors for these kids," Patty said, indicating the dancers, "to help them understand what happened."

"They aren't even going to be speaking English," Ben said. "Nicky could because he's a superhero, but none of these kids will."

"Can we give it to them in some sort of power?" I asked, trying to imagine fifty college kids trying to learn English while dealing with being centuries out of time and their entire country being destroyed and their families killed.

Ben nodded slowly. "We might. For the Atlantis Fifty, we might be able to make exceptions. I'll go find out.

"See if you can find something that will ease their memories as well," I said.

Ben looked at the group of frozen dancers and nodded sadly, understanding exactly what I was saying. With that, he turned and headed for the door and the stairwell for the long climb down.

I turned to Screamer. "We're going to need Johnny's help on this and any other police we can trust. And a bunch more we're going to have to fool with a cover story."

Johnny was Detective Johnny State. He was also a superhero working for the police department. I had worked with Johnny on numbers of cases, including the first case when I met Patty.

"That's going to take a really good cover story," Screamer said.

"Some sort of phony virus," I said, "that everyone in the building might have been exposed to, so we take everyone to a holding area and then when the time bubble jumps, we let them return, giving them all clear."

I was making this up as I went, but that sounded like it might work.

We get the Atlantis Fifty, as Ben called the dancers frozen around us, out first and isolated, then we work on the normal residents.

"I'll get some help from the gods of health," Patty said, "to come up with something logical, but not too bad, but that would require this kind of action."

"Stan," I said, turning to my boss. "If you can hold this time bubble inside Nicky's bubble, do you think it's going to be possible to release a set area of residents from his mechanical bubble?"

Stan shook his head, turning his attention from the dancers. "I don't think so. It doesn't work that way, and since this is mechanical, I doubt I can block it."

"How did I release Patty?" I asked.

"She's a superhero," Stan said.

I thought I was discouraged before, now I was really about to lose it.

"Oh, no," Patty said, shaking her head.

I took a deep breath and came up with the only solution I could think of.

"So we move maybe up to five hundred frozen people by stretcher to the entrance, down flights of stairs. Nothing to it, right?"

Silence in a room full of dancers.

I turned to the love of my life. "We're going to need even more help from the medical side of this than we thought," I said. "Because everyone has to be taken by ambulance to the hospital. Only way any cover story will work when they all snap back into real time going out that doorway Laverne is setting up."

Patty nodded.

"Our cover story could be some gas that knocked them all out," I said. "And has no lasting problems with it."

"Better than a virus," Screamer said, nodding.

I turned to Screamer. "Johnny's going to need his girlfriend from the paper to cover this as well. We're going to need help to keep this from turning into a panic that will empty the city."

Again everyone stood silently.

Then Patty said simply, "I don't think we have enough time."

"Time is the enemy no matter what we do," I said.

"Ain't that the truth," Screamer said.

I kissed Patty and told her to get going.

She nodded and went with Screamer out the door almost at a run.

I looked at my boss. "Can you hold the dancers?" I asked.

He nodded.

"I'm going to go scout out where the local residents are to save a little time while we're waiting for the cavalry to arrive."

He nodded and dropped down onto a couch, staring at the Atlantis Fifty, saying nothing.

There just wasn't any more to say at the moment. All I knew was that I didn't really want to see Atlantis. At least not on a one-way ticket to a time sixty years before it was destroyed.

Eight

I checked out the other penthouse apartments. They were really nice, and luckily no one was home in any of them.

On the floor below there were six apartments, all the size of Patty's apartment.

In two I found guys watching television. In two others I found only a woman home, both of them also watching television. The other two apartments were empty.

I was starting to understand how really lucky we had gotten that this happened on a Saturday afternoon.

On the floor above Patty's, I found twelve people in the six apartments. Four were playing cards in one, two kids about twenty-something were making love and were pretty tangled up together, which was going to get interesting to say the least.

They both might need counseling after this was over, one moment going at it with their partner, the next on a stretcher going out the front door of the building.

So in three floors I had sixteen people.

I heard some commotion in the staircase outside and went out to find Patty and Screamer headed back up.

I went with them back to the top floor and back into the room full of the brightly clothed dancers.

Stan was still just sitting there, seemingly lost in his own thoughts.

"Medical equipment and ambulances are headed this way," Patty said. "We've got all the gods and superheroes who could get free working this. But not everyone outside is with us, so we'll have to be careful outside the building."

"Are they coming up with stretchers?" I asked and Patty nodded. 'They should arrive here in about ten minutes."

"No one I could find on this floor," I said. "But we'll need to check again to make sure."

"Police already have the building surrounded and roads blocked off and press held back," Screamer said. "Johnny and two people he can trust are coming up in a few minutes."

Less than thirty minutes. I was impressed.

"So now we have to get these kids moving," Stan said.

"I think we should wait for Ben and Laverne," I said. "We have a language problem."

"I speak their language," Stan said softly.

I kind of looked at my boss, who seemed very, very upset by all this. Usually he was calm and clear, but now he just sat staring at the dancers.

I glanced at Patty and she shrugged.

"You want to tell me what's going on," I said to my boss, going over and dropping onto the couch beside him.

"We don't have time," he said, shaking his head, but not moving to stand.

"I want to wait for Laverne and Ben and help from other gods to help ease these kids' transition," I said firmly. "They can all walk down anyhow. So taking the time is worth the gamble."

He nodded, clearly agreeing.

"So what happened?"

My little voice sort of told me the answer, so I went ahead and asked anyway. "Did you know some of these kids?"

He nodded.

"Which ones?" I asked, my voice gentle. It never would have occurred to me that I would have to be gentle with my boss, the God of Poker.

"The two twins," he said, pointing to two brown-haired girls dancing almost back-to-back near the center.

Patty gasped and I sort of did the same the moment I focused on them.

They looked just like Stan.

"Are they superheroes?" I asked softly.

"Not yet," he said. "They will be."

"Your daughters?"

182

He nodded.

All I wanted to do was be sick.

Nine

All four of us remained silent after that until Ben and Laverne suddenly appeared on the edge of the room.

"Thank you," Ben said to her.

"We can teleport inside the bubble?" I asked.

Laverne nodded.

I turned to Patty.

She was ahead of me, already turning for the door. "I'll cancel the stretchers coming up, have them stage on the main floor. I'll get it set up."

Being able to teleport inside this bubble was the first good news we had gotten in this mess.

I stood and Laverne looked at Stan, a feeling of complete sadness on her face.

"Stan, you should be able to bring your daughters out before we do the rest," she said. "Get them out of here."

He nodded, took a deep breath and stood. "I'll explain what happened and they will help get their friends rescued. Give us a few minutes."

Laverne started to object, then nodded.

Then Stan moved into the dancers and touched one daughter on the shoulder, than the other, bringing them out of the time bubble he had the rest of the dancers in.

"Dad," the one closest to the window said, glancing around at her frozen friends. "What are you doing?"

"Yeah, does mom know you are breaking up our party?" the other asked.

Stan shuddered and then with another deep breath said, "Follow me."

I glanced at Ben and he waved that I should not ask, even though at that moment I would have never asked.

In my head I heard Laverne's voice. *His first wife killed herself when they lost their two daughters. Never ask him about it, ever.*

Understood, I thought back at her.

Stan took his two daughters toward a bedroom in the back of the huge penthouse. I did not envy him at all what he was about to tell those two girls.

I couldn't even comprehend it, to be honest. It just made my stomach twist into little knots.

Laverne looked at me, then nodded that I should go ahead with the plan.

"Let's give Stan the time," I said. "I will start clearing out residents, jumping them to the main floor. There should be a place down there we can store them until stretchers can take them outside."

Laverne nodded, staring at the door where Stan and his daughters had vanished.

"Ben, you stay here to help when Stan and his daughters need the help."

He nodded.

"Screamer," I said. "I know where people are on the two floors below. Go down to Patty's floor and start scouting. And work with Johnny when he gets here."

"Got it," Screamer said and turned and headed for the door.

"Stop a moment," Lady Luck said to Screamer. She waved a hand at him. "I just unblocked what was holding you from learning how to teleport."

She turned to me. "Have him jump with you on the first couple, then he can start moving people down as well. Have Johnny and his people do the scouting ahead."

Screamer started to open his mouth, his eyes wide, then he said simply, "Thank you."

Lady Luck waved her hand and sat down on the couch were Stan had been sitting. "You earned it and you would have figured it out eventually, and now you and my daughter can be together easier."

I smiled and grabbed his arm before he could say anything. He was married to Sherri, one of Lady Luck's daughters, and she lived in Reno while he lived here in Vegas.

I jumped us one floor down to where a guy was sitting in shorts and a tee-shirt watching a football game. The apartment was done in brown tones and had heavy tan drapes blocking out the sun. The television he was watching was huge and from what I could tell, the program was in commercial.

The guy looked to be around sixty and slightly overweight.

"Holy crap, what just happened?" Screamer asked, looking at me.

"Lady Luck just helped you get another power. Don't question it. You'll have time to figure it all out later. We got a lot of people and our own butts to save."

Screamer nodded.

I walked across the room. "See this spot?" I asked, pointing at the carpet beside me.

He nodded.

"Jump to it."

"How?" he asked, looking puzzled.

"I imagine myself in the new spot and then think I am there."

He nodded, focused at the spot beside me, and the next instant he was there, facing past me at the drawn drapes of the apartment.

"It worked," he said softly, shaking his head. "I thought the word *jump* and it happened."

"That sometimes works for me as well," I said. "Jump into the kitchen next." I pointed at the open kitchen on the other side of a brown counter with barstools against it.

Almost instantly he was there.

Then he jumped back beside me.

"Wow, just wow," he said. He was smiling like a kid at Christmas getting everything he asked for.

"I'm going to jump this guy and both of us to the main floor area," I said. "You can work on more there."

He nodded and I imagined the frozen guy and Screamer linked to me and I jumped to the main floor of the apartment building.

I was surprised to see so much activity going on. It was lucky I had tucked us off into a corner, otherwise someone might have seen us appear.

Patty sensed me at once and came running over.

The guy I had jumped with was on the floor, his back against the wall.

"Screamer can now teleport," I told her. "Where do we bring the residents down to so we aren't seen?"

Patty nodded to Screamer and smiled. "Great, we're going to need the help."

Then she showed us an area near the freight elevator where two people were setting up thick mats to help the residents of the building not get hurt. It was tucked around a corner and was big enough to get stretchers in close, but yet not be seen by anyone who shouldn't see people appearing and disappearing.

"We're telling people we're bringing people down the freight elevator and staircase here," she said. "We already have everyone who was on this level out and on the way to the hospital in ambulances."

I kissed her quickly. "Great job. We'll be back with more shortly."

She nodded and I turned to Screamer. "Remember the spot in that last apartment?"

He nodded.

"Jump there."

He vanished.

I followed him and he was standing there in the apartment smiling when I arrived.

"So how do I jump when I don't know where I'm going?" he asked.

"You know," I said.

He frowned.

"The apartment next door has a man in it," I said. "Can you sort of sense it, sense the apartment?"

After a moment he nodded slowly.

"Jump there, get the guy and I'll meet you downstairs."

"Do I have to touch the guy to jump him?" Screamer asked.

"Just imagine a link between you and the person. And then when you get ready to jump, imagine that link solid and that person coming with you."

"Wow, our minds are powerful, aren't they?"

"Don't question it," I said, smiling at him. "Like walking. Never think about it. Just do it."

He nodded and then vanished.

I went to get the woman from the apartment across the hall.

Screamer beat me to the main floor with his person, but not by much.

Ten

Johnny and two other superheroes working for the Las Vegas Police scouted apartments ahead of Screamer and me as we worked our way down the building floor-by-floor.

It seemed to be taking much, much longer than it needed to take, but we were making sure that no one was missed.

At one point Patty told me between jumps that Stan and Laverne and Ben had jumped all the kids to the main floor and had them all walk out into two waiting Greyhound buses. She said that they got safely away from the building and were being taken to a large lodge in the mountains where they could get the kids help and let them rest and get them started on learning what they were going to need to learn to survive in this new world.

"And counseling, I hope," I said.

"I can't imagine why not," Patty said, a very sad look on her face. "They all lost everything today. Their parents, their families, their entire world. Everything they knew and took for granted is gone."

I just shook my head. I didn't want to let myself think about the Atlantis Fifty at the moment. Screamer and I needed to keep going.

So I kissed her and thanked her for telling me and jumped to the next person.

Two other gods from hotel and apartment management areas joined in helping Screamer and me when we reached the eleventh floor since they could teleport. Four of us were about as fast as the ambulances could handle the load of people. Luckily the hospital was very close.

And since none of the residents of the building were actually sick, they all would be released fairly quickly.

As the hours went by, Patty made sure the main floor was cleared of anyone who didn't need to be in the building.

Screamer and I were bringing down the last two residents from the third floor. Both were young women who had been having coffee together at an apartment kitchen counter.

The second floor had already been emptied by the two gods from Patty's area. They were now all gone.

Patty and two others were waiting with stretchers. Both of the others looked like paramedics. Both paramedics were young women and intent in their job.

They helped the two residents we had brought down carefully on to the stretchers and covered them.

"This is it," I said. "Let's all get out of here."

We turned for the door.

We didn't make it.

So close.

Eleven

A shimmering went through the air.

It seemed the lights blinked, but I couldn't be sure on that.

The world spun for just a second, then snapped down solid again.

I glanced around.

Patty, Screamer, two superhero paramedics from the medical world, and the two building residents were standing around me in a cabin that smelled of pine and a cold fireplace. Everyone had a shocked and worried look.

I was sure I was no exception to that.

Only a couple lights were on in the big, high-ceilinged room and curtains were pulled tight over the big windows.

"Oh, no," Patty said softly.

"We didn't make it," Screamer said.

One of the residents of the building looked around and asked, "What just happened?"

Screamer nodded to the superhero paramedics and then reached over and touched the two residents lightly. They both fell instantly asleep.

The paramedics caught them both and stretched the residents safely out onto the floor.

That would take care of that problem for a while at least.

I wanted to just sit on the floor with them and bang my fists, but instead I walked over to the closed main door of the big wooden cabin and eased it open. The hinges on the big wooden door actually had the decency to squeak.

The air outside smelled fresh and warm, like the day might be getting warmer soon. The wonderful scent of pine needles hit me next.

The cabin sat on a hillside covered in tall pine-like trees and in the distance I could see the blue hint of a lake.

Tucked off to one side of the cabin were ten cars like I had never seen. They all looked like they had been designed by a 1950s movie guy trying to imagine what a car of the future would look like.

One of them even had a bubble on it that covered six different scats.

They looked very, very much out of place in the rustic mountain setting.

Those cars were the transportation for the Atlantis Fifty, more than likely.

A highway seemed to wind along the hill below. From where we were, I could hear high humming sounds that seemed to come from the vehicles buzzing past.

Not gas engines, that was for sure.

Patty stepped up beside me and looked around for a moment.

Then I pushed us both back into the cabin and shut the door.

"Are we where I think we are?" Screamer asked, standing next to the paramedics above the two residents stretched out on the floor.

"We're not in Kansas anymore, that's for sure," I said.

I took a deep breath and tried to think about jumping to my office hovering over Vegas.

Nothing. It wasn't there.

We were over eleven thousand years in the past. And who knew on what timeline.

In other words, we were screwed.

I looked around at the four others expecting me to lead them. I didn't have a clue what to do.

That silence just got too heavy.

"We stay here for a time," I said, finally, trying to sound decisive and in charge. Better than sitting on the floor pounding my fists.

But not much.

"You think Laverne might be able to get to us?" Screamer asked.

I shrugged. "Laverne or Chronos. We have no other hope otherwise, other than to get off this continent in the next sixty years and find a place to live and survive. So we sit tight for now and make it easier on them if they can rescue us."

All four of them nodded, clearly feeling as stunned as I felt. No one wanted to talk anymore about the fine mess we found ourselves in. I was okay with that.

"What happens when they come looking for the missing kids," Screamer asked.

I looked at him. "When that happens, we had better be gone. Somewhere."

That really nailed the silence so we all started looking around.

The place was bigger than it looked at first glance and that Nicky had described. It had a nice living room tucked over to one side with a large stone fireplace and a bunch of comfortable-looking couches and big chairs, all in dark brown tones that seemed to go well with the wood. The couches and chairs weren't shaped that different from anything you would see in a modern furniture store.

The ceiling was high and peaked and had wood beams.

On the opposite side was a kitchen and beyond that what looked like a bathroom. I had a hunch from the looks of those cars out front that using a bathroom in Atlantis might just be a learning experience.

Fifty people would have had no trouble being in here.

I turned to Screamer. "Help me find Nicky's machine."

He nodded and we started for a hallway that led off to what must be bedrooms of some sort.

"How long will they be out?" one of the paramedics asked, pointing at the two women on the floor.

"We haven't been introduced," I said, suddenly realizing I didn't know two of the people I was stuck with. I stopped and turned back. "I'm Poker Boy, this is Screamer, this is Patty."

The one paramedic with short blonde hair said, "My name is Katie."

"I'm Rocha," the taller one with short brown hair said.

Both were clearly in great shape and very strong from their handshakes.

We all did the pleasant stuff, as much as five people can do when trapped thousands of years from home in a world we didn't know. Then Screamer answered Katie's question.

"They will be out eight hours at least," Screamer said. "All harmless, I assure you."

The paramedic superhero nodded. "Let's get them back on a bed if there are any in this place."

"Hang on," I said, and went down the hallway and opened the first door on the right. It was a bedroom all right with a very comfortable large bed that seemed huge.

I jumped the two sleeping building residents onto the bed.

"Might want to straighten them out a little and cover them up," I said.

Katie nodded thanks at me and went into the bedroom.

"Can I do that?" Screamer asked.

I smiled at my friend. "I sure don't see why not."

"I'm going to check out the food supplies," Patty said.

"I'll help you," Rocha said, following her. "I'm hungry."

When she said that I realized I was as well, but I doubted I could eat at the moment.

Screamer and I quickly found Nicky's machine. It was in the bedroom on the left, sitting right in the middle of the floor.

Honestly, it looked more like someone had taken a motor out of a lawn mower and hooked it to the top of some plastic dome.

Only it was like no internal combustion engine I had ever seen. It had what looked like a big blue crystal sticking out of the top of it like a gearshift.

It wasn't humming or making any noise at all. In fact, it didn't even seem to have switches to turn it on or off. But it was glowing slightly.

"Any ideas?" I asked Screamer.

"Besides not touching it?" he said. "Not a one."

We headed back out and joined the other three in the kitchen area.

"Anyone here alive in Atlantis time?" I asked.

I had learned a long time ago that sometimes a superhero or a god could surprise you with how old they were. Since none of us aged much at all after we came into our powers, living a long time seemed to be an option. Ben looked moderately old, but he had been around for far longer than Atlantis. In fact, more than likely, he was here somewhere.

And we knew that Stan and Laverne were living here somewhere as well.

But I don't think we dared contact them. At least not until we gave Laverne some time to mount a rescue operation from our own time.

Of course, since it was time travel, the rescue might come in one hundred years of this time, but only in a half an hour of our Las Vegas time. No way of knowing.

If rescue came at all.

I pushed that thought away. I would deal with that possibility soon enough.

"Not even close to that old," Screamer said, answering my question about anyone being alive in Atlantis.

"I was born in 1930," Rocha said.

"I'm only slightly older," Katie said.

"Not even close," Patty said, smiling at me.

I always felt like the baby around gods and superheroes.

This time was no exception.

Twelve

I was about to suggest that Screamer and I explore the back rooms and around the outside of the cabin when Stan appeared.

The wrong Stan.

He was standing with his back to the front door and looked to be the same Stan from our time except for one major exception. He was wearing a brown toga and brown sandals. Even in a toga, he didn't wear anything but bland colors.

"Stan!" I said before my mind processed that more than likely this wasn't the Stan from our time period.

This was the Stan looking for his daughters. More than likely the angry dad Stan who didn't know any of us from a tree.

He frowned slightly, staring at me. "Who are you?"

I knew that tone in his voice. He was already angry.

I started to open my mouth, then stopped myself when warning bells went off in the back of my head.

I glanced at Patty and then Screamer. Both had wide eyes and both were shaking their heads.

The two paramedics were standing off toward the kitchen, just watching, clearly scared but saying nothing.

If we did something wrong here, we could really, really screw up a bunch of timelines. I knew enough about time travel to know that. I just hoped that we could keep Stan under control and thinking this through.

"I don't think I can tell you," I said. "Beyond that we are from your future."

Toga-Stan started to open his mouth, then shut it and stared at me like he was trying to get a read on me.

I had no idea if there was such a thing as poker in Atlantis, which meant I had no idea what area Stan was a god in.

The silence between us grew.

I flat had no idea what to do.

But I did know that anything I did right now that was stupid would doom us to remain in the past.

"Never thought I would ever get here," Stan said from my left.

All of us spun around.

Stan from our time was there, smiling at his toga-self. He had on the same plain clothes he had been wearing earlier.

I don't think I was ever so happy to see someone. I wanted to hug him, I really did.

He looked at me. "We needed that me to arrive here so we could track where and when you exactly were," regular Stan said.

Behind the toga-Stan, Laverne and another older man with a long white beard appeared. Laverne touched toga-Stan on the shoulder. That Stan then slumped gently to the ground.

I recognized the older man with Laverne as Chronos, the God of Time. Or Father Time as many called him. But instead of white robes, he had on a silk business suit with a vest and suspenders. He looked like any really rich old guy you would see on the street.

I couldn't believe how happy I was to see him as well. But not once did the thought of hugging him cross my mind.

A moment later toga-Stan vanished.

"I find him in an hour in my office," Laverne says. "I just put a memory block on him to forget all this until he sees Nicky today in the future. That way he doesn't tell me anything."

That made a lot of sense. It protected the timeline.

Then I thought about it. She had just planted the plan to rescue us in Stan's mind to carry for over eleven thousand years while he was in the middle of rescuing us. Have I ever said how much time travel gives me a headache?

"We need to get out of here," she said.

"Hold on, we have two residents of Patty's building with us," I said.

I nodded to the two paramedics to be ready and then instantly brought the two unconscious women to the front room. The two paramedics expertly caught the two women and held them like they did something like that every day.

"Got everyone now?" Laverne asked.

I nodded and took Patty's hand, feeling her calming influence on me.

Laverne turned to the white-bearded man who seemed to just be standing there smiling slightly as he watched like a grandfather pleased at the actions of his grandchildren.

"A ride home if you wouldn't mind, Burtram?" she asked.

Burtram Chronos? I was never getting that out of my mind.

He smiled and waved his hand.

Without even seeming to move, we were standing in front of the booth in my office that hovered over the Las Vegas Strip.

Laverne and Chronos were gone.

Stan was no longer with us either, more than likely with his daughters. I had a hunch we weren't going to be seeing him much for a time.

Around us the wonderful city of Las Vegas spread out across the desert. The sky was perfect blue, the desert perfect brown, and the planes were filling the sky on approaches to the airport. Below I could see the moving traffic and lights of The Strip.

It felt wonderful to be home.

Part of me had believed I would never see it again. Actually a very large part.

Ben and Madge were both sitting in the booth, sweating as if they had been running.

"Oh, thank heavens you are back," Ben said. "We couldn't hold this office up much longer."

I frowned and figured I would have them explain that later. It didn't feel like I was suddenly holding up the office.

Patty kissed me and then let go of my hand.

"Patty's building safe?" I asked Ben.

He nodded, using a napkin to wipe the sweat off his brow as Madge slid out of the booth and sort of staggered for the door to The Diner. "I'll get some milkshakes and fries started."

"I'll jump you two into the back area of the lobby," I said, turning to the two paramedics who were still holding up the two unconscious women residents. "From there you can get these two to the hospital."

They both nodded and I jumped them to the empty main floor of the building, thanked them for their help, and jumped back to my office.

It felt wonderful to be home.

Just wonderful.

Screamer was pulling a chair up to the booth and Patty had already slid into the side across from Ben.

"Go get Sherri," I said to Screamer as I slid into the big booth beside Patty. "Have her join us for a late lunch so we have someone to tell this story to."

He started to open his mouth, then remembered he could teleport and broke into a huge smile.

"Right back," he said, and vanished.

"Very good job today," Ben said, nodding and sipping on a glass of water in front of him. "You all saved a lot of people in a lot of time-lines. How did you like Atlantis?"

"Seemed pretty advanced," I said. "But we didn't luckily see much of it."

"How are the Atlantis Fifty going to be?" Patty asked.

"The Atlantis what?" Sherri asked as she appeared with Screamer and slid into the booth as Ben slid over. "And someone want to explain to me how my husband can now teleport?"

"The Atlantis Fifty," Ben said. "They were before your time."

"Considerably," Sherri said. "If they were actually from Atlantis. I'm not that old, thank you very much."

"But we were there today," Screamer said, smiling at his wife.

"Where?" Sherrie asked, looking very puzzled.

"Atlantis," Screamer said. "Nice place, but I wouldn't want to live there. I hear it had flooding problems."

Sherri opened her mouth, staring at her husband, then shut it and looked at me.

Patty and I both laughed.

Patty finally took pity on Sherri and looked at me. "How about we start from the beginning and tell her about our day."

"Should I start with the shower part?" I asked, remembering how wonderful she looked there, naked and not moving, covered in drops of water. "With you frozen in the shower and me just staring."

"Pervert," Patty said and smacked me on the shoulder and Ben smiled like he did when amused.

"After the shower," Patty said.

"Oh, bummer," Screamer said.

And with that the laughter drained away the last of the tension I was feeling.

It was wonderful to be home, wonderful to have stopped a horrid tragedy from happening, and wonderful to be back in this time.

And even though thousands of years before in Atlantis, fifty families had been torn apart with a horrid tragedy, the Atlantis Fifty had now found a new home. They were safe and would get the help they needed.

And Stan had two daughters back he thought he'd lost forever.

All in all, I figured it was a good Saturday afternoon.

DEAD EVEN

A Poker Boy Story

Superheroes in the gambling universe sometimes find themselves helping people who normally don't need help.

Poker Boy met Bob on Christmas Eve and proceeded to take his money at the table because Bob played horrid poker and did so while being a real jerk.

But Bob needed that money for a very special and personal reason. A reason Poker Boy found worthwhile.

BOB SHOWED up in the poker room at Spirit Winds Casino on Christmas Eve. Bob, like his name, was a very short man. I guessed he came up to my shoulder at best, even with heels on his boots. It's always interesting to me how names fit people. Bob fit Bob perfectly.

His black hair was short, the nails on his fingers were trimmed short, and even his nose was short. He wore a golf shirt that seemed a size too small, and brown slacks that covered brown dress shoes. He did not have the appearance of having money, but over the years I have come to not trust appearances very much, since I look like a slob most of the time, yet I have money and am a super hero.

In looks, I am, for lack of a better way of putting it, the cliché white male. I'm six feet tall, have brown hair that's graying slightly at the temples, and green eyes. Bob was the cliché short man who walked quick, talked quick, and had a flaring temper that might go off with just a wrong remark, or more likely, a bad beat at the table.

Cliché meet cliché.

Bob took every turn of the cards as if it was more than just a bad beat. He seemed to take it as an affront to his height. A ten would hit the table to give someone else a pair of tens to beat his pocket nines, and he acted if someone had just called him a runt.

It was a guaranteed way to lose money at a poker table.

Bad beats at poker tables are when a person thinks they should win, but the cards at the end of the hand say otherwise. Every poker player I know tells bad beat stories about how his pocket aces were beaten by jack/ten suited. Bad beats are the nature of poker, and I put them on people as often as people put them on me, so I pay no attention. Someone starts into a bad beat story and I just nod and think about what I'm planning on having for dinner.

All night long Bob kept complaining, and then continuing to play. He wasn't a bad player, but he wasn't a good one either. He knew just enough to think he was the best, and just enough to think he knew what he was doing, and just enough to think he could beat me and the rest of the group at the table. Of course he was wrong on all three counts. And he complained about it bitterly.

Clearly short Bob was not a happy man, either in poker or in life.

The turning point of the evening came when Bob had aces beat twenty minutes before midnight on Christmas Eve. He stared at the aces, then at the winning flush a guy named Carl had drawn into, then at the dealer, and for a moment I thought he was going to punch the dealer.

Now understand, during the evening so far, he had lost upwards of three grand in just under five hours, with about half of it sitting safely in the stack of chips in front of me. However, it was not my flush that had just put the bad beat on his aces.

I'm Poker Boy, and Christmas Eve or not, I played fair, and if someone wanted to give me their money across a poker table, I took it. There is no Santa in a poker game, but good old short Bob sure wanted to give me his money, so I was thinking kindly of him at that moment, even with him yelling at the dealer and complaining all the time.

I'm not sure yelling describes what Bob was actually doing. He was ranting, screaming, shouting, and even foaming at the mouth a little.

He had stood up and was even leaning over the table. For a tall man, this might have been threatening. For Bob, it made no difference.

The rake, a guy named Henry, watches over the dealers in a poker room. Henry came over and asked Bob to calm down. All the while the dealer named Scooter just sat there, staring ahead, ignoring Bob's ranting and shouting and carrying on.

"I'm not going to calm down!" Bob shouted.

At this point, Krissy, the room manager on duty showed up at the table. She was about Bob's height, with long blonde hair and a smile that could fill a room.

Scooter kept ignoring Bob, shuffled up, and got ready to deal the next hand.

"What's the problem?" Krissy asked Bob, as if she didn't know exactly what the problem was.

"Your dealer's cheatin' me!" Bob turned and shouted right into her face. Then he stepped toward her.

I just sat there watching. These situations were not the things that Poker Boy got involved with. My job was to save helpless people and dogs, not stop idiots from making fools of themselves.

Besides, Krissy was one tough broad who had many different colored belts from different martial arts disciplines. If Bob was stupid enough to take a swing at Krissy, he would be lucky to see it turn Christmas day.

"Our dealers do not cheat, sir," Krissy said, her voice low and level as she spoke right into Bob's face. "And we have cameras to make sure they don't."

"I don't care about no damned cameras!" Bob shouted. "For all I know, the dealer and the camera man are in this together."

I glanced around at the other seven players on the table. All of us had some of this idiot's money. Did he think we were all in on his great conspiracy as well? Of course, I didn't say that. Instead the rest of us just sat there as if nothing was happening, staring at either our hands, the felt tabletop, or the wall beyond the table. The number one rule when there's a problem at a poker table was to stay out of it.

"I think maybe a little walk might calm you down," Krissy said, moving to take Bob's elbow and turn him from the table.

"I don't need a walk!" Bob shouted, his face really red.

The next chain of events happened quickly.

Bob went to shove Krissy aside.

Krissy grabbed Bob's arm.

Bob tried to push Krissy.

Krissy moved a step out of the way, grabbing Bob in such a way that the man sort of lifted off the ground using his own forward motion, flew through the air with Krissy still holding on, and then came down flat, face first, on the empty table beside the one we were playing on.

Krissy now held Bob's arm behind his back with one hand and the back of his neck with the other, acting as if she had to do this every day.

Bob kicked for a moment trying to break free, but it looked like with each kick, he hurt himself, so he stopped.

Man, I was going to have to get to know Krissy better. She might come in handy as a sidekick on some of my adventures. Sure, I had super powers and all that, but sometimes a good hand-to-hand fighting master could beat a super power in the clinch.

"Deal this man out," Krissy said. She didn't seem excited or even winded. "And cash in his chips and give him his money."

Henry, the rake, moved to take what was left of Bob's chips. More than likely his anger had just saved him the last of his money.

A moment later, two large security men came in the poker room door, handcuffed Bob, and started to lead him away, with Henry carrying Bob's money right behind.

"Wait!" Bob shouted. "I have to stay. I have to win enough!"

Suddenly my Poker Boy alarm went off. I sometimes call this alarm my Ultra-Intuition Power. And right now that power was telling me in no uncertain terms that Bob needed my help, and not to escape the security guards.

I got up, leaving my chips on the table, and followed Bob, the guards, and Henry the rake. It felt as if we were having a little parade as the crowds parted to let us through.

The two large security men, with Bob walking between them like a small child being escorted to the principal's office, headed for the front door of the casino. When they had him safely out on the sidewalk and the handcuffs off, Henry gave Bob the remaining money and went back inside.

"Please don't return to this casino, sir," one big guard said.

"You're lucky Krissy's not going to press charges against you," the other said.

Bob just nodded, standing there in the cold evening air, the last of his money in his hand. He looked to be completely in shock and beaten, as if his world had just ended. Clearly he must have been playing poker with scared money, and the worst way to ever play poker is with scared money.

Scared money means the money you are using is not money you can afford to lose. You never gamble with rent or food or car payment money. Never. Ever. Only gamblers with problems do that.

"Where's your car, Bob?" I asked, stepping up between him and the guards and taking his arm. I turned him gently toward the closest parking lot.

"Around on the other side of the building," Bob said.

"I'll walk you," I said, glad I always wore my black leather coat and Fedora-like hat when playing, since we were going to have to go around the building and it was a cold Christmas Eve. It wasn't snowing or anything, but it felt cold enough to.

We walked in silence for a hundred yards or so, then finally Bob said softly, "I knew better."

"I know you did," I said. "How much did you need to win?"

"Six over the top of the four I had," he said, without looking at me.

We kept walking in silence, our breathing making frost waves ahead of us in the parking lot lights.

Now a couple times a year I have nights in live games where I win far over six thousand. And I've won numbers of tournaments with payouts a great distance over six thousand. But I doubted Bob had ever won that much in a casino, so whatever had made him try this stupidity on Christmas Eve had to be very important to him.

I clicked on my special Empathy Power.

To be honest, I just don't know what else to call the power. It makes people believe they can tell me anything, trust me with their very lives. And sometimes they do. But Empathy is the wrong name for it, but Trust Me Power just doesn't sound right. And neither does Make Them Talk Power. I'd figure it out some day.

With my Empathy Super Power on, I asked the next question. "Bob, what did you need the money for?"

Bob glanced at me. "What do you care?"

I notched up my Empathy Power. Little Bob needed a big dose. "Trust me, I care," I said, staring right at him to focus the strength.

He shrugged. "You wouldn't believe me if I told you."

I turned up the Empathy Power to the top of my capabilities and focused it at him like I was staring at a fly. Bob stood no chance. He was going to tell me.

"You would be surprised what I would *believe*," I said.

He shrugged. "I wanted to die even."

Now, of all the reasons he could have told me why he wanted ten thousand dollars, that was not one I expected. I wouldn't have been surprised at his daughter needing an operation, or his needing to replace money he took from his wife to bet on the horses, or maybe even he needed to buy a girlfriend a new sports car.

"You're going to have to explain that one," I said, keeping my Empathy Power cranked up.

"Christmas morning at six-ten," Bob said, his voice level and matter-of-fact. "Not long from now, actually, I'm going to die."

"And how do you know that?" I asked, even more stunned.

"I told you that you wouldn't believe me."

"Oh, I believe you," I said. "I'm just wondering how you know, or are you planning this exit from the here-and-now."

I really didn't want to spend Christmas Eve babysitting a short guy who wanted to kill himself because his life sucked and he was a bad poker player. I would do it to save his life, but I didn't want to.

He laughed, the sound echoing over the frost-covered cars as we headed down a row, clearly getting closer to his car.

"Not planning a thing," he said. "In fact, I wish I could stay around long enough to learn how to play poker like you do."

"But, you're not?" I said, ignoring his compliment.

"Nope." He glanced at his watch. "About six hours from now I'll be as dead as they come. I just know it, like I know the sun is going to come up tomorrow, and the tide is going to change. Call it a special power of mine. Most people never understand that I get these feelings about things, so a long time ago I quit telling people."

I knew that feeling. I dropped my Empathy Power and focused another of my super powers on him to see if he was telling me the truth.

After a moment I realized he seemed to be.

"All right," I said, "I buy that you think you're going to die in about six hours. And you need the ten grand to pay off one last debt?"

"Naw," he said. "Actually I got a bunch of money in stocks, good equity in my house, and both cars paid off. But when I add up the worth of everything, now that the market is down, the balance owed on my house is ten thousand over what I got in assets. I wanted to leave this life even, just like I came in. It seems that's too much to ask, isn't it?"

Again he laughed and stopped beside a late model SUV. For such a little guy, he sure drove a big, expensive car.

"You got a wife and kids?" I asked, still not completely clear on why this guy wanted ten thousand.

"Sure do," Bob said, smiling. "She's back in Minnesota visiting family, and both my kids are grown and married. They are both with their spouse's families this year."

"They left you alone?"

"I wanted them to," he said. "I sort of set it up, and let me tell you, it took some convincing. But I figured why have them hanging around when this heart of mine lets go? It's going to be hard enough on them as it is."

I nodded, not knowing exactly what to say. Either they watched him die, or they got a phone call saying that he was dead. I honestly didn't know which was worse either. But Bob clearly knew for him and his family, and I gave him that.

"Well, it was good playing cards with you," Bob said. "A real pleasure to get beaten by one of the best."

He beeped his SUV unlocked and opened the big door, getting ready to climb inside. I couldn't just let him go off like this, especially since I knew he was telling the truth.

"Bob, wait," I said. "I'm a gambling man, I'll make you a wager. How much do you have left?"

He reached into his pocket and pulled out the bills Henry had given him, made a quick count. "About a grand."

"All right, I'll give you ten to one odds you don't die this morning. If you do, you have ten thousand from me and go out even, if you don't, I get your thousand."

He stared at me for the longest time. Then he asked, "Why would you do that?"

I shrugged. "I'm a gambler. It sounds like a safe way to get that last thousand of yours, since you won't give it to me at the table."

An aside. Actually, I'm not a gambler. In fact, I never play if I don't have what's called "the-best-of-it." I never bet slots, or any other house game where the odds are in favor of the house. I am a poker player, and in poker, skill is everything. And since I'm one of the best in the country, I usually get the best of other people.

But tonight, I placed a bet to help someone.

Again he sort of stared at me for a moment. Then he said, "You're not kidding, are you?"

"Nope," I said. I dug into my pocket and brought out a roll of bills and counted off ten big ones.

I usually carry about twenty thousand in cash on me when I'm headed into a poker room. Then, no matter the size of the game I find, I can handle the buy-in. It never occurs to me that most people would be scared to death walking around with that much cash. I'm a super hero, so I don't have a lot of worries about getting mugged.

"Give me your card," I said.

I figured him for a businessman, and every businessman I knew had a card, and he was no exception.

He dug it out of his wallet and handed it to me.

"Robert Day," I said. "Portland, Oregon. That's you and a current phone number?"

"It is," he said, nodding.

"And this is your car?" I asked.

"It is," he said.

I went around back and recorded the license plate number of the big SUV, then moved back to where he stood.

"Here's the deal," I said, talking quick so he didn't have a chance to say anything. "I give you the ten thousand right now. You go home, do what you had planned on doing tonight, and if you're dead in the morning, the money is yours. If your fear is wrong, and you live through the morning, you come back here tomorrow night at eight and give me my ten grand back, plus one thousand of your own money."

He sort of stood there, his mouth open.

I knew I was just giving him the money. This was the biggest sham bet ever come up with, and I was doing my best to sell it to him. But I knew I had lost the ten big ones if he took this, and I didn't care.

An aside. Bob was a real jerk, of that I had no doubt, but he was a jerk who needed my help, and just because someone was a jerk, that didn't mean I shouldn't help that jerk.

I held up the card and smiled. "I know where you live. And I figure I can trust you. Just don't go offing yourself to win this."

At that he laughed. "Are you kidding? I'd love to come back here tomorrow, give you your money and a thousand, and buy you a drink. If they let me back in the casino, that is."

"I'll set it up so they will," I said. "But I doubt they're going to let you play poker for a while."

"Not a problem there," he said, laughing. "I needed my head examined to go up against the likes of you and the others at that table."

"So do we have a bet?" I asked, still shoving my sham bet, which was the only way I knew how to help him.

He again looked at me for the longest time. I had long ago turned off my Empathy Power, and I can't read minds, so I had no idea why he just sort of stared at me.

Then he stuck out his hand. "We have a bet."

His handshake was firm and quick, as you would expect from someone who moved and acted like Bob.

I handed him the ten thousand.

He handed me back one thousand of it. "Nine-to-one odds," he said. "I only need ten thousand total to be even in life, and I have one thousand already."

"Even better," I said.

Did I mention I wasn't a gambler? I could figure the math of a poker hand to exact figures, but a sham bet like this one, I had no clue.

"Thanks," he said, staring at the money. "I don't know why this is so important to me. Seems silly, actually, now that I think about it. No one's going to care that I went out even except me, and I'll be dead."

"Just make sure you're back here tomorrow night with my money. My nine and your grand. I'm going to collect on that drink as well."

"If I'm alive, I'll be here," he said. "Thank you."

With that he got into his big SUV and started it up. He backed out, and with a blink of his lights, drove off.

I went back inside, got myself a large mug of hot chocolate to cut the chill, and went back to the table. I had just given a guy nine thousand dollars to make him feel better during the last few hours of his life. I had no doubt he was going to die, just as he said he would. I had the same power he had, only I called my power Precog-Power.

He was going to die at the exact moment he told me he was, from a massive heart attack. Not even being in a hospital would change the result, that much I was sure of. Otherwise I would have been working to get him to one.

No, the only thing I could do for him was help him make his goal of going out the same way he came into the world: Dead even.

It cost me nine thousand, but what the hell, it was Christmas.

I waited around the next night at eight, just in case we were both wrong. He didn't show, and by midnight, in a very good game, I had won most of my money back.

His death was reported in the paper the next day, exactly as we had both known it would be.

Two weeks later, a very short man came into the casino poker room asking for me. He looked like a younger and shorter version of Bob. He handed me an envelope with nine thousand in it.

The guy looked puzzled, then said simply, "My father willed this to you. Said it had to be cash and left instructions that I was to buy you a drink after I gave it to you. And never play poker with you."

I laughed and steered Bob Junior out of the poker room and toward the bar. On the way he asked, "How well did you know my father?"

"Not that well," I said. "Played some cards with him is all, but I liked him. An honest man."

"That he was," his son said, smiling. "That he was."

IRON EYEBROWS: A ROMANCE WITH TOO MUCH HAIR

(Published under the name Dee W. Schofield)

Maria Webb hated men with too much body hair.

But then a magical guy with a lot of hair came striding nude toward her on the beach and everything changed.

This time she fell in love with a man with very bushy eyebrows and some special talents that no one would have expected to find with a nude man on a nude beach.

MARIA WEBB WATCHED with growing disgust as the brown-haired, naked man strolled down the beach along the water line toward her and Cindie. He seemed like he didn't have a care in the world, the white towel over his shoulder, his private parts swinging back and forth like a clapper in a church bell. The long brown hair that covered most of his body blew in the faint breeze and seemed to ripple over his body like waves on a glistening lake.

She hated hairy men. Her counselor said her hatred came from her short-lived first marriage to Ben. Seven months, actually, but they had only been together for two of those seven months. Ben had a lot of hair, and when they first met as freshmen in college, she had loved running her fingers through the long hair on his chest and back. Now, after he had gone and slept with five other women by the second month and then left her, the idea of running her fingers through any man's hair just made her shudder.

The guy walking toward them down the beach was certainly hairy. More than she had ever seen before, but she had to admit he was built better than Ben had been, not only in both muscles, but in other ways. She could tell that even from a hundred paces.

He had very broad shoulders and a walk that just sang of confidence. Maybe too much confidence. Arrogance was more like it.

Of course, he was completely naked, so he had to have confidence, even though they were on a nudist beach.

She went back to reading her Kindle, trying to lose herself in the newest J.D. Robb book, a blue towel over her naked butt, her breasts pressed enough into the towel and the sand below that she wasn't exposing anything.

Cindie, on the other hand sat upright, her knees up to her chin, exposing things that never should be seen on a public beach as she painted her toenails like she was sitting alone in their apartment back off the Oregon State University campus.

Maria couldn't believe she had she ever let Cindie talk her into getting an "overall tan" on a nudist beach while they were on spring break in California. Cindie might be tanning parts that shouldn't ever see the sun, but no way was Maria going to tan anything but her back. Just the idea of getting a sunburn on her butt scared her enough to keep that part covered.

As the guy got closer, Maria again glanced up and then flat stared. The guy's hair seemed to be vanishing. And with each step that he got closer, more of his hair disappeared. Including the brown hair on his head. Only his pubic hair seemed to be staying.

And his thick eyebrows.

He was going to walk along the waterline about ten paces in front of them.

Cindie, focused on her nails, hadn't even seen him.

Maria just stared. By the time he was almost even with them he was essentially hairless except for the two places. And his body was a stunner, his muscles rippling in the warm spring air.

Suddenly he looked over and smiled.

It felt like the old cliché electric shock had hit her. He was the most attractive man she had ever seen.

Ever.

But she was sure he had been covered with hair at first. But no one got rid of body hair like that. It must have been the sun and her over-active focus on ex-husband-Ben playing tricks with her mind.

Her counselor back in Oregon next week was going to have a field day with this.

"Is there something wrong?" the man asked as he stopped right in front of them and stared at Maria. He had the decency to bring his towel down and around his waist as she looked up.

Cindie also glanced up, then immediately put her legs down and together as she sucked in a breath.

"Excuse me?" Maria asked.

"You seemed to be frowning," the man said, his voice deep and almost hypnotic. "I noticed you watching me as I came up the beach; I hope I didn't do something wrong."

Cindie glanced at Maria, clearly shocked, then back at the man. Of the two of them, it was always Cindie who did the flirting while Maria held back and stayed out of the way.

"No, nothing," Maria said, shaking her head. "The light was such that I thought you were covered with a lot of hair is all."

"And you don't like men with a lot of hair?" he asked, smiling at her, and making her sweat even more in the warm afternoon sun. This guy was a real charmer.

"I don't," Maria said.

The man ran his hand over his bald head. "Not a problem then."

Maria laughed, a kind of high-school giggle. "No problem at all."

"I love your laugh," the man said, holding Maria's gaze.

Maria was sure she was blushing, but hoped her sun-red face didn't show it.

"My name is Jason," the man said.

"Maria and Cindie," Maria said before Cindie could say anything.

"Very nice to meet you both," he said, bowing slightly.

Maria could feel her mind spinning as she just couldn't look away from his eyes and that wonderful chiseled face and bald head. What she really wanted was to rub her hands over his head. Maybe he needed some suntan lotion on some of that exposed skin.

She shook her head, trying to clear the thoughts.

He continued to smile at Maria, then with that voice that seemed to just fill the warm air, he asked, "I assume you are not from around here."

"Oregon," Maria said, smiling back. "Not used to this sun, so we have to be careful. How do you manage to not burn?"

He laughed. "I'm from San Diego so I'm used to it, but it still takes lots of lotion. In fact, I've been walking for a ways. If you wouldn't mind, could I borrow a little of your lotion?"

"No problem," Maria said.

She reached over beside Cindie and grabbed the bottle, catching Cindie's puzzled expression. Cindie hadn't even said a word, which was very, very strange for her. In fact, Cindie started to open her mouth to say something, then just shook her head and closed it again.

Jason sat down on the sand next to Maria, keeping the white towel around his waist in perfect position to not show anything.

Maria actually felt both relief and disappointment. Again she shook the thought away

She started to hand the bottle to him, but he shifted slightly so his back was toward her with the shinning skin and rippling muscles.

"Would you mind putting some on my back?"

Beside her Cindie coughed lightly, but still said nothing.

"Sure. Would love to," Maria said.

She sat up, leaving the towel on the sand. Her breasts were now exposed to the California sun and the man sitting next to her.

As she started to rub the lotion over Jason's back, part of her mind was just enjoying the wonderful feeling of once again touching a man while another part of her mind kept asking, *What are you doing?*

It was Spring Break, she was enjoying herself, that's what she was doing.

"Would you get the back of my neck as well?" Jason asked.

"Glad to," she said, letting her hands roam all over his large, smooth back and up to his neck.

After a moment he broke the wonderful feeling and said, "Okay, my turn to get your back."

He turned around and took the bottle as Maria turned to face Cindie, who was sitting there staring, her mouth open. They had been roommates since Maria and Ben had broken up. Cindie knew more about Maria than anyone else, and Maria knew for a fact her actions were surprising her roommate right at this moment.

She was surprising herself, actually.

Then Jason's hands started rubbing in the lotion, working his strong fingers all over her back, and she wanted to just melt. It wasn't as if the afternoon sun wasn't hot enough, in a moment she was sweating like she was in a sauna just from his touch.

Twice he brushed near the sides of her breasts, both times her breath caught. And she damn near choked when his hands went down near the crack of her butt.

His fingers worked the lotion into her skin in a way that felt heavenly.

After what seemed like the shortest eternity she had ever lived through, he patted her shoulder and said, "That part is all protected for a while. Has anyone ever told you that you have wonderful skin?"

"You have fantastic hands," she said, turning as he poured more lotion on his hands and started to rub it on his chest.

"It's my job," he said. "I'm a massage therapist."

She took the bottle of lotion from him and sprayed some on both of her breasts and started to rub it around, hoping he would notice, which he seemed to a couple of times. But both times he quickly averted his gaze out over the calm ocean.

A real gentleman.

With very, very thick eyebrows. Now that she was sort of facing him up close, she couldn't believe the bushiness of his eyebrows. And they really stood out because of his bald head.

And then she remembered how she had thought he looked at first, covered in hair almost completely. But now he didn't even have any hair on his arms or legs.

And some voice in the back of her head warned her that something wasn't right. She just kept staring at his eyebrows, and with each passing second they seemed to get thicker and even bushier, if that was possible.

He smiled. "Some people think they are my best feature. Others have called me *Iron Eyebrows*."

She jerked and looked into his eyes. They were brown, deep brown, and his gaze was something she wanted to lose herself in. And in his wonderful body.

But the voice in the back of her mind kept bothering her. So she thought clearly at him. *Can you read my mind?*

He turned away, then his voice came back into her mind clearly. *Yes, but only surface thoughts. But I find you so attractive I just wanted to please you.*

Now that was enough to make her jump a little and glance at Cindie, who still just sat silently watching.

"I'll prove it to you," he said out loud. "Look at my eyes and let me open up to you."

She didn't want to. The chance that someone could really read her mind and all her secrets scared her to death.

But still she looked into his eyes and suddenly she was inside his head, knowing everything about him. He actually did work as a massage therapist in San Diego, and liked sunbathing and walking in the nude.

He had had an awful childhood, treated like a freak by everyone around him until he moved away from his Montana home to Southern California where he didn't let anyone know his secret.

He used his talents to read surface thoughts of customers' minds to give them perfect massages, exactly what they wanted.

He had suggested that Cindie not talk and implanted the thought in her head, so Cindie kept forgetting what she wanted to say when she opened her mouth.

He was single and had the ability to slightly change his appearance to please someone, something that he had only told three people. Two had run away. She was the third.

He hoped she wouldn't run as well.

And he was really, really attracted to her. He didn't understand why but he was.

Just as she was really, really attracted to him.

And he couldn't change his eyebrows.

"I could trim them, maybe," he said out loud. "But they grow back quickly, sometimes overnight."

She laughed. Then she asked, "Are you controlling my thoughts?"

"No," he said, shaking his head and looking worried. She liked that look on him almost as much as she liked his smile.

She could tell, since he left his mind open to her, that he really was concerned. Concerned he would scare her. That they were moving far, far too fast. That he had trusted someone he didn't know.

And suddenly she could tell that he had told the truth, he really hadn't looked into her mind past the surface thoughts.

He really didn't know her and hadn't pried.

"How do I open my mind to you?" she asked.

"Just give me permission," he said.

"That's damn scary," she said.

He nodded. "I know."

She took a deep breath and decided to go for it. "You've shown me around your place, you should see mine before we go any farther."

He nodded and suddenly she could feel another person in her mind, gently looking around. It felt very, very strange as thoughts and memories came up she hadn't thought of for a very long time. He could see everything about her short marriage, about graduate school, about what she liked about sex.

Within a few seconds he knew more about her than anyone ever had. He knew her favorite foods, her inability to ride a bike, even her deepest secret of lusting after a teacher when she was eighteen.

Then he was gone.

And his mind was closed to her as well.

For the first time in a long time she felt very alone.

And that surprised her. She was an independent woman who didn't mind being alone.

She had *loved* having him in her mind. She had loved seeing into his mind as well. It was like a speed date only really, *really* getting to know everything about someone in just seconds instead of years.

She knew so many things about him, she didn't want to be turned away now.

"Did you see something you didn't like?" she asked, very worried

He smiled and opened his mind to her again. What he was thinking was about how much more he liked her now, more than ever after seeing her true self. And how he wanted to get her into bed.

And spend time with her.

Lots of time.

That's why he had closed off his mind. He was embarrassed by those thoughts.

"I like that idea as well," she said out loud, smiling. "How about we go for a walk and get to know each other even better?"

"I would like that very much," he said, his smile beaming.

And she could tell he really, *really* meant that as well from his thoughts.

Maria stood, taking the towel that had been over her butt and tossing it over her shoulder.

"I'll be back in a half hour," she said to Cindie. "We're just going to take a walk."

Cindie, looking completely stunned at the sudden change in her roommate, nodded and didn't say anything.

I really love that you can silence my wonderful roommate. Normally she can really talk your ear off. Can you teach me that trick?

He smiled. *You never know.*

Jason took his towel and put it over his shoulder as well.

Then Maria took his hand and through his touch could feel his mind again, open and happy.

And with a thought she invited him back into her mind.

It felt right. Perfect, actually.

"I thought you didn't like being nude out in public," he said, smiling as they started off.

"After what you've seen in my head, there's no reason in covering up anything is there?"

"You have a point," he said, laughing. *Besides you have a wonderful body. You don't want to cover it up.*

"Thank you," she said. "Am I blushing?"

"Too much sun to tell."

She could tell from his mind that he was fibbing. She was blushing and he liked it.

"Do me a favor," Maria said. "Let the hair grow on your back as we walk away. Might as well really give Cindie something to talk about, when she can remember again what she wants to say."

He laughed and Maria knew, without looking, that the hair was long and thick on his back again. And maybe, just maybe some day, she would enjoy running her fingers through it.

"I hope so," he said. "I would enjoy that."

"I'm starting to think I would as well. Given time."

"We've got the time," he said.

Hand-in-hand and thought-to-thought, they walked down the beach together, naked, in more ways than one.

MOM'S PARADOX

She seduced her husband and changed the world.

But she remembers only the act, and how great it felt, but nothing about the why.

A story of time travel and a paradox beyond killing your own mother.

"Mom's Paradox" was first published in 2001 in a slightly different form in Men Writing Science Fiction As Women *from DAW Books, edited by Mike Resnick and Martin H. Greenburg*

One

I WOKE UP AS A WOMAN.

Not that I hadn't been a woman before that morning, before feeling those cotton sheets, smelling the faint scent of John beside me, hearing him snore deeply, the vibration shaking the queen-sized bed like a distant earthquake. It seemed I had a memory of going to sleep as a woman, lying there spent, but not satisfied from the too-short love-making.

I grew up a woman. The memories of my childhood, the pains of dating, of a first marriage, of childbirth were all there.

Yet—

For the first time this morning I awoke as a woman, *feeling* like a woman, as the sun filled the drapes with orange light. What a strange thing, to be a woman, yet have the feeling of waking up as one only this morning.

I lay there, letting John's snoring fill the small bedroom as I tried to place where the strange newness was coming from.

My name was Angie Sheldon. The man shaking the bed beside me was my husband. We had two kids, both just entering high school, a nice house just outside of Denver in an upscale neighborhood, not too many bills, and a decent retirement and college account. I could honestly say I wasn't unhappy with my marriage or with John, just not always satisfied. Yet that lack of satisfaction had never been strong enough to force me to make any changes. I loved John and my kids, so the feeling wasn't coming from there.

Yet I felt wonderful, freeing, almost as if I were alive for the first time just now, this morning.

I focused on more details. I took my creative energy and drive out on my job with a law firm downtown. Both John and I were attorneys, and had met in law school. Now he worked for the District Attorney and I spent my time on business cases for the state's third largest business law firm.

That wasn't it. Nothing felt right or new about the job either. It was just the job I had been doing for years.

But still it was wonderful to wake up a woman.

I eased over onto my side so my back was to John and stared at the dresser with the pictures of our kids, Beth and Danny. I could see them clearly in the morning light. My parents were dead, John's parents still lived in California. Nothing there to cause this wonderful emotion of newness and happiness.

I couldn't remember the last time I had just stopped and looked at my life. It felt as if I was starting fresh this morning.

Why?

Because I am starting fresh this morning. Or actually I will be shortly.

The other woman's voice inside my head damned near sent me screaming from the bed. Yet somehow my muscles didn't jerk, I didn't even jump or move, as if I were pinned there, staring at the dresser. But inside my head I was screaming. I could feel my heart pounding, like someone trying to beat her way out of my chest.

Calm down. This is strange enough as it is. Don't make it worse.

I'm dreaming. That's it, I'm just dreaming. I had to be. I tried to calm myself with that thought.

No, you're not dreaming. And neither am I.

I'm going insane!

The panic was a giant ball in my throat. I willed myself to climb out of bed and run toward the bathroom, but my body stayed on its side beside my snoring husband. Nothing I could do seemed to make even my fingers twitch.

You're not insane and you can't move because I have control of your body. And to be honest with you, it feels damned strange. I can also hear everything you think, so calm down, would you?

I'm dreaming. I have to be dreaming.

No, you're not.

I have to be, or I'm going insane. There are no other choices.

Oh, sure there are. A ton of them, just none that you've thought of. And if I don't get you moving soon, some of those choices won't happen.

The newness and good sensation started to drop away, leaving me empty. John had accused me of taking the joy out of just about any situation I got into, but inside I knew I wasn't joyless. I just had a hard time letting go.

No shit. I could give you a hundred examples of how I know that.

I'm going insane. All I wanted to do was scream.

Can't you just relax and go with it? This is strange enough for me without you making it even worse.

Now I knew I had flipped out. "Gone around the bend" as John would say. I was asking myself to relax. This was the strangest dream I had ever had.

I give up.

The good feeling I had woke up with was now completely gone. Suddenly my body jerked into motion, climbing out of bed, shedding my cotton nightgown before I even got across the room. I just left it on the floor. I tried to stop, to pick up the nightgown, but my body was moving on its own. I wanted to scream for John to wake up and help me, but I couldn't.

Thank heavens for some things.

Only on special nights, with the kids gone, had I allowed myself to be nude like this, yet now I was walking out of the bedroom in the morning light, across the hall and into the bathroom. Luckily neither of the kids was awake yet.

Just settle back in there and relax. A little stop here to get rid of what is pressuring your bladder, then we get to the job at hand, so to speak.

The door is open!

As I said, settle down. What, hasn't anyone ever seen you pee?

No.

Oh, man, I just could never believe you were always this uptight, but the more times I do this, the more proof I get.

More times you do what? What is happening to me?

Nothing you're going to remember, so don't sweat it. In fact, I think I'm just going to shut this conversation off for a few minutes until I get you ready.

The blackness crept up from the corners of my mind like a curtain being drawn over everything. I fought it, but everything just got blacker. The last thought I had was that they were going to find me, nude, on the bathroom floor. How embarrassing.

Oh, give it a rest.

Two

I came back to awareness looking into John's face. I was back in bed, the bedroom door was closed, and the covers on the bed were pulled back and off.

You're going to have to help with some of this. I don't really have the stomach or the inclination to watch.

"This is a nice surprise," John said, smiling up at me. His hands were firmly on my hips.

At that point I realized that I was wearing my special occasion black nightgown, the one that John had bought for me just after our honeymoon. John had lost his pajama bottoms, and I was sitting on him as he moved under me.

And inside me!

Tell him you always liked mornings.

I wanted to scream, yet at the same time what John was doing felt wonderful. The short love-making last night had left me wanting and excited. At least the door was closed and the children weren't up yet. But I had no idea how I got into the black nightgown and in this position.

Don't question it. Just enjoy it, because I can't watch. Sorry, too weird.

I should stop. This isn't right. What is happening to me? I must be going insane. Voices inside my head telling me to seduce my husband. We have never done anything like this before.

Or in this position.

More information than I need.

John moved a little faster under me. "What got into you this morning?" he asked, his voice husky from the way we were moving together.

Let me give you just a little more help, then I'm going to shut myself out of this. I've had enough counseling as it is.

Suddenly the good feeling I had when I woke up rushed back through me, pushing all my doubts, my worries away like leaves in a strong wind.

I was a woman making love to the man she had loved for years. It felt great.

No better than great, it felt wonderful.

Perfect. I'll be back when this is over.

I seemed to forget where I was and what I was doing.

I wanted to forget.

Everything I had focused on the intense sensations of John inside me, the movement of our bodies, and the pleasure of letting go and just being a woman.

"Is it safe?" John asked, his voice low, his face beaming in the morning light.

I didn't answer him, and I didn't care that it wasn't. I just wanted to keep going, not let these feelings ever end.

The morning seemed to vanish as everything focused down to just John and me.

Then the release that had eluded me last night swept up over my body as I rode John, grinding down into him and forcing him to come with me.

A few moments, maybe minutes later, I collapsed beside him, not even caring that I wasn't covered.

"Wow," John said between gasps.

"Yeah," I managed to reply.

In all the years of being with John it had never been like that. Passion, filled with love and caring and wonderful sensations. Right at that moment I loved being a woman. And I loved being with John.

He leaned over and kissed me, gently at first, then hard. After a few moments he pulled back and smiled. "I have no idea what caused that, but whatever it was, don't fight it."

"Okay," I said, remembering the voice I thought I had heard inside my head earlier. What had I been thinking? Maybe it all came from not being satisfied last night. Right now I felt so good I didn't care.

He kissed me again, then rolled away, and stood. He pulled the blankets back up over me, then grabbed his robe and headed for the bedroom door.

I let the morning light, the wonderful afterglow of the sex, and the warm blankets lull me almost back to sleep.

Looks like it was good for you.

I felt so good I didn't even care I was making up a voice in my head again.

Now that's the attitude, Mom. Relax. Learn how to roll with things.

Mom! Now the panic of hearing a voice swept up over me.

Yeah, Mom. Sorry for the slip. Thank heavens my job here is finished.

What's happening to me?

Like I said, nothing that you're going to remember. I just needed to make sure I was going to be born.

What? Now I was screaming, but again my body wouldn't move, and no sound came out. In the distance I could hear the shower running and John singing.

Calm down. About six timelines over, you and dad did that morning tango you just finished with, and got me as a little accident. I went on to be one of the major inventors of mind-jumping through time, a cheap but effective form of time travel.

Time travel? Mind jumping? I had no idea where the voice was coming from.

Of course you wouldn't understand what I'm saying. You never did understand me, or how smart I was. It took me five years of counseling just to get over being an unwanted child, something you never let me forget, I might add.

I could feel the anger boiling inside me, but I had no idea where it came from.

My anger. Sorry.

The feeling died away.

Anyway, since I was born in only one timeline that we explored, I decided to do the opposite of the old grandfather paradox, you know the one about going back and killing your own grandfather so you can't exist, thus you could never go back and kill him.

I had no idea what the voice was saying. I was going insane. I had to be.

Figures you'd think that. Oh well, the short of it is I jumped back here, into your mind on this timeline to make sure I am born. Otherwise you'd have gotten up a little while back, make breakfast, and been tense and angry all day for no reason anyone could figure out. And I would never happen in this timeline, and time travel would not exist here either. Not that any of that matters to you, or that you will even remember.

I've gone insane. I need help. Maybe professional help.

No, I'm the one who is insane, for even trying to explain the reason of my existence to her mother. You'd think after all these years I'd know better.

A feeling of disgust and anger filled me.

Oh, sorry, my issues, not yours.

The emotions faded quickly, again replaced with the intense joy of just being alive and satisfied.

I'll leave you feeling happy about the sex and not remembering anything about this conversation. That much I can do for Dad. See you in about nine months. Be nice to me, would you?

The morning sun bathed me and warmed the bedroom as I rolled over and stretched. There was a nagging feeling I had forgotten something, but what did it matter? I just wish we had tried this morning sex thing years ago.

I kicked the covers back and just lay there, exposed to the room, my black nightgown not even covering all of me. I wonder what had gotten into me this morning?

Besides John that is.

The thought had me laughing all the way to the bathroom.

THE KEEPER OF THE MORALS

Do you really need a lack of morals to climb the corporate ladder?

What happens if the morals you used to cherish get taken by the women you love?

A story of love, greed, corporate ladders, and blondes.

Lots of blondes.

"The Keeper of the Morals" was first published in the anthology Wizards, Inc. from Daw Books, edited by Martin H. Greenberg and Loren L. Coleman.

Chapter One

I NURSED the scotch-rocks like it was the last drink I was ever going to have instead of just the first for the night, twirling the glass and the golden liquid on its paper napkin like a kid's toy. More than likely, it was going to be the drink I remembered most in a long line of drinks, followed by picking up some blonde—they were always blondes—and taking her back to my big house in my Porsche for some fast, sloppy sex and then uncomfortable good-byes.

Around me, the party atmosphere of the "Danny's Crib Lounge," combined with the music from too many speakers, kept the noise level just under that of a jet taking off. I had been lucky tonight to find a place at the bar. Usually I ended up standing, drink in hand, pretending to actually talk to someone I mostly couldn't hear.

But tonight was special. That's what my six co-workers from the legal department had told me. I had closed negotiations on one of the company's biggest deals today, opening up a wildlife refuge for my company's oil rigs to go in and drill. Tomorrow, when the news got out, our stock would shoot up, the left-wing environmentalists would cry, I would get a bonus, and then I would go back to work on the next big deal.

But tonight I got to celebrate.

But I didn't feel like celebrating anything.

Thirty-six years old and I had no idea how I had gotten here.

In this bar.

Doing the job I did.

None. Not a clue.

I used to be one of those liberals who would think of the now-me as the devil. I started off using my legal degree to fight to keep wildlife refuges closed up to companies like the one I now worked for. I took the job with my current employer thinking I could stop some of the company practices from within.

Yeah, right.

What the hell had happened to me?

That wasn't a question I asked myself that often these days. I usually just thought about the money, the stock options, and buying a bigger house, even though alone, I rattled around in the one I had like a kid lost in a big, new school.

I had enough money, but I kept thinking I needed more.

Why?

A soft touch on my shoulder made me turn to my right and into the gaze of a beautiful woman with golden hair and large brown eyes.

My stomach twisted as she smiled a perfect smile showing off perfect teeth. I had barely sipped my first drink and this woman looked fantastic.

My type. She fit it perfectly. In looks as well as everything else. Side-by-side, walking down the street, we would look like Ken and Barbie. The perfect American couple. Her features were almost as chiseled as mine.

Could I get any more superficial? There was more to women than just blonde hair and a beautiful face. I used to look past all that surface stuff, looking for a soul mate, but now it seemed, I never did.

Just like I never really looked at what I did at work.

I felt like I knew her, then shook *that* thought away. I always felt like I knew every blonde I ended up with, but never did. Someday I'd have to get some counseling on that, figure out where in my past the blonde search started.

She leaned in real close and indicated she wanted to say something in my ear over the music and noise.

I turned my head just slightly

"James, Bob sent me," she said, her breath on my ear like what I imagined a whisper from an angel might feel like. "He thought you might need a little boost."

I turned to stare at her directly, then shouted into the music. "Bob? My boss?"

She nodded.

Bob, the short, fat bastard, had sent me a hooker. How crude was that? No matter how good-looking this woman was, I just wasn't interested. Even if she was bought and paid for already.

"Tell him thanks, but no thanks," I said into her perfectly formed ear. "I like to find my own dates."

She laughed, and the laugh seemed to cut through the noise like sharp scissors through tissue paper. "Not *that* kind of boost," she said, leaning in close again.

Her breath smelled of faint cloves mixed with vanilla.

"This kind of boost."

She touched me on the shoulder and I closed my eyes as her hand stroked my arm, filling me with the warmest sensation. Man, she could "boost" me any time she wanted.

Suddenly, all my doubts about what I had done were gone, my drive to get the bigger house was back, and my need to get laid by a beautiful blonde hit me like a sledgehammer.

I opened my eyes to thank her and suggest we go somewhere a little less noisy, but she was gone, vanished into the crowd like so much smoke.

"Well, not sure what old Bob was thinking," I said. "That was lame."

I downed the drink, ordered another, and turned on the bar stool to study the crowd, the memory of her already forgotten. I was looking for a companion for the night. After all, I had some celebrating to do.

Chapter Two

I awoke to my alarm the next morning, my head fuzzy from all the scotch and my tongue feeling like I had ran it through sawdust. The sheets on my massive bed still smelled of last night's conquest, a blonde with a chest twice the size of her IQ. She wore a perfume that, after six drinks, had driven me nuts. But this morning, the remains of it smelled like an air-freshener in a men's room urinal.

I vaguely remembered she had left at some point in the middle of the night, calling a cab and taking enough money from me to buy her own cab. I didn't care, it was only money, and after yesterday's closing of the big drilling deal, I was going to be making a lot more of it.

By the time I was through my morning routine and powering toward work in my Porsche, the remains of the scotch hangover were gone and I was looking forward to all the praise I was going to get at work, not counting the bonus. There had better be a damn big bonus.

Then, like a cloud lifting, I remembered the encounter with the woman Bob had sent. My bonus better be a lot bigger than some strange blonde in a bar, making promises and then not even hanging around to follow through. If Bob paid her more than a few bucks, he was going to have to get his money back, that was for sure.

It took me a few more blocks to really put her face back in my mind. It was as if the scotch had erased it. I prided myself on never forgetting a name or a face. Then what she had said came back. She had promised a "boost." She had touched me and my attitude had changed. Often just the touch of a woman did that to me. Or at least took my focus temporarily away from a problem.

But this time it had felt different, and there was just something about her I couldn't shake. That feeling that I knew her, that same feeling I had with every damn blonde-haired woman I met. That was part of it, sure. But there was more. Bob was going to do some explaining on this one.

As I expected, when I arrived in my office, on the seventh floor of the ten-story corporate headquarters, there was a message waiting with my secretary to join Bob in his office. I usually beat him into work, sometimes by hours, but on days after closing big deals, I gave myself the freedom to just get there when I wanted to. After all, I deserved that luxury for one day. Tomorrow, I would be back working harder than anyone in the place, coming in earlier, staying later, working weekends. It was the only way to get ahead in this business, and I planned on getting very, very far ahead by the time I was done.

Bob was sitting in his big chair, feet up on his desk as I knocked and then entered his office. He was almost as wide as he was tall, and had a face like a troll stuck in the mud. I tried hard to never stand beside him in any function or picture. It would just make him look bad, and making a boss look bad was never a good career move, even though I was after his job. He was number one in the corporation's legal department; I was number two.

"Nice job on closing that deal yesterday," he said. "Stock is going through the roof, and the guys upstairs are taking hundreds of phone calls from every media outlet there is."

"Great," I said, smiling and sitting down across his desk from him. But it didn't feel that great. It was done, I had managed to pull it off; now it was time to move on, get to the next big deal. The fun was in the chase, not in the having.

It was that way with women as well.

And with my cars and houses. What I owned or had at the moment didn't mean anything. All that mattered was what I was trying to get.

"Bonus check coming your way this afternoon, approved from upstairs," Bob said, smiling a smile that turned his wrinkled face into a mass of sneers. I knew that smile. It was sincere, even though it didn't look it.

"Thanks," I said. "And if you paid that blonde you sent my way last night more than ten bucks, you got taken. She vanished without so much as a kiss good-bye."

He actually jerked, glanced at me, then looked away, as if I had surprised him by remembering her.

"No big deal," Bob said, shifting his gaze to something in an open drawer beside his desk as he sat up.

I'd hit a very sensitive topic for some reason. I knew Bob after the last two years, and I had made it my job to know his moods and actions. I had surprised him.

"Who was she?" I asked, pushing the topic. "She was sure a looker."

He shrugged, which I knew meant he was going to flat out lie to me, or give me a half-truth.

"Just someone I know from personnel," he said. "I just suggested she stop by and see how the celebrating was doing."

"This someone have a name?" I asked.

He laughed and wagged a fat finger at me. "You know the rules on dating someone in the company."

I smiled. "You were the one that sent her, remember?"

"Not to screw your eyes out," Bob said, shaking his head and pretending to laugh. "Now, can we get to work and leave your personal life outside these walls? What little I already know about it scares hell out of me."

I dropped the subject and Bob and I started in on the next project, working to get right-of-ways through some old family farms for a pipeline. But I had no idea of letting the chase for the blonde from personnel go that easily. When I got my teeth into something like this, I never let go until it was finished.

While Bob was off with the higher-ups having a two-drink, two-hour lunch, I told my secretary I was not to be disturbed, then used my company security clearance to access employee records on a secure screen on my computer.

Sometimes certain legal work required me to do just that, so no one would think what I was doing odd if they noticed at all. It didn't take much of a scan of the people who worked in personnel to tell me that part of Bob's story had been a flat out lie. But I didn't doubt she worked for the company. The question was in what department, and why hadn't I seen her before?

I used the fact that I hadn't seen her to eliminate a dozen different departments I worked in and around regularly, depending on the project. But that still left over five hundred personnel photos to go through.

It took me until two in the afternoon.

She wasn't there.

So who was she, and why had Bob been surprised I had remembered her? She was clearly doing a favor of some sort for him. And the way he had acted, knowledge of her was not something Bob was willing to share.

I sat back, put my feet up on my desk, and covered my eyes, trying to sort out all the details like a giant legal puzzle.

I still believed she worked somewhere in the company. That was the way Bob lied, with half-truths, or truths that left out real basic information.

And I believed now that she had been sent to give me something she called a "boost." More than likely some sort of drug or something on her hands. The fog about last night had now completely cleared and I had a very real memory of what her touch had done to me. If it was a drug, I didn't much like that idea at all. I took my share of alcohol, but drugs were not something I did, or ever wanted to do. Too damn scary, and too much chance of messing with my mind. I made my money with my mind. I ruin that and it would be all over.

She had to work here somewhere, but where?

I looked up the official number of employees in the company from the records I had just gone through, then went into the payroll records and asked how many people were drawing official compensation.

Bingo.

The number was different by one.

So somewhere, this company had a secret employee, and I had no doubt that when I found that employee, it would be a beautiful blonde with wonderful brown eyes and a very scary touch.

Chapter Three

I had very little time over the next three days to continue the search for my elusive Blonde Booster, as I was starting to call her. But then, on Saturday, Bob didn't come in, and I was pretty much alone in the building. When I worked a Saturday or a Sunday, I was often one of the only few people in the big, ten-story building. I always got a lot done and liked the quiet. Besides, except for drinking at night and searching for blondes to take home, I didn't have a hell of a lot more to my life than work. Kind of sad when I thought about it, but I didn't much think about it that often.

This Saturday I liked the quiet for another reason. I had a quest.

Instead of going out last night, I had actually stayed at home with take-out Chinese food and studied floor plans and office layouts of the entire company building. There were only a few offices not clearly marked, and those would be my first targets.

I arrived at my office around ten, carrying a large mocha coffee and wearing jeans and a sweater. The old suit and tie were just not needed on a Saturday.

I took the floor plans out of my briefcase and spread them over my desk, studying them once again while I sipped the wonderful flavor of my coffee. Somewhere in this building the Blonde Booster might have an office. If she did, I was going to find it. If she worked from home, then I'd go into personnel records next, working through the payroll until I found out where her checks went. Having high-level security clearance sure came in handy sometimes.

I was staring at the map when a soft voice said from the door, "Looking for me?"

I somehow managed to remain fairly contained, and didn't snort any coffee out of my nose, which, considering the surprise I felt, was a miracle.

"Actually, I was," I said.

She was more beautiful than I remembered. Long, blonde hair flowed down over her shoulders, and her eyes were round, her smile real. She wore a baggy sweater and jeans with tennis shoes, but even that dressed down, nothing about her amazing body was really hidden.

She moved over to my desk, glanced down at the floor plans of the big structure, and then pointed with a fantastically perfect finger and short fingernail to one office that wasn't marked. "That's my office."

"That was going to be my second stop," I said. "Do you have a name?"

"Glenda," she said. "For now, just call me Glenda."

I pointed to a chair on the other side of my desk and then sat down as she did, keeping the desk between me and her. No way I wanted to get near that booster touch of hers again. Or at least not right away. I needed some answers first.

"I'm guessing from Bob's reaction that it's a surprise that I remembered you."

"Not really," she said, shrugging. "I can only do so much on the memory fogging aspects. But it really doesn't matter anymore, since I got the last of what you had at the bar the other night."

I didn't much like the sounds of *that*, but she went on before I could ask what exactly I was now missing completely.

"Since I did," she said, holding my gaze, "you're going to be promoted upstairs next week, over Bob and into a VP position in management, and then you would have been told about my presence here anyway."

I had so many questions about all that she had said, I couldn't think of which one to ask first, so instead I just sipped my coffee and stared at her beautiful face. My goal was to be a vice president, then maybe even higher, but I sure hadn't expected it this soon, and not over the top of Bob.

I did a quick run-through of all the questions, then settled on starting with the most basic. "So, what's your official title here?"

"Keeper of the Morals," she said with as straight a face as I had ever seen.

"And your job description?" I asked, trying not to laugh at her.

She looked me right in the eye. "I extract and contain employee personal morals, mostly in the legal and management departments, so that they can work with the full interest of the corporation at heart."

"And just how do you do that?" I asked, remembering what I had been thinking about at the bar, how I had changed, how I had no idea how I had become the person I had become. That memory scared hell out of me suddenly.

And made me angry at the same time. I didn't much like the idea of something being taken from me without my knowledge, especially under orders from Bob.

"Magic," she said. "Every major corporation has someone like me, a person of magic who can, for a fee, do as asked. And I have to admit, my fee is *very* high."

She smiled at that. She clearly enjoyed money as much as I did.

"I'll bet," I said, trying but failing to push all the memories of what I used to think, how I used to feel about the job I now did.

"Remembering your morals, aren't you?" she asked, smiling at me.

"I have to admit I am. And you're starting to scare me, to be honest with you."

She laughed. "Take a deep breath and look at those memories, at how you used to be. You're going to be a vice president of this company, with a big office two more floors up. Do you really care about how you used to feel when you drove that Volkswagen and camped out at music concerts?"

I started to say that I did, then realized she was right. I didn't care. But I didn't care because she had taken that caring from me. She and Bob.

"What did you do to me?" I asked.

"The first day you were here at work, we met. Remember?"

I started to shake my head, then suddenly the memory of her shaking my hand and holding onto it that first day came flooding back. We had spent a wonderful lunch and afternoon together, talking, laughing, touching.

The memory of that fantastic day flooded back over me like a wet dream. "We went back to my place that night, didn't we?"

She nodded.

I remembered now that I felt like I had fallen in love with her in that one short day. How could I have forgotten that? It still felt like I was in love with her now that I remembered. No wonder I kept going home with blondes. I had been looking for Glenda all this time.

I shook my head. I hadn't felt this far off balance in years. I looked into those wonderful eyes and managed to get out my question again. "What *exactly* did you do to me?"

She shrugged. "I used my magic to take your morals, so you could be a better attorney for the company. That's all. Got the last of a vast supply the other night in the bar."

I wanted to shout at her, call her a common thief, but my legal mind just wasn't believing what she was saying. My memories of my actions, of how I used to feel and think, were clear. I used to care about something more than money and a bigger house.

But now that was all I cared about.

That thought hit me like a hammer to the skull, and I knew, without a doubt, she had done just what she said she had done. She had taken all my caring away.

And the moment I accepted that, my mind snapped back to clear thinking and I knew what I had to do.

"I seem to remember that afternoon and evening as being very special, at least to me. You do that with all the lawyers?"

She actually had the decency to blush. "No, only you. You were my first, and the only since. I've been just waiting until this day came, so I could show myself to you again."

I stood and moved around my desk, kneeling at the side of her chair and touching her wonderful soft skin. "You could still care about a man who has had his morals destroyed?"

"I'm pretty sure that not having morals doesn't mean you can't still love," she said, putting her other hand on mine and holding me to her. "And I didn't destroy them. They're just stored, just like all the others."

"You're not kidding, are you?"

"Not kidding," she said softly.

"And you can put them back into people?"

She nodded and said nothing.

I laughed and stood, moving away from her, pacing, thinking. I often did some of my best thinking while pacing. I was angry, in love, and scared to death about what had been done to me. I needed to get those thoughts sorted out so that my next action wouldn't be completely stupid.

All the time I paced she sat silently, watching me.

Finally, I needed a little more information before I went any farther. I turned to her frowning and worried face. "How easy are these morals moved around and put into people?"

She held up what looked like a small fountain pen. "I have yours right in here. I promised myself I would give them back to you if you asked. That's how much I care about you."

That thought suddenly set me back.

"All my morals fit into a pen?" I asked, stunned. "Guess I didn't have that many, huh?"

"Highly compacted," she said. "You had an overabundance of them, to be honest."

"Yeah, I remember that," I said, laughing. "But for the time being, put that away. I don't want to accidentally get them back just yet."

She now looked puzzled, then the pen vanished back into her baggy sweater somehow. Maybe later, if things went the way I was hoping, I'd get to inspect those pockets a little closer.

"One more question," I said. "Who ordered you to take those from me?"

"Bob," she said. "With approval of the president of the company."

I nodded. That was all I needed.

"I think I owe you a long, early lunch, don't you?" I said, smiling at Glenda. "You saved me a lot of searching around the building."

She still looked worried, but I had a hunch if this woman could really do what she said she had done, and liked money as much as I did, then we were going to be very, very happy for a time in the very near future.

I took her by the arm, and like a modern version of Ken and Barbie, dressed down, we headed to lunch.

Chapter Four

I escorted Glenda to this fantastic, small restaurant where I knew we could talk for hours and not be disturbed. Over chicken slices and strong cups of mocha, we discovered we really liked each other. And that we both had the same goals, to be fantastically wealthy and powerful.

And I came to remember that even with my morals, I had wanted that same goal. Only I had planned on doing really good things with all the money once I got it.

I asked her why she just couldn't magic-up money and she said it didn't work that way. Her talents were more personal based, either giving someone good feelings or taking feelings from them. That's why the company had hired her to help them with the attorneys and management teams.

"Better than what a lot of my type do for money," she said, looking very alluringly at me.

"What's that?"

"Call girls, dating services," she said. "We can *really* make a man feel good."

"I've noticed that."

"I'm not doing anything," she said, laughing.

"I'm kind of wondering why not?"

"Yeah, me too," she said, smiling a smile at me that I would never forget.

With that, we moved to my house, with me breaking far too many speed limits along the way. We barely managed to get inside and to the bed before working as much magic on each other as we could do.

In the euphemistic sense of course.

More directly, we had great sex. Better than great, actually. But I won't go there.

Finally, after who knows how long, we both lay there exhausted. And for the first time, I didn't want this blonde to leave. I wanted her to stay right beside me.

"So, what exactly can you do with my morals?"

Naked, laying there with her golden body facing me, she suddenly become very worried again. No doubt she thought I might ask for them back, and to be honest, I had thought about getting them back into me as quickly as possible. Not much thought, but the idea did sound right. They had been taken, I wanted them back, just like anything else I owned that was taken.

"You said you can put them back, right?"

She nodded.

"Can you put mine, or Bob's, or the president's, or someone in general from the corporate supply into someone else?"

She now looked puzzled, then nodded. "I don't see why not."

"And even though what you give them is not their own morals, they would still work?"

"Sure. I'm sure it would be as if they got their own back."

I kissed her, then said, "How about we use that vast supply you have in storage to sabotage our company's rivals? Think we could do that?"

She blinked once, then twice, as if not really hearing me.

"You and me," I said, stroking the soft skin on her arm. "Working together. You get the morals into some of those decision-makers in other companies, cripple them with good intentions and feelings for the underdogs, and I'll take advantage of the situation. Together, we can make a fortune and just keep on moving up in the company."

Again she blinked, then she moved into me with her full body and kissed me like I had never been kissed before. Clearly, she liked my idea. I had no doubt that a woman who could steal other's morals for corporate and personal gain would like it.

The rest of that afternoon and evening we did things sexually I had never done before, or thought possible. Amazing how the promise of a lot of money and a little lack of morals can motivate a person. And I'm sure there was some magic involved as well.

Chapter Five

Six months later, I moved into my new corner office on the tenth floor, right next to Glenda's and two doors down from the president's office. Given a little time, that office could be mine as well if I wanted it. I didn't want it.

The view out my window was stunning, looking out over the city. I had gone through two levels of vice presidents since my move out of the legal department. My official title was now Executive Vice President in Charge of Corporate Acquisitions. And I had bought enough of the company stock that, if I wanted to, I could have a seat on the Board of Directors.

I didn't want that any more than I wanted to be president. And besides, most of my stock was in special holding corporations very hard to trace back to me.

I just wanted to be rich. Fantastically rich. And I was almost there.

In my top drawer was the pen that held my morals, locked away safely. Glenda had told me how the pen inserter worked and let me keep it just to make sure it didn't get mixed up with all the other morals we were taking from the corporate 'morals pool.'

Over the past six months, Glenda and I spent every night together in my big new mansion. Next month we had decided I was buying a yacht. All of it was in my name, of course.

I had taken care of dear old Bob quickly after moving upstairs. A little planted evidence and a double dose of morals from Glenda sent him scampering. The little bastard was working as a legal aide down in a shelter and living in a studio apartment after his wife had kicked him out. Served the bastard right for stealing from me.

Now, it was time to put the rest of my plan in motion. With one last look at the fantastic view from the office I had worked so hard to get to, I unlocked my drawer and took out the magic pen holding my morals, then tucked it safely in my pocket.

Then I quickly went over my resignation letter. It said what I needed it to say. I had moved nothing into my office that I wanted to keep. There was nothing about this job that I cared about. Nothing to pack. Having no morals could make you feel that way.

All I ever wanted was the chase, the hunt, the excitement of the search, keeping score with the money. I had been that way even before having my morals stolen.

Now, things were going to get really exciting.

After six months, I had convinced myself that I didn't much care about Glenda either. After all, she was the one who took from me what was mine. There would be other blondes I was sure. Granted, Glenda was damn fun in bed, but as she had told me that first afternoon, many witches were good in bed. It came with the magic.

Sally was almost as good as Glenda. I had met Sally two weeks ago, when she joined Glenda and me for a little three-way afternoon fling. And with a little training from me on some of Glenda's special moves, Sally would be almost as good.

I dropped off my resignation letter with the president's secretary. Then dropped off my good-bye letter in Glenda's office. I told her that her things had already been moved out of my house and which storage unit she could find them in. Granted, it was a cold way to end a relationship, but what did she expect from someone who didn't care? She knew what she had gotten into with me. After all, she was the one who took all my caring and stored it in a magic pen.

On the way down to the main entrance, I stopped off in the basement and slipped a tiny, but very powerful device into the main air flow duct. Glenda and I had come up with the device to use on other corporations, and it had worked wonderfully, spreading morals throughout a building in high doses; so high that often before I could schedule a corporate takeover, the company was dissolving into chaos.

This company, in a short time, would be experiencing the same thing. Glenda would be able to stop some of it if she wanted to, but not enough, and I doubted she would even try.

I had six more of the tiny morals bombs in my briefcase.

I made sure I was outside the building before the thing triggered and started giving back all the corporate executives and lawyers their morals. In very high doses.

The next morning I called my six different stock brokers and put in orders to short a large chunk of my corporate stock, buying options on some more and running puts. I had no doubt the stock was going down, and I was going to make a ton of money on the way down.

Six weeks later, I was richer than I had ever imagined as my former company stock hit bottom and was bought up by yet another rival. During those weeks, Glenda had tried to call me twice, but both times Sally answered the phone.

Sally said Glenda was crying, which meant that she too had been dosed. All I could do was shrug. What did Glenda expect, anyway? The sex had been good, she should let it go.

I didn't tell Sally that I dreamed of Glenda every night, and imagined having sex with her when I was with Sally. I figured that given enough time, that would change. But so far it hadn't.

Chapter Six

Ten months later, I had bought massive amounts of stock in six other companies, morals-bombed them, and then got even richer as they crashed and I shorted the stock all the way down. I had become a morals terrorist, destroying companies by making them do the right things. I was sure my bleeding-heart liberal self would be proud of me.

By this time, Sally was also a distant memory, just like I had hoped Glenda would become. Now I spent every night back at Danny's Crib, getting drunk and searching for that perfect woman. Blonde, of course.

None of them measured up to Glenda, but I still searched.

Tonight seemed to be no different than any of the others, yet it was. I knew I was done for the moment, the big plan finished, the last stock sold. I was so rich, it seemed almost silly to keep going. But I knew I wanted more.

I swirled my scotch, letting the ice clink against the side. I could feel it through the cold glass, but I couldn't hear the ice over the pounding of the loud music. I was sitting on the same bar stool that I had been on when Glenda had taken the last of my morals.

My world, it seemed, had come full circle. Now, finally tonight, over a year after that night, was as good a time as any to get who I really was back.

I took out the magic pen I had been carrying for the past month. It was time to retrieve what had been taken from me, to become a whole person again.

I was fantastically rich, I could use that money for some of the causes I supported before I took the corporate job. And the old me would be proud of the fact that I had brought seven greedy corporate giants to their knees. I was sure of that.

I took a quick drink of the scotch, set the glass on the napkin, then without another thought, placed the pen against my skin on my palm and triggered it.

It was as if I had a bad cold that suddenly had cleared up. Everything I had done over the past years in my corporate job came flashing back to me like a movie in fast forward.

And then I suddenly realized how many people I had hurt along the way.

I could almost feel their pain.

Bob, Glenda, Sally, a hundred different blondes, and thousands of employees with families and jobs.

I had hurt them all.

And suddenly I knew that. And suddenly I cared.

"Oh, no, what have I done?" I shouted into the loud music.

And with that I broke down right there on the bar.

And I couldn't stop sobbing into my arm. The bartender finally had me escorted outside and I sat in my new Porsche in the parking lot, banging my hands on the steering wheel and shouting at nothing while I sobbed.

I just couldn't stop.

I had hurt so many people. I could almost feel all their pain, understand everything I had put them through. It was like waves washing over me. Every memory, every deed suddenly was real, had real people attached, had real consequences.

I had nothing to live for any more.

I was the lowest of scum.

I had guns, lots of guns, back in my house. Just one with one bullet would end this, take these thoughts, these memories away, these feelings away.

As I reached to start the car, Glenda climbed into the passenger seat. It took me a moment to realize who it was.

"I was wondering how long it would be before you took back your morals."

All I could do was sob that I was sorry. So sorry.

I had never felt so sorry for anything in my entire life. I had loved Glenda, had hurt her.

I didn't deserve to live.

"I know you are sorry," she said, her voice cutting through the massive waves of self-pity and sadness for what I had done.

Her hand touched me, that wonderful hand, and I suddenly started feeling calmer.

"I'll take about half," she said. "Then we can talk. Is that all right with you?"

All I could do was nod. At this point, I needed anything to make this pain go away.

She kept stroking my arm and I calmed down, got a part of my brain back, got some basic control of myself.

Finally, she stopped. I could feel all the remorse and sadness for my actions, but only as background thoughts. My brain was back.

I turned to stare at her. "You knew I would take my morals back?"

"Of course," she said. "From that first moment in your office. I had money in dummy corporations and shorted our company's stock just like you did as it went down. I got almost as rich as you did."

I sat there for a moment, my mouth opening and closing, realizing just how smart Glenda was, how she had played me just as I had played her.

"And the other corporations?" I asked. "You were following me, weren't you?"

"Of course," she said. "I love you, remember? But that didn't stop me from making even more money while you were doing what you were doing."

I could feel the guilt starting to come up again from what morals she had left in me. She could clearly see it as well.

"You need another little bit drained off?"

I nodded, and she touched me again, and like climbing a long staircase, I got closer to thinking even clearer, like coming out of a dark basement into the light of day.

"Thanks," I said. "I would have killed myself if you hadn't come along."

"I know," she said, her voice sad. "No person with as many morals as you had to start with could live with what you've done over the last few years."

"So, after what I did to you, why did you save me?"

"Love," she said. And then she smiled that smile I had come to know so well. "And greed. We make a really great team."

"Yeah, but you'll never trust me again."

She laughed. "I didn't trust you the first time. Any more than you trusted me. But the sex was great. That's good enough to base a pretty good relationship on, don't you think?"

With that, she actually managed to make me laugh a little, which came out like a hiccup.

I turned in the car seat to face her. "Yeah, it was. I must admit, I've missed that. And I've missed you, every day. I was just so damn angry with you for taking something of mine."

"I know," she said. "But this time you wanted me to take them. And you can have them back any time you want."

I held up my hand. "No, let's just leave it at this level for the moment. Small enough to not control my thoughts, but not completely gone."

"That was the level I settled on for myself as well," she said.

I realized, right at that moment, staring into those golden eyes and smiling face, that I never wanted to hurt her in any way again.

"I really do love you," I said.

"I know," she said. "I love you as well."

"So how come I didn't feel that when I had no morals?"

She shrugged. "I have a hunch that without morals, you don't care about anyone else but yourself. And love requires that caring to work for any length of time."

I nodded, deciding I'd just accept that for the moment and think about it later, when all the swirling emotions were a little more under control.

"So what next?" I asked.

She laughed. "Well, I'm blonde."

"Right on that," I said.

"And I have it on good authority you like picking up blondes in this bar here." She pointed to the front door of Danny's Crib.

"Right again," I said, smiling at her.

"So how about you take me back to that obscenely large mansion of yours and show me what tricks you've learned in bed over the last ten months."

"I'd love to," I said. "And you can show me what you've learned."

"Not a thing," she said. "I've just been waiting for you."

Again, I just sat there, my mouth opening and closing like a damn fish out of water. I stared at her, into those wonderful golden eyes, taking in that fantastic smile. And I let myself feel the love for her, the emotions of sadness at what I had done to her, and the fantastic feeling of happiness that she actually wanted me back, and had waited.

It seems we had a lot of real feelings to talk about.

But that could wait. Sex came first.

Lots and lots of sex.

She was a blonde, I had picked her up at Danny's Crib, just like all the others. But I had a feeling, an honest feeling, that this time, she would be the last blonde I ever picked up there.

And it was a feeling I liked.

THE WAGES OF THE MOMENT

A Thunder Mountain/Jukebox Story

When Stout watches himself appear and disappear a bunch of times right in front of his own jukebox, he knows his time machine needs some repairs.
And in doing so, he finally gets to meet the inventors of the jukebox.
But first he must deal with himself, in more ways than one.

One

You know your time machine is screwed up when a person just starts appearing and disappearing at random times. And that person is you.

Jenny and I were back in town from San Francisco for the Christmas holidays, actually the first Christmas back since we had gotten married.

And I was back in the Garden. I still hadn't gotten used to not owning the place and being on the other side of the bar, but since I had sold the Garden Lounge to Richard Cone ten months before, I had made myself stay on the customer side unless Richard asked me to do otherwise.

The Garden Lounge is a very special bar that I had owned for over a decade. An old-fashioned neighborhood place with vinyl booths, a few tables, some artificial plants and a long, polished wooden bar with nine bar stools. Richard, to his credit, had changed nothing, even keeping the lights low all the time as I had done.

To the right side of the bar was an old Wurlitzer jukebox that was never turned on or plugged in except for very special occasions, usually Christmas Eve. That jukebox was a time travel machine of sorts. It could actually take a person back to the memory of a song for the length of the song.

And that person could change their future while in their past and maybe not end up back at the Garden Lounge, which was why the jukebox was so dangerous. And why it was almost never plugged in. It created new timelines if anything was changed.

But every Christmas Eve we plugged it in and let friends take rides back into their own pasts with instructions to change nothing. It had become a special evening for all of us and the reason why Jenny and I were back in town for the holiday.

But at one point there was a dark side to the Christmas Eve ceremony. I had lost a number of friends, friends that I could remember when the timeline changed because I had been touching the jukebox when they didn't return.

It was two in the afternoon, two days before Christmas. Richard had just opened and was sipping on an orange juice as he leaned against the back bar, just as I used to do when I owned the place.

I was sipping on my normal Christmas eggnog without alcohol, sitting on the bar stool closest to the jukebox that Richard used to sit on. We had just switched places. It felt weird, but somehow right.

Jenny was off shopping and wouldn't be here for a good hour. She liked to give me time with my old friends without her hanging around, even though all the regulars thought of her as just another member of the gang.

Dave, my best friend, a retired airline pilot, sat beside me at the bar and Big Carl, a contractor who had been a regular since I opened the place sat next to Dave. If I remember right, we were talking about a football game I had attended a month before in San Francisco when suddenly Richard's eyes got huge and he said softly, "Stout?"

I said, "Yeah."

And from the direction of the jukebox someone else said, "Hi, Richard."

I spun toward the voice.

That someone else was me, looking very dirty and a decade or more older.

If my mug of eggnog hadn't been sitting on the bar, I would have dropped it.

My older self looked at me, nodded and then said, "Good, got this one right. Glad you are here. I remember this now."

And with that he vanished.

Two

The silence in the bar seemed like a big thick weight.

I glanced at Richard whose eyes were huge, then back at where the old me had appeared beside the unplugged jukebox.

Dave cleared his throat. "Looks like you're going to have a rough time at some point in the future."

It did look that way, I had to admit. I had gotten dirty helping Jenny in her garden down in San Francisco last year, but even at my worst I hadn't looked as bad as I had looked a moment before.

Suddenly the air near the jukebox shimmered and the older me appeared again, just as dirty and dust-covered.

The older me smiled at me, then said, "Good, got this one right. Glad you are here. I remember this now."

The exact same thing he had said the first time.

Then he also vanished.

'Oh, oh," Richard said right before more versions of older me, or copies three-through-nine appeared in quick order, all saying exactly the same thing before vanishing.

We all just sat stunned. I mean, when nine copies of yourself suddenly appear, it takes a moment to get used to the idea. Actually, I doubt I would ever get used to the idea, but by the time number nine disappeared, I knew I had to do something to stop this and stop it quick before the numbers of me got really, really big.

When version number ten appeared and started to speak, I held up my hand. "You've said that and a bunch of you have already been here."

The older, dirtier me stopped, thought for a second, then said, "Damn, I remember that now."

And then he vanished.

The silence again filled the Garden Lounge as we all sat staring at the jukebox, waiting for another version of me to appear.

Nothing.

Finally, from down the bar Carl said, "You think he kept leaving because we didn't offer him a drink?"

Richard just shook his head and Dave chuckled.

"Got any idea what might be going on?" Dave asked as I sat staring at the jukebox.

"Not a clue," I said. "I've never opened up the real interior of that thing. Richard?"

Richard just shook his head. "I haven't touched it at all since you left, Stout. Wouldn't even begin to know what I was looking at."

"You looked older," Carl said. "Got any sense of how far into the future they are coming from?"

I shook my head. "Never tried to guess what I was going to look like. At this point I'm just happy getting out of bed every morning. But now I'm going to have nightmares for years."

I turned back to face Richard behind the bar and took a sip of my eggnog. I could see the jukebox out of the corner of my eye and if there was movement I would know it. I had a hunch this was far, far from over, whatever was going on.

"Might not be that far in the future," Richard said. "The gray hair and extra wrinkles on his face just might be dirt and dust."

'Possible," Carl said. "I got caught in some cement dust and looked like that once."

"But why now, why at this moment?" Richard asked.

I knew the answer instantly on that. "Listen."

"Silence," Carl said after a moment of all of us pausing.

"Exactly," Dave said, nodding, understanding what I was thinking.

Richard had not turned on the background music, so there was no music on to trigger the jukebox or to plant memories of this moment in any of our minds.

"I wonder why your statement stopped the appearances," Carl said.

I glanced past David at the big contractor. He clearly looked rattled and his drink was empty. I had a hunch Richard knew that and was pacing the big guy's consumption.

"You locked him into this timeline," David said.

All of us stared at him as if he had lost a bolt.

He just shrugged. "We all know that if we go back and change

243

something in the past, we create a new timeline. When Stout here let me go back and save my wife, I created a timeline different from the one I left. One where she lived and I never had come into the Garden. Right?"

We all nodded.

"But there are many timelines, more than likely millions, where I didn't go back, where Stout didn't open this bar, and so on and so on. Those versions of Stout were just from different timelines, all close, but yet different, where you are trying the same thing, whatever that may be, at some point in the future."

I could see where he was going. "So by talking and telling him what he was doing, I locked him and me together in this timeline, blocking out the others."

"At least the first nine," David said. "But this could be going on in millions of timelines in different ways right now. You just stopped the timelines from crossing into the same event."

"Richard, you don't have enough eggnog for that many Stouts," Carl said.

"This makes my head hurt," Richard said. "Have I ever said how much that machine worries me?"

"Me too," I said. "But if I know all of this in the future, what am I trying to do? And how am I getting back here without a song?"

"Seems to me you figured out how the jukebox works," Richard said and Dave nodded.

"But why would I do that?"

"Because the jukebox was full," my voice said from beside the jukebox. "It needed to be fixed."

Three

We all turned to see the dust-covered me standing beside the dark jukebox. I watched as my future self patted the jukebox and said, "In fact, it's full now. I'll fix it so you all can have Christmas Eve like normal."

"Sounds like we didn't have a normal one in your original timeline," I said to my older self.

"You got that right. The jukebox didn't work. It took me three years to track this actual jukebox to where it was made originally as a regular jukebox. Then I followed through old sales records what happened to it to make it into this special jukebox."

I nodded. I had thought of doing just that a few times, but had never really had a reason.

"Where are you coming from?" Dave asked.

"An old abandoned gold mine called the Trade Dollar above the old ghost town of Silver City, Idaho," the older me said. "That's why the dust. It's hard to get a crystal off a wall without doing damage to it."

I watched as the older me spread out his arms and sent dust flying in the air. With that he turned and with a key opened the jukebox, lifting the lid and showing the metal box inside that I had never had the courage to open.

As we watched, the older me clicked open the metal box with another key, showing a vast array of long crystals with wires running from the crystals out of the back of the box.

They looked like a mass of growing quartz crystals, only they had a slight rose color about them. And an odd light seemed to come from them, like they were almost alive.

Numbers of the larger crystals were a good half-foot long and thousands of small ones seemed to grow around the big ones, most the size of the tip of a pen.

I just stared, unable to speak.

"Wow," Richard said.

The older me pointed at the mass of crystals. "Each one is a different timeline created by the jukebox travelers. The machine was never meant to last this long and let this many timelines grow in it."

"How do you know that?" I asked my older self.

"I have talked to the guy and his wife who built all this. He's a twenty-something who lives a few miles from here, actually. His name is Duster Kendal and his wife's name is Bonnie. Wonderful people. His family owns the mine. He built the jukebox on one of his trips into the past, thought it might be kind of fun to attach songs to time travel. You ought to hear some of their stories. They have both actually lived hundreds and hundreds of years. Not kidding."

"Does he know the jukebox is here?" Dave asked over my shoulder.

"He has always known where it was," my older self said, smiling like a ghost, the white dust covering his face making me look just weird.

"He likes how we've been treating it and being careful using it, so he's helping me fix it. He didn't realize it had broke."

My older self pulled out a smaller crystal from his pocket and placed it carefully beside the jukebox, then as we watched, my older self unhooked the large mass of crystals and pulled the entire thing from the jukebox, placing it gently on the floor.

I stared at the mass of crystals, knowing that somehow in there was my entire life, and everyone who had known about the jukebox at the Garden, and all the lives we had changed.

My older self carefully installed the small crystal, then closed the interior box and locked it, then closed the jukebox.

Then he patted it and said, "Now you can have a normal Christmas Eve celebration."

"Wait!" I said as the older me started to pick up the mass of crystals. "We're not going to remember any of this, are we? Since you are changing this timeline."

"Not a bit of it," the older me said, smiling. "You know, by me doing this I am creating a different timeline for you, one where the jukebox will work on Christmas Eve."

"And you'll still have your memories of the jukebox not working?" Dave asked.

"Exactly," the older me said. "That's my timeline. Have a great time, so to speak."

I had to remember this.

I had to.

I wanted to see that gold mine, I wanted to talk to the man who built the jukebox. I couldn't let these memories vanish.

I just couldn't.

My older self picked up the mass of crystals from the floor as I jumped toward the jukebox.

I got my hands on the edge of the jukebox as he stood upright. He smiled at me and shrugged. "Just might work."

Then he vanished.

Four

A wave of energy, like a heat mirage, seemed to shift over the Garden Lounge. I knew that feeling well. It happened any time someone went back through the jukebox and changed the past and changed the timeline.

I stood there, both hands pressed as hard as I could against the glass of the old jukebox, letting the wave pass.

And when it did I could still remember everything that happened.

I knew where the mine was and everything.

Looks like Jenny and I had a trip to make up to an old Idaho ghost town next summer.

"What are you doing, Stout?" Richard asked from his position behind the bar.

Dave and Carl were also looking at me with puzzled looks.

Then Dave said, "You're touching the jukebox. Something happened, didn't it? That we don't remember."

"I hate it when that happens," Carl said.

I carefully took my hands off the unplugged machine, then smiled. "Yeah, we just had a visit from a jukebox mechanic. The old baby had to be tuned up for the Christmas Eve celebration."

All three men just stared at me like I had lost a bolt.

"So who was this imaginary mechanic," Richard asked. "And how much do I owe him?"

I sat back down on the stool and smiled up at my friend. "It was me," I said. "A future me. You owe me another eggnog and we'll call it even. And I promise I'll tell you all what just happened as soon as Jenny gets here."

"Sometimes that machine just scares hell out of me," Richard said, going for the eggnog.

"You met yourself?" Carl asked, shaking his head. "Now that would creep me out."

"Actually," I said, "he was a nice guy."

All three of my friends just groaned.

Behind us the front door to the Garden Lounge opened and I turned around to see a young couple enter. The man was wearing a long leather coat that swirled around his cowboy boots. A brown cowboy hat was tucked over his eyes, but he quickly pulled the hat off. The woman had on a long coat that looked like it was from the turn of the 19th century in fashion and high black boots. Both had long brown hair and both were very, very attractive people.

"We have new friends," I said, smiling at Richard, who looked puzzled.

"Who are they?" Dave asked.

"The inventors of the jukebox," I said.

Then I stood and headed toward them, sticking out my hand. "Duster and Bonnie Kendal I presume."

The young guy shook my hand, a huge smile filling his face.

"You look a lot younger not covered in dust," he said.

Bonnie also smiled as she shook my hand. "You are just amazing, you know that? I hope Jenny's on the way."

"Any time now," I said.

Duster shook his head. "I'll be damned, you told me it might have worked and you would remember yourself being here and I didn't believe you. Only reason we know as well was because we were touching our machine on our side. The one that doesn't require music."

I laughed. "I would love to see it. But that's an amazing jukebox you built here."

Then I turned and indicated that they should join us at the bar. "We've got some stories to tell you about your wonderful invention and how it has saved lives."

"And since you teased us with a few of those stories three years from now," Bonnie said, "we're dying to hear them."

Richard, Dave, and Carl all sat staring and listening.

Finally Richard said simply, "Does this stuff give anyone else a headache?"

Everyone laughed and I knew this first Christmas not owning the Garden Lounge was going to be as wonderful as any in the past.

BLACK BETSY

A Jukebox Story

Shoeless Joe Jackson made a mistake and was banned from baseball for life.

Sometimes, in the Garden Lounge, the special jukebox lets a customer go back in time to a mistake and fix it.

Shoeless Joe never had a chance to let the jukebox help him fix his mistake, but instead it allowed Shoeless Joe to do something even more important: Help a child become a better adult.

"Black Betsy" first appeared in the anthology Alternate Outlaws *from TOR Books edited by Mike Resnick.*

One

ELEVEN IN THE MORNING, *December 5th.*

The time and the day stuck in my head like the memory of my first kiss or the memory of my dad dying. The weather that morning had turned unseasonably cold. Not baseball weather at all. A storm coming down the west coast from Alaska was projected to bring four inches of snow to the valley floor and light snow was already falling. The storm would eventually drop almost a foot of snow and shut down the schools for two days. But that wasn't what I remembered about December 5th.

What I remembered about that morning was Edward Toole. I turned on the jukebox that morning and sent him back to 1951.

Back to a time when baseball was important to him and to one other very special man.

I had just finished the morning bookkeeping for the Garden Lounge, made the deposit from the night before, and started the prep work for the day. Light snowflakes swirled in a whirlwind just inside the front door as Edward entered. He brushed off his coat, stamped his feet hard twice, and then moved through the empty tables toward the bar. He was a big man, thick shoulders, thick waist, with thinning brown and gray hair, and dark, brooding eyes. He was the last person I would have expected to show up in the Garden at eleven in the morning. He worked as a house lawyer for the big computer firm to the south of town. He had a wife, two boys, and was the town's Little League baseball coach. His usual drink was bourbon and water, with a twist of lemon. He never had more than three in any given night and never before five.

He didn't look up as he approached the bar, which was also rare. Usually he was one of the most open and smiling people who came through the door.

"Morning, Stout," he said quietly as he pulled out a bar stool. He took his coat off and draped it over the stool next to him, then climbed onto the stool closest to where I was working at the well. I had been cutting fruit, so I still had limes, lemons, and oranges scattered on the waitress station next to him.

"Edward," I said. "Good to see you. Out of the office early today. Heading home before it gets too deep out there?" I wiped the lime juice off my hands and slid a bar napkin in front of him. "What can I get for you?"

"The usual," he said, then swung around on the stool and faced out over the empty lounge. "You know," he said, seeming to stare off at the front door. "This place looks the same during the day as it does at night." He laughed. "Even the same smell of smoke and cleaner. For some reason I thought it would be different."

I glanced around. The Garden was a small bar by current standards. More like a neighborhood bar in the old fifties tradition. It had a dozen vinyl booths, six tables, and a bunch of plants, mostly fake ferns. The walls were a natural wood, dark brown, and the carpet was the same dark brown color. The old oak bar filled the wall opposite the front door in front of a mirror and glass racks. A classic jukebox was framed in real plants to the right of the bar. Except for Christmas Eve, the jukebox was never plugged in. Background music was supplied by the stereo I hid behind the bar.

Most of the customers said the Garden felt comfortable, like an old sweater. For me it had been home for five years. And since I had never been married, my regular customers, like Edward, were the only family I had.

I cut a twist off a fresh lemon, slid it along the edge of the glass, dropped it in the golden bourbon, and set the glass on the napkin in front of him.

He twisted around to face me, holding a strained smile in place. "I suppose," he said, "since there are no windows, there would be no reason for this place to notice the time of day. I just hadn't thought about it before." He picked up the drink, nodding thank you, and downed half of it.

In all the years I had been serving him I had never seen him do anything but sip his bourbon. Not even the night his Little League team won the state championship. "Everything all right on the home front? Carol and the kids?" I asked, picking up a lime and going back to slicing.

He finished the rest of the drink and slid it toward me for a refill. "They're fine. Or at least they were this morning." He paused for a moment, then said hesitantly, "But I just got fired."

"Holy shit! You're kidding."

Edward gave me another strained smile as I picked up his empty glass and moved to refill it. "Wish I was. Seems I made a bad choice a couple months back. Since what I did seems to be unethical, they had no choice but to fire me. And it seems that the State Bar will yank my license to practice law, too."

I finished making the drink in silence and placed it in front of him. "It was that serious?"

He nodded. "Mostly stupid on my part. I guess I knew better. Just wasn't thinking."

I stood across from him, waiting for him to continue. Tell me what he had done. He took a sip off his drink, looked up at me and asked, "You ever hear of Shoeless Joe?"

"The old baseball player they made the movie about?"

Edward nodded. "That's the one. Joseph Jefferson Jackson—Shoeless Joe. I had a chance to meet him once, back when I was fifteen. Back in 1951 in South Carolina. But I was too afraid to go into his bedroom with my baseball coach and two of the other players. Back then I really wanted to be a professional ball player when I grew up and everyone knew that Shoeless Joe Jackson was the best left fielder to ever play the game. And one of the best hitters ever. I guess as a kid I just didn't have the courage to meet him. He died two days later and I always blamed myself."

I slowly shook my head, took a deep breath and looked down at the fruit I had been cutting. None of this was making sense. But sometimes that was what a bartender had to expect. When customers needed to talk about problems, very rarely did they make immediate sense. The best thing a bartender could do was just keep them talking until they talked themselves out.

"You blamed yourself?" I asked. "Why? How old was he?"

"He was sixty-three. And he was sick. I know all that. He died on December 5th. Forty years ago today. Interesting, huh? That I would get fired on the same day. I think it is a sort of poetic justice."

"But if he was sixty-three and sick, why would you blame yourself?"

Edward took a deep breath and looked quickly around the bar, as if to make sure no one could hear him. Then he looked me right in the eye and said, "I stole Black Betsy. His bat."

Two

Edward sipped on his entire second drink and he sipped his third through the lunch crowd and a fourth up until we were alone again at two. During that time we talked about what caused him to get fired, how stealing Shoeless Joe's bat from his house had caused Edward guilt for forty years. During lunch, Edward and two other regular customers filled me in on the entire Black Sox scandal of the 1919 World Series. I learned how Shoeless Joe was the leading hitter for that World Series with a .357 average. How he played errorless ball for the eight game series, yet was still thrown out of baseball for agreeing to take $5,000 to throw the series.

I learned about Comiskey Park, the White Sox, and Commissioner Kenesaw Mountain Landis. I learned about the other seven players that were thrown out with Shoeless Joe and about the Ten Day Clause in the old player contracts that led to the entire mess.

I also learned that Edward was a haunted man. He was haunted by a mistake he made as a kid. For his entire life he continued to make the same sort of bad decisions and mistakes. I also learned that he knew when he entered college that he really didn't have the talent to be a professional baseball player. He truly loved being a lawyer, but he never lost his love for baseball, and regretted not playing ball for a living.

At some point during that three-hour period, I decided to break one of my own rules: I would plug in the jukebox, and give Edward a chance to correct that one big mistake.

Three

The jukebox in the Garden Lounge was a time-travel device.

Actually, every jukebox is a time machine in a limited fashion. When a song is played on a regular jukebox, a person sort of travels back to the time and the memory associated with that song. The Garden jukebox does almost exactly that, with one major difference. It physically takes the person to the memory, and allows that person to be there inside their old body for the length of the song. They are actually there, smelling, tasting, and feeling the past.

And they can change it, too. Which is why I only allow myself to plug the jukebox in on Christmas Eve and then only for a few close friends every year. Changing the past is way too dangerous. And I have lost a couple of good friends because of it.

I inherited the jukebox from the junk in the basement of the first bar I owned. Ten minutes before the bank came in to close me down, I hauled the old jukebox out of the basement and into my garage at home, figuring I had the spare time to fix it up. A year later, when I finally got around to opening it up, I discovered a bunch of stuff inside that didn't belong in a normal jukebox. Stuff that seemed far beyond my limited electrical ability, so I just cleaned off the dust, fixed the electrical cord that looked as if someone had ripped it from the back of the machine, and turned it on.

Luck had it that the only forty-five I had around the house was a recording of a song that reminded me of the night I almost asked Jenny, the only woman I have ever loved, to marry me. It had been her favorite song. I had the record in a scrapbook with pictures of her and hadn't listened to it in years.

I fired up the song and the next thing I knew I was with Jenny. I could feel my fingers touching her hand. I could smell her light perfume. I licked my lips, and tasted the faint cherry from her lipstick. I was there, fumbling, trying to get up enough courage in my twenty-three year-old body to ask her to marry me. Yet I was also there as a thirty-seven year-old man, with the clear memory that I had not asked her. And the next week she had left me for college and eventually another man.

I sat there beside her, stunned, not talking, until the song ended and I found myself back in my garage.

The next day I finally got up the courage to play the record again and ended up sitting next to Jenny again. And again at the exact same time and place. That was where my memory from that song took me. That second time I almost asked her to marry me. Almost. It would have changed my life and my future. And I had no idea what that would have meant. My life really wasn't so bad. I have never had the courage to play Jenny's song again, even though it is on the jukebox, waiting.

Since then, every Christmas Eve I have given a few close friends the opportunity to go back and relive one memory. Sometimes they change something back there and don't come back. But most of the time they pop back into the bar as the song ends. Sometimes laughing, sometimes crying, but always more content then before they played the song.

Now I was going to break my own rule. It was December 5th, 1991, and I was going to plug in the jukebox and give Edward a chance to change his past and his life. I just hoped I was doing the right thing.

Four

"Well," Edward said, looking around as the last lunch customer went out into the blowing snow. "I suppose it's time for me to go home and tell Carol the news." He shook his head. "Damned if I know what we're going to do. I've never been fired before."

I set two dirty glasses in the sink and took a deep breath. "Humor me for a moment. What do you think would have happened if you hadn't stolen that bat?"

Edward shrugged. "I would have slept a lot better over the years, that's for sure."

I nodded and went on. "You have a song, or style of song that reminds you of that time you went to see Joe?"

Edward thought for a moment, then nodded. "Big band stuff. You know, like Dorsey. My mom was always playing it, and I remember a record player on real low, with one of those bands playing on it, when we visited Joe's house. Why?"

I pointed at the Wurlitzer jukebox to the right of the bar. "You ever have a song take you back to a memory?"

"Of course. Who hasn't?"

I moved out from behind the bar, reached in behind the polished chrome of the jukebox and plugged it in. A soft whirring came from inside and I could feel my stomach tightening up. I always felt sick every time I turned on the jukebox. The sickness of dread, of worry. The sickness of fear, like going into a bad situation, or knowing the moment before you are going to get hit that you will get hurt.

I stood and faced Edward as the green, red, and yellow lights flickered on, casting an odd rainbow on the floor and nearby booth. "I know you won't believe me, so just listen. This jukebox can take you back to that memory of Shoeless Joe."

Edward laughed. "I don't need a machine to do that. It is with me every day."

"It will actually take you there. Maybe this time you can leave the bat."

Edward looked at me for a moment, then snorted. "Right." He picked up his drink and downed it. Then reached into his pocket for his wallet. "I think I had better be getting home. Music there to face for sure."

"I told you that you wouldn't believe me. So just humor me. Play one song. Do that and the drinks and lunch are on me. I'll even supply the quarter." I held up a quarter for him to see.

He looked around at the empty bar. Then, after a long moment, he shrugged. "Stout, people said you were a strange bird. Now I guess I know why." He moved over to the jukebox, taking the quarter from me as he did.

"There are a number of big band tunes on there. Pick the one that reminds you the most of that moment you took the bat."

"Will do," he said, shaking his head.

I watched him as he looked over the selection, then dropped the quarter into the slot and punched the buttons. The jukebox clanked and then the sound of a small motor came from inside, followed by a bunch of clicks.

Now I felt as if I wanted to throw up. What happened if he changed something really major? Something that cost a lot of lives. Every damn time I plugged in the jukebox that fear hit me like a hammer.

I took a deep breath, placed both hands on the bar in front of me and faced him. He was a friend. He deserved the chance. "Just think about that moment in Joe's house," I told him. "And remember while you are there that you only have the length of the song that is playing. Not one moment longer."

"Sure," he said. "And then..."

The song started and Edward faded from the bar and was gone.

I took a deep breath and moved over to the well as the Jimmy Dorsey Band filled the room with the sounds of the past. I really wanted to break another one of my rules.

I needed a drink.

Five

Big band music played softly from an old record player in the cluttered dining room. The house smelled musty and closed in, with a faint medicine smell that seemed to coat everything. A big, overstuffed couch with doilies on the arms filled one wall. Glass cabinets with old trophies and pictures filled another. Outside, it was a cold December day in South Carolina.

In front of the glass case was a round umbrella stand. In that stand were five baseball bats, including a black one. Edward stared at that bat for a moment, not really understanding what it was, then glanced around the living room.

"Wow, Stout. You can really pull off an illusion." As he said it he realized his voice didn't sound right. It seemed too high and a different pitch to his ears. He glanced down at his younger body, the heavy coat, the boots, and the memories came flooding back. The memories of coming into Shoeless Joe's house with Coach and Dave and Johnny just a few minutes before. Yet those memories were overlaid by the forty years of the future and the very real memory of just getting fired from a job he really loved.

"Stout! How..."

The sound of laughing came from the back room over the top of the music. Stout had been right. Somehow he was here, yet he wasn't. He couldn't be. He was married, with two kids forty years in the future. He reached out and touched the arm of the couch. It felt real.

He looked around again, then moved over and pulled out the black bat. It was heavy and a little cold to his touch. The grip was rough with the old tape and felt almost sticky. Black Betsy. Joe's favorite bat.

He remembered looking at it forty years ago and then slipping it up inside his big coat and going out the front door. He had stashed the bat in a large bush and then waited for Coach and the others to come out. They had ribbed him a little about not going in to see Shoeless Joe, but not much. Mostly they just talked about how exciting it was to meet Shoeless Joe and how he couldn't have really thrown the series. He had gone back that night and picked up the bat. He still had it up in the attic forty years later.

Young Edward turned the bat over in his hands and looked at the initials S.J. carved in the handle. Many a night over the next few years he would hold that bat and run his fingers over those initials. He did so again, his young self treasuring the feel, his older self hating it. The two emotions battling inside his head and stomach.

The fight lasted for only a moment, but it seemed much longer. Finally the forty year-old memories won and he dropped the bat back into the umbrella stand.

It was as if the weight of an entire life lifted from his shoulders. "Thanks, Stout," he said to the air. He took a deep breath and let it out. It was time to face a few more things. The song was still playing, so with one last look at Black Betsy, he turned and headed for the back room.

Shoeless Joe's bedroom was filled with a huge dresser and a big, old, metal bed. The drapes were open to the gray December day. Joe was propped up on pillows and he was laughing. To Edward he looked like a skeleton, with large ears, an even bigger nose, and eyes that seemed to sparkle.

As Edward entered Joe looked over and nodded.

"Glad you came in," Coach said, and motioned for Edward to move up beside the bed. "Edward, this is Shoeless Joe Jackson. Mr.

Jackson, this is Edward Toole, one of my better players." Joe smiled and stuck out his hand. Edward shook it. Joe's grip was strong, but the skin was dry and rough.

The older Edward wanted to scream and shout for joy. He was actually meeting Shoeless Joe Jackson. Actually shaking his hand. But his fifteen year-old self was too embarrassed to talk. This time the young self won.

"Nice meeting you, Edward," Joe said. His voice was deep and powerful and surprised Edward, coming from the thin body.

"Nice meeting you, sir." Edward stammered.

Joe smiled as if he understood. And just maybe he did, because for a moment he looked into Edward's eyes. Then Joe's smile slowly turned to a frown, he shook his head and looked around. "I suppose you all are wondering the same question that everyone wonders. Did I really throw the series?"

"Sir," Coach said, "I made the boys promise to not ask about that."

Joe waved a large, thin hand in dismissal. "That's all right. After thirty years I have sort of got used to it."

In the other room the song was almost finished.

Joe looked directly at Edward. "Sometimes you make good choices and sometimes you make bad ones. Just like in a ball game. And with every play you must live with the choice. Sometimes only to the end of the inning. Sometimes for much longer. You understand me?" He was asking Edward directly.

Both young- and old-Edward could do nothing but nod.

The song had very few seconds left.

"I made a bad choice and it cost me," Joe said. "But I tried from that day forward to make good choices. And I kept on living. Just like in a game you must keep on playing, no matter what the mistake. What I learned is that you don't ever give up."

Edward nodded. "Thank you, sir." And Edward's older self added, "More than you will ever know."

The song ended and forty years of future memories slipped from the young Edward as Shoeless Joe nodded and smiled.

Six

The last notes of the big band song echoed around the Garden Lounge.

Edward did not reappear.

I let go of the warm chrome of the jukebox where I had been holding on to make sure I remembered Edward. He didn't come back so he had changed his past somehow. He probably didn't take the bat this time, and that had changed his present in some way. Now maybe he hadn't got fired. Or maybe he had never taken the job with the computer company in the first place, or he had never become a lawyer.

Anything could have happened, and I would not have even remembered him being in the bar this afternoon if I hadn't been holding onto the jukebox when the song ended. My memories would have switched over to this new world's. But by touching the jukebox I could remember the old world. And Edward.

I couldn't resist the temptation to go to the phone book and see if Edward's name was still in there. It was, only it also had an office number with it besides his home phone. It looked as if he had hung out his own shingle in this world. I hoped that meant he was happier. I unplugged the jukebox, finished my drink, and went back to cleaning up from lunch rush. If he didn't show up after five I would check around. Until then there wasn't anything I could do but wait.

Seven

At seven minutes after five Edward walked through the door. He looked the same, except that he wasn't wearing a suit. Instead he had on a casual dress sweater and golf slacks. He smiled and waved as he came through the door, and I waved back and started to make his normal drink.

There were about twenty of the regulars in the Garden, and he stopped for a moment to talk to a few of them at the first table. So by the time he was on the only empty stool to the right of the waitress station, I had the drink in front of him.

"Quick as always, Stout," he said. Then he held up the glass with the bourbon and a twist and looked at it. "But what's this. You forget after all these years that I drink Vodka tonics?"

A couple of the others at the bar laughed and I laughed right along with them as I took the drink back from him. "Just not with it today," I said, trying to act as normal as I could, even though my heart was pounding as if I had just run a hard five miles. I had about six hundred questions I wanted to ask him. Yet I knew he wouldn't understand a one of them.

I fixed him a new drink and slid it in front of him. He held it up and looked at me. "To Shoeless Joe Jackson," he said, making a toasting motion, then sipping his drink.

"Shoeless Joe?" I asked, somehow keeping my voice from shaking. "Wasn't he the one they made the movie about?"

Edward laughed. "You know, Stout, you have said that same thing every year. It's December 5th, forty years from the day Shoeless Joe Jackson died. Don't you remember we toast him every year on this date? He was the greatest left fielder to ever play the game." He paused for a moment, smiling to himself.

"Oh, God," one of the regulars down the bar said, shaking his head. "Here we go again."

Edward just kept on smiling. "You know," he said. "I met Shoeless Joe once."

JUST SHOOT ME NOW!

A Poker Boy Story

Poker Boy wants nothing more than to be left alone in a good game of poker. But a cherub circles overhead in the poker room wanting to talk.

And Poker Boy knows this cherub and knows the little guy represents trouble.

Even worse, the question the cherub asks Poker Boy could change a lot of futures.

How really, really annoying.

One

THE LITTLE JERK cherub just kept fluttering around near the ceiling of the poker room at Spirit Winds Casino. He acted like a bird trapped inside a small room with no windows. I know he was trying to get my attention, but the last thing I wanted to deal with tonight was a cherub.

And actually he had a couple small birds with very long beaks with him and they seemed to be flying in a figure-eight pattern, just missing each other as they moved around and around over my head.

The game was as good as a five-ten no limit gets. Three tourists who were drinking and wanting to have the action, two weak regulars, and two professionals. Plus me.

I had died and gone to heaven, cherub and all, it seemed. I was already three hundred up and the night was still young. Nothing can get my blood going more than a high-action poker game with players I know I can beat.

But nothing can put a player off his game more than a circling cherub.

I glanced up at the cherub and his two bird friends as I tossed a seven-four off-suit into the muck. No one else in the room could see the little idiot fluttering around the lights. He had golden hair and wore a white cloth wrapped around him that looked more like a diaper in places than anything else. The cloth started at one ankle and ended up over his shoulder.

His white wings were fluttering constantly like a humming bird's and he had on the traditional fake cherub halo that seemed to glow bright yellow. They could take those halo things off like a hat. He was about three feet tall at most and wore no shoes.

I even knew this one's name. Chadwick.

Chadwick the Cherub.

I had dealt with him once before on an assignment to help out a woman who thought she was dying and had started to give away her vast fortune. It turned out old Chadwick was just showing himself to her like a bad flasher, making her think she was seeing an angel with a very small penis.

He was sent to cherub counseling after I stopped him from forcing the poor woman to end up broke and insane and permanently put off of sex.

Now it seemed he was back. And was just as annoying. At least this time he was keeping his cloth diaper where it belonged.

I tried to ignore him again for another hand, but ignoring a kid-sized mythical creature fluttering over your head is hard to do.

Finally I couldn't handle it anymore. I flipped into the muck a couple suited connectors and froze time.

Actually I didn't really freeze time. No one could do that. But I did have the power to step between moments in time. It felt like I had frozen time because all the sounds of the casino stopped, and everyone froze in that moment.

Everyone but me and Chadwick.

His two bird friends remained frozen as well up near the ceiling. And some bird poop was stopped in midair headed for a spot right in front of my chips. Great, just great.

I stood and looked up at the cherub who had stopped flying around and was just hovering, looking down at me with a smile.

"All right, let's get to this," I said.

He came down and hovered in front of me, his white wings moving so fast that they looked like they were standing still. His smile was a cross between a worried grin and a smirk showing how happy he was I had come around.

"Nice trick on this time thing," he said, indicating the frozen people around us. "I thought only gods could do this."

"Just park it and take off that stupid halo," I said.

He stopped and stood on the nearest empty poker table. He folded his wings back behind him and stuffed the halo into his white cloth diaper strip where it wrapped up and over his shoulder like a sling.

"First off," I said, not even trying to hide how annoyed I was, "does Cherry know you are here?"

Cherry was the head cherub and one of the nicer creatures I had ever had the pleasure to meet.

Chadwick nodded. "She's the one who sent me."

His voice was deep and rough, not at all like what his image would project. He sounded more like a cigar-smoking old man. Most cherubs were thousands of years old. My boss, Stan the God of Poker had told me that Cherry was far older than he was which meant she was thousands and thousands of years old at least.

More than likely Chadwick was a few thousand years old as well.

"And I can check that?" I asked, calling Chadwick's bluff.

"Yes," he said.

He wasn't lying. I could tell a lie on a cherub's face from across the room. It seemed the sweet look didn't give them much chance to lie, especially to poker players. Cherry actually had suggested he come talk to me.

Great. Just great. A perfect night just ruined. Could someone just shoot me now?

Two

"So what do you need from me?" I asked, almost afraid of the question's answer.

Good old Chadwick looked me direct in the eyes with those round, innocent-looking brown eyes of his and said, "I want to be part of your team."

I actually managed to not break out into complete gales of laughter.

The team he was talking about consisted of three other superheroes and one god that helped me solve major cases. We often saved the world.

Me and my girlfriend and sidekick, Patty Ledgerwood, aka Front Desk Girl, led the team. Patty was a superhero working in the hospitality side of the world.

The third member was Screamer, a man able to read minds and connect minds at times. Screamer was a superhero who worked in the law enforcement branch of the gods.

The fourth member was The Smoke, a part dog, part human who was a superhero working for the gods of animals.

And then there was Stan, the God of Poker, my boss. He was our connection to Laverne, Lady Luck herself.

And now Chadwick the Flasher Cherub wanted to join the team.

Somehow I kept most of my poker face locked on and smiled and asked him the next question.

"Why would you want to do that?"

"Oh, I personally don't," Chadwick said. "But Cherry thinks it would be a good idea for me to start doing something constructive with my time now that I am mostly done with my counseling sessions."

I sort of stared at the chubby little cherub for a moment, trying to understand what I had just heard.

I must be dreaming. I had to be. I was at such a perfect table, a perfect poker game, the kind of game that just didn't happen every night. And now I was dealing with a converted flasher who wanted to join my team, but who really didn't want to join my team.

And a bird was about to poop on my poker table.

This had to be a nightmare, a really bad one.

I had no idea what to do.

I wanted to just laugh and send him back to Cherry, but my little voice was telling me that wouldn't be a good idea. There had to be some politics involved with all this and for a superhero to get involved with politics among the different gods was never a good idea.

I looked at Chadwick again.

"What can it hurt?" he asked, shrugging.

I couldn't begin to answer that, since most of the time that the team worked together on a problem, the entire world was at stake.

I looked up at the ceiling and shouted, "Stan!"

I needed help and I needed it fast. Before I said something I would regret and maybe cause a rift between different branches of gods, as if there weren't enough of those already.

Stan appeared beside me, inside the frozen time instant I had created. Stan wore his normal gray sweater, dark slacks, and blank expression. He was slightly shorter than I was and looked like any person you might see on the street. As the God of Poker, he could blend in anywhere and it was impossible to read any emotion on his face unless he wanted you to, or didn't care.

"Hi, Stan," Chadwick said, waving a chubby little hand at the God of Poker.

"I was afraid of this," Stan said.

"That's not making me feel any better," I said. "Chadwick here wants to join my team."

"Yeah, I heard," Stan said.

"But he really doesn't," I said. "Do you, Chadwick?"

"Oh, hell no," the cherub said. "It sounds like far too much work. It was just Cherry's idea."

"You know what I told you about swearing," a woman's voice said from above us.

I looked up as Cherry fluttered to a stop on the table next to a suddenly worried Chadwick.

She looked almost identical to Chadwick, except her golden hair was longer and the diaper-like cloth also covered her chest. Her face was thinner as well and she had a beauty to her that took my breath away.

"Sorry," Chadwick said, looking down.

"Nice seeing you again, Cherry," Stan said.

"I agree," I said, bowing slightly to her. "You look more radiant than ever."

She smiled and I could feel the warmth filling the air around me. "There's a real reason a lot of the gods like you, Poker Boy," she said.

"He's a charmer all right," Stan said, shaking his head. "So tell me why you think it would be a good idea for Chadwick here to join Poker Boy's team?"

"Keep Chadwick focused and out of trouble," Cherry said. "He needs something to hold his attention."

"Besides human women," Stan said before I could. Thankfully.

"Yes," Cherry said. "To be honest."

I knew now how to solve the problem. I just had to find good old Chadwick something to do. I had no idea what, but anything was better than him hanging around my team.

"You know we seldom put the team together," I said to Cherry. "In fact, it has been almost two months since the entire team has needed to be together for a problem."

"Oh," Cherry said, the smile vanishing from her face. "That's not going to work. I thought you met and worked every day together."

"Not even every month," Stan said, backing up my play.

Chadwick actually looked relieved. Cherry looked completely devastated for some reason.

I needed to come up with an idea and come up with it quick.

I sort of turned to Chadwick. "Besides human women, what do you like?"

"I don't even like them that much," Chadwick said.

Cherry turned slightly away and rolled her eyes, which made Stan grin.

Then Cherry said, "His mother married a Putti, so there is a lot of the old Cupid blood in him."

"So, Chadwick," I said. "What exactly are your powers that would help my team?"

I figured that if I could learn what he could do, I might be able to come up with a way to get him busy with something else. Anything else.

Chadwick looked annoyed, but Cherry looked at him and he took a deep breath and turned to face me directly.

"I can fly. I can be invisible. I can pass through any wall. I am an expert spy and can remember everything to the word anyone says that I am listening to and report that back exactly. Because of my father, I am an expert with the magical bow and arrow, but am not allowed to carry one because of an incident a number of decades back with a movie star and a president."

With that he glared at Cherry who only shrugged. "You tried to interfere with human events. You will serve your sentence to the fullest."

Chadwick just shook his head and looked down.

"How fast can you fly?" I asked.

"I can be in Las Vegas faster than you can jump there with your teleporting superpower."

Both Stan and Cherry nodded at that.

I was surprised. Now that I was actually thinking about it, there was no doubt Chadwick would be a good addition to the team on some problems. None of us had the abilities he had.

I glanced at Stan who actually looked like he was thinking the same thing.

"Chadwick," I said, "honestly I think we can use you at times on our team. We don't use every member every mission, but I think your powers would add to our team on certain missions."

Stan was nodding.

Cherry was looking surprised, and Chadwick looked shocked.

"You're kidding, right?" Chadwick asked.

"Not in the slightest," I said. "But the problem is we don't often have missions and you need something to keep you occupied."

"To help you keep that thing in your diapers," Stan said.

"It's not a diaper," Chadwick said in his gruff voice, glaring at Stan.

"Poker Boy is right," Cherry said, nodding to me with thanks. "If you want to be on Poker Boy's team, which is a very high honor, you need to stay out of trouble and do something constructive."

"And just what would that be?" Chadwick asked, looking disgusted. "I've been bored for most of the last thousand years. Being a cherub just doesn't have a lot of purpose these days. So I'm open to suggestions."

Because we were between a moment in time, the frozen poker room around us was deadly silent and now the four of us were as well. I just couldn't think of a thing for Chadwick to do.

Nothing.

Three

I glanced up and saw the two frozen birds that he had brought in with him. And the bird poop hanging in midair like a promise yet to be kept.

"What's with the birds?" I asked, trying to buy some time to think.

"I like birds and they like me," he said. "It's fun flying with them."

I had a faint glimmering of an idea, but I wasn't sure about it. I needed more information.

"Can you talk to them?"

"Not much," Chadwick said. "They aren't that smart."

I turned to Stan and Cherry. "Is there a god of birds? Or a god who looks over that area of the animal kingdom?"

Both Stan and Cherry looked puzzled.

"Not really," Stan said. "The Smoke's boss would be the most likely, but most gods tend to have one bird or another that they favor, but no one that I know is over all the birds in general."

"So they have no god really looking out for them?" I asked, surprised. I thought every aspect of the world had a god over it.

"I wouldn't think so," Cherry said looking very puzzled. "Odd, don't you think?"

I turned to Chadwick. "How about you make it your job to save birds and watch out over them?"

He just looked puzzled.

"You said you like them, right?" I asked.

He nodded.

"And you can fly faster than any bird, right?"

"Yeah," he said.

"So make it your job to save birds. If a bird is about to fly in front of a truck, save it. Save birds trapped in a cage in a burning house. Save birds from being shot by kids."

Both Cherry and Stan were smiling, so I knew I had them on board with the idea.

And Chadwick was nodding slowly as he thought about it.

"There is clearly no one else doing it," I said. "And from the number of dead birds I've seen over the years, clearly it needs to be done."

Chadwick nodded. "I've saved a few birds along the way and it always felt good."

"Cherry," I said, turning to Chadwick's boss, "you want to check with the appropriate god in charge to make sure it would be all right if Chadwick took up this great mission?"

"I think it will be," she said, smiling at me and looking very relieved.

I turned back to Chadwick. "And I'll still need you on my team on some missions if that's all right with you. Your special powers could really help at times."

Chadwick was nodding and smiling. "Sure, sure, and if I find something big that I need help on, I can get your help as well?"

"Of course," I said, smiling. "The entire team if need be."

"Great," he said.

He turned to Cherry. "I really like this idea. Much better than going around shooting people with stupid magic arrows like my dad does."

"I agree," Cherry said. "It is a perfect mission for you. Perfect, and will do a ton of good."

"Thanks, Poker Boy," Chadwick said.

"Yes, thank you," Cherry said.

And then they were both gone along with the two birds, but the big drop of bird poop still hung there.

"Looks like you have a new member of the team," Stan said, shaking his head. "Hard to imagine."

I just laughed. "Patty is never going to believe that I invited Chadwick the Famous Flashing Cherub to join the team."

"If he can keep the little thing in his diaper," Stan said, also laughing, "he just might be able to help at times."

"He might at that," I said. "But if nothing else we saved a lot of birds tonight."

Stan vanished, but I could still hear him laughing.

I grabbed a couple handfuls of napkins and went back to my chair at the poker table. I placed the napkin under the bird poop and then let myself slip back into the time stream.

The noise of the casino crashed in around me as the bird poop hit the napkins and I swept them up before anyone noticed.

I just hoped that cleaning up crap wasn't a sign of the times ahead with Chadwick the Flashing Cherub.

MY SOCKS ROLLED DOWN

When a fella wins the lottery, he learns all sorts of things, including how his magic socks really feel and how much they want some companion magic socks.

But sometimes, even after winning the lottery, magic socks don't always get what they want.

When socks go rogue. Never a pretty sight.

A PERSON CAN ONLY GO SO FAR in life with only one pair of magic socks. I know, I know, it's tough to imagine anyone only having one pair of magic socks, but you can come and search the three drawers in my small bedroom of my trailer, or look under my old second-hand green couch, or even check the coin-op laundry where I do my clothes. You won't find more than one pair. And I wear them every day and have for my entire life, all twenty-three years of it.

Sad, huh?

I've never had more than one pair. My mom gave them to me on her deathbed when I was born, rolling my little feet into the magic white cotton like putting little rubbers on two small penises. I don't remember the act, of course, but for some reason, that pair of magic socks are the only pair I have ever had.

As with all magic socks, they fit me perfectly and always have, growing perfectly with me right up until I stopped growing at five-four and a half.

And they never wear out. I wash them once a week, never leaving the washer or dryer while they are in there. I've heard of people stealing magic socks. It's bad enough only having one pair. I really can't imagine those few poor souls who have none.

What scares me is that I am only one pair of magic socks away from those poor, sockless souls. It would really be better if I could find a second pair. And three pair would be perfect. I might be able to do something with my life if I had three. That way I wouldn't have to do laundry so often.

Well, my dream to have enough money to buy more magic socks finally came true on January 13th at five in the evening. I was sitting there, watching my old television, hoping a truck didn't go by outside on the gravel road and shake the rabbit ears I had made of tin foil.

Every week I bought a lottery ticket, and every week I played the same numbers and watched the lottery drawing on television before turning the channel over to *Wheel*. Can't let a night go by without staring at Vanna's tits, you understand.

If I just had more than one pair of magic socks, she might talk to me.

I had my feet kicked up on the old pine coffee table while I sat on the couch drinking a Pabst, the best beer anywhere for the price. My boots were by the front door and my magic socks looked like it was time for another trip to the coin-op.

The first number was six, and the magic socks on my feet tingled a little. The last time they tingled like that I found a five-dollar bill on the sidewalk.

Six was the first number I always picked. It was how old I was when I shot my first rabbit with Grandad's twenty-two.

Next number was eight, and my old magic socks were giving me a real itchy feel. Last time they did that, when I was sixteen, I got laid for the first time by the mother of my best friend at the time.

Eight was the age I was when Dad brought home my new step-mother who stayed for two years before she disappeared one night and Dad came back kind of muddy and smiling.

I took a swallow of the Pabst and set it down on the coffee table as the next number came up.

Fourteen, and my magic socks were rubbing my feet so hard they were getting almost hot. In all my years I'd never had my magic socks get so excited.

"Down, boys, down," I said, reaching for the drawer and pulling out this week's ticket to make sure I had the numbers right. I did. The first three were six, eight, fourteen. Fourteen was when they arrested Dad for killing stepmom number three, or maybe it was number four, I wasn't sure.

The police talked to me for a while, then said that I was going to a foster home, but I ran off, got my clothes and hunting equipment and Dad's hidden rifle and ammunition and made it off into the mountains along the coast. I camped out until I turned eighteen, which was my next number.

The guy on the television watched the old ping-pong ball slide up the tube and he said, "Eighteen."

My magic socks felt like dancing, so that was what I did, got up and danced around the living room for a moment, letting them celebrate. I really liked how they were hugging my feet like a woman hugging a long lost lover. That felt great to be honest.

With four right numbers I had already won a few thousand. Just one more of the two and things would be really fine.

My next number was twenty. That's when I moved into this doublewide trailer up Jenson Creek.

The old guy that lived here before me is buried out back, and so far no one has missed him at all. I told two neighbors he got sick and moved into Portland and I was renting the trailer. That seemed to keep them happy, and I buried the old man deep enough no coyotes were going to dig him up. Now after three years, a tree was growing on his grave. Nice little thing, too.

The old guy had on his one pair of magic socks when I shot him, but weirdly enough, when I went to shoot him, my aim suddenly went bad and instead of hitting the old guy in the chest, I hit him in the foot, right through one magic sock, blowing it all apart.

As the old guy jumped backwards, screaming and swearing and holding his torn-up foot, I shot again.

And again the gun seemed to have a mind of its own and it shot the guy in the other foot. I gave up shooting him and tried to pound his head, but I just kept missing like he was moving around, even though he wasn't. The old guy bled out after a few minutes and died anyway, and his magic socks were worthless and dead as well. A real bummer and to this day I have no idea why I couldn't shoot straight that day.

The announcer said, "Twenty."

My magic socks sort of flipped my feet up in the air so hard I went over backwards, smashed into the wall and hit the floor hard.

Then, even though I was hurting something awful, the socks got me to my feet and ran around the small living room of the trailer, bouncing me off the walls like I was so much kindling.

"Slow down!" I shouted at the white socks on my feet, but they didn't.

I heard a thought clear as a bell in my mind. *You dumb idiot, don't you realize you've just won enough money to buy a dozen more magic socks and I won't have to put up with your smelly feet all the damned time.*

My magic socks could talk to me. Wow!

"How come you've never said anything before now?"

What for? Holding a conversation with you would be like talking to an outhouse wall, like you did for all those years we were camping.

"Hey, nothing wrong with—"

Shut the hell up and let's see if you've won the entire thing!

The announcer said, "Twenty-three."

My final number, because that's how old I am now.

An instant later my magic socks had me walking on the ceiling, then doing a moon-walk backwards across my ceiling and down the wall.

Now you can buy a thousand pairs of magic socks. And you can retire me.

"What happens if I don't want a thousand pair?"

The magic socks stopped me cold in the middle of the floor. *What did you mean by that?*

"I didn't know socks could talk. I'm not so sure I want all them living here and talking to me."

There was a nice silence in my mind, like normal, then my magic socks sort of growled low and deep, like a wild animal ready to attack.

Then I decided something real clear like. "You know, I could buy a huge house and have rooms full of magic socks and tell them that none of them could ever talk to me. Only to each other."

I smiled for a moment before I realized that my magic socks had made me say all that.

"I'm not going to do that and you can't make me," I said.

Again there was a low growl, then the socks said inside my head.

That's it. I'm still young, I have a life to live, other socks to meet, baby magic socks to create. I don't need to stay here with you anymore.

"You're my socks and I'm not taking you off," I said.

You are such an idiot. You think you are in control. All of you humans believe that, letting us live off your energy, giving us special places in your life. But we control you, every last one of you. And idiot boy, it's time I moved on.

Now I was getting mad. "And just how do you think you're going to do that if I don't take you off?"

The voice of the socks sort of gave off a snorting sound, then I walked against my will over to the wall, up the wall, and out onto the middle of the ceiling, hanging upside down from my white socks.

Oops, the voice inside my head said, and suddenly I was hurtling toward the green shag carpet. I tried to get my arms up to break my fall, but I couldn't. I hit on the top of my head and flopped sideways.

"That hurt!" I shouted.

Damn it all, the voice said.

My magic socks were trying to kill me!

No, shit, Sherlock.

With that my magic socks walked me to my phone and made me pick it up and dial 911.

Then, when the operator asked what was my emergency, I said without wanting to, "I killed an old guy and he's buried out under a small tree in my backyard. I can't take the guilt. I'm going to kill myself."

Then I laid the phone down and walked down the hall to where I kept my rifles, all of them loaded.

My magic socks weren't allowing me to say anything, so instead I just thought at the socks really, really hard that they should stop.

Wow, a thought, the socks said. *From the idiot. Stunning.*

"Why are you doing this?" I asked as at the same time I dug into the guns and pulled out my favorite without wanting to.

Because I'm tired of your sweating feet, I want to meet other magic socks as you call them. Actually we are called Yekcoj, a race millions of years older than humans.

I just didn't believe that. My magic socks had lost it, gone off the deep end.

You want to know what we really look like?

Suddenly my white socks shifted around my feet and combined, with both of my legs fitting into the teeth-lined mouth of what looked like a nasty groundhog, only with scales and ten eyes and four arms.

To be honest, I'm tired of you standing and walking around in my mouth. Why my people thought this was a good idea is beyond me.

One long black eye blinked at me and then my magic socks were back, white as ever.

The socks walked me back out to the living room. The operator on the phone was saying, "Sir! Sir! Help is on the way."

I sat down on the couch against my will, put the gun in my mouth against my will, and put my finger on the trigger against my will.

Thanks for the worst twenty-three years any socks could ever dream of living. See ya.

I pulled the trigger.

The socks laughed and pulled themselves off of my body's feet.

I could see my body through the eyes of the magic socks, or weird groundhog or whatever it was. The gunshot had blown most of my brain against the front window and some part of my skull was hanging off the drapes.

Now you've done it, I thought at the socks.

What…? What…? What are you doing here? You can't still be here, in my mind, you're dead.

Never heard of the Four Laws of Magic Socks, have you?

I hadn't known them either until I died. Now I knew them and a lot more stuff I had never known when alive. Weird how dying made me a lot smarter.

What four laws? the magic socks asked.

It was part of the treaty with humans when they allowed your people to come here to live.

I hadn't known that either until that gun blew my brains out.

Law #1: You must always let humans wear you at any time.

Yeah, yeah, the magic socks said.

Law #2: You can't speak to any humans or let them know of your presence. Broke that one, didn't you?

Just go on, my magic socks said.

Law #3: You must always follow the orders of your human unless it conflicts with Law #4, which is that Magic Socks cannot allow harm to come to humans unless otherwise avoided.

Oh, my magic socks said softly.

Let's get back into place on my feet, I thought at my not-so-faithful magic sock companion, *so when the Magic Sock police get here, they'll know what to do with you and with me.*

275

Together we moved over to my body and formed clean white socks around my now very dead feet.

Outside, coming up the dirt road, the police sirens filled the narrow valley. Back when I was alive, that would have scared me enough to go get my gun. Now it just made me laugh.

Too bad I'm never going to get to collect the winnings on that ticket. I might have bought a big place and lots of your friends for you to play with.

Please, please, please would you just shut up for a few minutes? my magic socks said, clearly angry.

Nah, I thought at my magic socks as together we rested around the feet of my dead body. *I figure we can spend our last few hours together going over all the great years we had together.*

My magic socks made a groaning sound.

Remember that day when I was four and had to take a crap really bad, and didn't make it to the bathroom and crapped all over you? Wasn't that a great time? I think that pulled us closer together, don't you?

My magic socks said nothing, once again following the Second Law of Magic Socks.

The police knocked hard on the door, then shoved it open, covering their mouths when they saw the mess my brains left on the window and drapes.

"He's got magic socks on," one cop said, pointing to my feet and me and my magic sock companion.

"How could he do this, then? Magic socks won't let you hurt yourself."

Both cops looked at each other, then one of them said, "Rogue Socks."

"Call the Magic Sock Police representative," another cop said. "If his socks went rogue, it means this guy is still in there with the socks."

I made old magic socks move what used to be my big toe up and down like I was doing a mini-nod.

"Shit," one cop said and both backed up.

So they call you rogues, huh? I thought at my magic socks.

My socks said nothing.

Remember that time I was all out of toilet paper and needed to use you to wipe my ass? Great fun, huh?

Hey, idiot-boy, my magic socks thought at me, *with all your new knowledge you should know what's going to happen next, now that you told those cops I was a rogue and you were trapped in here with me.*

"We do it together," one cop said.

"Count of three," the other cop said as they stepped closer to me and my magic socks.

Suddenly I realized what the two cops planned to do. When magic socks went rogue and killed a human, they had to be killed at once, not only to stop the rogue socks, but to release the soul of the departed.

Hey! I thought at my magic socks, suddenly very panicked. *Get us out of here. Make a run for it!*

I'm not allowed to talk to you, remember?

But you're supposed to follow my instructions. Run!

The two cops got closer and both aimed their pistols, one at my right foot, one at my left.

I don't have to, my magic socks said. *I'm rogue, remember?*

"One," a cop said, pointing a big gun at my old right foot while the other cop pointed at my left foot.

Don't you want to live?

My magic socks laughed. *With you? Not any more. Twenty-three years was more than enough.*

"Two," the cop said.

I should have used you for toilet paper more often, I thought at my magic socks.

I should have killed you long before now, my magic socks thought back.

Screw you, I thought at my magic socks.

Another original thought, my magic socks thought back.

"Three," the cop said.

There was a huge explosion and I could feel myself slipping away, fading into the darkness.

And the last thing I heard before I vanished into the blackness was the last thought of my magic socks.

Oh, thank the Great Sock this is over!

THE ROMANCE NOVEL CHALLENGE

Hanna had a job and a life that just didn't let her meet men. So her boss invited her into a very special book club.

One night Hanna decided to take The Romance Novel Challenge. With luck she just might live happily ever after.

This might just change forever how you look at book clubs.

Published under the pen name Dee W. Schofield.

One

HANNA WURMBRAND SAT on her couch staring at the thick, brown envelope that had just been delivered. The special delivery package lay on her apartment's brown carpet next to her front door like it was a snake ready to bite her.

She had dropped the package once she realized what it was.

She had been expecting the package, yet it still had surprised her when the Fed Ex guy handed it to her.

She had closed the door, dropped the package, and then backed to her couch like moving away from a wild animal.

The entire idea had seemed like such a good idea at the time. A daytime-talk-show-idea to spice up her sex life.

Problem was Hanna Wurmbrand never watched daytime talk shows. In fact, she seldom watched television and she had no sex life.

At least she hadn't until tonight.

Tonight, thanks to that package, she might actually have a sex life again.

Hanna didn't even have a boyfriend and she hadn't had a date in a year at least, even though at five-three, long black hair, and a model's body, she was very attractive.

She got lots of those "looks" and some women called her "stunning."

She had had more than her share of dates back in high school, even though she was considered one of the "brains" of the place. And in college she went with Dave Pennant for most of the five years before he went slightly crazy and joined the Marines.

He had told her that killing the enemy took precedence over their relationship. She would have been fine if he had said, "defending the country" or "doing his civic duty" was more important. She could understand that, but Dave had said he would rather kill people than be with her.

That didn't do a girl's self respect any good at all.

She had had sex with exactly nine different men in her twenty-four years, with most of the encounters being short and nothing to even bother writing in a diary if she bothered to write in a diary, which she didn't.

Over the last year of no sex she had tried to remember a few of those encounters, but the only thing that came to mind was sweat dripping in her eyes and a lot of grunting.

Nothing at all romantic.

Every time she had felt like more of a conquest for the guy instead of a heroine being swept off her feet by a hero of a romance novel. Was there anything wrong about wanting to be swept off her feet? Clearly there must be, because it had never happened to her.

She had graduated from college a year before with three degrees, one in English and two in computer science.

She had the degrees after five years of college, but no boyfriend.

No hero.

She took the first job offered right out of college, a government job doing computer work for the CIA trying to track down any kind of threat to the country.

Mostly the job was her sitting in front of large computer screens and trying to find patterns in massive amounts of data. It had sounded exciting at first, being on the front lines of the war against terror, but that excitement wore off after a few weeks.

She was good at her job and she did feel she was helping her country. And it paid well, but wow was it boring.

Every day she drove alone to work in her fancy new red Mustang, on nice days letting her long black hair fly in the breeze just like a romance heroine.

She always parked in a large parking lot in her assigned spot, went to a gray-walled office, and sat in front of two large computer screens. She only talked to the other three women in the office and her boss, Constance, all of whom were happily married and who mostly talked about their kids.

Sometimes the women around her talked about trying to find her a man, but it never had gone anywhere.

There were a lot of men in the building, mostly wearing gray suits with tight collars and thin ties. They seemed to all carry briefcases and not a one of them seemed to give her a second look.

She usually had lunch alone or with her coworkers, then went home alone at night and read romance novels until she fell asleep to wake in the morning and start the routine over again.

On the weekends she either worked extra or went from Washington up to Newark to her parents' home where she couldn't talk about her work and never met anyone.

Twice her parents had tried to set her up on blind dates. Both times had been a disaster. One guy she had tossed her drink on before the salads arrived at dinner.

It had been one year of the same routine at work. She was shut off from the world, friendships, and any chance of meeting a man even for casual sex.

It was enough to drive any normal young woman to extremes and a growing collection of vibrators.

Three months ago she had finally tried a dating service, only to cancel before all three dates the service set up for her. With Constance's permission, Hanna had run background checks on the three men while at work and all three had turned out to be losers.

One even had a stalking case pending.

Now, thanks to Constance, she had decided to do what was called *The Romance Novel Challenge*.

After Hanna's last attempt at the dating service, Constance had called Hanna into her office, closed the door so no one could overhear them, and then had sworn Hanna to secrecy.

Hanna had thought it was about something going on at work until Constance asked, "You getting tired of spending the night with vibrating appliances?"

Hanna started to deny everything, then laughed. "I have a few special ones I've grown fond of."

"I thought so," Constance said, smiling.

Constance was an attractive blond with extra large breasts that she kept tightly contained in gray or brown suits. Just as Hanna did, Constance kept her hair pulled back tight and pinned while at work and kept her makeup at work to a minimum.

But under that hidden shell, Hanna knew Constance had a spirit of adventure.

She was married to a man named Ben whom Hanna had never met, but he looked handsome in the photo on Constance's desk. Hanna had heard all kinds of stories about the two of them going skiing, camping, surfing, and other things. They didn't yet have kids, so they liked to have "adventures" as Constance called them.

"So why such a personal question?" Hanna had asked.

"I have a special invite to extend to you," Constance said and then went on to tell Hanna about *The Romance Novel Challenge*, calling it the best thing she did for her marriage.

It seemed that Constance and her husband were both members of a very *special* book club.

"The rules of the book club are simple," Constance had said. "A new romance novel is mailed sealed to two members. By the luck of the draw, two members of the club, one man, one woman, are paired up."

"And you have no idea who does the pairing?" Hanna had asked, still thinking Constance was pulling some sort of joke, even though it wasn't her style.

"No idea and I don't want to know," Constance had said. "With the unopened package, the book club member is sent to an assigned hotel suite where he or she meets a partner for the night."

"A dating book club?"

Constance had just shaken her head no and went on.

"The hotel suite is always fancy and is paid for by the monthly dues required to join the club. Both members of the book club, without talking, open their package at the same time and then take turns reading the supplied novel in the package to the other person while sipping champagne in the hotel suite."

"Now that's kinky," Hanna had said and Constance just kept going.

"No names are allowed except for the character names in the novel. The woman takes the heroine's name, the man takes the hero's name. When they reach the first kissing scene, they have to follow and act out what happens in the scene."

"And if it's a sex scene?" Hanna had asked, now starting to understand what this *book club* was all about.

Constance had just smiled. "They have to act that out as much as is possible inside the hotel suite. Then, without exchanging any names or personal information, they have to leave the hotel room, taking their books with them."

Hanna had been shocked and Constance could tell.

"Come on, Hanna," Constance had said. "You can't tell me you're a prude?"

"Far from it," Hanna had said. But inside she wasn't so sure.

Constance went on to tell how she and her husband attended the book club night once a month with different partners, then took their books home and finished the two books with each other the rest of the month, acting out every scene.

"And you never ask about the other person?" Hanna had asked.

"Never," Constance had said. "We both know what happens. The reason we are members is the excitement. And we both love to read, of course."

"Of course," Hanna had said.

Now Hanna sat on her couch staring at the special delivery package on her floor by her apartment front door.

It contained a book, a romance novel that would change her life if she let it.

Tonight was the night. She had gone through all the steps, been vetted by who knew who, signed all kinds of papers, and had paid the first month's fee of three hundred.

Since she had started the process, Hanna had to admit she had gotten more and more excited at the idea.

Constance had told her that some nights were pretty mild, other nights were wild and crazy. It all depended on the novel. And how much each person got into their character's role.

Hanna went over and picked up the package, resisting the impulse to hold it at arm's length.

It clearly had a book inside. She really wanted to open it, but instead she just looked at the address typed in the return address area.

Suite 611, Hyatt Regency Hotel. Seven P.M.

She glanced at her watch. It was four now and it would take her an hour to get to the Hyatt if traffic was bad. She had better get going.

She turned toward the bathroom, dropping the package back on the floor near the door.

She had a new book to read this Saturday night.

She just didn't know what the title or the plot was yet.

Two

By the time Hanna made it across town to the Hyatt, she was early and scared to death. Her stomach was doing flip-flops and even with the night air being cool and the roof up and air conditioning on in her Mustang, she was sweating.

She got the key to the room from the front desk and then ducked into the restroom off the plush, plant-filled lobby. She put cold water on a towel to try to cool her face. But even the cold towel and two Tums didn't help the twisting in her stomach.

This had just seemed like such a good idea at the time.

And she did so love romance novels.

But even though she worked at the CIA, she just wasn't the adventurous type. She much more wanted a real hero to come along and sweep her off her feet to live happily every after.

Tonight might have a happy ending or two involved, but it sure wasn't a romance, anymore than a night home alone with her favorite vibrating appliance was a romance.

She stared at herself in the mirror.

She looked good, ready for a night on the town. He long black hair flowed around her face. Her shoulders were naked and the lace along the top of her black dress accented her breasts. Plus she had on her best underwear.

"You've gone this far, Hanna," she said to herself.

Her voice sounded as hollow as she felt.

This was stupid, but after a year, even stupid started to sound good.

She turned and headed back out into the lobby.

Hanna knew that all romances had meet-cutes where the two characters would meet and fall in love and then eventually hop into the sack, sometimes before trouble hit them, sometimes after.

Meeting her date tonight would be far from a meet-cute. More like a meet-scared-to-death.

As she went toward the elevators, she happened to glance up to see a very nervous-looking-man waiting for the elevator, an identical package to hers in his hand.

She stepped to one side behind a stone column protected by a large plant and watched him for a moment.

He was handsome and tall and he did have dark hair.

He could be the perfect hero of any romance novel. He even a little chiseled jaw.

But she could tell he was as frightened as Hanna felt.

Maybe more so.

And Hanna knew him.

She wasn't sure where, but she felt she knew him from somewhere.

He paced, waiting for the elevator and his nervousness calmed hers. For some reason it made him seem even more attractive. And he was already into Greek God country.

But wow did he look familiar.

She had never met him. She would remember meeting someone as good-looking as he was.

Then she gasped and wanted to throw up.

Now she knew why he looked familiar.

The man she was supposed to meet was Ben, Constance's husband.

Oh, no. Now what was she supposed to do?

The rules of the club were that no one was to know each other.

The elevator doors opened and Ben just stood there, not getting on.

After the doors closed he shook his head, took a deep breath, and pushed the button again.

The poor guy was scared to death.

How could a man that good-looking be that scared?

This time when the doors opened he stepped inside.

Hanna felt her own fear vanishing.

If Constance and Ben were so experienced at this book club thing, Ben never would have been acting like that.

He had never done this before either.

This book club thing was all a fake.

Constance had made up this entire thing, more than likely to try to spice up their marriage, and who more gullible to fall for it and help her and Ben out than Hanna, the shy recluse with too many vibrators.

Suddenly Hanna felt herself getting angry.

It would serve Constance right if Hanna did go up there and seduce her husband. They needed marriage counseling, not a book club.

Hanna started to toss the book into the garbage can next to the elevators and head for her car, then stopped.

Not showing up wouldn't help either.

She actually considered Constance a friend. An office friend, maybe, but at least some sort of friend. And clearly Constance and Ben needed some help. If Hanna didn't show, Constance and Ben would just try it with someone who might actually show up. And maybe destroy their marriage.

She had no plans on sleeping with that hunk of a man who had just gone upstairs, but she could at least help him and Constance out.

A few moments later she was pushing open the door to the suite on the 6th floor, the book club package in her hand.

The suite was fantastic. A huge, plush living room with far too many large, green plants accenting the tans and browns of the couches and chairs. The drapes were pulled, the lighting lower than normal to set a mood, the wide double-doors to the bedroom completely open showing a bed large enough to sleep a family of six on.

Facing her across the carpet was the guy she had seen getting on the elevator. Ben, Constance's husband.

He was clearly one of the most handsome men Hanna had ever seen. He was dressed perfectly in an expensive suit and a silk tie that matched the handkerchief tucked perfectly in his pocket. Up close he not only had a chiseled chin, but deep green eyes.

He could pose for covers of romance novels.

Hanna felt her stomach twist again. Maybe, just maybe she might spend a little time with him before calling his bluff. Someone like him she could have great fantasies about later with her vibrator collection.

Then she shook her head and cleared out that thought.

He nodded and nervously smiled with a smile that could just about break anyone's heart.

Wow!

The package in his hands looked like it might explode at any moment the way he squeezed and twisted it.

She smiled at him.

Maybe she should just jump his bones. Constance didn't know how lucky she had it. What was she thinking letting this man near another woman?

Hanna smiled back, then turned and shut the suite door and locked it.

Then she turned and tossed her book package on a small table near the door.

"All right, Ben," she said. "Let's drop the act and call Constance."

The man facing her for a moment looked puzzled. "You know Constance?"

His voice was deep and rich enough to give a person a sugar high.

"Of course I know Constance," Hanna said, heading past the hunk toward the bottle of champagne on the table. She needed a drink more than anything except sex at the moment.

"How?" he asked, still holding the book package.

"She's my boss and the one who pulled this book club scam on me. And I've seen pictures of you on her desk."

The hunk sort of looked at the book package in his hands, then tossed it on the closest couch like it would burn him if he held it any longer.

"So call her and tell her to get her ass down here," Hanna said. "We all have some talking to do."

The guy opened his mouth to say something, then shook his head and closed it. He took out his cell phone and hit a speed-dial number as Hanna poured herself a glass and then filled one for him as well. Might as well get a little something for her money. There was no doubt this night was going to be a bust.

Three

"Constance," he said. "Hi."

He paused. Then he said, "Not so well. She says she recognized me from a picture on your desk and wants to talk to you down here."

He nodded and listened, then said, "All right. Thanks."

He clicked off the cell phone as Hanna watched.

"She said it would take her twenty minutes."

Hanna nodded and handed him a glass of champagne.

She had about a thousand questions she wanted to ask him, but most of them would wait until Constance got her. For the moment she was just going to stare at the guy and pretend he really was her date for the evening.

He took the glass and walked over to the window and opened the heavy drapes.

For the first time she noticed the faint background music playing in the suite. Romantic string music not too loud, but there.

Someone really had gone to a lot of work with every detail.

After taking a sip and staring out the window for a moment, he turned. "So you were willing to go through with this crazy book club idea?"

She shook her head. "More than likely not. I was about to chicken out when I recognized you getting on the elevator. I figured I was a friend of Constance and you two, if you were going to this level of planning and deception, really needed some marriage help."

For the second time he smiled and again she felt things melt inside her that shouldn't be melting in public.

He sipped his champagne. "Since you seem to know me, can I have the pleasure?"

"Sorry," she said, smiling back at him. "Hanna Wurmbrand. I work with Constance at the CIA and can't tell you any more without killing you."

He actually laughed softly at her stupid joke, the nervousness now long gone, replaced by a confidence that sort of radiated from every wonderful pore of his wonderful body.

And she was starting to feel more nervous by the moment.

She took another sip of the expensive champagne and then went back to the package she had tossed on the table near the door. She held it up. "Did you open yours?"

"No," he said. "I followed the rules."

She looked at him and frowned. "So you don't know which book Constance put in these packages?"

"Not a clue," he said, again smiling. "But I have to admit, this is a very, very elaborate set-up don't you think? I wonder how she got the idea?"

Hanna now felt even more confused. It was starting to sound like Ben hadn't been in on what Constance was doing. Or at least it seemed that way.

She put the package down without opening it yet again.

He took a sip, then excused himself and headed for the bathroom. "Nervous bladder and too much coffee on the way over here."

He vanished into the bathroom and closed the door, leaving her alone in the huge suite that now felt completely empty. It was stunning how one man could fill such a huge space with his presence.

Constance had no idea how lucky she was.

Hanna opened the door into the hallway and blocked it open with the security latch, then took her glass and went over to the window to stare out at the beautiful Washington DC night. If nothing else about this city, it could be beautiful.

Behind her there was a knock on the hotel room door.

She didn't know how she felt right now, but anger was just below the surface. More than likely she was going to be without a job in a few minutes, but she didn't care. She couldn't work with Constance anymore, not after this.

"Come on in, it's open."

Hanna turned as Constance and Ben came through the door from the hallway.

Hanna glanced at the bathroom door, which was still closed.

And Ben had changed into a sweater and tan slacks.

Constance looked around, worried, then stepped forward leaving Ben in the entry. "Are you all right?"

Hanna went to open her mouth to yell at her boss but didn't get out a word as the bathroom door opened and a second Ben stepped out.

"Constance, Ben," the man said. "This sure was an elaborate trick to play on us."

Hanna just stood there, her mouth open, staring at the three other people in the suite.

Two who were clearly twins. Identical twins.

"Sorry, brother," Ben said, stepping forward. "We figured it was the only way we could get you two together."

Constance nodded, smiling first at Hanna, then turning to the man who would have been Hanna's date. "You both hated blind dates and had had such bad luck with dating services. We felt you would be a perfect match if we could just get you together."

"So you tricked us," the man said, clearly some anger in his voice as he moved up to stand near Hanna, his champagne glass in his hand. "Why didn't you just introduce me to this wonderful and smart woman and let us see what might happen?"

Hanna looked over at him. She didn't even know his name.

"And how would we have done that?" Constance asked. "You two are impossible to break out of your schedules."

"A backyard cookout might have been an idea," he said. "You do barbeque, don't you, Ben?"

Ben, standing behind Constance, just nodded, clearly embarrassed.

Hanna held up her hand for silence.

"Constance, could I get a complete story please?" And then she turned to the man standing beside her. "And a name?"

"Gary," the man said, looking at her with those wonderful green eyes and a smile that could melt steel off a high-rise. "I am Ben's twin-and-clearly-smarter brother."

He reached out and they shook hands.

At that moment Hanna didn't want to let go of Gary's hand and he didn't seem to want to look away or let go of her hand as well.

She could get lost in those eyes if he let her. Wow, what a horrid romance novel cliché, but now she understood it. The swirling green of those eyes were just hypnotic.

Finally he did let go and she felt disappointment go to places of her body she didn't know could feel disappointment.

Constance shrugged. "We thought it would be impossible to get you two together, so we came up with the book club idea. It seemed like a great idea at the time."

"Hanna thought I was Ben," Gary said, "and was willing to stay here and help talk her friend through her marriage troubles."

Constance looked at Hanna, then just blushed and looked down. "Thank you," she said softly.

A very tense silence settled over the large suite with only the faint romantic background music floating through the roughness of the moment.

Hanna knew that it was up to her to do something to break this.

Her job and the future of their family happiness and trust depended on her taking some action now.

She turned to the handsome hunk beside her. "I am all dressed up and so hungry I could eat the cork off that bottle."

Gary smiled and said nothing.

"How about we go get dinner, just you and me?"

"I would love that," he said, smiling, offering his arm.

She took it with a flourish, and she had to admit it felt wonderful. He felt strong and solid.

As they walked across the suite toward the door, she smiled at Constance and then at Ben. "Thank you for the very kind thoughts."

"Yes," Gary said to his brother and sister-in-law. "Weird, but interesting. Thank you."

As Gary opened the door for her, Hanna smiled at her boss. "And we expect a new bottle of champagne by the time we get back."

"And you two long gone," Gary said.

Constance and Ben both smiled huge smiles of relief.

"And leave the books," Hanna said, winking at Constance and making her blush as the door swung closed.

Hanna and Gary both laughed all the way down the hall, which Hanna knew was just the romance novel way of saying they lived happily-ever-after.

And she liked that idea a great deal.

IN THE SHADE OF THE SLOWBOAT MAN

For a vampire, saying goodbye to your mortal lover can be the hardest thing you ever have to do.

First published in The Magazine of Fantasy and Science Fiction, *the story was on the final ballot for the Nebula Award.*

One

I WAS USED to the sweet smell of blood, to the sharp taste of disgust, to the wide-eyed look of lust. But the tight, small room of the nursing home covered me in new sensations like a mad mother covering her sleeping young child tenderly with a blanket before pressing a pillow hard over the face.

I eased the heavy door closed and stood silently for a moment, my clutch purse tight against my chest. One hospital bed, a small metal dresser, and an aluminum walker were all the furniture in the room. The green drapes over the window were slightly open and I silently moved to stand in the beam of silver moonlight cutting the night. I wanted more than anything else to run. But I calmed myself, took a deep breath, and worked to pull in and study my surroundings as I would on any night in any city alley or street.

As with all of the cesspools of humanity, the smell was the most overwhelming detail. The odor of human rot filled the building and the room, not so much different than a dead animal beside the road on a hot summer's day. Death and nature doing its work. But in this building, in this small room, the natural work was disguised by layer after layer of biting poison antiseptic. I suppose it was meant to clean the smell of death away so as not to disturb the sensitive living who visited from the fresh air outside. But instead of clearing, the two smells combined to form a thick aroma that filled my mouth with disgust.

I blocked the smell and focused my attention on the form in the bed.

John, my dear, sweet Slowboat Man, my husband once, lay under the white sheet of the room's only bed. His frame shrunken from the robust, healthy man I remembered from so many short years ago. He smelled of piss and decay. His face, rough with old skin and white whiskers, seemed to fight an enemy unseen on the battleground of this tiny room. He jerked, then moaned softly, his labored breathing working to pull enough air to get to the next breath.

I moved to him, my ex-husband, my Slowboat Man, and lightly brushed his wrinkled forehead to ease his sleep. I used to do that as we lay together in our featherbed. I would need him to sleep so that I could go out and feed on the blood of others. He never awoke while I was gone, not once in the twenty years we were together.

Or at least he never told me he had.

I had never asked.

Two

I was hunting the night we met. The spring of 1946, a time of promise and good cheer around the country. The war was won, the evil vanquished, and the living bathed in the feeling of a wonderful future. I had spent the last thirty years before and during the war in St. Louis, but my friends had aged, as always happened, and it was becoming too hard to continue to answer the questions and the looks. I had moved on many times in the past and I would continue to do so many times in the future. It was my curse for making mortal friends and enjoying the pleasures of the mortal world.

I pleaded to my friends in St. Louis a sick mother in a faraway city, and booked passage under another name on an old-fashioned Missis-sippi riverboat named *Joe Henry*. I had loved the boats when they were working the river the first time, and now, again, loved them as they came back again for the tourists and gambling.

For the first few days I stayed mostly to my small cabin, sleeping on the small bed during the day and reading at night. But on the third day, hunger finally drove me into the narrow hallways and lighted party rooms of the huge riverboat.

Many soldiers and sailors filled the boat, most still in uniform, and most with women of their own age holding onto their arms and laughing at their every word. The boat literally reeked of health and good cheer and I still remember how that smell drove my hunger.

I supposed events could have turned another way and I might have met Johnny before feeding. But almost immediately upon leaving my cabin, I had gotten lucky and found a young sailor standing alone on the lower deck.

I walked up to the rail and pretended to stare out over the black waters of the river and the lights beyond. The air felt alive, full of humidity and insects, thick air that carried the young sailor's scent clearly to me.

He moved closer and struck up a conversation. After a minute I stroked his arm, building his lust and desire while at the same time blocking his mind of my image. I asked him to help me with a problem with the mattress on my bed in my cabin and even though he kept a straight face the smell of sexual lust almost choked me.

Within two minutes he was asleep on my bed and I was feeding, drinking light to not hurt him, but yet getting enough of his blood to fill my immediate hunger.

After I finished I brushed over the marks on his neck with a lick so that no sign would show, then cleaned up myself while letting him rest. Then I roused him just enough to walk him up a few decks, where I slipped away, happy that I might repeat the same act numbers of times during this voyage. It was an intoxicating time and I felt better than I had ever remembered feeling in years.

I decided that an after-dinner stroll along the moonlit deck would be nice before returning to my cabin. I moved slowly, drinking in the warmth of the night air, listening to the churning of the paddle wheel, feeling the boat slice through the muddy water of the river.

Johnny leaned against the rail about mid-ship, smoking a pipe.

Under the silver moon, his Navy officer's white uniform seemed to glow with a light of its own. I started to pass him and realized that I needed to stop, to speak to him, to let him hold me.

He affected me like I imagined I affected my prey when feeding. I was drawn to him with such intensity that resisting didn't seem possible.

I hesitated and he glanced over at me and laughed, a soft laugh as if he could read my every thought, as if he knew that I wanted him with me that instant, without reason, without cause. He just laughed, not at me, but in merriment at the situation, at the delight, at the beauty of the night.

He laughed easily and for the next twenty years I would enjoy that laugh every day.

I turned and he was smiling, a first smile that I will always remember. He had the simple ability to smile and light up the darkest place, he had a smile that I would lose myself in many a night while he told me story after story after story. I never tired of that smile, and that first exposure to it melted my every will. I would be his slave and never care as long as he kept smiling at me.

"Beautiful evening, isn't it?" he said, his voice solid and genuine, like his smile.

"Now it is," I said. I had to catch my breath even after something that simple.

Again he laughed and made a motion that I should join him at the rail gazing out over the river and the trees and farmland beyond.

I did. And for twenty years, except to feed on others while he slept, I never left his side.

Three

The smell of the room pulled me from the past and back to my mission of the evening. I looked at his weathered, time-beaten form on the bed and felt sadness and love. A large part of me regretted missing the aging time of his life, of not sharing that time with him, like I had regretted missing the years before I met him. But on both I had had no choice. Or I had felt I had had no choice. I might have been wrong, but it was the choice I had made.

Since the time I left him I had never found another to be my husband. Actually I never really tried, never really wanted to fill that huge hole in my chest and my very being that leaving him had caused.

But now he was dying and now I also had to move on, change cities and friends again. I had always felt regret with each move, yet the regret was controlled by the certainty that the decision was the only right one, that I would make new friends, find new lovers. But this time it was harder. Much harder.

I sat lightly on the side of his bed and he stirred, moaning softly. I again brushed his forehead easing his pain, giving him a fuller rest, a more peaceful rest. It was the least I could do for him. He deserved so much more.

This time he moaned with contentment and that moan took me back to those lovely nights on the *Joe Henry*, slowly making our way down the river, nestled in each other's arms. We made love three, sometimes four times a day and spent the rest of the time talking and laughing and just being with each other, as if every moment was the most precious moment we had.

During those wonderful talks I had immediately wanted to tell him of my true nature, but didn't. The very desire to tell him surprised me. In all the years it had not happened before. So I only told him of the twenty years in St. Louis, letting him think that was where I had been raised. As the years together went by that lie became as truth between us and he never questioned me on it.

He was born in San Francisco and wanted to return there where his family had property and some wealth. I told him I was alone in the world, as was the true case, just drifting and looking for a new home. He seemed to admire that about me. But he also knew I was free to move where he wanted.

I wanted him to know that.

The day before we were to dock in Vicksburg, I mentioned to him that I wished the boat would slow down so that our time together would last. The days and nights since meeting him had been truly magical, and in my life that was a very rare occurrence.

He had again laughed at my thought, but in a good way. Then he hugged me. "We will be together for a long time," he had said, "but I will return in a moment."

With that he dressed and abruptly left the cabin, leaving me surrounded by his things and his wonderful life-odor. After a short time he returned, smiling, standing over me, casting his shadow across my naked form. "Your wish is granted," he had said. "The boat has slowed."

I didn't know how he had managed it, and never really asked what it had cost him. But somehow he had managed to delay the boat getting into Vicksburg by an extra day. A long wonderful extra day that turned into a wonderful marriage.

From that day forward I called him my Slowboat Man and he never seemed to tire of it.

Four

"Beautiful evening, isn't it?" he said hoarsely from the bed beside me. His words yanked me from the past and back to the smell of death and antiseptic in the small nursing home room. Johnny was smiling up at me, lightly, his sunken eyes still full of the light and the mischief that I had loved so much.

"It is now," I said, stroking him, soothing him.

He started to laugh, but instead coughed and I soothed him with a touch again.

He blinked a few times, focusing on me, staring at me, touching my arm. "You are as beautiful as I remembered," he said, his voice clearing as he used it, gaining more and more power. "I've missed you."

"I've missed you, too," I somehow managed to say. I could feel his weak grip on my arm.

He smiled and then his eyes closed.

I touched his forehead and again he was dozing. I sat on the bed beside him and thought back to that last time I had sat beside him on our marriage bed, almost thirty years earlier.

That last night, as with any other night I went out to feed, I had put him to sleep with a few strokes on the forehead and then stayed with him to make sure his sleep was deep. But that last night I had also packed a few things, very few, actually, because I had hoped to take very little of our life together to remind me of him. It had made no difference. I saw his face, his smile, heard his laugh and his voice everywhere I went.

I had known for years that the day of leaving was coming. And many times over the years we were together I thought of telling him about my true nature. But I could never overcome the fear. I feared that if he knew he would hate me, fight me, even try to kill me. I feared that he would find a way to expose those of us like me in the city and around the country. But my biggest fear was that he would never be able to stand my youth as he aged.

I could not have stood the look of his hate and disgust.

At least that was what I told myself. As the years passed since I left him I came to believe that my fear had been a stupid one. But I never overcame that fear, at least not until now.

I know my leaving to him must have felt sudden and without reason. I know he spent vast sums of money looking for me. I know he didn't truly understand.

But for me I had no choice. During the month before I left, comments about my youth were suddenly everywhere; Johnny and our friends had aged, I hadn't. I even caught Johnny staring at me when he thought I wouldn't notice.

Three nights before I left, one waitress asked him, while I was in the ladies room, what his daughter, meaning me, wanted for dessert. He had laughed about it, but I could tell he didn't understand and was bothered. As again he should have been.

The night I left, hidden in a pile of magazines recycled from his office, I found a book about vampires. A well-read book.

I could wait no longer and I knew then that I could never talk to him about it. I had to go that night and I did so, leaving only a note to him that I would always love him.

I moved quickly, silently, in an untraceable fashion, to the East Coast. But less than a year later, no longer able to even fight the fight of keeping him out of my mind, I returned to San Francisco under a new name and began to watch him from afar.

As with me, he never remarried. Many nights he would walk the streets of the city alone, just smiling, almost content. I paced him, watching him, protecting him from others of my kind and from the mortal criminals. I imagined that he knew I was watching him. Pacing him. Walking with him. Protecting him. I pretended that knowing I was there made him happy. Many nights I even thought of actually showing myself to him, holding him again.

But I never did.

I never had the courage.

Five

He stirred under the nursing home sheet and I watched him as he awoke. He opened his eyes, saw me, and then smiled. "Good. I was hoping you were more than a dream."

"No, Slowboat Man, you aren't dreaming."

He laughed and gripped my hand and I could feel the warmth flowing between us. I leaned down and kissed him on the cheek, his rough skin warm against my face. As I pulled back I could see a single tear in the corner of his right eye. But in both eyes the look was love. I was amazed.

And very glad.

I had feared he would hate me after I had left him without warning. I had feared that when I came to visit tonight he would ask the questions about my youth and how I had stayed so young, questions that I had always been so afraid to answer. I had feared most of all that he would send me away.

But he didn't. And the relief flooded through my every cell. Even after almost thirty years he still loved me. I wanted to shout it to the entire world. But instead I just sat there smiling at him.

In the century I had been alive I had never felt or seen a love so complete and total as his love for me.

It saddened me to think that in the centuries to come I might never find it again.

"I'm glad you decided to come and say good-bye," he said. "I was hoping you would."

I gently touched his arm. "You know I wanted to when——"

He waved me quiet. "Don't. You did what you had to do."

My head was spinning and I wanted to ask him a thousand questions: How he knew? What he knew?

But instead I just sat beside him on the bed and stared at him. After a moment he laughed.

"Now say good-bye properly," he said. "Then be on your way. I overheard the doctor telling one of the nurses that I might not make it through the night and I don't want you here when I leave. Might not be a pretty sight."

I just shook my head at him. I had seen more death than he could ever imagine, but I didn't want to tell him that.

A long spell of coughing caught him and he half sat up in bed with the pain. I stroked his forehead and he calmed and worked to catch his breath. After a moment he said, "I loved it when you used to do that to me. Always thought it was one of your nicer gifts to me, even though I never understood just how or what you did."

Again he laughed lightly at what must have been my shocked look. Even after all these years, even with very little force behind it, his laugh could still gladden my heart, make me smile, ease my worries. Again this time it took only a moment before I smiled and then laughed with him.

"Now be on your way," he said. "The nurse will be here shortly and I have a long journey to make into the next world. I'm ready to go, you know? Actually looking forward to it. You would too if you had an old body like this one."

I nodded and stood. "Good-bye, my Slowboat Man." I leaned down and kissed him solidly on his rough, chapped lips.

"Good-bye, my beautiful wife."

He smiled at me one last time and I smiled back, as I always had.

Then I turned and headed for the door. I knew that I had to leave immediately, because if I didn't I never would. But this time he wanted me to go. I wasn't running away.

As I pulled the handle open to the dimly-lit hallway, he called out to me. "Beautiful?"

I stopped and turned.

"I'm sorry I couldn't slow the boat down this time."

"That's all right," I said, just loud enough for him to hear. "No matter how long or how short the lifetime, sometimes once is enough. Sleep well my Slowboat Man. Sleep well."

And as the door to his final room closed behind me I added to myself. "And thank you."

IT'S A STORY ABOUT A GUY WHO . . .

Danny Evans needs a good grade in creative writing.

His assignment? He must write about any person he sees in a public place, and really get inside that person's head. He must make up a character.

It seemed like such a simple assignment.

But sometimes some stories don't end well.

THE FIRST START

MR. HAROLD HERMAN SCREWS *sat silently in the crowded old train station, his back straight against the hard wooden bench.*

The sounds of fifty other people talking and a few children playing seemed to only bounce off Mr. Screws like raindrops off a yellow police slicker. The large room of the historical station seemed filled with life, the high ceiling and wooden rafters softened the sound, making even the loudest cry from a newborn baby seem like a distant sound of joy.

Mr. Screws wanted no part of the life around him. His disdain for all other members of humanity radiated from him like a bad smell, keeping anyone from sitting within ten feet. He wore a dark brown suit with matching slacks, a white shirt, and a simple white bow tie. His brown hat sat on the bench beside him guarding his brown plaid suitcase on the floor beside him.

His attire had clearly been chosen carefully to draw no undue attention and his five-foot-four-inch height also kept him well hidden in crowds.

Yet Mr. Harold Herman Screws stood out, sitting alone on the wooden bench, a sea of emptiness around him like there were walls holding back the rest of humanity.

Mr. Screws did not notice the distance, but there was little doubt he secretly felt glad for it.

Pretty much everyone else in the room noticed Mr. Screws, at least enough to hope that he would not sit beside them on the outgoing train from Boise, Idaho, headed east.

REALITY

I tucked the pen into the notebook I had been writing in and reread what I had put down about the strange man sitting on the bench two rows in front and to the right of me. Even though I had no idea what his real name was, I liked the name I had called him. Harold Herman Screws. A distinctive name for a man who was impossible to miss in a crowd.

The assignment for the creative writing class I was taking at Boise State University was to go to a public place, observe, and then write a character sketch about a person we saw there.

Mrs. Wilson, my instructor and published author of six literary short stories in university presses, had told us we should try to get inside the head of the person we were observing.

I had no idea how to do that.

Once again I reread what I had written.

Damn.

Not one word from inside the guy's head. That wasn't going to up my grade. And I needed to get the "B" I had at the moment up to an "A" if I had a decent chance at getting into a good law school in two years. Otherwise I would be stuck up in Northern Idaho going to law school there.

And somehow I needed to get into the first part that the air in the terminal was cool compared to the unusually hot, sticky April day outside. Mrs. Wilson really liked setting and feeling details.

I glanced over at the big board on the wall showing the arrival time for the train. It was fifteen minutes delayed and wouldn't arrive for almost another forty-five minutes. I had time to get more from the guy.

In an hour I had to be downtown to meet Barb, my girlfriend, for dinner.

Perfect.

I took a deep breath and tried to get myself to relax.

"Come on, Danny, this writing thing isn't rocket science."

No one was close enough to me to hear me talking to myself in the noise of the train station.

I stared around at the people in the terminal reading or trying to nap. A couple men to one side were actually reading paper newspapers just like this was 1960 or something.

There was a dark area in one corner of the old terminal. I could make this character sketch into a Rod Serling description. Barb and I had done a marathon of old *Twilight Zone* episodes. I loved that old show.

That might work.

I went back to writing in my notebook. I hated writing by hand, but Mrs. Wilson thought it would get us more in touch with what we were writing.

SECOND DRAFT

The short, handsome man with the cigarette stepped from the shadows into a spotlight as Mr. Harold Herman Screws sat staring ahead at the windows leading out to the train platform.

"For your consideration," the man said, his voice deep and distinctive, "one Mr. Harold Herman Screws. A man waiting calmly and patiently for a train to take him away from the body of the elderly mother he has just killed, the dull job at the accounting office, the daily ritual of sameness that can drive a man to the brink and beyond."

The handsome man half smiled, the smoke from his cigarette curling up around him.

Then he went on. "But Mr. Harold Herman Screws isn't just waiting to escape from his dull life and his recent crime. He is waiting for a train that will carry him, luggage and all, directly into..."

(Pause, wait for it...)

"...The Twilight Zone."

REALITY...PART TWO

I looked at what I had written and had no idea how I would include it in the assignment. And it still wouldn't help. Once again it didn't do what Mrs. Wilson wanted.

She had said that if we couldn't get into a person's head by making it up, we might need to talk to them.

I looked at the guy in the brown suit staring silently ahead at the windows. Why had I picked him, anyway? Of all the people in the train station to pick, he looked like the last guy who might want to talk to me.

"You want the grade?" I asked myself. "And a good law school or you want to be stuck in northern Idaho for three years?"

I took a deep breath and stood.

"Good law school."

I headed over to the bench with the guy in the brown suit staring ahead at the windows. To one side a couple of kids played with a red rubber ball, kicking it back and forth, laughing.

I could do this. Any kind of response from the guy with the bow tie would help me and I could make up the rest.

I stopped a step from him and cleared my throat.

He looked up at me, the dark, brown eyes boring through me like I was tissue.

He said nothing.

"I'm very sorry to bother you," I said.

He just stared at me and I could feel my heart beating like the first time I had kissed Barb. Or the first time I had tried to learn how to ski.

Fear.

Just plain old fear, like talking to a guy was going to kill me or something.

Stupid.

There was nothing to be afraid of. The guy could be rude, ignore me, and it would make no difference to me.

"My name is Danny Evans," I said to him and thankfully my voice didn't crack. "I'm a student at Boise State and I have an assignment from one of my teachers to talk to a perfect stranger to help me learn how to write a story."

He kept staring at me.

Then he blinked and a slight smile cracked the corners of his mouth like concrete being hammered into dust.

Then he nodded and indicated I should sit on the bench beside him.

"Thanks," I said. "I won't take up much of your time. This is only for a character sketch."

"It is no issue," the man said, his voice high as I would have expected of a man wearing a bow tie waiting to ride a train. "I seem to have more time than I need."

I nodded, not really understanding that statement at all. But I could use it in the story.

I flipped to a clean page in my notebook. "Would you mind telling me anything you would feel comfortable telling me about yourself?"

He nodded. "I suppose I could do that."

"Good," I said. "Are you from here in Boise?"

He nodded. "Born and raised. Until today. Today I am moving on."

Then he seemed to pause and catch himself. "Please pardon my bad manners. I am preoccupied."

He stuck out his hand.

I took it as he said, "My name is Harold Herman Screws. Former accountant."

Then he smiled.

Not Possible!

I wanted to pull away, but couldn't.

Around me the room seemed to darken.

The voices of the other people in the room seemed to fade and just vanish.

A short, well-dressed man in a gray suit stepped from the shadows in the corner of the station and into a spotlight that had not existed a moment before.

The smoke from the man's cigarette drifted up and around him in the bright light.

I couldn't move. It was as if my body was frozen in place.

Frozen by fear, by disbelief of what I was seeing.

The man started talking in that very familiar voice.

"Meet one Danny Evans, student and hopeful law student, tasked with interviewing a character who has come a little too close to reality for comfort. Little does Danny know that with one stroke of the pen, a writer can open doors into new worlds of the imagination."

The man with the cigarette in the spotlight paused.

Then he went on. "Danny Evans is about to step through one of those doors he has created. Only this door leads directly into..."

The man paused.

The smoke swirled in the spotlight.

I shouted, "Don't say it!"

He didn't hear me.

NONEXISTENT NO MORE

A Poker Boy Story

When the wife of one the guardians of humanity, herself one of the most powerful beings in the universe, comes looking for help, a superhero does what he can.

Poker Boy and his sidekick (and girlfriend), Front Desk Girl, must help with no idea why.

One

WHO KNEW that Wolfgang Sucker had a wife? A Mrs. Sucker.

And since Wolfgang was a blue-skinned Searchlight, if I had thought of him having a wife, I would have assumed that Mrs. Sucker would be blue as well.

Wrong. Mrs. Wolfgang Sucker was bright pink, and depending on the light, the pink shifted to bright purple, very bright purple. And she had wide brown eyes instead of blue eyes.

Just as the first time I saw her husband, I first saw Mrs. Sucker walking toward me across the lobby of the MGM Grand Hotel and Casino in Las Vegas. I was leaning against one of the stone pillars in the lobby waiting for my girlfriend and sidekick, Patty Ledgerwood, aka Front Desk Girl to get off work.

Stunning didn't begin to describe Mrs. Sucker, even though no one in the lobby seemed to even notice her, and they should have. Every man in the room should have been staring. Her body suit, or at least I hoped it was a body suit, blended perfectly with her pink/purple skin making her look to be a very bright nude, only with no real details showing.

Maybe she didn't have any of those details. I just didn't know. In fact, what I knew about Searchlights wasn't much, other than they were very, very powerful.

She stood as thin and as tall as her husband, at least six-six, and she couldn't have weighed more than one-hundred-and-twenty pounds.

And I was sure that most of that weight she carried on the front of her chest.

She was the wet dream of every modeling agency on the planet. Even with the bright pink/purple skin color. It was just weird how the color kept changing from shade to shade the closer she got.

And on her completely bald head she had the same patterns of white marks as her husband. The patterns shifted as she moved her head slowly from one side to the other, making different scenes.

Searchlights were a race that no one in the superheroes and gods seemed to know much about, or even where on Earth they lived. They seemed to exist in nowhere land.

The Searchlights were called the guardians of the human race, and usually worked with the different deities when a problem threatened humanity.

I first met her husband, Wolfgang Sucker, during the big fight against the Fuzzy-Wuzzy bugs from another dimension. He had been assigned to the Gambling Gods, and since as Poker Boy, I work for them, I got a chance to work with him.

"Poker Boy," the female Searchlight said, her voice as raspy as her husband's, and her breath just as bad. "My name is Emmanuel Sucker, the wife, as you humans would call it, of Wolfgang Sucker."

I wanted to back away to get out of the smell of rotted garlic and dead fish that was her breath, but instead I somehow managed to bow slightly as is a traditional show of respect when talking to a Searchlight.

Then I said, "Very nice to meet you."

"My husband spoke highly of you and your team in our last mating."

I opened my mouth to say something, then closed it and decided that a nod was safer. I was learning far more about the Searchlight society and relationships than I wanted to at that moment. And any question I might ask might cause a lot of problems—or more likely, answers I just didn't want to hear.

And I didn't need my imagination going any farther thinking about a tall pink woman and blue man mating, constantly turning their heads from side to side.

"I need to talk to Front Desk Girl, if you don't mind?" Emmanuel Sucker asked.

"Of course," I said. "Would you wait here while I jump and get her? It will take only a moment."

She nodded.

I knew exactly where Patty was, and could have easily marched the ten or fifteen steps to the front desk and asked for her, but I wanted to practice my newly discovered superpower of jumping around in space.

And besides, when a Searchlight started asking to talk with other superheroes, it usually meant they wanted to talk to the major gods as well. And that meant something very bad was about to happen to humanity in general.

So I winked out, appearing beside Patty in the employee lounge at the same moment taking us out of time so that no other employee saw me appear.

Taking myself out of time used to be my most fun superpower before I learned how to jump around in space. Now I was doing both and that just made me happy. It's not often a simple poker player can learn to teleport and step between moments in time.

Around us a half-dozen of Patty's co-employees were frozen in positions of that moment in time. One woman was chewing on a candy bar and her mouth was half open and it wasn't a pretty sight.

"I love doing that," I said, smiling at Patty's wonderful brown eyes. She had her long brown hair let down and was wearing the standard black slacks and white blouse of the MGM front desk employee.

"You are getting pretty good at it," Patty said, smiling and kissing me. "Just like many other things."

I think I blushed. In fact I was sure I blushed. And that simple hint of suggestion almost made me forget about Emmanuel Sucker standing in the front lobby.

"We have a problem," I said. "Did you know Searchlights have mates?"

"No, I didn't," Patty said, frowning. Even with a frown on her face, she was the best-looking woman I had ever seen.

"Well, they do, and Emmanuel Sucker, Wolfgang Sucker's wife, is out front in the lobby and wants to talk to you."

Patty's eyes got wide. "Me? Why?"

"I didn't ask."

Patty was a superhero like I was. There was little if any reason a Searchlight would ask for one of us.

Then I looked up and shouted "Stan! Need help!"

Patty nodded and I flicked us back to a position in front of the Searchlight, then took all three of us out of time so we could talk without all the noise of the lobby.

An instant later, Stan, the God of Poker, joined us, going through the ritual slight bowing to the Searchlight.

Then Emmanuel Sucker, her bald purple head moving slowly from side to side, the patterns on her head moving and changing, bowed slightly to Patty. "Thank you for seeing me."

Patty bowed slightly in return. "It is my honor to meet you. What can we do for you? Is there a problem we are going to need help with?"

"To be most honest," Emmanuel said to Patty, the patterns on her head seeming to move slightly faster than normal, "I only need your help concerning a problem with my husband."

I glanced at Stan, who looked as shocked as I felt.

As far as the little bit of history I knew, no Searchlight had ever come to just talk with one superhero before. They always contacted superheroes first to be taken to the higher gods of each deity. Sort of like going to a servant to be taken to the Queen.

"That will be no problem," Patty said. She turned to Stan. "Can you jump Mrs. Sucker and myself to the meeting room off the main corridor near the lobby? I will call for you when we are finished."

Stan nodded, and an instant later the two women were gone.

"You have any idea what that is about?" Stan asked.

"No more than you do," I said.

He nodded, then said, "I had better tell Laverne and Patty's boss what's happening."

Then he too was gone.

Two

I let myself drop back into real time.

The sounds of the lobby of the MGM Grand smashed into me. It was always a shock going from the complete silence of between-time and back to real time when it came to the noise. All the people who had been frozen in mid-stride or mid-sentence a moment before were now suddenly moving and talking again.

I stood against the stone pillar off to one side of the grand lobby, no longer waiting for Patty to get off work, but to work her superhero magic with a Searchlight.

I had a sinking feeling about this, and I couldn't tell if that sinking feeling was one of my superpowers trying to warn me, or my normal guy worries about his girlfriend being in some sort of trouble.

I was just starting to try to sort that out when Stan appeared again and took us back out of time, freezing all the movement in the lobby and silencing all the noise.

"I talked to Laverne," he said. "She didn't seem worried, and told me to keep her informed."

Laverne was Lady Luck herself, one of the most powerful gods anywhere.

"Did you tell Judy what was happening?" I asked.

Judy was the God of Hospitality, the top deity that covered everything to do with lodging and guests staying anywhere. Patty was a superhero under the hospitality gods, working directly under the God of Front Desks, Benson, just like I worked directly under Stan, the God of Poker.

"All Judy said was she was wondering when this was going to happen," Stan said, "and told me to keep her informed as well."

"What was going to happen?" I asked.

Stan shrugged. "Now you know exactly as much as I do. Neither of them would say another word."

"Did you know Searchlights were married?" I asked Stan.

"I assumed they had something like that, otherwise how would they have little Searchlights."

"I thought they lived forever."

"No one lives forever," Stan said. "Even gods have to be born."

I just shook my head as Stan dropped us back into real time and everyone in the lobby started moving again and the noise of regular people doing regular things washed over us.

We both leaned back against the stone pillar and using the skill of calm that all good poker players have, we just waited while Patty talked with the bright pink Mrs. Sucker.

But I had to say, the curiosity was killing me.

And the worry for Patty was making my stomach twist into knots.

Three

About fifteen minutes of intense worry later, Stan nodded to something I couldn't hear and jumped us both to the meeting room.

Patty was alone, sitting at the head of the long oak table in the ornate MGM Grand meeting room. The only sign that Emmanuel Sucker had been there was the lingering odor of her bad breath.

Patty looked worried and tired. I had rarely seen her look like that.

"She wants a place to live," Patty said, looking up at me and giving me a tired smile. "And a job."

Okay, I had to admit, my mouth sort of gaped open at that. The idea of a Searchlight wanting a job was just nuts. They were the beings that gods bowed to, that watched over humanity against all the threats that might harm us regular people.

Why would Emmanuel Sucker, a Searchlight, need a place to live and a job?

Patty signed and said, "She wants to live here in Vegas for the next twenty-one plus years. She likes it here. And she's pregnant."

Like that was going to explain everything.

"You mean Wolfgang kicked her out for getting pregnant?" I asked.

Behind me Laverne and Judy both laughed.

Stan and I both spun around, moving quickly aside to let Lady Luck and the God of Hospitality closer to Patty. There was a real disadvantage to jumping through space. You could really sneak up on someone. And those two had snuck up on both me and the God of Poker.

Lady Luck had on a black pants suit and black business jacket and looked like every powerful businesswoman tended to look. And she was thin enough and had her hair pulled back tight, making her look like she was even more in control of everything.

Judy, on the other hand, looked like everyone's image of a matronly grandmother. She was even wearing an apron over her plaid dress. And Judy was way, way overweight, something you didn't see often in the gods.

"How far along is she?" Laverne asked Patty as she and Judy sat down on either side of Patty.

"Two months," Patty said. "She and Wolfgang were picked for the honor right after the battle with the Fuzzy-Wuzzy."

"So we're going to have to move rather quickly," Judy said, nodding and smiling like this was the best news she had ever heard. "She's going to be leaving home within the next month at most."

Patty nodded. "She says she's already beginning to change. She feels she has less than a week."

Both Laverne and Judy nodded sagely, clearly thinking. About what, I had no clue at all.

I glanced at Stan and he was looking just as puzzled as I felt. But darned if I was going to ask any more stupid questions after my last one.

"First things first," Judy said. "We need to get her a house that she can use for a home for the next twenty-one plus years at a rental payment. The Searchlights will not take any charity from any human or god, even though they help us all the time."

Laverne nodded and turned and looked at me. "Poker Boy, would you mind being Emmanuel's landlord? You and Patty could find her a comfortable home and get her approval before buying it. And make sure it's in a good school district."

Now it was Patty's turn to look puzzled at me.

I had just kept forgetting to tell her that even though I lived in an old double-wide trailer next to a casino in the Oregon coast mountain range, I was very, very rich. She had always just assumed I was a poor poker player. Actually, my poker playing had made me very, very rich; I just seldom spent any of my money.

I had always meant to tell her, but the subject just never came up.

"I'd be honored to do so," I said to Lady Luck.

Laverne nodded. "Make sure her rent is reasonable, but not too low."

Then Laverne turned to Judy, the God of Hospitality. "You think Emmanuel could find a job in your area?"

"I'm sure she could," Judy said. "But with those looks and that build, she might be better served dealing cards. Tips would be a lot better and she would be more comfortable then with the monetary aspects of living here."

I wanted to know how a bright pink bald woman who always turned her head slowly from side-to-side and had horrid breath could deal cards, but I kept my mouth shut again.

"Actually, Judy" Laverne said, nodding, "you are right." Lady Luck turned to Stan. "After Emmanuel is settled, I'll leave it up to you to teach her how to deal poker so she is ready to go after the baby is old enough for her to go to work. I'll loan her some money to last her until then."

"A couple of quick questions," Stan said.

I wanted to say, "Thank you." I had a hundred questions, but I just didn't have the guts to ask anything. Even Patty was looking relieved that she wasn't the one to ask some of the more obvious questions.

Laverne and Judy both laughed at even that much from Stan. For some reason all this was just too much fun for the two of them, while it was driving the rest of us crazy.

"Shall we tell them?" Laverne asked, clearly enjoying the frowns on our faces.

Judy nodded. "I sure don't see why not. Might help them sleep tonight."

Laverne laughed and then said, "When a Searchlight becomes pregnant, she basically turns into a human. Emmanuel will lose her color and grow hair on her head in the next few weeks."

Well, that was going to help with the poker dealing.

The God of Hospitality smiled and said, "Emmanuel will give birth to a normal-looking human child and will need to raise her child with humans until the child's twenty-first birthday. Then they will both regain their color and head patterns and join their own kind."

"Why?" Patty asked a half second before Stan and I could.

"This has always been their way," Laverne said, "from the beginning of humanity. It allows them to understand those they are protecting."

"When was the last Searchlight born?" Patty asked.

"There hasn't been a new Searchlight baby since the days of Atlantis," Judy said. "But I expect more in the next few centuries; maybe one even sooner, since this child will need a mate."

"And Poker Boy," Laverne said, smiling at me, "you might consider including Emmanuel on your team in the future for some missions. She will have some special powers, although it might take a little time to figure out exactly what they are."

"Be glad to," I said, trying to imagine Emmanuel Sucker joining the rest of us at The Diner for milkshakes while we tried to solve dangerous problems.

"Keep us informed as to your progress," Laverne said.

Patty and I and Stan all nodded and an instant later the two major gods were gone.

"Too weird, just too weird," Stan said, shaking his head and then he also vanished, leaving me with my wonderful girlfriend.

I dropped into the chair beside Patty. "You all right?"

She nodded. "Just stunned is all. Not sure why Emmanuel picked me."

"I think her husband liked you," I said, smiling.

"Looks like we will have a new charge very shortly," Patty said. "And maybe a new member of the team."

"Could be interesting," I said, still not sure how she might help us. But she was a Searchlight. Even a human Searchlight might be of help.

"I have a hunch," Patty said, "from a few things Emmanuel mentioned, that she will need lots of coaching in our modern world."

"Breath mints as well," I said.

"We can hope that changes with her skin color," Patty said.

Patty then turned to face me, a serious look on her face. "Laverne wants you to buy Emmanuel Sucker a house? You want to explain how that is possible?"

I sort of coughed under the intense gaze of those superhero brown eyes. "I can easily afford it," I said, smiling. "You know, poker winnings."

"I think we need to talk," Patty said, clearly not happy that I hadn't told her I had money.

Lots and lots of money. So much money, in fact, I wasn't sure how much I had anymore.

But I had a hunch, since Patty was a hundred years older than I was, that there were some things she hasn't told me as well. It might be a very, very interesting conversation, one we had needed to have for a while now.

"Your place or my trailer?" I asked, smiling.

She just glared at me, clearly not even happy at the question. So I picked her place and jumped us there.

Just safer.

And somewhere I was sure I could hear Lady Luck and the God of Hospitality laughing.

STANDING IN LINE AT THE INTERSECTION

Harold wants to end his life because he knows he will never attain perfection. Then, while waiting, he meets Linda, a woman who wants to end it all because she hates her perfection.

When perfection meets imperfection, anything might be possible.

Even living.

TODAY, Wednesday, the nineteenth day of July, the line of people at the intersection stretched only a few city blocks, back past the front door of the triplex theater showing reruns of *Heaven Can Wait, It's a Wonderful Life,* and *You Can't Take It With You.*

Harold Jones had decided to wear his best work suit, the one with the dark pinstripes, to stand in line. He had polished his shoes and combed his newly cut gray hair twice. He had left home to join the line at ten minutes after seven and ended up standing behind a beautiful and very nude young woman. She had dark skin, long dark hair, and a perfect all-over tan, plus a slight dimple in her left butt cheek.

The big electric sign on the bank a block from the intersection read 78 degrees at two minutes before eight a.m.. Two short minutes before the traffic started and the line of people began to move. Those standing in line who wanted to talk complained about the heat. "Muggy," they muttered to each other. Harold agreed and nodded his agreement to those he could hear muttering.

Harold had decided to stand in line on a Wednesday because Wednesday symbolized the middle and nothing different at the same time. Every day people stood in the line. This particular Wednesday was a hot, muggy day in the city, but still a day just like any other in the fact that people stood in the line to step into the intersection. However today was different for Harold because he stood with them behind a naked woman with a slight dimple on her ass.

As with every day, the people around Harold in line were all types and nationalities. Eighteen was the youngest, as was the law, but the oldest sometimes could barely walk. They were short, fat, thin, tall and almost every color of the rainbow. In other words, the line always seemed to be a basic cross-section of the human race.

The people in the line dressed in everything from full suits to nothing at all, with a large majority choosing to stand in line in their bathrobes. A few dressed formally, figuring it would save time later, and a few stood nude, choosing that form of expression as a symbol of their lives.

Harold and the beautiful naked woman were at least a block from the intersection, standing in front of a laundry called Mun Chings Dry Cleaning and Laundry Service. No matter how much Harold concentrated on what was going to happen at the intersection, no matter how hard he tried to look at the others in line, his gaze kept returning to the beautiful little dimple in the left cheek in front of him.

Every time she moved, shifted her weight from one foot to the other, the dimple seemed to smile at him, talk to him. "You're wasting your life," it said. "Leave the line, call off the ex-brother-in-law, find a new job, a new wife. Most of all *keep living.*"

The dimple on her ass said all of that to him every time she moved. She moved a lot and the dimple just kept right on talking.

Of course, since his wife had left him a year before he had been constantly horny. He figured that might have had something to do with the lecture. But after a few minutes he discarded that theory and decided the dimple truly was speaking to him.

For the first time the line eased slightly closer to the intersection and Harold noticed over the dimple lecture the squeal of brakes. Everyone in the line started to look and act a little more nervous.

Harold took a deep breath and smiled, glad the waiting was almost over.

Slowly, much slower than a wedding march, the line moved forward.

Harold just kept staring at the dimple, listening to it lecture him like a young boy being scolded by his mother.

Finally, while passing in front of a Taco John's, he couldn't take it any longer. He had to, in the final moments of his life, know the woman who owned that dimple.

"Excuse me," he said to the back of her dark hair.

The dimple instantly shut up.

She turned and smiled at Harold. She had a full, white-toothed grin, beautiful dark tanned skin, and almost no pubic hair. He took that all in at once before his gaze moved quickly back up to her deep brown eyes and colored eye shadow she wore.

She smiled and nodded. "You like what you see?" she asked, holding her arms up in the classic look-at-me gesture.

"Of course," he said. "What human being wouldn't like the perfection of another human body, especially one as proportioned as yours."

She appeared a little startled at his answer, letting her arms drop back to her sides. For the first time she seemed to look at him. Then her gaze moved down his front, taking in *his* suit, *his* shoes, *his* very stance on the hot sidewalk.

"Corporate?"

"Dressed like this," this time it was his turn to hold his arms up in the look-at-me expression, "what else? Twenty-eight empty years with the same company, a failed marriage, and enough money so that money doesn't matter any more."

She nodded. "Who gets the honor?"

"My ex-brother-in-law," Harold said. "He hated me more than anything else, mostly because he is a total failure in his life and too afraid and stupid to do anything about it. He's using his beat up old pickup, if he can keep it running long enough. I liked the symbolism of it."

She nodded again, obviously thinking deeply about what he had said. "Yes, that does have a nice feel to it. Failure meets success, with the winner being failure, of course, on both sides. Nice."

"Thank you," Harold said, bowing slightly. "How about you?"

"Love," she said, matter-of-factly.

Harold was actually puzzled. "Love?"

She smiled and lightly touched his arm as they, and the line around them, moved up, their place on the sidewalk now less than a half block from the intersection. "I'm twenty-six, have had five boyfriends and two fiancées, all of whom were jerks. They only wanted me for this body." She raised her arms again for a moment. "I left them all and now I can trust no man."

Harold nodded, thinking about what she had said. "So going out nude expresses your revulsion of every man's inability to see beyond your body to the true *you* under the skin."

"Exactly," she said. "It's so nice you understand."

"So who is doing you?"

"My younger sister. She has always been jealous of how I looked and how I always got the boys when she didn't. I promised her all of my clothes and jewelry if she did the driving and she jumped at the chance. I don't think I have ever seen her so happy."

The line moved forward and now there were fewer than twenty people between them and the intersection crosswalk. Up ahead a man wearing a pink bathrobe waited quietly for the walk light. When he got the green he stepped into the street, never looking to either side.

As he neared the center of the crosswalk a huge pink Cadillac sped through the intersection and hit him right at the hood ornament. The crumbling, crunching, and thumping sound echoed down the block between the city buildings. The Cadillac did a four-wheel slide, coming to a stop near the body. The driver of the Cadillac was a woman and she was smiling and laughing.

After a short pause, the cleanup crew ran into the street and Harold turned back to face the woman with the beautiful talking dimple on her butt.

"Great, huh?" she asked, then turned to face the front of the line so that again Harold could stare at the indentation, the talking dent in her ass.

But now it wasn't saying a word.

Two more people stepped into the intersection, were hit and killed, and the line moved up. Harold decided he couldn't stand it any longer. He had to tell her what he was thinking. He had to clear his mind and his conscience before he could ever step into that road.

"Excuse me," he said again to the mass of dark hair that cascaded in perfect lines over her shoulders. She turned, this time smiling for real.

"My name is Linda," she said, extending her hand.

"Harold." Her skin felt soft and moist in his hand and she squeezed in a fondness-like way before she let go.

Harold cleared his throat. "You know," he said, taking his time while trying to gain his courage, "that you have a dimple on your butt."

She frowned at him. "I do? Where?" She tried to turn her head over her right shoulder so that she could see her own ass.

"The other side," Harold said. "Right there." He pointed without touching, even though he really, *really* wanted to touch.

"Wow," she said, pulling her perfect skin on her ass around so that she could see the dimple. "I didn't know that."

She and Harold both looked at the dimple on her ass for a moment, Harold expecting it to talk, but it didn't.

She let go of her butt and faced him. "Why did you tell me that at this moment?"

Harold shrugged. "I'm not exactly sure. Your body is beautiful, but that indentation in your otherwise perfect skin became the focus for me earlier." He decided he didn't want to tell her that her dimple had talked to him. Too much to explain in such a short time.

"Go on," she said, looking even more puzzled.

"I think," Harold said, doing his best to put his deepest and most private thoughts into words, "that the dimple, a flaw in such an other-wise perfect body, symbolized to me that the world is not a perfect place. I had always strived for the world to *be* perfect and for me to be one hundred percent successful in everything I ever did."

Harold shrugged. "When I wasn't perfect, as I saw the world to be, I could no longer live in that perfect world." He held his hand up at the line. "Thus this decision."

The look on her face seemed dazed, and for a moment Harold was afraid he had made her very angry, or even worse, made a fool of himself ten minutes before he was to die.

"So," she said, "the dimple on my ass is a symbol that the world is not a perfect place, and that symbol, my dimple, is giving you hope again?"

Harold thought for a moment and then realized it was doing exactly that. Her dimple *was* giving him hope, giving him a reason to continue living. He smiled at her. "That's right. And I think in a moment I will get out of the line."

Again she looked very thoughtful, then asked, "My imperfection is giving you a reason to live?"

Harold nodded.

"That's wonderful. For the first time a man wants me for something besides my perfect figure, my perfect skin, my perfect teeth. For the first time a man wants me for something besides sex. I didn't think that was possible."

"It is very much true and very much possible," Harold said. "As I have just learned, it is not a perfect world, even when you have an *almost* perfect body such as yours."

"And," she said, "as I have now learned, a man can want me for something besides my perfection." She smiled and pulled her butt cheek around so she could see her dimple again. "My almost perfection."

Harold held out his hand for her. "I think we need to step out of line."

She glanced around and realized the cleanup crew was just finishing sweeping up a mechanic who had died with his tools in front of a plumbing truck. The only person left in line ahead of her was an older woman in a housedress and an apron.

"Come," Harold said. "How could you deprive me of looking at my symbol of imperfection?"

She laughed. "I couldn't, of course."

She took his hand and he instantly knew they would be together for a long, long time. He had found his soul mate.

Laughing and talking all the way, the man who had always desired perfection, but had learned he could never attain it, walked up the hot sidewalk with the naked woman, who had always thought she was perfect, but had suddenly understood she had a flaw.

A GOLDEN DREAM

A Jukebox Story

Sometimes very special friends, even friends you can't remember, give you a chance to change your past by following the memory of a special song.

Should you take the special Christmas gift, take the trip, and change your own history?

Or maybe take a look at tomorrow and change that instead.

"A Golden Dream" was first published under the title "The Song of a Gift Horse" in Black Cats and Broken Mirrors *anthology edited by Martin H. Greenberg and John Helfers.*

Also, a very altered version of this story was part of the novel Melody Ridge: A Thunder Mountain Novel.

One

SHE CAME through the heavy front door of the old hotel with a face as young as yesterday. And for just a moment the stale piss-smell of the thick air, the stained and faded linoleum floors, the peeling paint on the smoke-yellowed walls were forgotten by the three of us in the front foyer.

For just a moment we forgot our long, dull days of old men's boredom, moving like zombies from our rooms, to the sitting room with the television, to the front stoop, back to the sitting room, then back to our rooms, punctuated only by a silent lunch and an even more silent dinner in the small kitchen.

Mitchel, Hank and me. When she came through that door we forgot we were three corpses too damn old to just lie down and be done with it. We forgot we were the last residents of The Golden Dream Hotel for men.

We even forgot it was Christmas Eve.

A year ago crusty Jamison bought the old hotel from a development agency. We all had an understanding that the four of us would be able to live in the hotel until we all died. Jamison died the next month at the age of sixty-eight, giving me the hotel in his will. Now all the three of us did was sit around and wonder who would be next. But no one talked about it. Since I am the youngest at sixty-six, I figured I would have the longest to wait. Since I owned the place that sort of made sense.

And now, as she stood there on this cold winter evening, her short, perfect-skinned nose wrinkling at the smell of old age, even the thought of dying was forgotten.

She blinked in the dim light and then focused on the old black and white television flickering in the corner. I could see she had bright, large eyes, thick eyebrows, and a full mouth. The kind of mouth I remembered that Alice had back what seemed like a million years ago. Alice was my first love, my first sexual partner, my first real girlfriend. We never married and I always wondered why.

The young woman brushed a long slender hand against her nose, then straightened her shoulders as if she were going to face a firing squad. She stepped toward the three of us. Her high heels clicked on the linoleum floor and I wondered when that floor had last felt the steps of a woman.

"Excuse me," she said. Her clear, soft voice seemed to fill the old hotel with life. She stopped and glanced around, as if startled by the sound of her own words. "I'm.... I am looking for a Mister Fred Thorpe."

I thought I was going to swallow my teeth. She was looking for me, as if I actually existed to someone outside of these walls besides the social security department. "That's me," I said, sort of waving a hand in her direction. My voice sounded really odd following hers.

She seemed relieved and took another step toward me. "Would it be possible for us to talk?"

I shrugged and pointed to the vacant chair that had been Jamison's.

She shook her head. "In private, if you don't mind."

Again I shrugged and without looking at the others pushed myself up from my chair in the most dignified manner I had managed in years. I nodded toward the hall that led past the old front desk cage. "We can talk back in the kitchen."

She said fine and I shuffled ahead of her distinct and firm footsteps down the hall and into the kitchen.

After we were both settled at the old wood table she took a deep breath. She started out saying that I wasn't going to believe her.

She was right.

I didn't.

Two

The old Wurlitzer jukebox sat like a king at the end of the oak bar in the Garden Lounge. Radley Stout, the owner of the Garden polished the old jukebox every week and the chrome and glass sparkled as if the machine had a life and energy of its own.

Above the jukebox was a polished wood and glass case that held four drinking glasses with the old Garden Lounge logo and a name etched on each.

Carl, Dave, Jess, and Fred.

Except for Christmas Eve, the jukebox was always unplugged and the glass case always locked.

The Garden Lounge was a local, quiet bar. It had old-styled booths, a hundred regular customers and enough atmosphere in plants and low lighting that everyone felt safe when they came in.

Radley Stout had owned the bar for eleven years and for ten Christmas Eves he had plugged in the jukebox. Tonight was to be the eleventh and he hoped it would be something special.

Three

The kitchen smelled of the hot dogs we had had for lunch, and the dirty pan and plates were still in the sink. I couldn't remember if it had been my turn to do dishes or Hank's. It was Christmas Eve. What did it matter?

"My name is Sandy Reeves," the good-looking young woman said to me across the kitchen table. "I am a private investigator and I was hired to find you by a Mr. Radley Stout."

I laughed and leaned toward the woman who looked like she might be barely old enough to be out of high school. "Right. So what is the gimmick? What are you selling?"

She didn't seem bothered by my rude question at all. Calmly she reached into her large purse and pulled out at small, black pistol. With a thump she placed it on the table between us. "I have a permit for that," she said, smiling slightly.

All I could do was stare at the black gun while she pulled her wallet out of her purse, flipped it open, and slid it across the table at me. Then she scooped the gun back into her purse.

Open in front of me was her driver's license and her private investigator's license from the state. I glanced at her birth date. She was twenty-six. At lot younger than any child Alice and I might have had. I nodded and slid her wallet back at her. "So what does this Mr. Stout want from me?"

She sort of shrugged. "Actually, I am not exactly sure. He owns a place called the Garden Lounge, down on Main. He said he just wanted to buy you a Christmas Eve drink."

"That's all?" I shook my head. "He hired a private investigator to find me to buy me a drink?"

She nodded, almost looking embarrassed. "I am just supposed to take you down to the Garden Lounge. And Mr. Stout gave me strict instructions to not force you in any way. He knows nothing about how you are living or even that you are alive. So are you interested in having a drink?"

I glanced at her and then around at the old kitchen and the dishes in the sink. It was Christmas Eve and I had absolutely nothing better to do. "What the hell," I said. "I've always believed that you never look a gift horse in the mouth."

"True," she said. "You just never know when a miracle might happen."

I stared at her, but she only smiled, not explaining at all. Slowly I pushed myself back from the table and stood. "I could use a drink tonight."

She nodded. "So could I."

Four

Jukeboxes, by their very nature, are time machines.

Not only do they look as if they belong in another decade, but by playing songs, they sometimes take the listeners back to the memories associated with those songs.

The jukebox in the Garden Lounge did a little more than that. It physically took the listener back to their memory from a song. And the listener could be there, inside the listener's younger body, until the song finished.

The listener could also change events that occurred during the time the song was playing. And by changing those events, change the future.

That was what made the jukebox so dangerous. That was also the reason the jukebox was never plugged in. When new customers in the Garden asked about the jukebox, Stout just told them it was broken.

Stout, the owner and only bartender of the Garden Lounge, originally saved the old jukebox from the bankruptcy court a good hour before the bank locked up his first bar. For one full year in which he had tried to run the bar, the jukebox had sat in the back hall, covered with a blanket and a good inch of dust and grime. It had been just part of the old furniture and things that came with the bar. Almost as a lark, he took the jukebox to his garage, hiding it from the bank, figuring that he would fix it up some day.

That day came another year later on a Saturday.

He was thinking about buying a second bar and giving the bar business another try. The old jukebox would make a great item to have in the new place if he could get the jukebox to work.

When he opened the jukebox up, he found a lot of sealed boxes and weird looking electronics that seemed far beyond anything needed or standard in an old Wurlitzer jukebox.

He studied the insides for a few hours without figuring any of it out. Finally he just dusted everything off, fixed the electrical cord that looked as if someone had ripped it from the back, and plugged the jukebox in.

The jukebox blinked a few times, the colored lights came on, and nothing blew up.

So Radley went in search of a record to play on it. Luck would have it that the only forty-five record Radley owned was an old song he and Jenny had bought. It was their song and it reminded him of the day in the student union that he wanted to ask Jenny to stay with him, not leave town, but hadn't. The next day she went back to college and eventually met another man.

He dug the old record out of his scrapbook, cleaned it off, put it on A-1, and punched the buttons. With the first note the world shifted, his garage disappeared, and he suddenly found himself sitting in the old Student Union café, facing Jenny across a scarred table.

The air in the room felt warm and seemed to close in on him. He could smell Jenny's wonderful perfume. Her light brown hair was pulled back and off her face. She was nodding in time with the beat of the song, waiting for me to say something.

And smiling. Night after night for years Radley had remembered, and would remember, that smile.

The chair felt hot and sticky under him and his hands seemed to be glued to the table top. The song, their song, was on, echoing through the large room, and he stared around at the others studying or eating at tables nearby before turning to stare at Jenny. He could not believe this. He could remember all of his older memories and his younger ones, too. He knew exactly that he wanted to ask her to stay with him, maybe even marry him.

And he knew exactly what his future held because he hadn't.

The thought of that future scared him even more than asking her to stay with him.

He sat there, not saying a word, staring at Jenny and her smile until the song ended and he found himself back in his garage. He took a deep shuddering breath and then barely made it to the back door before he threw up.

The next day, after a long night of no sleep, he finally got up the courage to play the record again.

And again he did nothing but sit across from Jenny and stare.

He never played their song again, even though it remained for eleven years as A-1 on the jukebox.

Except on Christmas Eve.

On Christmas Eve, the only night he plugged in the jukebox for his friends, he takes that special record off and places it in the safe. He didn't want to ever take a chance of anyone else playing it.

Five

Sandy Reeves, Miss Private Eye with the Big Black Gun, held the front door of the Garden Lounge open for me to shuffle through. I had passed by the Garden a hundred times and always thought about stopping. Never had. It had just not been the right time. I never expected Christmas Eve to be that right time.

The place smelled of smoke and green plants and I immediately felt at home. Much more than at the hotel.

Empty tables cluttered the center of the room and booths filled both side walls. Christmas candles were lit on every table. An old-looking polished-wood bar filled the wall opposite the front door and three men sat on stools near the bar's center with their backs to the door. They were the only three customers. A medium-sized man in a white apron was standing behind the bar and when I came through the door he looked up and said, "Holy Shit."

The three men at the bar turned around as if pulled by the same string and the bartender put a glass on the bar and headed around the end to meet me.

He dodged around a few tables with ease and we met in the middle of the bar. He grabbed my hand and shook it as if we were old friends seeing each other again after many years.

I studied his face as he stared at mine. He looked to be in his early fifties, with thinning gray and brown hair. His eyes were green and his smile seemed to fill his entire face.

After what seemed like a long moment he took a breath and sort of shook himself. "I'm sorry. I'm Radley Stout. I own this place. And I'm really glad you came."

All I could do was shrug. "Not as if I had much else to do," I said. "And you did offer a free drink."

He just laughed and patted me on the back. "Come on up to the bar. I have a few friends I want you to meet."

I took the stool on the left of the three men and the lady P.I. took the open stool to their right.

Radley Stout went around behind the bar as he did the introductions. Dave was the closest to me. He was an airline pilot and his daughter was the private investigator who had found me. Next to him was a big guy named Carl who did construction and beside him was a convict-looking man by the name of Billy. I nodded at them without really noting what any of them looked like, then turned to Radley Stout.

"All right," I said. "Why bring me here?"

Again Stout laughed. "As you said, to have a Christmas drink. Give me a moment and I will explain."

He rummaged in the drawer under the cash register and came up with a key. Then he went to the end of the bar and unlocked a glass case that was mounted on the wall over an old jukebox.

Everyone at the bar watched in silence as he pulled out three of the four glasses that were in there and walked back to the sink in front of us. He rinsed out one of the glasses and held it up for me to see.

It was a crystal-type glass, with the Garden Lounge logo etched near the center and the name Fred over the logo.

"So you needed a Fred to join the toast this year. That it?"

Stout shook his head, set the glass down on the mat above the ice and started to rinse out the other glasses. "No, actually that glass was yours eleven years ago."

No one else said a word. They either watched Stout wash the glasses, or they stared down into their own drink, as if slightly uneasy about something.

I had never seen that glass before and had never met Stout before or been in this bar before. This gift horse was starting to look like a bust, just as most of them had in my life. I laughed for a short moment and then said, "Not highly likely."

"That's true," Dave said from beside me. "It isn't highly likely. But I think it's true."

I turned to Dave. He was a clean-cut sort, with short hair and wrinkles on his forehead that cut lines across his tanned skin. "Were you there when I supposedly owned that glass?" I pointed in the direction of Stout and the glass. He had just finished washing out a glass that had the name Dave over the logo.

"In a manner of speaking," Dave said. "I was. But I too do not remember the first time. However, I do remember the second."

I just stared at him for a moment before shaking my head and pushing myself back off my stool. Free drink or not, this was just a little too much. "I knew this entire thing was crazy, but you folks are all a bunch of loonies."

Stout put the third glass on the rubber mat. It had the name Carl etched on it. "Fred. Please just hold on for a moment. I just want to buy you a drink and tell you a story. I know you won't believe me, but what can it hurt? It's Christmas Eve."

Sandy looked down the bar at me and sort of smiled. "I told you that you wouldn't believe this."

I stopped with one hand still holding onto the back of the bar stool and looked down the line of faces staring at me. It seemed clear that everyone wanted me to stay and everyone was taking this craziness very, very seriously. I took a deep breath and let it out in a noisy sigh.

Sandy laughed. "You said never look a gift horse in the mouth. So stop looking."

At that I laughed. "All right. One drink and then Miss Private Investigator there can take me back."

"And a story, too," Stout said. "Don't forget."

I nodded and climbed back up on the stool. "A story too. As long as you don't want me to buy anything."

Stout nodded and smiled. "I promise. Now what would you like to drink?"

I ordered a vodka tonic and for the next half hour the conversation was light and fun. I could feel the heaviness and gloom of the Golden Dream Hotel lifting from my shoulders as everyone laughed and talked and sipped their drinks. There seemed to be a friendship among these people that I had not felt before. A closeness that went far beyond customers in a bar.

I ended up asking for a second drink and Stout refilled my special glass. As he placed it on the napkin in front of me he said, "I think it's time for the story."

Everyone nodded as Stout went back to stand in front of the well where he was sipping on a glass of eggnog. He leaned against the backbar and raised his glass. "First, a toast. To friends again united."

I drank to the toast not knowing what he was talking about. I assumed the united friend he was talking about was me, but since I had never met the man before, that was going to be some story.

"I had the Garden for just over a year," Stout said. "And I had some really good, regular customers. But four of those customers had become my good friends. Dave. Carl. You, Fred. And Jess." With each name Stout tipped his drink in the person's direction. With the last name he tipped it in the direction of the glass case that still held one glass over the jukebox. I assumed the name on that glass was Jess.

"Fred," Stout said, "you see that jukebox there?" I nodded as he went on. "Everyone here except you knows just how special that jukebox is. This is the part of the story that you will not believe no matter how hard or well I explain it, so just think of this part as fiction. All right?"

Again, I just nodded, so he went on. "That jukebox can take a person back to a memory. Not just in your mind, but in real flesh and blood. It's a sort of time machine."

"Fiction is right," I said and Stout just held up his hand.

"I discovered how the jukebox worked by accident before I ever opened the Garden. Ten years ago on Christmas Eve I decided I would give my four friends a chance to go back into their pasts. A special Christmas present from me. At that time you were divorced from a woman by the name of Alice and you had two kids."

Suddenly the bar felt very warm. He was assuming that I had been a regular in here for almost a year and once been married to Alice. But I knew that wasn't true. I must have had too much to drink with just two drinks, since it felt as if the room was spinning. How could he know about Alice? And he was saying that I had married her and divorced her after having two kids.

Stout was watching me and after I looked up at him he went on. "You had been divorced from Alice for ten years and you hated her. Completely and totally hated her. It was a standing joke among the five of us. You also had a daughter by the name of Jenny."

"So what happened to her in this crazy world of yours?" I asked. My voice had more anger in it than I could remember.

Stout just shrugged. "I assume she was never born. When you left here through the jukebox, you said the song reminded you of the night you and Alice first made love. The night you conceived Jenny which forced you two to get married out of high school."

Again the room felt too warm. The night Alice and I first made love was the night her parents were gone to a Christmas party. Right before going over to her house, I had gone to the drugstore to buy some rubbers. I remember almost chickening out and then the next thing I knew I had a pack of them in my hand and was heading out of the store. Alice and I always used one every time we made love. She met another guy a year later and left me because she said I was never going to ask her to marry me. She was right. I never did.

"You all right?" Stout asked. I glanced up. He had moved down the bar and was standing in front of me. Everyone was looking at me. I tried to laugh, but it sounded sort of weak, even to me. "You did your research real well. Sandy there must be a really good investigator."

"She's good all right," Stout said and Sandy held up her glass in a thank-you gesture. "But she didn't find any of this information out. I knew about Alice and your divorce because you told us over and over for almost a year."

"So how come I didn't live any of this?"

Stout just sighed. "Because you lived a different life after you changed whatever it was you changed that evening. The only reason I remember you is because I was touching the jukebox when the song ended. For some reason that allows me to remember the old timeline. I remember you being in here, but no one else does."

He pointed at the glass in front of me. "I was holding onto the glass, too, when you didn't come back."

"Didn't come back? What do you mean I didn't come back?" Again I was trying to keep the anger out of my voice. But all of this was making me mad. And damn tired.

"You changed something while you were back there. And whatever you changed did not lead you to the Garden again in your new life. At least not until now. If you had not changed anything, you would have come back when the song ended."

Dave was nodding beside me. "That happens every year to me. This year I plan to go back and watch Sandy being born. It will be a Christmas present to myself. Trust me, I will be very careful to not change anything."

I looked at Dave for a moment and then shook my head. "So why bring me back here now. Assuming that all this is true, which I find not likely, why now?"

Now it was Stout's turn to look slightly embarrassed. "I guess I just wanted the old group back together again on Christmas Eve. Selfish, I guess."

"Looks like you didn't pull it off," I said. "What about that other glass? Didn't your P.I. there find the guy?"

Stout took a sip of his eggnog and then looked up at me. I could see the pain in his eyes and the sadness that coated his face. The silence in the bar seemed to fill the room with a thick, heavy feel. "Sandy found him all right," Stout said. "He changed something, also, when he went back that Christmas Eve ten years ago. In the new world he created he was killed by a drunk driver. We found him up in Memorial Cemetery."

I shook my head in disbelief and looked down at my name in the old glass. "So what did I do in the previous life? Be a lawyer or something?"

Stout took a deep breath and then laughed. "Not hardly. You worked for the city. I think you had something to do with streets or something like that."

It was my turn to laugh. "I did that in this life, too. Fancy that. So how come, if that machine can change someone's past, you just don't go back and stop that guy from getting killed?"

Stout shook his head. "I am actually glad it doesn't work that way. Way too much responsibility. No, you can only go back to your own memories. You can't change other people's memories. Or their lives."

Dave stood. "Tell you what, Stout. Plug in that jukebox and I will go watch my daughter being born. That might just give old Fred here a new outlook on life."

Stout shrugged and walked down the length of the bar to the jukebox. Dave downed the last of his drink and joined him.

"You got the record I brought on there?" Dave asked as Stout reached around behind the jukebox and plugged it in. The colored lights flickered for a moment and then held steady. It was a beautiful old Wurlitzer, with the chrome arch, red, green and blue colored lights, and bright red buttons. Inside I could see the disk full of forty-five records all waiting to be played.

"Just punch up old B-4," Stout said and handed Dave a quarter.

Everyone at the bar had swung around on their stools and were watching intently. I felt uneasy and nervous, even though I knew the only thing that would happen was that the song would start playing and that would be that.

Dave dropped the quarter into the slot, punched the two buttons and then stood back as the machine clicked and whirred. Inside I could see a record being picked up and placed on the turntable.

Stout saluted Dave.

"Don't go changing anything, Dad," Sandy said. I want to be here when you get back."

Dave laughed. "Don't worry. Just going to watch."

The jukebox clicked and the song started. I recognized it immediately. An old Rick Nelson song called, "It's Up To You." That song reminded me of...

The bar shifted and was gone. For a quick instant I felt dizzy and then everything went black.

And then came back to a bright white spotlight. Right in my eyes.

Six

"God damn it!" Stout shouted as the song started. Sandy, Billy, and Carl had all been looking at Dave and Stout. But as one they turned to look at the bar stool where a moment before Fred had been sitting.

"Oh, no," big Carl said.

Sandy just shook her head. "Every year we do this and every year something weird happens."

Stout moved down the bar and put his hand on Fred's bar stool, as if that would help bring him back. "Damn it! I forgot to ask him if he had a memory with that song. What the hell was I thinking?"

"Don't worry about it, Stout." Sandy said. "He'll be back."

Stout picked up Fred's glass and looked at the name. "He didn't come back last time he left here through the jukebox." Stout reached over and picked up Dave's glass. Then he headed back for the jukebox. "I want everyone holding onto the jukebox when the song ends. If he doesn't come back this time, I want someone besides me remembering him."

Sandy laughed. "Boy won't Dad be in for a surprise when he gets back."

Seven

When a spotlight hits you square in the eyes, your first instinct is to raise your arm to cover your face. And that is what I did. Only my arm hit the steering wheel of my '57 Chevy.

"What...?" I said out loud as I glanced around like a frightened deer caught in a hunter's sights.

The car's engine and lights were off and the windows were rolled up tight. Rick Nelson belted out the song on the radio. Sweat trickled down the side of my face and down my bare chest. The temperature inside the car must have been that of a steam bath and the spotlight was coming through the fogged-up front window.

"Oh, no!" A young woman's voice said from beside me and I turned to look at her. That was when the memories flooded in like light pouring through an open door between a dark room and a lit one.

Marcy was struggling to get her bra back on. We had dated for two years after Alice left me. She worked at the department store downtown in the men's section and wanted me to be her husband more than almost anything. That fact had suited me just fine because it made parking with her a lot of fun. She ended up marrying a guy from the appliance section of the store and had three kids last I heard.

Tonight was our first anniversary of going out and we were parked on the canal bank behind the orchard to the south of town. It was the only night we ever got caught parking by the police.

"This can't be," I said. I looked completely around the car. It was my '57 Chevy all right. The one I wrecked in 1969 while driving drunk on New Year's Eve. A moment ago I was sitting in the Garden Lounge with a bunch of people who I thought were nuts and now I was back here parking with Marcy.

I held onto the steering wheel with sweaty hands. I could still freshly remember getting here and what Marcy and I had been doing just a few short moments ago. I remembered taking her bra off and almost putting my hand up her skirt. In fact I was still aroused from all of it and I hadn't had anything but a piss-erection in years back at the old Golden Dream Hotel.

I had said I never looked a gift horse in the mouth. The Private Investigator's words now echoed back through my mind: "You just never know when a miracle might happen."

So this was what she was talking about.

Marcy smacked my arm. "Hurry! Get your shirt on."

Outside I heard the car door close and a vague shape through the fogged window started toward the door. I had a clear memory that we had gotten dressed before the cop got to the window and he let us go with a strict warning to be moving along. We had laughed about it for days.

Stout had warned Dave not to change anything when he punched up the song. And he said that the reason I didn't end up back at the

Garden was because I changed something when I did this music/time-travel thing the last time.

If what Stout had been saying back there at the Garden was true, and it looked like it was, I had better do some fast dressing.

Real fast.

Marcy was already buttoning her blouse as I turned around and grabbed my shirt off the back seat where my younger self had tossed it a short time before. I had it on and buttoned, in what seemed like impossible speed to my sixty-two-year-old brain, just as the cop tapped on the window.

Marcy straightened her hair as I rolled down the window and looked into the cop's flashlight. "Wow, that's bright."

I remembered that was the exact same thing I had said when I didn't have sixty years of memories to draw upon.

The cop shined his light on me, then on Marcy.

She smiled at him.

I turned and smiled at him.

Then Ricky Nelson stopped singing.

And I was back on my bar stool at the Garden Lounge.

Stout, Sandy, Carl, and Billy stood around the jukebox, touching it.

Dave stood in front of the jukebox staring at them.

"Wow," was all I could say.

All four cheered and Stout held up my empty glass as if in a toast.

It felt really good to be back.

Eight

I had another drink as I told them about my adventure with Marcy, getting caught parking, and who she was to me and my life now. I explained that my two years with Marcy had mostly been trying to forget about being in love with Alice. It was a fun time, but nothing really important, or life altering.

After I got done telling my story, and Dave told his about how great it was to watch his daughter being born, Sandy went back through the jukebox to visit her senior prom. She came back smiling and laughing and told us all about it, right down to where she and her girlfriends spiked the punch to get the guys drunk.

I remembered in my time that the guys were the ones who put booze in the punch. Things do change.

Carl went back to visit his mother and when he came back he didn't say much and no one really pushed him.

It shocked me both times when they just sort of popped out of existence and then back again when the song ended. And before each song Stout asked me if I had any memories associated with the song.

Stout and Billy both declined to play a song, so when Carl returned and dropped back onto his bar stool, Stout moved down the bar and stood in front of me.

"Usually," he said, "we only go back once, but since your first trip was an accident, are you interested in giving it another try this year?"

His question surprised me, for some reason. "Give me just a second to think about it." I slid my glass toward him. "How about a refill?"

He nodded and moved down the bar with my glass as I thought about Alice. She had turned out to be the one woman, over all the years, that I truly loved. Now Stout was giving me a chance to go see her again. And maybe tell her how I really felt. Maybe keep her from leaving me.

He was offering me another gift. And this was a very special gift.

I turned on my stool and looked out over the empty Garden Lounge. This evening had been one of the nicest, and wildest, I had spent in more years than I cared to remember. I enjoyed the people and I enjoyed the place.

Why leave it at the moment?

Besides, if Stout was right, Alice and I ended up in a really ugly divorce that I hated enough to change once. Maybe I was just cut out in this life to live alone, as I had done. Maybe on this gift, this year, it was better to look the old horse in the mouth.

Stout set the glass on the napkin and I turned around to face him again. "Thanks for the offer," I said. "But I think I will pass this year. One was enough. Maybe next year if you want me back."

Stout broke into a huge smile. "Every year. You are always welcome."

He moved down the bar and unplugged the jukebox. "That's it for another year," he said.

We all toasted the jukebox and then we spent the next hour laughing and talking about anything and everything, including what

Stout could remember of my previous life, including how really unhappy I had been with Alice.

At a little after midnight on Christmas morning, Sandy dropped me off in front of the Golden Dream Hotel for Men.

I almost bounded up the front stairs, feeling younger and more alive than I had in years. I'm not sure why a few drinks and a trip into my own past would make me feel that way. But it did.

And for the moment that was all that mattered.

I unlocked the front door and went into the front foyer.

The place was dark, the only light the one over the old front desk cage. Hank and Mitchell were long asleep. In fact this was the latest I had stayed up in years.

I looked around at the deep shadows and the worn furniture. It was as if I was seeing it for the first time. Seeing the age and the stagnation. Nothing had changed in this room for as long as I had lived here.

I patted the back of Hank's chair and a small cloud of dust rose in the dim light. Maybe it was time to bring some life back here.

I wandered over to the open area beside the cage and looked up at the high ceiling. Twenty feet, maybe. More than enough room for a Christmas tree.

Tomorrow the three of us would stop down at the Garden to have a Christmas drink with Stout. He had promised he would fix us his special eggnog. And then we would go buy a Christmas tree for the hotel. It was time we started a few traditions of our own. The guys would piss and moan, but they would enjoy it.

And then maybe the following week I might find an old jukebox. A real one that only gave you memories instead of trips through time.

You didn't always have to go into the past to change the present. As I discovered tonight, with a very special gift from the strangest gift horse I had ever met, sometimes you can do it right now.

FIGHTING THE FUZZY-WUZZY

A Poker Boy Story

The world about to be destroyed. What can a poker player do?

When a blue Searchlight appears and says the world hangs on the edge of destruction, even a great poker face feels hard to keep. Until Poker Boy discovers the blue guy doesn't bluff.

Can a simple superhero save the world? Sometimes playing poker might be the answer for just about everything.

One

I FIRST MET Wolfgang Sucker two nights before the great Fuzzy-Wuzzy war.

Now, as Poker Boy, I meet my share of strange beings, mostly just people sitting around poker tables as I try to earn enough to get to the next place where I have to do my superhero thing and rescue someone or fight the bad guy. (And sometimes along the way I even save a dog or two, but that's not part of my job description. It just sort of happens.)

But Wolfgang Sucker was one of the stranger people who ever walked up to me and asked for help.

Honestly, I didn't see him until he was standing in front of me. I was standing against one of the large stone columns in the main lobby of the MGM Grand Hotel and Casino on the Strip in Las Vegas. My girlfriend and sidekick, Patty Ledgerwood, aka Front Desk Girl, had a couple of things to finish before she got off work and we headed back to her place.

I have no idea how Wolfgang Sucker knew who I was, and I sure didn't notice him until he was standing in front of me.

"Poker Boy?" he asked, his voice sounding like someone sanding a piece of furniture. "I need your help if you don't mind. My name is Wolfgang Sucker."

Actually, what he really needed was a couple bottles of Scope and a bath. His breath smelled like he had bathed in onions, but I didn't say anything. Not my place to judge people who are asking for my help.

That was the exact moment, as the crowds of people moved around and past us in the huge lobby, talking and laughing, that I actually focused on Wolfgang Sucker for the first time.

And actually saw him, in all of his blueness.

Not kidding. He was blue, skin and all, and there was a lot of skin showing. He only wore a pair of tight pants that seemed more like skin than pants, showing parts that no man should show in public without getting arrested.

If the blue had been painted on I would have thought him to be a refugee from the Blue Man Group that performed all the time in Vegas. But his skin was a real blue.

He had on no shirt at all, but security in the MGM Grand didn't seem to even notice. In fact no one seemed to notice.

He stood about six inches taller than my six-foot frame and weighed far under my weight, which gave Wolfgang the look of a tall stick with arms. I had seen skinnier people, but not many. Skinnier people were usually high school basketball players, and Wolfgang looked to be a ways from high school age, even though his skin was as blue and smooth as it comes.

Besides being blue, what made Wolfgang really stand out was his nervous tick of constantly turning his head from side to side, not fast, but slowly, like a lighthouse beacon moving around.

He seldom looked at anyone directly with his deep blue eyes. His gaze just sort of passed over you until his head was completely sideways to you, then it slowly came back the other direction.

After about two minutes of talking with him that first time, I wanted to just grab his head and hold it still, but I was afraid his body would start rotating under it. And I didn't want to get that close to that breath, either.

But worse yet, if that and the bad breath wasn't bad enough, his head was completely bald and covered in white tattoo patterns of some weird alien design that looked at first a little like a giant net with a squid in the middle. But every time he turned his head and then started back, the tattoos seemed to shift without really shifting so that by the time his head was turned one hundred and eighty degrees in the other direction, the scars gave a different image.

And they moved around, all over his face, his head, down his neck.

Never once did the image repeat that I could tell.

I have no idea how the tattoos changed, but I sure watched them a lot trying to figure it out since there was no point trying to look the guy in the eyes. At one point I actually thought about fighting my way upstream into the onions to get closer to see how those marks were shifting like that. But I didn't.

After a moment or two of staring at Wolfgang Sucker's head, I realized he had been talking about something, but his rasping voice was so low I couldn't hear it over the loud sounds of the huge lobby and the casino down the hallway.

I held up my hand for him to stop. "We're going to need to get to a place where we can talk in a little more quiet. I'm having trouble hearing you. Can you hold on for less than one minute?"

I could see Patty heading toward us across the lobby, and I most certainly wanted her to hear what kind of help this guy needed from me. And I wanted her to meet him, otherwise she would just never believe me.

As she approached, Wolfgang Sucker turned and bowed just slightly at the waist. "Front Desk Girl. Good, I was also hoping you might help as well."

Patty's eyes got round and she glanced at me before going back to staring at Wolfgang Sucker as he introduced himself.

I just shrugged and indicated I didn't know what the guy wanted.

It was a nice, comfortable October night outside, so I figured there would be less noise out through the front doors than in the lobby, so I indicated we should all move that way.

He wouldn't budge. "No," he said firmly. "The Fuzzy-Wuzzys are going to be arriving out there, near the front door."

Now Patty's eyes really got large, and I'm sure I had the worst puzzled look on my face. It was then that it occurred to me that this might be some practical joke, played on us by one of the gambling gods.

In fact, the more I thought about, the more I was sure it was a joke. The only "Fuzzy-Wuzzy" I knew came from an old children's rhyme about a bald bear or something like that.

I slipped Patty and me out of time, leaving old Wolfgang frozen with the rest of the lobby.

I always got a kick out of doing that. It was a real power, compared to some of my other powers like getting someone to believe me or reading their faces to see if they were telling the truth. Slipping into a moment in time was just fun and cool. I couldn't hold it very long, not more than a few minutes, but each time I did it, I got stronger. And since all my power came from casinos, it was pretty easy to do while standing inside one of the bigger ones on the planet.

"Is this guy for real?" Patty asked, staring at the scars on his head that were now frozen in the moment into a picture of some sort of alien cow being eaten by some other creature with fangs.

"I have no idea," I said. "I'm guessing it's a joke someone's pulling on us. It finally dawned on me that with a name like Wolfgang Sucker, we might be the real suckers. And it was the Fuzzy-Wuzzy part that convinced me."

Patty nodded, so I shouted into the air, "Stan!"

An instant later Stan appeared beside us. It only took him a second to notice Wolfgang and start staring, his mouth open.

"So what's the joke?" I asked.

Stan didn't answer, just sort of walked around Wolfgang, then came back to me.

"No joke," Stan said. "This guy is a Searchlight. I've only seen one and that was a number of centuries back."

"Searchlight?" Patty asked.

"Yeah, the name we call them, more than likely because of that annoying head movement they do. There are only a few thousand of them and they live forever, or so the myths say. No one knows where they came from, where they live, or what they even do. Or what those changing pictures on their heads mean."

"You're serious?" I asked, still thinking this was an elaborate joke that Stan was part of.

"Completely," Stan said, still staring at Wolfgang. "Did he say what he wanted?"

"My help is all I managed to hear because he talks so softly."

Stan frowned. "Not good, really not good."

"And he wanted me to help as well," Patty said. "And he knew who I was."

Okay, maybe this wasn't a joke. I sure didn't like the sound of the God of Poker saying "Not good, really not good." In all the years I had worked as a superhero for him, he had never said anything like that. Even joking.

"He wouldn't go outside to talk because he said the Fuzzy-Wuzzys were going to be out there, or something like that."

"Oh, shit," Stan said, his normally calm face now almost pale.

Having the God of Poker looked scared about a guy named after a hairless bear didn't make me feel any better about this situation either. I had no idea what the problem even was and I was starting to panic.

Stan turned to Patty. "Get our guest to a meeting room. I'll be back with Laverne and some other help as soon as I can. And you had better call in your team."

At that Stan vanished.

"Seems our nice evening at your place has just been postponed," I said.

All Patty could do was nod as I stuck us back into real time and let the noise of the crowd wash back over us like a pounding wave. Being in the silence of between-time was always nice.

Patty indicated that Wolfgang Sucker should follow her. "I have a meeting room we can talk in."

"Have you contacted Laverne and the others?" Wolfgang asked in his raspy voice, barely loud enough for me to hear.

"We have," I said. "They'll join us in the meeting room."

He said simply, "Good. We will need everyone if we are to survive this coming battle."

I stared at him as we walked, not liking the sound of that either. And if he wanted to contact Laverne, why didn't he just go to her?

And then he said, just loud enough for me to hear, "And we are called Searchlights because we stand guard over humanity, always watching for trouble, not because of our head movement."

I walked a few steps with my mouth open. Even with Patty and me out of time, he had overheard what we had said.

That was creepy, just creepy.

Two

The meeting room that Patty led us to was off the main corridor leading to the casino from the lobby, and it could hold fifty people, if needed. It was the standard business meeting room that you saw everywhere in every hotel. Only this one had the bright MGM Grand Hotel colors and logo on the carpet and a huge polished wooden table in the middle of the room with about thirty leather chairs around it.

When Patty closed the door, the sounds from outside shut off as if someone had thrown a switch. I had no doubt that in this place I would be able to actually hear Wolfgang speak clearly in his rasping voice, but he didn't say anything and I had no idea what to ask him.

I was still trying to get over the fact that he could hear us between moments in time.

He moved with gliding steps to the head of the table and stood behind the leather chair there and said nothing. His head just kept shifting from side to side, slowly.

Patty jumped on her cell phone and called both Screamer and The Smoke and told them where we were.

"They are both about ten minutes away," Patty said.

"Good," I said. I didn't say that I wished I knew what we were up against so I could tell them what was going on.

A moment later Stan, the God of Poker, appeared with Burt, the God of Casino Operations, and Laverne, Lady Luck herself. Laverne was dressed in a black pants suit.

Now I knew for sure this was no joke.

Stan and Burt just looked worried.

"Wolfgang," she said, moving toward our guest. "It is always a pleasure to see you again."

Then Lady Luck bowed slightly in a show of respect, which flat stunned me. Laverne was one of the most powerful gods there was in all the deities. She didn't bow to anyone I knew of.

At least until now.

Wolfgang bowed slightly in the same way to Laverne as he had done to Patty. "It is also good to see you," he said, his voice clear even though it sounded more like someone was taking sandpaper to the large wooden meeting table in the room.

Laverne got right to the point. "Am I to understand that the Fuzzy-Wuzzys are coming back?"

"They are," Wolfgang said, his head never stopping for an instant.

"How long until they reach this plane of existence?" Laverne asked.

"They will become clear to you in five hours, and to the rest of the human race in two days; just under forty-nine of your hours. If they cannot be stopped before that point, I fear for the human race."

I glanced at my watch. It was just past eleven in the evening. So they would appear to humans in two days at midnight. Whatever they were. And Laverne would be able to see them coming in five hours.

And I assumed something called a Fuzzy-Wuzzy appearing suddenly to humans was a bad thing from the way everyone was acting and talking. But at this point I didn't have a clue why or how we were all going to die.

And I also didn't know where they were appearing from exactly. Laverne and Wolfgang sure seemed to think all this was serious. For the moment, since Laverne was the big boss, that was good enough for me.

"Are there other Searchlights involved?" Laverne asked.

"We all are," Wolfgang Sucker said. "At the moment they are contacting all the other deities, and a delegation has been sent to the Fates. We have little time."

Now I really wanted to know why this guy came to me first.

Laverne nodded. "I assume this is a worldwide attack this time?"

"It is," Wolfgang said. "They are stronger and are coming in more numbers than before. They will not be easily tricked or defeated this time."

"Humanity barely survived the last time," Laverne said, shaking her head.

Now that didn't sound good at all.

Patty took my hand and squeezed it.

"And why are you here?" Laverne asked. "Is this an attack point?"

"Yes, they are opening a portal just in front of this building. One of a thousand such portals around the world."

"A thousand?" Laverne asked softly, more to herself than to Wolfgang.

He said nothing.

Laverne again bowed slightly to Wolfgang Sucker. "Thank you and your people for the warning and the help in this coming fight. As always, it is appreciated."

"Unless I am needed before, I will come back to this room in twelve hours," he said, returning the bow.

Then he vanished.

"Damn," Laverne said, turning to the rest of us shaking her head. "I worried about this day coming again. I just hoped it never would."

Now the silence in the large meeting room felt like a huge weight just pressing down on everything.

"Stan," Laverne said, "please explain to Poker Boy and his team what's happening."

Then she and Burt vanished.

Stan moved over to the table and sat down hard.

Seeing the God of Poker completely shaken and hearing Lady Luck herself actually swear wasn't a good sign.

Not good at all.

Three

Patty and I went around the big table and sat facing Stan. Patty kept her hand in mine and I liked that. Together we were a lot stronger than we were apart. And from the sounds of whatever we were fighting, we were going to need all the strength we could muster.

I wanted to ask Stan about a thousand questions starting off with why something that could destroy mankind was called a "Fuzzy-Wuzzy" and why, if this Searchlight guy wanted to talk to Laverne, did he come to me first, but I decided to just wait. It sounded like these blue guys were a lot older than some silly children's rhyme and more than likely had some ritual they had to follow.

Both Screamer and The Smoke came through the door two minutes later, for a moment letting in the loud sounds from the hallway and casino before closing the door.

Screamer was a superhero as well and his main power was the ability to connect minds of people and put images in people's heads. He got his name from a time when the police asked him to get the location of a buried-alive woman from a killer's mind. He made the guy scream and the nickname stuck.

The Smoke is a superhero working for the animal deities. He's actually a werewolf of sorts, with complete control of which form he is in, and he can go through walls with ease. That's a nifty trick that has come in handy a few times since he became part of our team.

"So what are we in for this time?" Screamer asked dropping into one of the soft leather chairs and smiling.

Then he noticed that Patty and I and Stan were all looking very upset.

"I fear this is no good," The Smoke said, moving around and standing off to my right near the wall. The Smoke liked to stand, and only sat when he needed to.

Stan nodded and took a deep breath. "It's bad and everyone is working on this. The Fuzzy-Wuzzys are coming back."

"Oh, no," The Smoke said, coming over and also dropping into a chair beside me.

It seemed clear that he knew what the Fuzzy-Wuzzys were. Screamer just looked as puzzled as I felt.

"Okay," I said to Stan. "Time to tell us what these things are."

"History first. Do you know the story of the continent of Atlantis?"

"Was that a real place?" Patty asked a fraction of a moment before I did.

"It was the home of most humans on the planet at the time," Stan said. "A wonderful place, very beautiful. It was mankind's third home on this planet, and it was destroyed in the first Fuzzy-Wuzzy invasion."

I desperately wanted to ask him what the first two homes were and where they were and how old was he, but I managed to stay on topic somehow. At this point I had so many questions there was no chance I was going to remember them all.

"How did they destroy Atlantis?" Patty asked.

"They didn't, we did," Stan said. "We sank it to kill them and drive them back."

I could hear a pin drop in that huge meeting room at that moment. Stan seemed very far away and didn't want to meet my gaze at all.

"You sank it?"

He nodded. "All the gods combined, along with the Fates and help from the Searchlights. We all sank it. We killed almost a billion humans to save everyone else. Humanity almost didn't recover."

Again the silence filled the room, and my stomach felt like it was going to crawl up through my throat and lodge in my nose. I just couldn't think of one damn thing to say.

Patty squeezed my hand really, really hard.

"Why are these Fuzzy-Wuzzy things so bad?" Screamer finally asked.

"Humans are a giant buffet to them," Stan said. "They eat everything except bones and fingernails and hair."

"They also eat most animals," The Smoke said. "And trees and brush and everything."

"Where do they come from?" Patty asked.

"They are coming from the alternation dimension over down the time stream," Stan said.

I felt like a kid in school and the teacher was talking, but nothing was making sense. "Do you want to try to explain that?" I asked, "or for now can we just say they come from another dimension?"

Stan nodded. "Just say another parallel dimension, only the humans in all the dimensions in that direction along the time stream lost the war to the Fuzzy-Wuzzys and are gone. We are their next meal. But we managed to stop them so soundly last time that it has taken them thousands of years to recover."

Again the silence.

"So what do these things look like?" I asked. "Why the name Fuzzy-Wuzzy? And why can't we get the armies of the world to pitch into this fight?"

Stan pointed to the nail on his little finger. "They are bugs, covered in a light fur, and over a hundred of them could fit on my little fingernail."

I just stared at him. "You are telling me this great threat to humanity is a mass invasion of tiny, tiny, furry bed bugs?"

He nodded. "They can take a human body down to a pile of bones and Fuzzy-Wuzzy black shit in two seconds. And once here they can move faster than any man can run. In Atlantis I watched them mow through a crowd of thousands before the crowd knew what hit it. The more they eat and digest, the smarter they get and the harder they are to stop."

I opened my mouth and again could think of nothing to say.

"So you drowned them the last time?" Screamer finally asked.

Stan nodded. "We did, and poured an awful lot of ocean water through the dimensional portals. But they only came through five portals last time, not like the thousands they are attacking through this time."

It finally dawned on me what was bothering me.

"You are telling me these things are very, very tiny. Yet you are acting like they are intelligent. That's not possible."

"Hive mind," Stan said. "Alone or in groups of only a few thousand, they have no ability to think and can be easily killed. In fact, in groups of under a thousand they don't eat. But in masses, they are eating and thinking machines of fantastic ability and intellect. Somehow they transport the energy from eating to the hive mind. No one is sure how that works."

"So what weapons kill them?" Screamer asked. "And can anything protect a human from them?"

"Stepping on them kills them," Stan said. "Drowning, flame, anything with any force. And chemicals of all types kill them. Just like any other tiny bugs. The problem is that they move so fast and together that they can lose millions and not be bothered in the slightest."

"And protection?"

"They can't eat through anything inorganic," Stan said. "Stone, rock, rubber, things like that. But they can go through wood like it doesn't exist."

Again the intense silence.

I couldn't think of another question to ask Stan, and neither could anyone else it seemed, so Stan nodded and said, "I'll be back in an hour to see if you four have any ideas on how to fight these things."

Then he vanished.

The silence again. I was starting to really, really hate the silence.

Finally I said, "We are so screwed."

None of my team challenged me on that.

Four

After we all sat there in the silence for what seemed like the longest time, I finally couldn't take it anymore. "Anyone up for a milkshake?"

Normally we met downtown, at The Diner, to plan operations and work to save people. It just seemed natural to go there now. It wasn't more than a small hole-in-the-wall around the corner on a side street from the Horseshoe Casino. The Diner was decorated in fake

1960sstuff and had a phony jukebox playing in the background all the time.

Before anyone could say anything, Stan showed back up. "I would love a milkshake."

A moment later we all appeared in The Diner sitting at our favorite booth while Stan sat in a chair in front of the booth. Madge, our normal waitress, was sitting at the counter shaking her head. In all the years we had been coming into this little place, I had never seen Madge sit down. She was a superhero working for the Gods of Food and Beverage, and she knew about us.

Madge always had an attitude, and was the best waitress I had ever met. And when in the 1960s diner uniform, she always wore too much make-up and light slacks three sizes too tight. She was a large woman both top and bottom, and it was a standing joke that no one should be allowed to watch Madge walk away or bend over.

Since we discovered she was a superhero as well, she had become a sort of unofficial member of my team.

We were the only ones in The Diner, and it was clear the place was closed, something I had also never seen. At least the oldies station was still playing softly on the radio.

Stan shouted over to Madge. "Our regular, then come join us. We've got planning to do."

Madge glanced around and it was clear from the black streaks of thick make-up on her face that she had been crying. She must have heard about humanity's upcoming doom.

She nodded and got to her feet, using a napkin to smear the make-up even more.

"So when are you going to teach me that jumping around in space trick?" I asked Stan. I'd been bugging him about learning that now for a while, but he had just never gotten around to showing me how that power worked. He had never said I didn't have the power, only that I needed to learn how to do it.

"Next week," he said, 'if we can figure out a way to win this war, and there is a next week."

I nodded. "Deal. Now tell me why the Searchlight came to me instead of going straight to Laverne?"

"Custom," Stan said. "When you want to see the queen, you don't just barge into the throne room, you talk to her guards."

"Real old school," I said.

Stan just nodded.

From the counter the milkshake machines started up.

"So how come you are back here with us?" Patty asked.

"I'm worthless with the gods," he said. "I told Laverne I'd do better back here with your team, and she agreed."

Over the years, our team had saved the planet a couple of times, and saved Lady Luck herself more than once. She clearly had a lot of faith in us to send Stan to help us. I just wished I had as much faith in us right now as Lady Luck did.

I was just a lowly poker-playing superhero. What could I do against an invasion of tiny bugs? I couldn't read their faces because more than likely they didn't have any. I couldn't take their money, or bluff them off their chips. And I...

"Bluff," I said out loud.

Everyone at the table looked at me.

I had zero idea what I meant by that, but my little voice, the voice that told me when to bet and when to fold, was shouting that the key to all this was bluffing. And I trusted that little voice.

But how the hell do you bluff a hive mind of millions of bugs?

"You want to explain that outburst?" Stan said.

I glanced around the booth, realizing that everyone was just staring at me. Madge was just finishing the milkshakes.

"Not sure what I meant," I said. "I need more information. Wolfgang said that they are coming through one thousand portals? How big is a portal?"

"In Atlantis a portal was about five feet around, but impossible to block."

"And we know where all these portals are going to appear?" I asked.

Stan nodded. "The Searchlights do, and the top gods will be able to see them forming in a few more hours as well."

I wish I could figure out what I was thinking. It was just there, at the back of my mind, but darned if I could figure it out.

Then I had another idea.

I took Patty's hand that had been resting on my right leg and placed it on the top of the table with my hand on top of hers. Then I looked at Screamer.

"I have an idea, but can't quite get it to form. Come on in with Patty and help me figure it out."

Screamer nodded, reached across the table, and put his hand on top of ours.

Suddenly Screamer and Patty were in my mind. We had joined minds so many times on missions over the last few years, the sensation almost felt familiar.

Weird, but familiar.

Bluff. What am I thinking about, bluffing the Fuzzy-Wuzzy?

I focused, trying to dig up the idea as Screamer and Patty searched inside my head. After what seemed like only an instant Screamer thought at me directly, Just what the word means. To mislead.

He's right, Patty thought at me. You are thinking we can mislead the Fuzzy-Wuzzy.

Screamer took his hand away and I was again alone in my own head. But I did have a part of an idea.

"Stan, do any of the gods or Fates have the ability to open one of these portals?"

"I wouldn't know why not," he said. "It's similar to the power needed to slip between a moment in time. I've never tried it since I have no desire to meet myself in another dimension."

Suddenly I was confused again.

"Are you saying that the dimension to our left has never been attacked by these things?"

"No, it would take you moving over thousands of millions of billions of dimensions to find one that was never attacked. Think of a river. Every time there is a new event, it splits off two dimensions, like two almost-identical branches of the same river. When you all saved Lady Luck from the Bookkeepers' little mistake, you created two dimensions, this one where you saved her, and one where you didn't. So since the last attack on Atlantis, billions of new timelines have formed to the left of this one."

"Every major event creates a new timeline, a new dimension?" Patty asked. "Every event? Anywhere?"

My head hurt.

"That's right," Stan said. "If we stop these things this time, there will be a new dimension where we don't stop them. And in that timeline over, those of us existing in the neighboring dimension will have to fight them. And so on. The Fuzzy-Wuzzy need to keep eating, thus their need and ability to keep moving from dimension to dimension and eating entire populations. There are a lot of dimensions out there."

"I'm really sorry I asked that question," I said.

"I am sorry you asked it as well," The Smoke said. "But we must focus on this dimension and let the others fight their own fights."

At that moment Madge brought the milkshakes. She had managed to wash her face, but still looked completely distraught.

"Any ideas?" she asked, sliding a vanilla milkshake in front of me.

"A couple," I said.

At that she brightened up. Then she turned to The Smoke. "It's going to be a minute on the hamburger. I had the grill turned off."

The Smoke's regular was a hamburger, almost rare, instead of a milkshake.

The Smoke nodded and said, "Pull up a chair."

"So what's the idea?" Stan asked.

"I need one more piece of information. When these things run out of human food, do they attack each other?"

He shrugged. "I honestly don't know. Let me find out about both questions."

He vanished, and then a moment later he and Lady Luck herself appeared back. Lady Luck sat down in Stan's chair and Stan quickly pulled over another chair.

"So what are you thinking?" Laverne asked.

I took a deep breath and stared at the most frightening god that existed, as far as I was concerned. "We need to bluff the Fuzzy-Wuzzy into going to another dimension, one where they have already eaten us all. Stan says we can form these gates to other dimensions."

"Easily," she said. "We don't as a general rule."

"Can the portals be made to be one way?" I asked. The idea was starting to form and I was getting excited.

"They can be," Laverne said, looking puzzled.

"I asked Stan if these things ever got hungry enough to eat each other," I said, "and he went to ask you."

Wolfgang Sucker appeared in all his bright blue glory, standing beside the booth next to Stan, his onion breath covering us all instantly as his head turned slowly from side-to-side.

Madge jumped up and took a couple of steps back, the look of shock on her face very clear.

"They must eat every fifty years or they will turn on each other," Wolfgang said, his voice again like sandpaper on a hard surface. "It takes them almost a half year to form the portals."

"How long does it take us to form a portal?" I asked.

"Instantly," Laverne said.

"One more question," I said. "When they leave a dimension, do they leave anyone behind?"

"Nothing but a stripped planet with nothing alive remaining," Wolfgang said.

I smiled. This idea just might work if there wasn't something I didn't know.

"Can you form a portal to one hundred dimensions back along the line of the Fuzzy-Wuzzy conquests?"

"We can go back thousands of dimensions, but all the worlds would still be dead," the Searchlight said.

I nodded. "Okay, here's the idea. "Form a portal to one of the destroyed worlds a thousand worlds away, and put that portal directly over their portal and somehow seal the connection. You won't be blocking it. They just won't know they haven't arrived here yet."

Stan and Laverne were nodding so I went on. "That way when they come through their portal, trying to get to us, they instead end up in a dead dimension without their knowing it. We bluff them."

"Actually," Screamer asked, smiling, "why not divide them into a thousand different dead worlds over a thousand dimensions, so far back they will only be able to eat themselves?"

Laverne stared at me for a moment, her dark eyes seeming to cut through me like I didn't exist. Then she said softly, "That might work."

At the same instant she and Stan and the Searchlight vanished.

Patty squeezed my hand and Screamer and The Smoke just smiled.

"You guys are really something," Madge said, shaking her head. "Milkshakes are on me."

I just hoped my idea worked and this wasn't going to be my last milkshake ever.

Five

Forty-eight hours later, I stood with Stan, Patty, Screamer, The Smoke, and Wolfgang Sucker in a "you can't see us" bubble around the portal forming in the driveway to the MGM Grand Hotel valet parking.

Around us, Las Vegas went on with its normal, noisy life. The night air was warm, but thankfully not hot.

I was the one holding the "can't-see-us" bubble. Up until yesterday I didn't know I had that power.

Stan, with help from the Searchlight, and with energy support from all of us, had formed a dimensional portal that fit tightly over the Fuzzy-Wuzzy's portal. Stan's portal shifted the Fuzzy-Wuzzy almost a thousand dimensions back.

From what I understood, the Fuzzy-Wuzzy could only move from one dimension to the next every half-year; so if this worked, it would take them hundreds and hundreds of years to get back. And since they would turn on each other to eat long before that, they might never make it back.

And we were splitting the entire invasion force up into a thousand parts over thousands of dead dimensions.

All over the planet right now, Searchlights and gods were forming dimensional portals over the Fuzzy-Wuzzy portals.

It was our only plan of defense, and it had been my idea. I just hoped it worked. I hadn't slept, worrying about it.

If this plan didn't work, we were all going to be the first appetizer for a very hungry horde of bugs.

"Five, four, three," Patty said, counting down.

All of us poured energy to Stan as we had practiced, while the Searchlight held the connection between the two portals.

Since I wasn't a god, I couldn't see the forming Fuzzy-Wuzzy portal until suddenly it formed directly under the one Stan had formed.

A blur of black seemed to fill the opening of the portal. It went on and on and on.

And then nothing.

"I think they have all gone through," Stan said, beads of sweat forming on his face.

Suddenly the dimensional portal formed by the Fuzzy-Wuzzy closed and Stan slumped to the ground, breathing hard.

"I hate those bugs," he said, panting.

For a moment the Searchlight stood there, then he said, with his rough voice loud enough to hear even against all the noise of a Las Vegas night:

"It has worked."

Then he turned to all of us as Stan climbed back to his feet.

Suddenly Wolfgang Sucker's head stopped moving, and his blue eyes stared directly at us.

"This great battle will be shown on the heads of a thousand of my brothers for centuries to come. It has been my honor to be a member of your team, Poker Boy."

With that he vanished.

"Well, you all did it again," Laverne said from directly behind me.

We all spun to face Lady Luck.

She was smiling, and when Lady Luck smiles on you, you know it.

"Someday we might have to start paying all of you if this keeps up."

She laughed at her own joke, since superheroes don't get paid.

Then she winked at Stan. "Teach him how to jump through space, would you? I worry about him taking so many airplane flights."

Then she got serious. "Thank you. Every one of you. It was a perfect bluff, and a perfect idea. I just wish you all had been around in Atlantis' time."

With that she vanished.

Stan turned to me, smiling. "Well done, as usual."

I didn't know what to say. I was so stunned that my idea had worked, I just sort of felt nothing.

"Milkshakes are on me," Stan said. Then he smiled even larger, "If you can get us there, Poker Boy, without calling a cab."

And suddenly I knew how to jump through space, from one location to another. I don't know how I knew, but I just did.

"That's a deal," I said. I took Patty's hand in mine and said to Stan, "Race you."

An instant later, I had my team sitting in our regular booth in The Diner as a fraction of a second later Stan appeared, still smiling.

Wow, that felt good.

Patty just squeezed my hand and smiled. Then she whispered in my ear, "Now we can see a lot more of each other."

I liked that idea. I liked it a lot.

The sound of crashing glass made us all turn around as one.

Madge was dancing on the counter in front of the kitchen. She seemed to be doing dance moves not thought of in years, and considering she always wore slacks three sizes too tight, it wasn't a scene that any sane person could watch for very long.

Stan started laughing and The Smoke just covered his eyes.

After a moment, all of us started laughing.

"Why not?" Screamer asked, and got up and started dancing as well, quickly joining Madge on the countertop.

"Looks like milkshakes are going to be a minute," I said between huge laughs of relief.

"Thanks to all of you," Stan said, "we have the time to wait."

HUSBAND DUMMIES

When two couples decide to play the Bob and Carol and Ted and Alice pretend game, things can take a nasty turn for the worse.

Especially when the wives want to change the movie.

A very strange crime story with a movie twist.

One

"WHY IN THE world does anyone live in this god-forsaken humidity?"

My words drifted through the thick air with no wind to take it away. Two midwestern natives—used to this thick, water-filled air—sat next to me in the drainage culvert under the concrete bridge as above us trucks thundered over, swimming through the thick air down I-70. The two men ignored my question without even pretending not to hear it.

Bob-from-Minnesota, my husband and a real jerk, just shook his head and stared at the ground, blood dripping down his arm. It had already soaked his white T-shirt, mixing with the sweat-stains growing under his arms. It looked like a lot, but it wasn't that much blood loss. He had just dislocated his shoulder and had a few surface wounds. I figured it served him right for being such a screw-up. And the worst driver I had ever seen, especially for a getaway car driver.

I wanted to just slap him, but instead I sat on the ground with my back against the rough concrete side of the culvert and just sweated. Humidity had to be one hundred percent in this tunnel. Why hadn't I planned this robbery for October instead of August?

Ted, Bob's best friend, adjusted his Cub's baseball cap and then pulled the shoelace from his right dress shoe free and flipped it away. He had twisted his ankle so badly in the getaway that his foot was too swollen to even stay in his shoes. His blue dress shirt was soaked with sweat, turning it even darker, and his usually perfectly combed brown hair was messed up and had a weed caught in it.

He was going to live as well. None of us were injured enough to die.

My two men, my two lovers, sat across the small space from me. Both looked a mess, more than any morning-after hangover look, and I had seen both of them like that. Hell, I had seen those two in just about every position possible and to be honest, I was sick of it. Jail time might actually be a relief.

As bad as they looked, I had to admit, I wasn't doing much better. The getaway from my perfectly planned bank robbery had turned sour, ending up in a car wreck because my stupid husband somehow forgot how to drive. I was so angry I could hardly think. I just hadn't expected Bob to screw things up that way. It had sure changed my plans in a hurry.

And Alice's plans as well. She was Ted's wife and my best friend. We had left her stuck in the car, shouting at us to get out and run before the cops got there. She wasn't actually stuck, but the men didn't know that. Alice was just flowing with the changes in my plan caused by my dear husband's bad driving.

Alice had a body men lusted after, wore clothes that were always in perfect style, and bought the best jewelry. I just hoped she was better at getting out of that van and getting away than Bob was at driving it.

Now, because of his bad driving, the three of us were all injured. I figured I had a broken arm. I had tucked the arm inside my white blouse and downed four Advil from my now long-lost purse to hold back most of the pain. Sitting still, the pain just throbbed and I could ignore it.

Amazing the things I could just ignore. I was a master at it.

That didn't much matter at this point. I couldn't ignore the fact that, more than likely, the only place I was going was to jail, thanks to

Bob's awful driving. Sitting under the freeway in a drainage ditch in the middle of midwestern farmland didn't offer us much chance of escape without a miracle and I didn't expect that.

I hoped for it for myself, but didn't expect it.

But one thing was for sure, I wasn't going to make the miracle happen just sitting in this culvert. I had to get moving.

"I'm going to go up and jump in front of a speeding truck," Ted said. "Get this over with."

"Don't," Bob said. "We'll be out in four years; three if we behave."

"Alice might be dead," Ted said. "Shot by the police or something."

"She's not dead," Bob said, his voice firm. "Besides, Carol here can handle us both, can't you, baby?"

"Screw you," I said. "Ted, Alice is just fine. And I'm going to be glad to go to jail just to get away from you two."

"So, brilliant master-planner," Bob said, staring at me. "What do we do next?"

I stared back, wondering what the hell I ever saw in the guy. Sure, he was good in bed, knew how to make me come more times than a doorbell being pushed by a bill collector. And he was damn good-looking. But he was also a real wimp and a really bad driver. How the hell had I ended up marrying a shitty-driving jerk with no courage?

"We give up," I said. "Go up and sit on the edge of the road until some lame-ass cop comes and arrests us. At least they'll get us out of this heat."

I managed to move my broken arm enough to get a look at my watch. It was about time to hope for the miracle. Past time, actually. I needed to move.

"And then what do we do?" Bob asked, being his usual annoying, snide self. Snideness and humidity just didn't mix. Nothing mixed with heat and humidity as far as I was concerned.

"Serve our sentences and get back together after we're out," I said, doing my best not to sneer at him.

"Brilliant!" Bob said. "Wish I could think that well."

"Screw you," I said.

"Children," Ted said, pushing himself up and balancing on his one good foot while leaning against the concrete wall of the culvert, "After this wonderful conversation, I think I'll face that truck grille now. Someone want to help me up there?"

"Sure," Bob said, standing and moving to get under his best friend's arm. "But don't expect me to push you. I'm not doing time for murder as well."

"You know," I said, "I'm beginning to hate both of you as much as this heat."

Two

I tried to push myself to my feet, but the sharp pain from my broken arm took my breath away and made me stop. I sat there, staring at the ground, trying to cram the pain down and into a place I could just ignore it. I needed to move, to keep going, and I couldn't let some pain stop me.

"You going to make it, babe?" Bob asked, actual concern in his wimp-ass voice.

"Yeah." I took a deep breath, gritted everything in my body that I could grit, and stood.

Damn, that hurt.

Damn my arm.

Damn my stupid-ass husband.

The heat seemed to get even worse, if that was possible. I was sweating so bad, I had a small river running down between my breasts and into my crotch.

I used my good hand to brace my bad arm up tight under my breasts and keep it from moving as much as possible, then nodded to my husband. "Let's go."

"Well, this was sure fun while it lasted," Bob said, smiling at me.

"It was," Ted said.

"Except it didn't end like this in the movie," I said. "Make sure you give the cops your real names."

"Yeah," Bob said, smiling. "Less bad press if we don't get known as the Bad-Sex Bandits."

"And we're worried about press coverage now?" Ted asked, shaking his head. "I'm getting more and more serious about facing the grille of that speeding truck."

"Who said the sex was bad?" I asked.

"All right," Bob said. "The Good-Sex Bandits. You happy?"

"Purring like a drowning kitten." I took a step and let the pain wave wash over me, braced my broken arm even tighter and kept going toward the opening of the ditch.

Bob and Ted stumbled over the uneven dirt behind me, both men grunting from the pain of the movement. During the sex play between the four of us, I loved to listen to them grunt in unison as they pounded me or Alice. Now it sounded just sad, especially echoing between the sounds of the cars and trucks overhead.

Damn I hoped Alice was all right. Imitating that old movie wasn't such a bright idea in hindsight. Bob and Carol and Ted and Alice. We even took their names and it became such a fun game, such a major part of our lives, that I now thought of my husband Danny as Bob. If we had just left the fun with the sex and the names and the games, we'd have all been fine. But no, we had to come up with a foolproof plan to get rich, move to the Bahamas and live the good life forever as Bob and Carol and Ted and Alice. None of us liked how the movie ended, so we figured we could change it.

Well, this was sure ending much worse.

Now, if a miracle didn't happen, it would be years of jail ahead of me without Bob or Ted and especially Alice. Every movie had to end, I guess. I just wished it wouldn't end like this.

This ending sucked. Unless I got my miracle and Alice had done her part of the plan.

I stopped and wiped the sweat out of my eyes. Who the hell lives in this kind of humidity? I wanted to go back to Southern California so bad I could taste it. Now that wasn't going to happen for years, either, thanks to Bob's shitty driving.

I stopped and rested in the hot, glaring sunshine outside of the culvert, waiting for the two men to catch up. Bob had lost a lot of blood and Ted looked white from the pain. As I had figured, I doubted either of them could make it up the twenty-foot bank to the edge of the highway.

"You two stay back in the shade," I said. "I'll climb up and get the police."

"You sure, Babe?" Bob asked.

"As sure as I'm ever going to be," I said.

I turned my back on the two men I had slept with and slowly started to climb. The nightmare of just a simple movement was almost too much for me to keep going.

Twice I slipped and had to stop as the jarring pain blinded me and took my breath away. Getting to a jail and a hospital would be a relief after this.

I stumbled up onto the edge of the hot freeway and glanced back at my husband and Ted. They were nowhere to be seen. They had done as I had told them and moved back into that hot culvert to sit and wait.

What wimps. What did I ever see in those two men?

Three

Cars flashed past, then a big truck, kicking up a hard wind filled with fine sand.

There wasn't a cop in sight.

Good.

Suddenly, in the other lane, a blue camper braked hard, swerved to the inside lane and then off the road and across the shallow ditch between the two sides of the freeway. It hesitated for just a moment to let a big truck flash past, then spinning dirt and dust, it accelerated toward me, cutting across the two lanes and sliding to a halt off the freeway near me.

Alice.

Right on time. My miracle had arrived.

And, I hoped, with all the money.

"I thought I'd never find you," Alice said as she jumped out of the camper and ran toward me. "I've been cruising this freeway for the past half-hour looking for you."

I didn't quite stop her from hugging me, a wonderful, sweaty hug that almost caused me to pass out from the pain in my arm.

"Oh, man, are you all right?" Alice asked, stepping back.

"Bob broke my arm in that stupid wreck. It took a little longer to get everything set up."

"And where are the two love machines?" Alice asked.

"Down in the ditch right under us," I said. "Both hurt, but not that seriously. They just think they are. A couple of wimps."

Alice nodded. "Nothing new there."

"They thought you were captured."

"And we're going to be," Alice said, her control voice in full force, "if you don't get into the camper before too many more people see you."

I didn't argue.

The first movie was over. Bob and Carol and Ted and Alice was rolling the credits now.

But we just hadn't bothered to tell our dear husbands that this was a double feature. Thanks to Bob's shitty driving, though, we still had a few twists and turns to make it through.

The camper Alice had found was one of those small things with a small back bedroom, another bed or storage area over the driver, a tiny kitchen area, and a bathroom so small, you couldn't sit down without scarring your knees. It looked new, so new in fact that it had a price and features list glued to the counter.

I knew exactly where she had gotten it, which dealer lot, which dealer, and how. I had planned it, and it seemed that Alice had carried out my plans perfectly, even after the wreck.

Alice slammed the door and scampered into the driver's seat. The van was still running and I could feel the air-conditioning flowing over my sweating face and arms. Between the pain, the excitement of being rescued instead of arrested, and the air-conditioning on my skin, I almost had an orgasm right there.

I moved to the copilot chair as Alice kicked the van into gear, waited for traffic to speed past, then got onto the freeway. The movement of the camper and the roughness of the road forced me to again hold my broken arm tight up under my breasts.

"I'm going to need a doctor to set this before we go too far."

Alice nodded. "So do I. That husband of yours sure can't drive."

It was at that moment I noticed the dried blood and the bandage wrapped around her leg.

"You got any idea of where we might find one?" I asked as I turned both dashboard vents to face me, blowing cold, wonderful air over my skin.

"If you can make it, I have an old friend who's a doctor about six hours south of here. He'll help us if we give him a little side treat, if you know what I mean?"

"After a shower, that will be a pleasure."

Alice laughed. "Better than what old Bob and Ted are going to get. You feel bad about them?"

"Are you kidding?" I asked. I didn't feel bad in the slightest. Relieved, actually, to be away from them.

Alice laughed. "Yeah, know what you mean. When should we tell the police where they are at?"

I smiled at the idea of the two of them coming up out of that culvert to find the police waiting and me not there. "Let's give them a half hour to sweat."

"Good," Alice said. "We'll be across the state line by then as well."

"And the money?"

Alice nodded toward the back. "More than we're ever going to be able to spend, tucked safely under the bed in the back."

All I could do was laugh. Except for the car wreck, the plan had gone perfectly. The only robbers the bank saw were Bob and Ted, and no amount of talking on their part was ever going to convince anyone that their wives had taken part. In fact, with the blood that I splattered around our house before we left, it's going to look like the two of them killed us and dumped our bodies before their little bank robbery.

I braced my arm and sat back, enjoying the cool air and the smooth ride of the camper. Alice and I had money, and we were free.

Completely free.

With new identities already made up and set.

Judy Freeman, a.k.a. Carol, wife of Bob was now dead. Welcome to the world Thelma Downer, rich widow of oil tycoon Bobbie Downer.

I closed my eyes and just let myself relax.

"Carol, you all right?"

"Carol's dead," I said, glancing at the woman I loved more than anything in the world. "Remember?"

Alice laughed. "That's right. The new movie starts now, doesn't it?"

"That it does, Louise."

She smiled as I turned to face her. "So, after the doctor, where would you like to go, Thelma?"

"Anywhere but the Grand Canyon."

LAST CAR FOR THIS TIME

A Thunder Mountain Story

When men start getting run over by slow-moving train cars in a gold rush town in the mountains of Idaho, Marshal Duster Kendal must solve the murders.

But there might not be a motive besides the fact that Duster Kendal lives.

Duster knows exactly what to do about that.

And he needs to do it fast before things get much, much worse.

An early story of when Bonnie and Duster were first testing time travel and a problem they had early on.

One

MARSHAL "DUSTER" Kendal really had no great desire to see the death scene. He stepped off the wooden porch of the Dewey Hotel and moved his six-foot frame as slow as he could down the dry dirt of the Main Street of the tiny town of Dewey, Idaho. With each step his boots kicked up a small cloud into the hot, morning air.

Lately he'd seen far too many deaths and he had a hunch this one wouldn't look much different than the other two he'd seen here and others he'd seen over the last year.

Things seemed to be unraveling. He knew the signs.

This time he had met the dead guy two nights before in the Benson

Saloon in Silver City. It was one thing to see a body of a stranger. Another to look on the dead face of a man Duster had watched pour drinks for two hours.

The morning sun beat down through the clear August sky with such force Duster could almost feel it like a weight on his shoulders, pressing him down into the dirt of the street. The day would be a scorcher before it was finished.

People thought him odd to wear his light, oilcloth duster even on hot summer days, but he had learned while in the Arizona territory a long, long time ago that it actually kept him cooler in the hot sun. His wide-brimmed Texas cowhand hat kept the sun off his face as well.

Wearing the long, brown coat had gotten him the nickname "Duster" and he had no intention of changing that now. He actually had grown to like the name and the coat. Both fit him like a comfortable old pair of boots.

He wore his gray and brown hair long and streaming out the back of his hat to cover his neck, and his face and chiseled features gave away very little of his actual age, which was north of forty-five now. Only his bright green eyes let his intelligence shine through and he was known for the intensity of his gaze. Sometimes he could stare a man down enough to kill a growing problem.

Today he had no plan on being out in the sun much longer than he needed. If this death followed the pattern of the others, he wouldn't need to be out long.

And this morning just maybe he might figure out what was causing these men to die.

Or at least why.

He had a hunch he knew, and with no train due back in the valley for six days, he had time to find out if his hunch was right and set everything on the correct path again.

In his years of wearing a badge, he'd never seen anything quite like this. Of course, no place else in the west, or in the world for that matter, was like the Owyhee Mountains. They had been mostly ignored by the huge rush on the Oregon Trail close by in the 1860s and if it hadn't been for the gold found in the streams and deep veins here, Duster doubted anyone would be in this hostile place.

And if no one had come here, he wouldn't be here either.

These deaths by train were the reason he was up here from Boise in the mining district of Silver City. The only law in the valley was a constable in Silver City named Ben and his deputy. The poor guy had called for help after the first death. Ben's job was to break up bar fights, not figure out why someone died under the wheels of a train.

What bothered Duster even more was that there didn't seem to be anything going on in the town that would cause this. No fights beyond drunken brawls, no mine-labor disputes beyond normal. Yet four men in three weeks had been run over by slow-moving freight trains just down the hill from Dewey, Idaho.

Dewey was a silver-and-gold-mining boomtown tucked in the bottom of a valley leading up between War Eagle and Florida Mountains in the Owyhee Mountain Range in Southern Idaho. The town straddled Jordon Creek like it couldn't decide which way to step.

The main attraction of the town beside the huge twenty-stamp ore mill and the Blaine tunnel was the Dewey Hotel. Colonel Dewey had built the hotel tucked up against the west side of the narrow valley. Two stories and as plush as anything Duster had seen in San Francisco or back east. Colonel Dewey himself lived in a large house beside the hotel and seemed just as upset at all the deaths as everyone.

Maybe more. Colonel Dewey had brought in the railroad in the first place. He knew that if the deaths didn't stop soon, there wouldn't be a person left in the valley to work his mines. This was scaring everyone and Colonel Dewey had offered Duster extra to solve this fast.

Duster had turned him down, of course.

If Colonel Dewey actually knew how fantastically rich Duster was, and where he actually came from, he would have never offered. But Duster played the role of marshal well, even though he always stayed in the best hotels when he traveled and only ate at the best restaurants and drank the finest brandy.

Duster felt that just because he worked as a marshal didn't mean he couldn't fully live life as well. And no one really questioned the money he spent and he didn't offer an explanation.

The railroad had put a spur line up the valley to the Dewey Mill in 1881. All the ore from Silver City and all the mines farther up either had to be hauled out over forty miles by wagon down to Murphy or taken the short three miles down to Dewey in the summer months when the train could get up the valley. In a few months the snow would start flying and the train wouldn't return until late spring.

If it returned then.

The town of Dewey was dying. Duster had seen it before around the west. Towns sprang up and then vanished, often within years. In a hundred plus years there wouldn't be anything left here but a bend in the road.

Silver City, the county seat three miles up Jordon Creek above Dewey, wasn't in much better shape. He had no doubt that the winter would kill most everything in this valley and the mines that were marginal wouldn't open again. And after the snow started flying the train wouldn't be back.

Plus, with the Bank of California going down a few years back and payrolls for most of the mines in this area being lost, people were already not trusting anyone.

The valley had a few more generations in it as it slowly died, but not much beyond that.

And now the deaths of four good men weren't helping.

This area was about to go down and would become a ghost town.

Duster just needed to figure out why people kept dying under the wheels of slow-moving ore cars so he could get back to his wonderful suite in the luxurious Boise Hotel.

He really wanted to get back to the life he had picked and the restaurants and the women in Boise as well. Everyone knew how Duster loved his food, and his friends wondered how he could eat so much and stay so rail thin. He had his secrets he would say.

Duster had a lot of secrets.

Two

Duster kept trudging down the street thinking about the deaths. None of this made a lick of sense. If someone wanted to drive people out of the valley ahead of when they would naturally leave, what would they gain besides changing the natural history of this valley? The mines were pinching off. The death of this valley was only a matter of time, so these deaths couldn't be about that.

Duster walked past the big mill and down the rail line to where a group of bystanders gathered near the edge of the almost-dry creek across from the tracks.

Just as with the others before, this body wasn't a pretty sight.

The head and upper torso were on one side of the track, the waist and legs on the other. The train had pretty much cut old Benny in half, leaving his toes pointing down and a stunned look on Benny's face as he stared with blank eyes at the morning sky.

Benny had to be at least fifty and his face and hands showed many rough years in the mines.

The blood had stained the rock fill around the ties slightly darker than normal for about ten feet along the track. No telling which stains were Benny's and which were from the other three men. All of them had died in the same place.

The train had left parts of Benny's guts strung out along the rail. That smelled just downright awful, like an overfull outhouse baking in the afternoon heat. The nasty odor had kept the gawkers back a distance. And the hot morning sun wasn't helping matters.

Duster had no desire or need to go any closer, so he stopped about twenty paces away and just studied the scene. He knew what he would find if he went in closer. Nothing.

The same as every man who had died before Benny in the same spot in the same way.

Benny wouldn't have a mark on him. And no ropes had held him in place under the train. And the railroad men wouldn't have seen him on the tracks when they walked the train before starting down the valley.

Somehow Benny had gotten under the car on the tracks in broad daylight just as the train started.

And without anyone seeing him.

Then he had turned face up and let the train cut him in half.

What a horrid way to die.

Duster shook his head and turned to look at the silent crowd.

"Marshal," one man said, fear clearly in his eyes. And some anger as well. "When is the great Duster Kendal going to stop this?"

"Yeah," another guy said. "I got a family that's starting to get spooked."

"They should have gotten worried after the first one," Duster said, glaring at the man. "Someone wants all of us to be scared. Seems to me it's working just fine."

Duster watched the faces of the twenty people, watched their eyes in the hot sun. Not a one of them seemed satisfied at what he had said. All showed fear.

Damn. He shook his head and turned away from the crowd. It would have been too easy to have the murderer standing around watching. He hadn't been in the crowd at the previous murder either and that had been larger. This was happening so often now, fewer and fewer people were going out to look and stand in the odor of a man's guts cut open and baking in the hot sun.

Duster turned and headed back up the road toward the hotel and the bar there. He had four men to meet and if luck held, they would have his answer.

He just didn't want to hear what he was afraid it might be.

This all might be his fault.

Three

The air felt cooler inside the hotel and out of the hot sun.

Duster pulled off his hat and coat and carried them into the bar over his left arm, his right arm free to reach for his gun on his hip. Over the decades he had become one of the most accurate shots with a Colt around. Luckily, he seldom had to use that skill.

The bar smelled of cigar smoke and a faint odor of puke. None of the windows were open yet, trying to hold off the heat of the day as long as possible.

The four men were sitting at the bar, clearly drinking and not talking, their heads down. He motioned for them to follow him and he went out and into the dining room and to a large table in the back.

The dining room was even cooler since the drapes were pulled closed and it still smelled of the breakfast bacon. It was empty.

Bonnie, a middle-aged woman with a bright smile and bright red hair, saw him coming and got up from where she was reading the Silver Avalanche paper. Her blue dress had been protected from a couple of morning spills by a stained apron tied around her neck and her waist. Her wonderful brown eyes looked very, very worried.

She looked as good as always. He had known Bonnie for a very long time and every time he saw her, his heart skipped a beat. Being in love with Bonnie was a normal thing for him.

And lately he had been missing her a lot. More than he wanted to admit to even himself.

"Another one, Marshal?" she asked standing across the table from him, her smooth hands on the back of the chair.

Duster nodded. "Not anything you'd want to see."

She shook her head, worry and fear filling her eyes. "You think it might be against us?"

"It might be," Duster said, nodding. "I'm about to find out for sure. Could I get a big glass of water if you wouldn't mind? Actually, make that two and add a couple chips of ice."

"Never a problem for you, Marshal," she said, smiling and turning as the four men followed him into the room carrying their drinks from the bar.

She would have to go down into the cellar to where they stored the ice from the winter, and it would cost him, but after that walk in the sun, it would be worth it.

And he tipped well. Everyone in the valley knew he tipped well. It got him a lot of extras he didn't even ask for.

Bonnie knew a lot more about him than that as well, but in public they stayed in their parts, their lives.

The four men pulled out chairs and sat at the table with him, their eyes down, trying to find the bottom of their shots of whiskey like there were answers there, clearly not liking what they had to report to him.

He had stationed the four men on the hillsides above the parked ore train, two on one hillside, two on the other. He had paid them all good money to stay out there from sunset last night until the train moved this morning. Where they had been on the hillsides, all four of them should have seen the death.

"So what happened?" Duster asked.

Not a word as all four stared at their drinks. These men were miners, rough men, strong men, able to handle the dangers of deep rock tunnels, yet all four were afraid to talk at that very moment.

He didn't blame them. They were good men, not men used to seeing things that they didn't understand. They had all seen death, he knew that. But how this death had happened they weren't used to seeing and that was what was bothering them.

They didn't think he would believe what they had seen and then be mad at them and maybe even blame them.

The silence in the dining room was broken by Bonnie coming back and bringing Duster his two large tumblers of ice water. The water was naturally cold from the spring up the hill above the hotel, but the ice made it even better.

"Thanks," he said to Bonnie, then took a long swig out of one. Then he pressed the sweating cold glass against his forehead.

That felt wonderful. It had been even hotter out there than he had thought.

He took a handkerchief from his pocket and wiped off his face, then took another drink.

All the while the four big miners sat silently, not even bothering to take a drink of their whisky shots.

"Well," he finally said as Bonnie moved back over to her paper. She could hear from there clearly, which was good. She would need to know if this was what he thought it was.

"You wouldn't believe us, Marshal," Dave Jennings said and the other three nodded, not looking up.

Duster decided to just let them off the hook. "Benny just appeared on the tracks, right before he was run over. No one put him there. Am I correct?"

All four of the miner's heads snapped up to look at him like he had lost a screw.

"That's right," Dave said. "One second he wasn't there and I thought nothing would happen and the next moment he was on the tracks and the train was running him through like so much soft butter on a hot day. That vision will haunt my dreams, let me tell ya, Marshal."

The other men nodded in agreement, clearly seeing again what had happened out there on those tracks.

"I was afraid of that," Duster said, sighing. Damn it all, he had just settled into a nice routine in Boise.

He glanced over at Bonnie who was just shaking her head as well. She knew they were in trouble.

He reached into his breast pocket and took out four gold coins, each coin the equivalent of two-week's work in the mines for these men. He had already paid them an equal amount for their night's watch, but now he had to buy their silence, let things get back to normal here.

He slid one coin each to the men. "This is to get you to forget what you saw and not mention it to anyone."

All four looked at him with a puzzled look.

"I don't think anyone would believe us even if we wanted to speak, Marshal," Dave said, picking up the coin and looking at it.

"There is another just like that for each of you if I don't hear a word of what you saw for the next month. Understand? Not even a rumor."

All four nodded.

Good, that would give things time to calm and change and be forgotten and winter would be that much closer by then.

"So where did that guy come from, Marshal?" Dave asked, his voice a whisper. "How'd he get under those wheels? Do you know?"

"Not exactly," Duster said, being truthful. "But thanks to you four, I now have a lead. Now not a word."

All four nodded, picked up their coins, and headed back for the bar. He didn't blame them for drinking after what they had just seen. It was bad enough a man had died like that. But just appearing out of thin air in that spot was something no sane man could grasp.

At least not someone from 1898.

After they had left, Bonnie came over and sat down beside him as he finished off his first glass of water and started on the second.

"We going up to the mine?" she asked.

"Looks like we have no choice," Duster said. "Things are twisting bad around here."

She sighed and looked around. "I was really starting to enjoy this timeline."

"Yeah, me too. But it's coming apart really fast," Duster said. He knew that the moment he arrived in Dewey and saw the ore train. In the real timeline, the original timeline, Colonel Dewey had never managed to get the spur line up Jordon Creek.

And those four men were still alive in 1898.

Four

At midnight, Duster and Bonnie left the Silver Nugget in Silver City arm in arm. A couple people saw them and tipped their hats to them as they passed. This time was such a polite society. It was one of the many charms Duster liked about it.

They angled up the hill toward Florida Mountain to the west, following a wagon trail, pretending to just be out for a walk together under the spread of stars on the warm summer night.

The slight moon and the sky painted with stars was enough to let them see where they were walking. After they were a distance from the buildings of town, they stopped talking and just walked in silence, her arm tucked into his left arm.

To Duster it felt comfortable. They had done this walk many, many times over the decades and centuries. He hadn't realized until just now how much he enjoyed it.

And missed, really missed her company.

The stars seemed to just fill every ounce of the sky, cutting out the dark shape of Florida Mountain to the west and War Eagle Mountain to the east like a cookie cutter cut out shapes from white dough on a black table.

The temperature had dropped from the high of the day, but it was still a warm night with very little breeze.

The climb soon winded both of them.

"Not used to this altitude," Bonnie said.

"How long were you working at the hotel before I got here?" Duster asked.

"Just a month. Came up here from San Francisco when I noticed some history going wrong. Small things, but enough to send me here."

"Amazing how two people can change so much in just a few short decades," Duster said, laughing.

"It never seems to fail, does it?" Bonnie said. "Luckily there are an unlimited number of timelines."

"Infinite number," Duster said.

"So how come the mine is killing people this time around? It's never done that before."

"Not that we know of," Duster said.

"Yeah, good point," Bonnie said. "But is someone in there running the deaths?"

"Infinite timelines," Duster said. "Remember? How could anyone from the future even find us?"

"Oh, yeah," she said.

"I just think it's the timeline trying to adjust is all. Spit us out in a manner of speaking."

She laughed. "Sometimes I do feel like something stuck in someone's tooth."

He laughed. "You always know how to kill a good metaphor."

"I've had a lot of practice," she said, also laughing. Her wonderful laugh carried over the barren mountainside and faded under the stars.

They walked the rest of the way in silence, both sweating slightly and panting from the climb.

At about eight hundred feet up the open face of the mountain above the mining town, they moved off the main wagon trail to the right and followed what was not much more than a trail up a gulley.

At one point a lot of Florida Mountain had been covered in different trees, but all of them were gone at this point in history, used in building the towns along the creek and stoking the ore mill fires.

Now they were walking along in scrub brush, following a trail that was left over from when the Trade Dollar had been a going concern. It had been closed down now for over forty years, the gold vein officially pinched off.

Actually, when they came back into a timeline, Duster always bought the mine and then willed it to his grandfather. This very afternoon he had sent the deed to Boise to be delivered to his grandfather in twenty years.

Duster always felt it was better to get the mine in control when he could and then lock it up.

"I'll never get used to the difference," Bonnie said, indicating the hillside around them.

"Me neither," Duster said.

In their original time in 2014, all the trees had grown back over this mountain, at least most of it. Silver City was only a ghost town with a few buildings left and a tourist trap in the summer. The Trade Dollar Mine was only a name on a map and a tailing pile covered in scrub brush.

Duster's father had taken him to the mine when Duster turned twenty-one and showed him what the mine was capable of doing.

And how to do it.

Duster and Bonnie had been married at the time for only a year, and when they first started going back in time, they went as a couple, him working as a marshal, her the marshal's wife.

But after a dozen timelines and a few hundred or so of their own years, they decided to go their own ways. For the last ten timelines and two hundred plus years or more, they had gone in different directions.

Often they didn't see each other for decades, until the end of each timeline that is, when their very presence started to unbalance things.

And cause things like those poor men's deaths for no reason.

When Duster and Bonnie left, the timelines stabilized.

They finally reached the top of the old mine tailings. A small shack sat to one side of the tunnel entrance and small ore car rail tracks came out of the mine tunnel, went through the shack and to the end of the tailing pile.

Nothing looked disturbed as far as Duster could tell in the dark, even though neither of them had been up here in thirty years.

But he didn't feel the need to check. Besides, up here on the mountain he had no plan on shining a light on anything. A dozen people around the valley would see it and wonder and maybe investigate and that was the last thing they needed.

This mine just needed to sit abandoned until his grandfather came to investigate it and follow the instructions Duster had given him with the deed to get in.

Duster and Bonnie moved over to the mine entrance. It looked like it was solidly boarded up and in the starlight and faint moonlight nothing had bothered the old wood.

Duster took a skeleton key from the lining of his coat.

Bonnie had two of the very same thing and Duster had another sewn into his hat as well. They had also hidden a key a couple hundred yards from the mine just in case.

Duster pointed the skeleton key at the door and then turned the top head of the key.

There was a click and a slice of rock moved aside near the entrance. Duster moved over and put his palm print on the exposed panel.

Another click and what looked like a boarded-up mine entrance swung open. The wood was attached on the outside to a vault-like metal door that would withstand a lot of dynamite blasts.

Bonnie and Duster stepped inside and the door slid closed behind them, plunging them for a moment into blackness before the automatic light came up.

It still looked like an old mine tunnel inside at this point, even though Duster had reinforced the walls completely when they first came back to this timeline. The ore car tracks ran down the middle of the tunnel and lights strung along one side gave the tunnel a golden look.

"Good to be home," Duster said.

"I liked my place in San Francisco," Bonnie said.

Duster didn't say anything. This time around he hadn't settled down anywhere, but instead had just kept moving around, living in luxury hotels and being waited on. But even that had gotten old now that he thought about it.

They headed deeper into the mountain, the lights in front of them turning on as the lights behind them shut off.

The tunnel and the ore car tracks along the floor at one point turned right, but both Bonnie and Duster kept walking straight and through a wall that was nothing more than a hologram. Another level of protection in case someone got inside.

Beyond the hologram was a large chamber with tables and supplies stacked along the walls. Supplies they hadn't needed.

They just kept walking in silence into another small tunnel on the other side of the room and through another hologram that looked like the tunnel had dead-ended.

Beyond that was a large metal door that Duster unlocked and pushed open and then stepped through.

The lights came on and they were greeted with a sight very few people had ever seen.

They faced all of time.

The sight always took his breath away.

Seemingly every inch of the huge chamber walls were covered in crystals that reflected the light into a thousand colors over and over. The human mind couldn't really hold everything it saw in this room.

The chamber stretched slightly downward into the distance as far as anyone could see. The ceiling was a dome thirty feet over his head, the floor flat and dirt-covered. Every inch covered in those fantastic crystals.

His father had told Duster the chamber just kept on going and going and going since his grandfather had tried to hike it and gotten lost and never returned.

Duster had studied the physics of time and space at MIT for three years after his father had shown him this chamber the first time. Duster had come to figure that more than likely the chamber went through many dimensions of space and just expanded as it needed to.

The crystals looked like quartz crystals on first glance, only rose colored and multi-sized. They were of no mineral anyone had ever heard of and could not be removed from the walls. Some crystals were huge, others smaller than a tiny finger.

The amazing thing was that every crystal was an alternate timeline.

Every time anyone made a decision, a new crystal was formed for that timeline and that decision. If the decision was minor, the crystal stopped growing and was absorbed back into the larger crystal.

But when decisions had an impact down through time, then the crystal kept growing and millions and millions of new crystals were formed from it.

An infinite number of alternate universes, an infinite number of chambers stretching into infinite numbers of universes.

And every alternate timeline represented by a single crystal somewhere in this vast and unending cave.

It made Duster's mind hurt every time he thought about it.

In the middle of the room near the door was a long wooden table and on the table was a simple-looking machine. It drew power from the crystals when attached.

Duster often wondered in how many other timelines his father or someone else had discovered this room, built a machine like the one he and his father had built.

More than likely millions or billions.

And he kept thinking someday he and Bonnie would meet up with themselves if they kept living like this long enough.

But with an infinite number of alternate timelines, the odds were so large, it would be hard to calculate.

Duster moved to the machine and then glanced at Bonnie. "You ready?"

"As always," she said, moving over and holding onto the edge of the machine near his hand. If they were touching the machine, they would keep the memories from that timeline.

He flipped the switch on the machine and then carefully unhooked the wire that led from the machine across the floor to a crystal about head-high on the wall. When they had hooked the machine up to that crystal, it had been a tiny side crystal off a larger one. Now it covered most of fifty feet of wall with hundreds of thousands and thousands of smaller crystals around it.

As they watched, many crystals were absorbed into the larger crystals as that alternate universe reset itself because of their absence.

Basically, that alternate universe had spit them out like a watermelon seed.

Duster glanced around at Bonnie. Even though she was still

wearing the waitress uniform of the Dewey Hotel, it no longer fit her. She was back to her twenty-five-year-old body.

They were now back in 2014. In this time, this timeline, they hadn't been gone for more than a few minutes, even though he had clear memories of living for over thirty years in that other timeline.

He stared at Bonnie. She looked damned good, he had to admit that. He had missed her.

He still had on the duster and his hat, but it felt larger as well. He was also in his twenty-five-year-old body.

"You want to head home?" he asked, smiling at her. Home being their house in Boise in 2014. He could barely remember what it looked like, they had been gone so long. "Get caught up on what has happened to each other the last few decades?"

She smiled back, her eyes gleaming. "You know it's been almost three hundred years our time since we went home?"

"Really?" he asked, then realized she was right. No wonder he could barely remember their house and this modern world. The last five times they had just reset, connected to a new alternate universe crystal and gone back. And each time had lasted over thirty years. Once they had actually made it long enough for their presence to not sink the Titanic in 1912.

"Really," she said, glancing at a watch she had left on the table. "We've aged here about five hours, but been gone almost two hundred years. Wild, huh?"

"Then we really have some catching up to do," he said, pulling off his duster and laying it across one end of the table, then taking off his hat and dropping it on the table as well.

She took off her apron and tossed it beside his coat and hat.

He offered her his arm. "Think you can remember how to drive after two hundred years?"

"Not a chance. That's up to you," she said, laughing. "I'm not trying to drive any new-fangled contraption off this hill. But I do want to feel air-conditioning again."

"Oh, wouldn't that be nice," Duster said. "And the taste of a giant hamburger with pickles."

She laughed. "A shower. Just a simple shower instead of a bath. And real hot water not heated over an open fire."

Duster laughed, starting to remember all the things he had forgotten about while living in the past.

"That sounds heavenly," he said, "now that I think of it. We just have to come home more often. And maybe stay home a little longer," he said, squeezing her hand.

"I'd like that, Marshal," she said, laughing.

As they left the huge cavern that contained all of time, the automatic lights dimmed behind them.

On one wall to the left of the metal door a very small, very simple new crystal formed.

ON TOP OF THE DEAD

Benny Slade came out of his vault one December afternoon to find the world changed.

Something instantly killed almost everyone in the city, including his two employees. The death stretched beyond the city. The event killed almost all the humans on the planet.

Benny has to figure out how to survive in a city full of dead bodies.

And maybe help build a new future for humanity.

A vastly altered version of this story was part of the Seeder's Universe novel The High Edge.

One

SOMEHOW I SURVIVED everyone else in the world dying.

One minute everyone was alive, the streets of New York were teeming with all sorts as is the case with this fine city; Then I went into my old steel vault at Benny Slade's Personal Loans to get some cash for my next loan, and when I come out, everyone was dead.

Car alarms were going off and the street in front of my place was a mess. Bodies littered the sidewalks, dead people filled wrecked cars, slumped over their steering wheels, or heads back, bodies held up by their seat belts.

And both Madge and Maggie, my two right hands, were both face down on my newly installed brown carpet.

Madge, who looked more like my old mother used to look before she got hit by that cab, had fallen next to her desk; while Maggie, about two years younger than my thirty-five years of age, had sprawled in the middle of the floor, her short skirt riding up and showing me a little of those wonderful white panties of hers that I liked so much.

I called out to Maggie and checked her first, then Madge. Both were dead. I sat back, feeling that cold, hard feeling come over me like it did when I had been in a firefight in the Gulf. Emotions got shoved back and I just stared.

It took me a minute to figure out what was different, what was wrong besides two healthy women being suddenly dead. There was no blood. Nothing. Now that I had turned them over, they just lay face up, eyes wide open, completely dead.

My first thought was gas attack, so I scrambled back into the vault; but I had left the vault door slightly open when I came out, so if it was some sort of terrorist gas attack, I was as good as dead as well.

After a minute sitting in the dark, I got disgusted at myself. "Come on, Benny, get it together," I said out loud. Madge had always complained I talked to myself too much, but Maggie thought it cute.

Maggie thought anything I did cute, and I thought she was cute, and we had flirted since the first day I hired her six months before. She was as sharp as they came and knew money and books and computers. I had somehow managed to keep the relationship on only flirt level.

I stared at Maggie for a moment. I was going to miss those white panties she flashed at me all day. I was going to miss her laugh and her smile and that wonderful blonde hair.

The coldness inside me whelmed upwards and I pushed those thoughts away. As my sergeant used to say, "Time to fight: time to think later if you survive the fight."

Clearly this was some sort of strange fight I was in.

I turned away from Maggie and headed for the door.

The moment I opened the door, the wave of sound hit me like a hammer. Hundreds and hundreds of car alarms were all going off at the same time.

Cars engines were still running, some racing as if their dead occupant still had a foot on the gas. Up Lexington Avenue I could see a fire starting to take hold of a building.

But what I didn't hear were police and ambulance sirens.

And no one around me in the cars or on the sidewalk was moving.

No one.

The day was a nice cold but comfortable December afternoon, some faint sun beating down on the buildings, so I didn't need any coat at the moment.

I checked a couple of young girls on the sidewalk to be sure they were dead. They were as gone as Madge and Maggie.

Then up the street I saw some movement as people came up out of the subway and sort of stopped and stared.

"So I'm not the only one," I said, feeling fantastically relieved.

I started toward the other people, then saw a couple of them panic and flee back down into the subway, followed by the others.

"Won't help," I shouted. But no one was going to hear anything I said over the noise of the car alarms and engines.

But they were doing exactly as I had done when I ran back into my old safe.

I glanced around at the buildings towering over the canyon of Lexington Ave. I couldn't see one window opening, or anyone even peeking out at all the noise.

And as far as I could see in both directions, everything was stopped and bodies covered the sidewalks.

I walked up to the corner of 54th and looked both directions. Same thing along the tree-lined street.

Everyone was dead, knocked down by some sort of giant killer in an instant. From what I could tell, not a one knew what hit them. None of them looked shocked or panicked or showing any fear at all. Just normal expressions on very dead people.

"What happened?" I said out loud, but the words barely made it to my own ears in the noise of alarms and running cars.

Who knew that the end of the world was going to be so damned loud?

Two

"I need to find out how far this spreads," I said into the noise of the running engines and car alarms.

I could feel the panic I had learned to hold down when I was a kid in fights on the street start to ease up into my gut. I hadn't felt that in many years. It wasn't the dead bodies that bothered me, I had seen worse in the Gulf. Much worse.

After the first few months in Iraq, dead bodies had stopped bothering me, at least on the surface. My counselor at the VA said I had a lot of buried anger and that the only way to get healthy was to let out some of the anger and tell him what I had seen. I didn't want to tell anyone, so he and I hadn't gotten too far in the last few years.

Death didn't really scare me; but there were dead bodies on my street, in my own business, and I was still alive. Now that scared hell out of me.

I started to head back to lock up my safe, then laughed at myself and looked around. Unless this was the second coming and everyone was going to suddenly spring back to life, locking up my money was the least of my worries.

But I went in and locked the safe anyway, tossing the money back inside that I had taken out to loan Mrs. Tenny for her grandkid's operation. More than likely, Mrs. Tenny and her grandkid weren't going to be needing much of anything anymore.

Then I headed downtown along Lexington, stepping over and around the dead bodies on the sidewalks. I thought these sidewalks used to be crowded when people were alive. When the same people are sprawled all over the place, the sidewalks got even smaller.

Down a dozen blocks I saw a few more people gathered near the subway entrance, looking terrified and very panicked, but at least this group had gotten over the desire to flee back into the tunnels.

I crossed the street. "Anyone have any idea what happened?"

All four of them, including a nice-looking young thing with a backpack over her shoulder, shook their heads no.

One guy held up his cell phone. He looked to be about five years older than me and had more hair than any guy his age should ever have. "Phones are working, but no one is answering anything. Anywhere."

He stressed the word "anywhere."

He seemed to be the one who had taken charge of the little group. Besides the college-age girl, there were two boys about the same age, all looking stunned. More than likely this had been some sort of field trip for a class, and the older guy was the professor.

He stressed the word "anywhere" again, more than I wanted him to.

The other three nodded, all holding their cell phones as if they were lifelines. After walking a dozen blocks, I was starting to get the idea that no one was going to toss any of us a lifeline.

"Anyone try tuning in a radio?" I asked.

The guy nodded. "Nothing. The internet is still working, so is Facebook and Twitter, but not one new post from anyone anywhere in the world that we can tell. We are searching. And no one, including family across the country, is answering any of us."

"Are they all dead?" the young college-age girl asked, the look of panic in her eyes. I had seen that look a number of times in soldiers' eyes in Iraq. She was about to flip and I wanted no part of that.

"They might be," I said. "I'd head off the island, get away from the city."

The professor-guy nodded.

"We can't drive, and the subways aren't working," the girl said, her voice higher than a moment ago.

The guy who seemed in charge of his little group said softly, "Let's walk."

He turned them toward the river. "You coming?"

"Got to check on a few people first," I said.

"We'll head south if you want to join us."

"Thanks," I said to him. "I might."

I reached into my wallet and handed him my card. "Cell phone number. Call me if you hear anything or end up back this way—if the phones are still working."

I had no intention at that moment of joining anyone, but better to leave the options open. At least this group seemed to be holding together, except for the girl.

He nodded and tucked my card into his pocket. "Good luck," he said and followed his little flock.

I was starting to think the human race needed the luck now. No one online, no emergency declared, and no announcements coming across any emergency bands or over the radio. I had a hunch that no help was coming. That group could walk all the way to Florida and never find help other than other survivors.

I had a hunch that most of the human race had just bought the farm in a really big way.

Clearly being down in the subway had saved a number of people, and me being in my vault had saved me from whatever killed all these people. It hadn't been gas and it hadn't been an attack. That much was clear. I had read an article last week about some huge burst of energy that might take out the entire planet coming from some other sun. Maybe something like that had happened without warning.

Or maybe this had been an alien attack. That thought made me smile. I had clearly watched far too many late night movies. Maggie really liked those old bug-eyed monster movies. I had really liked when she sat on my couch watching television. It had been a fair trade.

I was never going to know the answer to the question of what happened, I was certain. And to be honest, I didn't much care. What I did care about was staying alive now that I had drawn the lucky straw.

I headed toward Broadway along 42nd Street, working my way among the bodies.

What was really creepy about the bodies was the lack of blood. All the bodies I had seen in the past had become dead bodies because of holes that let out a lot of blood. No one sprawled on the sidewalk around me now had anything more than a slight bloody nose from hitting their face when they fell.

And since it was December, they had all mostly been bundled up, so most of them looked like nothing more than piles of clothing with an arm or a couple legs sticking out.

I wandered all the way over to Broadway, seeing only a few survivors picking their way through the streets of dead. I turned and went up Broadway, then finally, a couple hours later as the sun was starting to set, I found myself back at my loan company on Lexington.

It had been a nice little business, funded by investors to help those on the streets who needed help to get by with short-term, interest-free loans. I had felt good running the little shop, helping out people, and Madge had been fantastic at getting us grants and donors to keep us going.

I went into my little business and pulled both Madge and Maggie out onto the sidewalk and sat them with their backs against the front of the business, like they were taking a break and just looking out over the street. I smoothed down Maggie's dress so her white panties didn't show.

I had been around enough dead bodies to know that after a while they would start smelling. No point in having Madge and Maggie smell up my office.

I stood on the sidewalk and looked in both directions, suddenly realizing something that was very obvious. This entire city was going to be one stinking mess in very short order. It was scheduled to freeze tonight, and that would help with the people outside, but everyone who had died with the heat on in their apartments and businesses were going to start smelling really, really bad very shortly.

I had smelled my share of three-or-four-day-dead bodies and didn't much care for it.

I sat in my chair behind my desk, put my feet up, and tried to think while keeping the cold of the "emotion screen," as my counselor called it, in place. Breaking down now might just end up getting me as dead as everyone else.

Outside the car alarms had calmed down and the city was actually much quieter than I ever remembered hearing it, even late at night.

I looked around at the business I had put my heart into since getting out of the service, and sighed. "Not much to do here. I think you need to figure out what to do with the next part of your life, Benny. Right?"

No one answered me. My voice just echoed, and that seemed damn creepy as well.

I stood and headed back out into the light of the city, heading home. Luckily the electrical systems were still working, the stoplights still going through their cycles, the streetlights and building lights still making the night in the city seem like daylight.

More than likely that wouldn't last very long without people maintaining the power systems and lines. First good winter storm, and this place would be a giant frozen city of dead meat.

My apartment felt unusually silent, so I clicked on the television, hoping to find something or someone to tell me what happened.

Nothing. Some stations that had automatic programming were running, but the rest were just dead air.

The radio was the same, so I finally tuned the radio to an automatic light jazz station and let it play just to have some background music.

Then using my computer, another appliance that would soon be worthless, I pulled up some maps of New York and the area going south.

After an hour of studying those, I decided the idea was too stupid for words. Assuming I made the hike all the way to Florida, even taking some cars once I was outside of the city, what was I going to do down there with alligators and snakes and rotting-in-the-sun bodies?

"Think, Benny, think!"

I couldn't think of one darned thing, so I decided to make sure this was as bad as I had a hunch it was. I started dialing friends I knew in Southern California, Chicago, even Texas. I even dialed five of my old buddies who were still stationed overseas. Not a one answered.

I dialed twenty people. All machines or no answer. Not rock-solid proof things were bad everywhere, but adding in the internet and television silence, enough for me.

So I grabbed a yellow pad and asked myself, "What are you going to need to survive this winter?"

Then I started making a list.

—I was going to need power for lights and heat for long term.

—I was going to somehow need to figure out a way to get a place that I could hold back the smell until that passed, which was going to take some time and help from Mother Nature.

—I was going to need a place to store food and lots of canned supplies and safe drinking water.

—And considering the nut cases in this town that might still be alive, I was going to need a place I could protect.

—And from the faint glow out my window from the building on fire ten blocks up the street, I would need a place that wouldn't easily burn.

And maybe I could get a band of other survivors together who could work together to search for food and for defense.

Now I liked the sound of that.

I walked over to the window and stared toward the center of the city. Suddenly I could see it. The answer was right there in front of me. I knew exactly the place that fit the bill perfectly. But I was going to have to move fast, before anyone else had the same idea.

Three

I cooked myself a good steak dinner and scanned the television and radio channels again as I ate, coming up blank yet again. Nothing was working besides automatic systems, and those weren't going to last long at all.

I put my coat on with my trusty .45 in one pocket and a flashlight in the other, and headed out.

At night, even with the lights of the city still completely on, the bodies looked even stranger, piled and sprawled on the sidewalk. It took me a good hour to reach the Empire State Building.

I figured the Empire State Building had pretty much everything I would need. It was a secured building so I could defend it. It would have a pretty fine security system and extra supply of weapons for the guards, and it would have generators. Lots of generators to run all those elevators during power failures. I think the building had something like eighty different elevators or something like that. Also it was high enough and windy enough that even at the worst of the smell, it should be survivable.

The biggest problem was going to be clearing out the bodies. I was going to need to do that quickly as soon as I made sure the building actually did have everything I needed.

By ten in the evening I had borrowed the keys off a guard's body and found the security room. It had a lot of cameras that all seemed to be working.

Nothing was moving on any of the cameras.

Nothing.

"Benny, you've got yourself into a real mess this time."

Staring at all the bodies showing on those cameras, I almost decided to just pack and head for Florida. Then I shook that thought away. This city was my home and I'd be damned if I was going to let the fact that most everyone was dead scare me off.

It took me another half hour in the security room to clear out the guards' bodies and then to find all the generators for all the floors and the ones that ran the elevator. They had more than enough fuel, and when that ran out I could re-supply easily.

And there was a good-sized water tank up high that had electrical pumps. I was going to have to check every room to make sure all the water was turned off so that didn't drain out when the power shut off.

The Empire State Building was all offices and meeting rooms and tourist stuff. No apartments, so I would have to find a really high office and clean that out and set myself up an apartment. That would be easy to do.

For the next hour I went around taking all the keys and guns from the guards and then locking the five main entrances to the building. That felt weird, like I was locking out the dead, but if I wanted to be secure, no point in taking any chances that some other survivors had this idea.

The last thing I needed was survivors with more guns than I had.

I went back to the main security area and spent the rest of the night making sure I knew all the details of the building, or at least as much as I could find. I didn't want to be on an elevator with no chance of rescue when the power went out. I needed to know that the backup generators would kick in, and if that didn't happen, how to do an emergency escape. I was going to be spending a lot of time in those elevators. Being trapped alive in one with no chance of rescue scared me cold.

Four

Somewhere along the way, I fell asleep for a few hours on a cot in a side room off the security area.

An alarm woke me up.

I scrambled to the screens, at first not remembering where I was or what had happened. Then I saw all the bodies and nothing moving.

An alarm was flashing that it was time to open the doors.

I shut it off, dropping the room back into silence.

A radio in the back gave me no more hope than it had yesterday.

Outside it looked cold and overcast. That was good for the moment, since it would slow down the decay on the people in the streets.

I banged open a candy machine in the break room and feasted on a breakfast of a couple packs of nuts and a Diet Coke.

From what I could tell from the ever-changing monitors, there had to have been thousands of people in this building when humanity's number came up. No way I was going to be able to move all of them before they would start smelling.

I was just going to have to go up high, to the 102nd-floor observatory, and work my way down, clearing every body I could find from as many of the top floors as I could.

About a third of the way up, you have to change elevators, and there were a lot of bodies in that area, so I just figured a few more there wouldn't hurt.

But when I got to that lobby, I decided that was a bad idea. I was going to have to go through that transition floor all the time. I needed to clear that first.

I went down three floors, then using a large fire ax, I broke out some of the windows in an office there, letting in the cold wind from outside.

First I dragged all the bodies in that large office area to the window and just dumped them out. After about thirty bodies, a couple of which could have used less pasta when alive, I decided I was going to need a better system.

I had no doubt that some of the protections built into the side of the Empire State building to catch falling bodies would stop some of the ones I'd tossed, but after about twenty, the bodies would make it all the way to the street below.

I got a large cart from the shipping and receiving area and went all the way to the top. It took me two hours to clear off the two-dozen people on the top observation deck and take them down a dozen floors to another empty office suite, where I again broke out a window. Only this time I just stacked the poor souls near the window to take care of later.

By eleven in the morning I knew that stacking those bodies there wouldn't help my situation at all. I had to toss them outside. Which meant that by the time I got done clearing out the bodies in this building, there would be a stack of human flesh a story tall around north base. I would be living on a pile of the dead.

I was moving like a zombie, and considering what I was doing, that seemed about right. Like we used to say in the service, I was walking dead. Not a way to keep from making a mistake and getting injured or killed. I was going to need more food and more rest, if that was possible.

I went back down to the security area and did a check of the area outside the building.

Nothing but death.

I ate a quick lunch of some guard's sandwich stored in the fridge and then took another nap. Two hours later I was just about ready to go again when my cell phone rang in my pocket and scared hell out of me.

"Yeah," I said.

"This is the man you met yesterday with the three college kids," the voice on the other end said.

"Find anything?" I asked, for a moment excited at the idea that I might be wrong about everyone being dead.

"Nothing," the man said. "We're coming back to the city. It's where we all live, doesn't seem right leaving it. You got any ideas on where to hole up to get through the winter?"

My stomach twisted in disappointment, then pushed that aside as I had been pushing all feeling aside since this started.

I glanced at the security cameras showing room after room of bodies and shrugged. Why not? I could use the help.

"I'm setting up in the Empire State Building," I said. "It won't burn, it's got generators, a great security system, and a good water supply. It can be defended."

"And it's high enough to escape some of the smell," the guy said.

I was impressed. He had been worrying about the same thing.

"You and your merry band want to join me?" I asked. "There's a lot of work to do."

"It will take us about three hours to get there," he said. "Thanks."

"Pick up anyone else you see that looks sane along the way," I said. "This is one big building. Go to the South Entrance. I'll be waiting there in three hours."

"Okay," the professor said.

"And one more thing. Stay away from the north side of the building."

"Why?" he asked, then before I could tell him he said, "Oh, I understand."

This guy really was smart. That was good. It was going to take my street smarts and military training and his brains to keep any of us alive through the winter.

"Three hours; call me if you get stuck or run into problems."

"Three hours," he said and hung up.

I once again checked the television and radio. Nothing.

At least I was going to have help.

Five

I took some lumber from the maintenance area and went back up to the floor where I had broken out the window. There I spent an hour building a ramp for the shipping cart that slanted slowly up to the broken window.

Then I went back to the floor under the top observation platform and worked my way down, room-by-room, office-by-office, floor-by-floor, using the cart to take the bodies I found to the ramp and dumping them out the window. Luckily for me, some of those floors were empty, thanks to the recession.

Or a slow day at the office.

In one office, it made me sad when I found twenty very attractive women. I would have dated any of them. And that thought made me miss Maggie.

I even missed Madge.

I just hoped that some women had survived besides that panicked college girl. With luck, we would build a nice little community right here in the Empire State building.

With luck.

I found a nice hide-a-bed couch in one executive's office on the seventy-ninth floor, and decided that's where I would bunk for the night later. The office also had a really nice bathroom and shower, and I was really needing a shower.

Exhausted, I went downstairs to the south entrance at three hours, making sure my .45 was still tucked in my pocket.

No sign of the professor and his class; so I went across the street to a deli and got some great roast beef from the fridge and made myself a sandwich. I was really going to miss fresh meat.

I got enough food for three meals tomorrow and went back across the street.

There were three bodies in the deli, and another near the door, but I just didn't have the energy to do anything with them at the moment. But I would have to, since that deli had a back room full of supplies and some nice freezers full of meat. If I could get a couple of those freezers across the street and hooked up to a generator, maybe I'd have meat for the winter.

I was back inside the lobby of the Empire State Building, and was about to lock the door, when I saw the professor and his three charges winding their way along the sidewalk.

They all looked tired and clearly depressed, and the girl had lost her backpack along the way.

I propped the door open and waited for them, chewing on the sandwich.

"Thanks, Benny," the professor said, extending his hand. "My name is Professor C.M. Green." He laughed. "Not sure what I'm a professor of anymore."

He had managed to pull back his long hair and tie it, and I could tell he had been a gym rat. He was strong, of that I had no doubt. He had a firm grip, but I could tell that the last day had really worn on him. I'm sure I looked just as bad to him.

He quickly introduced me to the two college boys. The redhead with bright freckles who stood about six foot high, was called David. The other kid, shorter with a lot of pimples, was Freddy. Both looked like they could use some muscle and about fifty pounds. The girl was named Constance. She had long brown hair, long fingernails, and the remains of some makeup on her brown eyes. She looked like she was about to pass out.

"You had any food?" I asked them.

The professor shook his head. "Just snacks is all."

"So that's job one," I said.

I had them leave their stuff just inside the building entrance, tossed the professor a group of keys from a guard, locked up the building, then headed across the street to the deli.

"Boys," I said, "can you clear out those bodies and move them a little ways down the sidewalk while the professor and I fix you something to eat?"

Both boys looked horrified that they would have to touch a dead body, and the professor didn't look too pleased himself.

"Do it this way," I said, grabbing the man's body near the door by both feet right at the ankle. Then I just dragged him away from the door and down the sidewalk. "Don't try to pick them up, and if you don't want to use your bare hands, there's a store two doors down that has leather gloves. Bring me and the professor back two pair of larges each as well."

I stopped dragging the body, then led the professor and the girl into the deli as the two boys went for gloves.

"There's a lot of work to get that building ready," I said as the professor and I went in behind the counter.

"I can't even imagine," he said.

"You won't have to imagine," I said. "You're going to get to see it for yourself as soon as we're done eating."

The boys cleared the bodies out of the deli and then we all sat and ate sandwiches with soda. It almost seemed normal. The professor told me how far they had walked before turning back. They had stayed the night in a furniture store, but most of them hadn't slept much.

All of them had families they were convinced were dead, and the professor had a wife. "We're all going to need to find our families and check on them," he said. "It's why we came back."

My only family had been Madge and Maggie. Both my parents had died in a boating accident while I was in Iraq. I knew Maggie and Madge were dead. I would have looked for them as well if I hadn't known. Especially Maggie.

"I can understand that," I said.

He nodded thanks.

"Any idea at all what caused this?" I asked as the conversation lagged.

"Quasar pulse," Freddy said.

"Aliens," David said.

The professor shook his head. "All kinds of theories; no facts."

I nodded. "Well, back to the task of survival then. We need to get as much of the building cleared and set up before things turn really sour."

"You mean everything smells?" the girl asked.

"It will. Worse than you can imagine," I said. "We'll work some more tonight, and then you all need some rest. How about tomorrow you take a student and go out one at a time to find that person's family? And maybe look for more sane people to join us. The rest of us will keep working."

"That's a really good plan," the professor said, trying and failing to sound upbeat. "Everyone up for that?"

They all just nodded and kept eating. If nothing else, this was the most well-behaved and smallest class I had ever seen.

After dinner, I first took them up to the security room and made sure they all knew the same things I did about the emergency generators and how to escape if they were stuck in an elevator when the power went out.

Then, pulling the professor aside, I suggested that the two boys start working on clearing out the main lobbies downstairs, dragging the bodies away from the main doors, that sort of thing. I then suggested that he and Constance start on the floor where I'd left off and check every bathroom in every office to make sure the water was turned off in every bathroom and lunchroom. Even the public ones in the lobbies.

"What are you going to do?" he asked, after he sent the two boys off with their assignments and instructions to call him on his cell if they needed him.

"I am going to keep working my way down, floor-by-floor, clearing bodies."

All three of us went all the way back to the top, double-checking to make sure I hadn't missed anyone in a maintenance area or in a back office, and that all the water was turned off. We worked our way down by taking the stairs.

I showed the professor and Constance my cart set-up and ramp when we reached that floor, then they went off checking the water and I kept working my way down, one body, one floor at a time. By the time two hours had gone by and it was dark, I had the top thirty floors completely cleared of bodies.

I had scouted the neighborhood a little, mostly with the exterior security cameras, and I knew there was another restaurant nearby, so we all headed there to scrounge for food, then a couple stores down to find bedding and to a neighboring store to find changes of clothes.

We cleared the bodies out of both places in only minutes, since we were going to need to use both places in the future.

I was starting to feel better by the minute.

It had only been a little over a day since the world ended and I had a hunch this new way of living just might work. We might actually have a way to survive, with enough help.

And a little more time.

Six

We got the time.

For the next five days we tried to prepare the big building as much as we could. After dumping a few hundred bodies through windows, you started to get numb to what you were doing. And after the first few days, we were wearing masks and tossing our clothes out after working and taking long hot showers to try to clear the smell from our noses.

But we finally got every body we could find out of the big building.

The city was starting to smell as well, mostly from the bodies inside the other buildings. So after clearing the bodies from the entire building, our focus turned completely to stocking up on bedding, food, clothing, and just about anything else we thought we might need and could get on carts or carry.

I took the top office floor and the professor and his kids stocked up the twenty-second floor, since there were six bathrooms and lots of offices that could be made into bedrooms.

I wanted us to be prepared for a hundred people living in the building instead of just five, even though we hadn't seen anyone else since the first day. And the professor agreed. So we stocked food and blankets and propane heaters and lighting and everything else on a dozen different floors.

"The moment the lights go out in the city and lights are on in this building, people from all over will see us. We need to be ready."

All the kids had found their families, all dead. And every so often I would run across one of them crying. Nothing I could say to cheer them up. They were either going to make it or they weren't.

My counselor had taught me that. I had decided after that session that I would be one of the soldiers that made it. And I would make it this time as well.

Constance just slowly withdrew, working and eating less and less, no matter what any of us said. On the fifth morning she vanished, going out the south door before any of us got up. I had no doubt she wouldn't be back, but the professor wanted to go in search of her.

He took two gas masks we had gotten for long trips outside into the smell and he and Freddy went looking for her without luck.

As he and David were about to go out on a third search party trip, I stopped him. "It's safe out there. She knows where we are. If she wants to come back, she will."

We both knew by that point she never would.

Seven

The power cut out on the tenth day.

We all went to using propane lanterns and climbing stairs. The smell outside was getting so bad, none of us wanted to go out there.

I had set up a portable generator on a balcony outside of an office suite that I had converted to a very large apartment, with a big screen television and a movie library that would take me ten years to watch if I never stopped.

I had all the staircases boarded and sealed on my floor except for one, and that one I had fitted with steel bars locking it at night. And I had enough firepower to hold off a pretty good-sized attack. Not that I thought one was coming. I actually doubted it was, but in the Gulf I had seen my share of the underside of humanity. I had survived this, which meant scum might have as well. Not everyone was going to be nice guys like the professor and his kids.

When the power went out we made sure all the doors were locked again, then set up a twenty-four-hour guard system in the security room and kept the exterior and lobby camera systems running on generators. If anyone wanted in, we would see them.

It was on the twelfth day after humanity had been destroyed that the aliens showed up.

The day had broken clear and crisp, one of those wonderful New York winter days that made you want to go outside. And I would have, except for the smell.

The alien ships seemed to settle over the entire city, their massive shadows cutting off the sun completely. A couple of the ships had to be almost as big as the entire island and just hovered overhead.

The damn kid had been right. Aliens had wiped out humanity.

I called the professor on the walkie-talkies we had set up, and twenty minutes later he and the boys joined me in my apartment, staring out the large window at the alien ship closest to us.

I wouldn't even begin to try to describe it. Dark black with lots of different elevations on the bottom, like a city in and of itself was stuck to the bottom of the ship.

"They are here to rescue us," David said.

I glanced at David who was smiling. "Why would you say that?"

He kept his eyes on the huge ship. "They've been taking our kind to another planet for centuries. They knew we would be destroyed. They planned for it."

"And you know all this how?"

"He doesn't," Freddy said. "Since they are here it's pretty clear they were the ones that wiped us out like stepping on an ant hill. They just missed a few of us."

I was about to ask the kid why he thought that when a blue beam shot down from the ship and hit somewhere in the city. I was expecting noise or flash or smoke, but nothing.

"Now what are they doing?" I asked the two boys.

One said, "Rescuing."

The other said, "Killing."

The professor said nothing.

Then more and more beams slashed down on the city. But again that didn't seem to be like any weapon I had ever seen before. No smoke, no destruction.

Then a blue beam hit the professor and he vanished.

A moment later the two boys were gone.

Then suddenly there was a blue light around me, and the city and my office apartment and the alien spaceship vanished.

Eight

Damn, I wish I could say that was the end of it, that the kid who thought the blue beam was a weapon had been right. But, of course, it wasn't.

The blue beam was some sort of transportation device right out of Star Trek, only without the stupid music and sound effects.

I found myself standing beside the professor and the two boys, along with hundreds of other very tired and scared-looking humans who had survived the destruction of the world, only to be kidnapped by aliens.

"Perfect," I said. "Are we in the frying pan or in the fire?"

"I'm guessing fire," the professor said.

"We're lunch," Freddy said.

"I doubt they have a cookbook," David said.

I had no idea what they were talking about, but it didn't sound good that the aliens with the blue beam could want to eat humans.

Then one of the doors on one side of the room slid back, and one of the aliens walked into the room. Only it wasn't an alien. The guy looked as human as I do, only he was clearly more rested and clean in his white shirt and dark slacks and military hat.

The two or three hundred of us in the room just stared as he jumped up on a low stage. You could have heard the old pin drop in that room.

"Fine people of the great city of New York," he said. "Very sorry to startle you like this, but the next wave of the pulsar will be hitting Earth in just under four hours. We have over a hundred ships circling the planet, pulling all survivors from the first wave to safety."

"How come you couldn't get here before the first wave?" one guy shouted.

"And who are you, anyway?" someone else shouted.

The officer just smiled. "Let's just say I'm as human as the rest of you, and from a very distant place. We could not save everyone from the first wave, although we have saved millions over the centuries and humanity is flourishing just fine on five other planets around other stars. But we can save all of you who survived and let the second and final wave pass with no more deaths, and then put you back on Earth to rebuild."

"What happens if we don't want to go back to that graveyard?" one woman shouted.

A lot of people shouted "Yeah, what happens?"

Again the officer smiled and said, "We'll deal with that problem when the time comes. But for now, there is food and drink against the far wall and cots to take naps. This entire process will take about ten hours. Please relax, and I will be back to talk with you as soon as I can."

"One last question," the professor beside me shouted at the officer. "How many survived the first wave?"

"Worldwide," the officer said, smiling, "almost two million. And we'll get them all, I promise."

As the noise of three hundred people talking at once filled the room like a hard wave, I turned to David who had been talking about the aliens.

"Well, now what?"

"I have no idea," he said.

At that moment, a girl's voice called out, "Professor," and Constance hit the professor with a hug, sobbing.

Even I was glad to see she was still alive, but not as much as the boys in her class. She looked like she had gone through hell, and she smelled awful, like she had been sitting next to a dead body for days.

"Where have you been?" he asked, clearly fantastically glad to see her,

"At my mom's apartment," she said between sobs. "I hid when you came there looking for me."

That made sense. She had simply gone home to die beside her mother.

The owners of this big ship clearly were going to make sure that didn't happen. At least not for the next ten hours.

Nine

I had no idea how the hundreds of other people in the room felt, but I kept verging on sheer panic that came close to cutting through the black screen in my head and then five minutes later I would be elated to be a survivor.

After we had stood in line for some of the best-tasting food I had ever had, I asked the professor why he had asked the question about how many survivors.

"Because there is a magic number of humans that it takes to build a population and to survive and have a large enough gene pool to make the effort even worthwhile."

"And you know this how?"

"It's my field," he said, smiling. "Or it used to be."

"Is two million enough?"

He laughed. "Far, far more than enough."

At least that was good to hear.

During the next six hours, both the professor and I mentioned to numbers of people that we had set up the Empire State Building for survival, and if we were put back, they were welcome to join us. He and I had talked days before about how it would be an advantage to have a few hundred people in the building, all working toward the same goal of survival.

At nine hours, true to his word, the officer of the big spaceship came back in and everyone got quiet.

"Everyone has survived the second and final wave of deadly electromagnetic waves. We are returning to Earth and will be in orbit in about fifteen minutes."

"So do we have an option of going to another planet?" someone shouted.

"No," the officer said, which caused my heart to sink and the room to explode in shouting. I loved New York, but not in the condition it was right now. Anywhere would be better than that killing field.

The officer held up his hand for silence and got it. "We will take the wounded and the sick, but all of you, and the two million others on this ship and the other ships, are the future of humanity on Earth. We can't rob Earth of that."

"How do we survive?" someone shouted from behind where I stood, staring at the man in the white uniform who was sealing my fate.

"Some of you won't," he said bluntly. "But many will; enough to rebuild a wonderful culture and society and preserve much of what is already there. Your job is to save the old art and culture and build new on top of it."

Building on the dead was all I could think of, just as every society did.

Suddenly, beside the Professor, Freddy shouted out, "We won't remember any of this, will we?"

The officer smiled. "A few of you will," he said. "Most of you won't. And the ones that do remember won't be believed by the others."

That stunned everyone even more than the death sentence he had just declared on many people in the room.

"I wish each and every one of you luck," he said. "The future of the human race on the planet Earth depends on all of you."

With that, a wave of purple beams swept over the room and I knew I was going home, to the city I loved, and my new home near the top of the Empire State Building.

Ten

I awoke with a slight headache on the carpet of my new office suite apartment. The professor and the two boys were sprawled on the carpet beside me.

The aliens had sent us all back to the exact spot we had been when taken.

"Aliens!" I said, jumping to my feet and looking out the window. The night sky looked bright, with many stars. Below most of the city was dark. No sign of any spaceship or anything odd.

Except for the fact that the professor and the two boys were passed out on the carpet behind me.

Crap, I was one of the people who would remember. Damn, that was all I needed inside my screwed up head. Had I imagined it all?

The professor moaned and sat up, holding his head. "What happened? How did I get up here?"

Beside him the boys were starting to stir.

I was about to tell him about the aliens, then decided against it. "What do you remember?"

"Nothing," he said.

"Boys," I said, "do you remember how you got up here?"

"No," both said at almost the same time, looking around.

"I think a milder version of what killed everyone hit us and knocked us out. I don't remember anything either."

"Maybe the aliens came," Freddy said.

Dave and the professor both just shook their heads.

"We'll figure out what happened tomorrow," I said. "We need to go hunt for Constance in the morning. I woke up with an idea of where she might be. And I also have a hunch we're going to have some new tenants in the building soon."

"Bad dream?" the professor asked. "I didn't dream anything." He glanced at his watch. "We were out for a good twelve hours."

"Yeah," both boys said. "I doubt I could get any sleep."

I nodded in agreement. I had no doubt I could sleep. We had a very large world to rebuild, one person at a time.

"All right then," I said. "We need to go save Constance right now. Boys, you guard the security system, professor, get your gas mask on. You and I will go to her mother's apartment. I'm sure she's there."

"I always wondered about that," the professor said, shaking his head. "But we checked there."

"I think she was hiding from you the first time," I said.

Moving slowly toward the stairs with the boys following him, the professor said, "I sure wish I knew what happened."

"Aliens," Freddy said.

"A second weaker pulsar blast," David said.

I didn't want to try to tell them that they were both partially right. I wasn't sure if I believed it myself.

"We'll figure it out," I said. "Eventually. But right now my gut is telling me Constance needs our help. We do that first."

All three nodded and started down the stairs ahead of me.

I had once asked my counselor at the VA how he did his job every day, digging in the trash of people's minds trying to save them.

He just smiled and said, "I just do it one person at a time."

I had followed that motto when I opened my little loan office to help people, one person at a time. Now we had to dig around in the junk of a ruined planet and give a helping hand up to one person at a time.

And by doing that, given time, we just might build something a lot bigger.

NEWSLETTER SIGN-UP

Be the first to know!

Just sign up for the Dean Wesley Smith newsletter, and keep up with the latest news, releases and so much more—even the occasional giveaway.

So, what are you waiting for? Go to deanwesleysmith.com to sign up.

But wait! There's more. Sign up for the WMG Publishing newsletter, too, and get the latest news and releases from all of the WMG authors and lines, including Kristine Kathryn Rusch, Kristine Grayson, Kris Nelscott, *Fiction River: An Original Anthology Magazine, Smith's Monthly, Pulphouse Fiction Magazine,* and so much more.

To sign up, go to wmgpublishing.com.

ALSO BY DEAN WESLEY SMITH

COLD POKER GANG MYSTERIES:

Kill Game

Cold Call

Calling Dead

Bad Beat

Dead Hand

Freezeout

Ace High

Burn Card

Heads Up

COLD POKER GANG STORIES:

The Case of the Pleasant Hills Murder

A Bad Day for the Dream

THUNDER MOUNTAIN NOVELS:

Thunder Mountain

Monumental Summit

Avalanche Creek

The Edwards Mansion

Lake Roosevelt

Warm Springs

Melody Ridge

Grapevine Springs

The Idanha Hotel

The Taft Ranch

Tombstone Canyon

Miss Smallwood's Goodies

DOC HILL THRILLERS:

Dead Money

DOC HILL STORIES:

The Road Back

Eyes on My Cards

POKER BOY NOVELS:

The Slots of Saturn

They're Back

POKER BOY STORIES:

The Old Girlfriend of Doom

Dead Even

Gods Aren't Funny

Gambling Hell

Luck Be A Lady

Sighed the Snake

The Smoke That Doesn't Bark

The War of Poker

Daddy is an Undertaker

Nonexistent No More

Fighting the Fuzzy-Wuzzy

Pink Shoes and Hot Chocolate

Dried Up

The Empty Mummy Murders

Living Time

Not Saleable For Sale

Just Shoot Me Now!

For the Balance of a Heart

Black Betsy

The Ghost of the Garden Lounge

A Golden Dream

She Arrived Without a Song

The Songs of Memory

He Could Have Coped With Dragons

The Wages of the Moment

BUCKEY THE SPACE PIRATE STORIES:

Cutting Down Fred

The Waiting of the Wind

Long Dead New Love

The Lady of Whispering Valley

Cucumber Party

The Last Man

BRYANT STREET STORIES:

The Man Who Used Shrill Whispers

A Study of an Accident

An Obscene Crime Against Passion

Why Delay? Just Rub?

He Meant No Harm

I Killed the Clockwork Key

For Your Consideration

Call Me Unfixable

A Pity About the Delusion

Bryant Street

They Were Divided by Cold Debt

A Long Ways Down

The Man Who Laughed on a Rainy Night

Not Easy to Kill the Light Next Door

Through the For Sale Sign

In the Dream of Many Bodies

Wings Out: A Bryant Street Story

Mary Jo Assassin Novels:

Death Takes a Partner

Death Takes a Diamond

MARY JO ASSASSIN STORIES:

Death in the Morning

The Remodeling of a Life

Make Myself Just One More

MARBLE GRANT STORIES:

A Lady in Heat: A Marble Grant Story

A Look at His Heart: A Marble Grant Story

OTHER SHORT STORIES:

The Big Tick of Time

Long Shadow

The Matchbox Agenda

Out of Coffee Experience

Sleeping with the Goddess

If Sex is All a Dream, Then Who Cleans Up the Mess

Love with the Proper Napkin

Neighborhood

Remember

A Bubble for a Minute

Waiting for the Coin to Drop

A Pinch of How Rosie Lived

In Case of Emergency

The Mouth that Walked

A Pathetic Fallacy

As the Robot Rubs

Music in Time

The Tragic Tale of a Man in a Duster

Skiing the Graveyard of Souls

Marriage in Six Floors

Well, Maybe Not

Butchered Whale on a Red Bedspread

Two Roads, No Choices

Who's Holding Donna Now

Ambassador to the Promised Land

Santa's Snack

Sprinkle on a Memory

I'm Her Dead Husband

Variations of a Scream

Gus

The Last Burp of a Very Good Woman

A Vanilla Three-Way With a Cherry

Nostalgia 101

A Life in Whoopees

Between Showers

Squatter's Rights on the Street of Broken Men

After the Dance

Mated from the Morgue

Me and Beans and Great Big Melons

Don't Rust on Me Now

Shopping Cart Lover

Iron Eyebrows: A Romance with Too Much Hair

Mom's Paradox

The Keeper of the Morals

My Socks Rolled Down

The Romance Novel Challenge

In the Shade of the Slowboat Man

It's a Story About a Guy Who...

Standing in Line at the Intersection

Husband Dummies

On Top of the Dead

The Yellow of the Flickering Past

Cheerleader Revelation

Dead Post Bumper

Clicking Sticks

Peter the Hermit

In Search of the Perfect Orgasm

The Life and Death of Fortune Cookie Tyrant

Tumbling Down the Nighttime

Growing Pains of the Dead

The Call of the Track Ahead

Dinner on a Flying Saucer

The Great Alien Vibration

Cold Comfort

For the Delusion that Waited

The Face in the Fullness of Time

Playing in the Street

Best Eaten on a Slow Tuesday

Here to Stay on the Edge

The Stone Slept Here

To Remember a Single Minute

Something Wasted On

A Parker House Roll

The Thickness of a Warp

Unlocked Gate

Last Man Out

Shadow in the City

Another Damn Deal

Habit

Smile

The Last Short Putt of a Fearful Man

Keep Hoping for a New Tomorrow

The Wait

ABOUT THE AUTHOR

Considered one of the most prolific writers working in modern fiction, *USA Today* bestselling writer Dean Wesley Smith published almost two hundred novels in forty years, and hundreds and hundreds of short stories across many genres.

At the moment he produces novels in several major series, including the time travel Thunder Mountain novels set in the Old West, the galaxy-spanning Seeders Universe series, the urban fantasy Ghost of a Chance series, a superhero series starring Poker Boy, and a mystery series featuring the retired detectives of the Cold Poker Gang.

His monthly magazine, *Smith's Monthly*, which consists of only his own fiction, premiered in October 2013 and offers readers more than 70,000 words per issue, including a new and original novel every month.

During his career, Dean also wrote a couple dozen *Star Trek* novels, the only two original *Men in Black* novels, Spider-Man and X-Men novels, plus novels set in gaming and television worlds. Writing with his wife Kristine Kathryn Rusch under the name Kathryn Wesley, he wrote the novel for the NBC miniseries The Tenth Kingdom and other books for *Hallmark Hall of Fame* movies.

He wrote novels under dozens of pen names in the worlds of comic books and movies, including novelizations of almost a dozen films, from *The Final Fantasy* to *Steel* to *Rundown*.

Dean also worked as a fiction editor off and on, starting at Pulphouse Publishing, then at *VB Tech Journal*, then Pocket Books, and now at WMG Publishing, where he and Kristine Kathryn Rusch serve as series editors for the acclaimed *Fiction River* anthology series, which launched in 2013. In 2018, WMG Publishing Inc. launched the first issue of the reincarnated *Pulphouse Fiction Magazine*, with Dean reprising his role as editor.

For more information about Dean's books and ongoing projects, please visit his website at www.deanwesleysmith.com and sign up for his newsletter.